KILLER KAYFABE

A ZOEY WILDE MYSTERY: BOOK TWO

RANDEE GREEN

CAMEL PRESS
KENMORE, WA

A Camel Press book published by Epicenter Press

Epicenter Press
6524 NE 181st St.
Suite 2
Kenmore, WA 98028

For more information go to:
www.Camelpress.com
www.randeegreen.com

Killer Kayfabe

Library of Congress Control Number: 2026935962

ISBN: 978-1-68492-356-4 (Trade Paper)
ISBN: 978-1-68492-357-1 (eBook)

For Daisy. You are the light of my life.

ACKNOWLEDGEMENTS

LIMITLESS THANKS AND SMOOCHES to Daisy, Molly, and Snookums for the love and support that only pets can provide.

Thank you to my mom for (mostly) not complaining every time that I've handed you a new manuscript with the expectation that you find and correct all my grammatical and punctuation errors. And thank you to my dad for subjecting me to professional wrestling at such a young age and for taking me to all those events. The cage should remain standing . . .

Jennifer McCord at Coffeetown Press for believing in me and my wild characters.

Huge thanks to Nick "Sicend" Taylor of Riot City for giving me an insider's view of the business and for answering all my pro wrestling questions over the years.

And to all the professional wrestlers who have inspired me . . . None of his would have happened without you.

ONE

Monday December 3rd, 2018

"We aren't even open yet, and you're already sleeping on the job." Zoey Wilde opened her eyes and watched her twin brother stroll through the combined office and reception area of 3 Count Tattoos. Zack was two minutes younger than she, and a few inches taller. His long, brown hair was pulled back into a sloppy ponytail, and he had purple bags under his eyes. He looked about as exhausted as Zoey felt. Even though three other artists worked at the shop, Zack had carried the brunt of the business over the past few months. The stress and long hours were catching up to him.

"I had a grueling weekend," Zoey said. "Normally, I have Mondays off to recover. But my inconsiderate boss temporarily changed the schedule—"

"The same inconsiderate boss who lets you nap on the job, make your own schedule, and live upstairs rent-free?"

Zoey stuck out her tongue. "One and the same."

3 Count was typically closed on Mondays; but, thanks to the holidays—Thanksgiving last month, and now Christmas and the new year coming up—the shop's regular schedule of Tuesday through Saturday had been thrown out of whack. As majority owner, Zack decided to open the shop on Mondays in December to help make up for the holidays when they would be closed.

When Zoey wasn't managing the tattoo shop in exchange for a free place to live, she could most often be found in a wrestling ring. For as far back as she could remember, she had dreamt of being a professional wrestler. She'd spent her childhood training and had her debut match not long after her eighteenth birthday. That had been almost thirteen years ago. Despite all the years of hard work both in and out of the ring, Zoey had not made it past the independent scene. Though she had wrestled for several of the top independent companies in North America. She'd also wrestled for promotions across the world.

"You know you've been leaving me in a bit of a bind lately," Zack said. "With everything you've got going on, you haven't been here all that much the past few months."

"Yes, I have." Zoey flipped her long, dark brown hair over her shoulder. "Sure I haven't been here as much as usual—"

"And you weren't around all that much to begin with," Zack said, causing Zoey to roll her eyes at the exaggeration. She was still putting in fifteen to twenty hours at the tattoo shop every week. "But ever since you and Justin suddenly became two of the hottest wrestlers on the independent scene, you've been on the road more than you've been home."

Over the past few months, Zoey and her younger brother, Justin, had teamed up together several times in intergender and mixed tag matches for promotions across the country. They were a solid team. There was no denying that, but they weren't as good as she and Zack had been. The twins could practically read each other's minds. They had been nearly flawless in the ring. She and Justin did not have that same precision.

Teaming together forced Zoey to spend more time with Justin, and it had helped them to finally get along with each other. Yes, she had always loved her younger brother; but, since the day he was born, Justin had been an exasperating pain in her backside. When they were kids, Justin had been the annoying younger brother who wanted to tag along everywhere and always got in the way of his siblings. As he got older, Justin morphed into an immature and selfish adult. Justin's childish antics infuriated Zoey, and she'd found it hard to get along with him. Lately, Justin seemed to be maturing and was showing some promise that he might turn into a semi-decent human being. Zoey credited Justin's girlfriend for the transformation.

Regardless of who or what was responsible for Justin's sudden maturity, Zoey's bond with her younger brother had strengthened over the past few months. Back in August, their wrestling careers were tied together following the death of Zoey's ex-boyfriend. Devon Isler's murder—and their positions at the top of the suspect list—had been an unexpected boost to their careers. The dirt sheets—wrestling magazines and websites that covered the real-life perspective of wrestling and the wrestlers' lives—had covered Devon's murder. Because of their past relationship, Zoey's name came up in most articles, and, as Devon's final in-ring opponent, Justin was mentioned almost as many times as his sister.

Justin wanted to take advantage of their newfound fame, but Zoey had been reluctant. She didn't want to profit from Devon's death. That seemed callous. Justin would only grudgingly admit it, but he knew Zoey was the top draw of the two of them. The sudden interest in him would quickly crash and burn without Zoey by his side. Determined to ride the coattails of his sister's wrestling career, Justin forced Zoey to take advantage of the situation before interest in them waned.

In the weeks following Devon's murder, promoters from outside the Wildes' normal stomping grounds of the Mid-Atlantic region scrambled to book them. Throughout the past months, Zoey and Justin had wrestled at shows in the Southeast and in Canada. In the upcoming months, they were scheduled to spend a week in Mexico City and had bookings on the West Coast and across Texas. They'd even received calls from promotions in Japan, Australia, and Europe.

This past weekend, Zoey had wrestled four matches in three days. Friday night she had wrestled at a show in Baltimore. Then on Saturday and Sunday, she was part of a two-day event in Philadelphia. On Saturday, she had teamed with her younger brother in a mixed-tag match. The match—as well as the rest of the show—had been broadcast live over the internet. Zoey and Justin had won the match, as well as bragging rights as the top intergender team in the company. Then, on Sunday, she and Justin had taken part in taping four one-hour long episodes that would be aired online over the next four Fridays. They'd wrestled on two of those episodes and made an appearance on a third.

"Okay, maybe I haven't been here as much as you'd prefer. But I've kept up with my work." Zoey jutted out her chin. "I've kept the schedule updated and made frequent posts on social media. All the bills have gotten paid on time. I've returned all the calls and emails from clients. And I've kept the supply closet stocked."

"Yeah, but you're not *here*." Zack pointed at the desk. "And that's the reason I hired you. To be *here*. To answer the phone when it rings opposed to returning messages. To greet the clients when they come in. Without you here, the guys and I have to stop in the middle of our sessions to deal with anyone who walks in the door. And you know how I hate having to stop when I'm tattooing."

"I get that. But you know that most of the time I'm here, I have nothing to do. I'm just twiddling my thumbs and waiting for the phone to ring." Zoey smacked her hand on the desktop. "And are you really going to give me a hard time about this, Zack? I mean, I'm more popular than I've ever been. I've been getting booked by some of the top independent companies again. All the bloggers have been talking about me. This could be it. This could be my last chance at making it."

At almost thirty-one, Zoey knew that she was running out of time to get called up to one of the premier wrestling companies. By the time they reached their mid-thirties, a lot of the top women's wrestlers were retiring. With her nagging knee issues and her body slowing down, Zoey worried how many more years she still had left of her career. She wanted to make the most of it. Yes, she'd had a successful career on the independent circuit. As long as she could get in the ring and entertain the fans, she was happy. She wrestled because it was her passion. She didn't do it for the money—though she was thankful that she made enough to cover her bills and support a decent living. Despite all that, she still dreamed of making it to the big leagues of professional wrestling before having to retire.

"No, I would never want to hold you back or cause you to miss an opportunity," Zack said. "Trust me, I get it. I used to want the same thing that you do. I want you to make it. It's just hard not having you around."

Zoey shifted forward in her seat. "Do you miss it?"

"Of course, I miss it. At least, I miss most of it." Zack stepped into the storage closet behind Zoey's desk. "I don't miss the long hours on the road getting to and from the shows. Or all the time wasted sitting around backstage. And I really do not miss the injuries or spending the week feeling like I'm recovering from a minor car accident. You have no idea how nice it is to not to be living in constant pain anymore."

"But you do miss the actual wrestling?"

"You know I loved it as much as you do. And wanted it just as badly." Zack continued to rummage around in the closet. "But I had to be realistic. As of two years ago, I hadn't made it yet. And I probably wasn't going to. Plus, I make a lot more money running this shop than I ever did in the ring. It might not be a normal nine-to-five, but I can make my own hours. I'm home at a decent time most nights. It wasn't so bad when it was just me and Arielle, but when Paige came along . . . I didn't want to do to my daughter what our dad did to us."

"But we loved going to shows to watch Dad wrestle."

Wrestling under the name Maverick Marlon, their father had spent over twenty years on the independent circuit. Marlon had wrestled mostly in the Mid-Atlantic region. When they were kids, Zoey and her brothers spent almost every weekend traveling to shows with their dad. They had been born and raised in the wrestling business—as had Marlon. His parents were Kazimir "The Wilde Man" Wilde and Vivacious Vivian. Kazimir's father had been a wrestling promoter, and his grandparents had wrestled in the sideshow act of a traveling carnival. Professional wrestling was in the Wildes' DNA.

"It was fun. But you have to admit, it was not a normal childhood. And it wasn't easy on Mom. Don't you remember around the time Justin was born when Dad and Uncle Leland were wrestling for that promotion in Japan? They'd be gone for weeks at a time. That left Mom home alone with three kids."

"Nana and Pops were next door," Zoey said. "It wasn't like Mom was totally alone."

"No, but it was still hard on her. And Dad, too. I know he hated missing out on stuff because he was off wrestling somewhere."

"Did he tell you that?"

"Yeah. He did. Dad and I had a long talk around the time Paige was born. He also told me that he regrets dragging us along to all those shows. He thinks he deprived us of a lot of things. You know, the things that all of our friends got to do because they weren't traveling around to wrestling shows most weekends. I want my daughter to be able to play sports, join clubs, and hang out with her friends . . . And I don't want to miss out on being there for Paige. And Arielle." Zack grumbled something about how the storage closet needed reorganized. "If it hadn't been for my shoulder,

I might have wrestled for a few more years. But that was the deciding factor for me. Not being able to tattoo for months while I recovered from surgery . . ."

A little over two years earlier, Zack tore his rotator cuff during a match. He required surgery to fix the tear, and the following recovery period kept him out of the ring. It had also kept him from tattooing. The injury had been to his right shoulder, and Zack was right-handed. It was weeks before he could move his shoulder around enough to comfortably sketch, and it was months before he could resume tattooing. During that time, his daughter had been born. After Paige's birth, Zack decided to hang up his wrestling boots.

"Would you consider getting back in the ring for just one more match? You never did get to have an actual retirement match."

"I'll admit that it is tempting. Watching you and Justin tag together really makes me miss it. I miss the days when it was you and me tagging together."

"Me, too," Zoey said. "I mean, I like teaming with Justin. But it's just not the same."

Zack emerged from the closet carrying a handful of bottles containing brightly colored inks. "Don't you be getting any ideas."

"And what kind of ideas would I be getting?"

"Maybe you're hoping that I'll jump at the chance to get back in the ring, now that you're running your own promotion." Zack bopped his sister on the forehead with a large bottle of black ink. "Don't deny that you've thought about asking. Remember, Zoey, I know how you think."

"Of course, I'm thinking it," Zoey said. She'd recently taken over running the Linville Association of Wrestling. It was a small independent company that put on shows at the local VFW Hall. "Just hear me out, Zack. You know how Justin and I are wrestling Mama and Tiny at the next LAW show?"

"I'm aware. What does that have to do with me?"

"I talked to Mama this morning. Bubba is medically cleared to wrestle again."

Mama, Bubba, and Tiny were part of a pro wrestling stable with a hillbilly gimmick. Zoey, Zack, and Justin had wrestled them countless times throughout their careers.

"Let me guess," Zack said. "You want to make it a six-person intergender tag match."

"Will you do it? For old time's sake?" Zoey asked. "It'll just be the one match, I swear. I won't ask again."

Before Zack could respond, the front door swung open and his client walked into the foyer. Without saying anything to his sister, Zack stepped out of the office and ushered his client across the hall and into his private room.

The tattoo shop was housed in a two-story Craftsman-style house that had been built in the early 1900s. The house, on one of the main streets in Linville, was a few blocks away from the downtown area. Marlon had purchased the house going on eight years ago. While wrestling, Marlon had worked for a construction company. After retiring from the ring, he'd opened his own home improvement business. He also occasionally flipped houses. Marlon's original plan had been to fix up the rundown house and flip it for a profit.

After seeing the property, Zack talked Marlon into remodeling the first floor into a tattoo shop with the front office, a breakroom, and four private rooms. The second floor was converted into an apartment. Zack and Arielle had lived upstairs for a few years. When they've moved out over three years earlier, Zoey moved in. Prior to that, Zoey had still been living with her parents. She loved having freedom and privacy now. She also relished the short commute down the interior staircase—especially on these bitter cold winter days.

Turning her attention to her work, Zoey booted up the shop's laptop. She had just opened the day's schedule when her younger brother strolled into the front office. He was dressed in ripped-up, paint-splattered jeans and a leather jacket. His long, brown hair hung about his shoulders in unruly waves, but his scruffy beard was a little less scraggly looking than usual. Zoey figured his girlfriend had something to do with that.

"You're late," Zoey said as she glared at Justin. "I told you to be here at quarter *of* twelve. Not quarter *after* twelve."

"Give me a break," Justin said. "Dad wouldn't let me leave for my lunchbreak until after I finished tearing out the old kitchen cabinets."

When he wasn't working, Justin worked for Marlon as a general contractor. Marlon hoped that Justin would one day take over Wilde Home

Improvements. He did a lot of the demolition work as well as installing flooring.

"You missed your chance to talk to Zack. He's with his client."

Justin swore. "Did you say anything to him?"

"I did."

"And . . ."

"And I would have been a lot more convincing if you had been here to back me up."

Justin swore a second time. "We've got almost two weeks to talk him into it."

"We better be pretty convincing. You know how stubborn Zack can be."

"Don't worry. I'm sure he'll come around." Justin propped his elbows on the counter and leaned against the front of Zoey's desk. "Are you ready to run your own show?"

"I think so," Zoey said. "But it's turning out to be a lot tougher and time consuming than I originally thought it would be. There's a lot more to it than I realized."

"But you helped Uncle Leland run the show . . . Didn't you already know what all was involved?"

"You know I really only helped Uncle Leland promote the show online. And I handled the ticket sales," Zoey said. Since the first LAW show—which had been over a year earlier—3 Count Tattoos had been the only place to purchase advanced tickets. "But he took care of all the booking duties and dealt with the wrestlers."

Leland Freeman was not Zoey's or Justin's biological uncle, but he was Marlon's former tag team partner, and that made him family. The two had been like brothers for over thirty years. Together they had been known as Wilde and Free. Back in August, the friendship went down for the count when Leland's self-centered ways caught up to him. His selfish actions had also cost him his marriage. Realizing that he had burned too many bridges, Leland hightailed it out of Pennsylvania. The last the Wildes had heard, Leland had moved to Arizona and was living with a woman half his age.

Had it not been for the Wildes, the Linville Association of Wrestling would have folded. When Leland took off at the end of October, he already had wrestlers booked for the November show. Marlon agreed to take charge of that show, but he didn't want to take on running his own promotion.

Instead of letting LAW die, Zoey decided she would take over. Running a promotion was a whole new experience and something she could continue doing after her in-ring career finally came to an end.

The December show would be the first one that Zoey managed on her own. As the booker, she was responsible for hiring wrestlers to compete. She had to figure out the matches and winners along with how to continue the previous storylines and create new ones. She also had to babysit the wrestlers by making sure that they plugged the show on their social media pages as well post promotional videos. After weeks of hard work, Zoey was fairly certain that she was ready to go for next Saturday night.

"You know I'd do whatever I could to help you out. But you know how Dad keeps me busy during the day," Justin said. "Speaking of which . . . I should probably grab something to eat and get back to the jobsite."

"And I should make it look like I'm doing the job that Zack doesn't pay me for," Zoey said. "I'll see you tonight for a practice session."

TWO

After seeing Justin out through the side door, Zoey returned to the office and switched on the neon "open" sign that hung in the window. With 3 Count officially open for business, she turned her attention to the shop's email and Facebook messages. As usual, there were inquiries about openings and pricing. Zoey took a few minutes to respond to each message and jot down notes for the artists.

Caught up on the most pressing of her work, Zoey turned her attention to her Wilde Woman website and social media accounts. She'd received countless notifications since Saturday afternoon, but she had not had the time or the inclination to check her email or any of her accounts. Now, she scrolled through the pictures that fans had posted from the weekend's events.

Zoey was examining a decent action shot—one in which she wasn't making too weird of a face—when the bells above the front door jangled.

"Welcome to 3 Count Tattoos," Zoey called out.

A man in his late-twenties or early-thirties strolled into the room. His navy blue peacoat strained across his barrel chest, and the top button threatened to pop off. The man yanked off his knit hat and then used it to wipe away the fog that had formed on his thick glasses.

"Oh, God . . ." After replacing his glasses, the man used his hat to swat at the action figures that stood at one end of the counter. The Rock tumbled off the counter and landed face down on a pile of junk mail. "Don't tell me you're still into this pro wrestling crap, Zoey."

"Yes, I am." Zoey picked up The Rock and set him back on the counter next to Shawn Michaels and Stone Cold Steve Austin. She then pointed at the framed poster of herself, Zack, and Justin that hung on the wall above the black leather couch. The posed picture had been taken in the ring not long before Zack hung up his wrestling boots. "I'm also a wrestler."

"I see that." The man—Zoey had no idea who he was, but it was obvious that he knew her—walked across the room to get a better look at the picture. Muttering under his breath, he said, "Man, you Wildes are still total freaks."

"Excuse me?"

The man spun around to face Zoey. "You don't recognize me, do you?"

"No. I don't." And she wasn't sure that she wanted to. Not after he called her a freak.

"It's Lucas." The man patted himself on the chest and grinned. "Lucas Jennings."

"From high school?"

"The one and only."

No way, Zoey thought. *There is no way this is the same Lucas Jennings.*

Once upon a time, Lucas had been the most popular guy in Zoey's graduating class. He'd played football in the fall, ice hockey in the winter, and baseball in the spring. If Zoey remembered correctly, Lucas had been the captain of all three teams during their senior year. He had also gotten a full scholarship to play NCAA Division 1 baseball at Virginia University. The small town of Linville, Pennsylvania, had high hopes for their native son. It was expected that Lucas would go on to play in the MLB.

"It's been a long time, Lucas." Zoey plastered a fake smile on her face. "Did you ever make it to the major league?"

"Nah. I got drafted by a minor league team right out of college. I played one season and then I blew out my pitching arm. That was the end of my baseball career."

"That's too bad." Zoey genuinely felt for him. "What have you been up to since then?"

"Oh, you know . . . This and that. Nothing too interesting. But enough about me." Lucas gave Zoey the once over, and then wolf whistled. "You're looking good. How come we never hooked up in high school?"

The smile slipped from Zoey's face. "Because, back in seventh grade, you told me that you only dated pretty girls."

Lucas chuckled. "That sounds like something I would have said."

"It's not funny," Zoey snapped. "I was humiliated."

Lucas's insulting comment had been a blow to young Zoey's fragile self-confidence. Along with most of the other girls in her grade, Zoey had developed a crush on Lucas during the first few weeks of middle school. With his naturally wavy brown hair, dark brown eyes, and emerging muscles, Lucas had been the cutest boy in their grade. Zoey had made the mistake of telling one of her friends about her budding crush. Instead of keeping the information to herself, Olivia Kreider went right to Lucas with the news that Zoey liked him. The next day, Lucas approached Zoey in the hallway between classes. In front of several dozen of their classmates, Lucas proclaimed that he only dated "pretty girls," and would, therefore, never go out with Zoey. He had not directly called her unattractive, but he had implied it. Zoey had been mortified—and some of her classmates rubbed salt in the raw wound when they mocked her over it. Up through graduation, some of them had not allowed Zoey to forget it.

"I was a jerk back then, wasn't I? But I was the big man on campus. I had an image to maintain. A role to fill." Lucas chuckled. "And I said hook up. Not date. Guys like me didn't exactly date girls like you—"

"You mean the freaks?"

"I was going to say the outcasts."

"Same difference according to the people you hung out with," Zoey muttered. "The outcasts. The freaks. The emo kids. The punks. The goths. We were all the same to you."

"Yeah, yeah. We looked down on everyone who wasn't part of our crowd." Lucas waved his hat around. "You probably won't believe it considering what I said and how I acted . . . But I actually had a bit of a crush on you in high school. You were so different from the girls I hung out with. They were—"

"Fake?"

"I was going to say stuck up snobs. But, yeah, 'fake' describes most of them."

"You should know considering you dated the queen of the fakes."

"Yeah, Jocelyn . . . Not only was she fake, she was also insanely toxic and manipulative. But she was hot, and that's all I really cared about." Lucas said. Jocelyn Hershey had been the most popular girl in their graduating class. Lucas had dated her throughout all four years of high school. "Anyway, you had that 'bad girl' vibe. And you weren't afraid to be yourself. Even if people like me and Jocelyn picked on you for it. Looking back, it would have been so much easier to have dropped the act and just been myself. But high school was a long time ago. And we've both changed a lot since then. We should go out sometime."

"I haven't changed that much since high school. And, as for all those things you and your friends gave me a hard time about . . ." Zoey stood up and stepped out from behind the desk. She then gestured towards her leopard print leggings. "I still wear animal print clothing almost every day. I still paint my fingernails black. And I still love pro wrestling. I've also gotten a lot more tattoos since we graduated."

"I don't remember giving you a hard time about any of that. I mean, other than the wrestling. And I still think that's stupid." Lucas grinned. "But come on, Zoey. Go out with me sometime."

"Not interested. Plus, I'm . . . uhh . . . I'm seeing someone." The lie easily rolled off Zoey's tongue. She hadn't seriously dated anyone in years, but that was none of Lucas's business. She wasn't sure why she lied other than, thanks to previous experiences, she had learned it was easier to get rid of unwanted attention by claiming she was already in a relationship than simply stating she wasn't interested. Changing the subject, Zoey asked, "Are you in town for the holidays?"

Lucas shook his head. "I'm back for good. For the past few years, my old man has been bugging me about moving back and taking over his used car dealership. I kept putting him off. Lately he's threatening to sell. I figured it was time to come home and do my duty."

"Didn't you have a job wherever it was you've been living."

"Well, yeah, of course. I didn't say I wasn't making some serious sacrifices to come back and take over the dealership. But I'm doing what needs to be done. Plus I was getting sick of living in the Midwest."

Catching movement out of the corner of her eye, Zoey glanced towards the doorway and found that one of the tattoo artists had slipped into the room on silent feet. Chester Neidigh's foot-high purple mohawk brushed the underside of the arched doorway. The sides of his head were shaved, and he had a short beard. He also had a labret piercing. A silver ball sat in the crease between his lower lip and chin.

"Lucas . . ."

"Chester . . ." The corner of Lucas's mouth twitched up in a sneer. "I figured I'd never see you again."

"And I'd hoped I'd never see you. But here we are."

"Yeah . . . Here we are."

Chester gestured for Lucas to follow him.

Zoey trailed them into the hallway that had been painted a dark red. Three private rooms lined the wall opposite the office. Chester's room was in the middle. Zoey watched as Chester and Lucas disappeared inside. She wanted to press her ear against the closed door and eavesdrop. No doubt it would be an interesting conversation—and it probably would not have anything to do with tattoos.

Instead of eavesdropping—which she knew would be wrong—Zoey jogged up the interior staircase and unlocked the door to her apartment. Directly across from the door was a bookcase. She grabbed a large, hard-cover book off the bottom shelf and hustled back downstairs.

"Is that our old yearbook?" Zack asked as Zoey returned to the office. He was back to rummaging around in the storage closet. "Why did you get that out?"

"Remember Lucas Jennings?"

Zoey flipped through the yearbook's pages until she came to Lucas's senior picture. His brown hair was slicked back, and he had a smug expression on his face. While attractive, he was nowhere near as good looking as she recollected.

"Yeah, I remember that asshole," Zack said as he looked at the yearbook. "Why do you suddenly care about him?"

"Because he's in there with Chester right now. And he looks way different."

"How different?"

"Like you need to see it to believe it."

"Chester hardly looks like he did in high school." Zack held up the yearbook and pointed at Chester's picture. Back in high school, he'd had shaggy brown hair, and his eyes were hidden behind glasses. "Admit it, you didn't recognize him when he showed up a few months ago."

"No, I didn't," Zoey said. "And neither did you."

Three months earlier, Chester Neidigh—formerly known as Chester Hartman—had walked into 3 Count Tattoos and asked for a job. Even though he looked familiar, it had taken Zoey a minute to dig through her memories and dredge up his ghost. Yes, she remembered him from high school, but she didn't remember much about him.

Chester had been in Zoey's and Zack's graduating class of just under three hundred students. Because they had attended different elementary schools, they had not encountered each other until they started seventh grade at Linville Area Middle School. The only reason Zoey was aware of Chester's existence in middle school was because he was so heavily picked on for his bowl-style haircut, thrift store clothes, and his loner status.

It was in high school that Zoey and Zack befriended Chester. During the fall semester of ninth grade, they were in the same Foundations of Art class. Zack had inherited all the artistic talent in the Wilde family, and he would go on to take almost every art class that the high school had to offer. Zoey had only signed up for the basic level art class because it was a prerequisite for the print photography classes that were offered to juniors and seniors. If she was going to take the photography classes, she would have to pass Foundations—even if it meant feeling like a failure when her sorry attempts at art projects paled in comparison to Zack's masterpieces.

Because there hadn't been anywhere else for him to sit—or anyone else who was willing to make room for him— Chester had shared a workbench with the twins. Zack had also invited him to sit with their group of friends at lunch—saving Chester from the ultimate adolescent embarrassment of having no one to sit with in the cafeteria.

Even though they'd had a few classes together and would sit at the same table if they had the same lunch period, Zoey had never really gotten to know Chester. Zack, who had probably been the closest thing that Chester had to a best friend, had barely known anything about his personal life.

In the days following high school graduation, Chester packed up his belongings and took off. Neither Zoey nor Zack had heard from him or about him until he showed up at the tattoo shop a little over twelve years after they had graduated. After seeing Chester's portfolio and confirming that he had worked at a tattoo shop in Venice Beach, California, for almost ten years, Zack hired his former classmate.

"Chester and Lucas aren't the only ones who look different." Zack flipped forward a few more pages in the yearbook. "Look how much we've changed since high school."

Zoey snatched the yearbook away from her brother and then held it up next to her face. "What are you talking about? I look the same."

"Not exactly . . . Your face has gotten thinner. And you've toned down the makeup." Zack leaned in for a closer look at the yearbook. "I forgot you had your nose pierced back then."

"It didn't last long." Zoey ran her finger along the side of her nose, feeling for the slightly raised scar. "Don't you remember it getting ripped out during a match?"

"Oh, yeah . . . There was blood everywhere. It's why I stopped wearing my lip ring. I was afraid mine would get ripped out, too." Zack pulled the yearbook away from Zoey and held it up. "But look at me. How could I have ever thought that spiked hair with purple tips was a good idea? And what the heck pattern is on my tie? It's hideous."

Zoey giggled. She was about to say more when she heard a door open and then someone say, "if you know what's good for you, you'll keep your mouth shut." Seconds later, Lucas trudged by the office on his way to the front door. He gave Zoey a quick wave before he stepped outside.

"Whoa . . ." Zack rushed over to the front window and peered between the blinds. "*That's* Lucas Jennings."

"Told you he's unrecognizable."

Zoey grabbed Zack's arm and dragged him down the hallway to Chester's room. They found Chester slumped in his chair next to the battered metal desk. He was staring at a school picture of a redheaded boy who looked to be about eleven or twelve years old. As Zoey barged across the room, she got a quick glimpse of the picture before Chester slapped it face down on his desk.

"Who's the kid?" Zoey asked. "He looks kinda familiar."

"He's . . . uh . . ." Chester said as he spun the chair around to face her. "He's no one."

"He has to be someone."

Zack elbowed Zoey in the side. "You good, bro?"

"Peachy dandy."

Zoey fought back a giggle. Since he had first walked through the door at 3 Count, Chester had used "peachy dandy" as his answer to almost every question. The phrase was infectious.

"So that was Lucas, huh? He's changed a lot since high school," Zack said. "What kind of tattoo does he want?"

"He doesn't want one," Chester said. "He'd just heard that I was back in the area and stopped by to confirm it."

"Why would Lucas care?" Zack asked. "It's not like you guys were friends."

"No. We weren't. Not since elementary school," Chester said. "You guys probably don't remember, but Lucas and I grew up next door to each other. We were best friends until seventh grade. Then he decided I wasn't cool enough to be his friend anymore. At least not in public."

"Does that mean you and Lucas still hung out outside of school?" Zoey asked.

"I don't know if I would call it 'hanging out.' But I spent most afternoons at his house because his parents paid me to tutor him in some of his classes. And Lucas paid me to do his homework. That's one of the only things I was still good for. To do his homework while he focused on playing sports."

"That explains his good grades," Zack said. "I remember having a few classes with Lucas, and he never seemed like he was all that smart."

"But why would he tell you to keep your mouth shut about that?" Zoey asked. "I mean, all these years later, who would care?"

"It's not the homework that Lucas told me to keep my mouth shut about. You're right, Zoey. No one would care about that now," Chester said. "But there are some things that people might still care about. Including how his dad's Lamborghini really got totaled the summer before senior year."

"Didn't someone break into the Jenningses' house?" Zack asked. "They stole the car and then wrecked it a few miles up the road. I remember Lucas talking about it on the first day of senior year. He was home alone, and the intruders beat him up."

"That's what Lucas wants everyone to think happened." Chester laughed. "Now that he's broke and relying on his parents again—"

Interrupting, Zoey said, "Lucas told me that this dad was begging him to come home and take over the dealership."

"Yeah, I heard him lying to you about that." Chester laughed. "But I know the real reason why he's back. That's another thing he wants me to keep my mouth shut about. He's afraid I'll tell the two of you and then you'll tell some of our other former classmates. He doesn't want word getting around that he's back because his life totally fell apart and he had nowhere else to go. But mainly he's worried I'll finally tell his dad what really happened to the Lamborghini. His mom might forgive him, but I know his dad won't. Then he'd really be shit-out-of-luck."

"So, what actually happened to the car?" Zack asked.

"That's between me and Lucas. I've already said too much," Chester said as he turned back to his desk. "But there are so many things I could tell you about him . . . Heck, I could tell you about the skeletons a few of our former classmates and teachers have hidden in their closets. Stuff they wouldn't want you or anyone else to know. Secrets that could ruin their lives."

Zack shot Zoey a concerned look. "Chester, are you blackmailing Lucas?"

Chester shook his head. "Blackmailing implies that I'm extorting Lucas for money or some other type of payment. I'm not doing that. Lucas doesn't have anything I want. Truthfully, he barely has anything at all anymore. I was just reminding him that I know his secrets and can deprive him of what little he has left."

"And you're not blackmailing anyone else?" Zack asked.

"No. Though I easily could," Chester said. "I could very easily open my mouth and ruin some people's lives. But I'm not forcing anyone to pay for my silence. I just like watching them squirm. It's my way of getting revenge for how they treated me back in high school."

"So, you're just threatening to break kayfabe?" Zoey asked. "You're not actually going to do it."

"What the heck is kayfabe?" Chester asked.

"It's a wrestling term," Zoey said before she launched into an explanation.

In the pro wrestling world, keeping kayfabe meant maintaining that the matches and storylines were reality. When breaking kayfabe, a wrestler does or says something that is legitimately real or unscripted. It shatters the illusion that the matches, characters, and storylines are real and, instead, shows that they are predetermined and scripted. The internet and social media had mostly killed kayfabe, but, back in the day, the wrestlers were expected to be in character at all times. Their personal lives needed to remain a secret. Even their families and friends would be kept in the dark. The unwritten rule was that rival wrestlers couldn't travel together, eat in the same restaurants, or stay in the same hotels because the fans might see them. Then kayfabe would be broken.

Kayfabe had to be maintained. Secrets needed to be kept.

Because they'd basically been raised in a wrestling ring, Zoey and her brothers used wrestling jargon on a regular basis. Since they were little kids, they'd used "kayfabe" to signify secrets. "Keep it kayfabe" meant whatever was said or happened was to remain between them. "Breaking kayfabe" meant that one of them tattled on the others or revealed secrets to someone who wasn't supposed to know. As adults, they continued to use the term. Their family and close friends understood what "kayfabe" represented. If Chester had known what it meant back when they were in high school, he'd forgotten about it over the past twelve years.

"Lucas . . . And whoever else's secrets you know . . . They've created their own reality based around their secrets or lies or whatever—"

"Don't we all do that, Zoey?" Chester asked. "Don't we all get up in the morning, put on our masks, and play the character we've created? We all have multiple versions of ourselves. Let's face it, you guys only see one side of me. You have no idea what I'm up to when I'm not here—"

"You're right," Zoey said. She didn't want to admit it out loud, but Chester made a good point. Everyone acted differently in public than they did in private. Zoey knew that she did to a certain extent. "But now that I know you're going around threatening people, I'm a little concerned."

"Maybe we all wear a mask, but not all of us have secrets," Zack said.

"You sure about that?" Chester asked. "Are you telling me you don't have any secrets, Zack? Things you wouldn't want anyone else to know."

"Well, yeah . . . But none of them could potentially ruin my life."

"Same here." Zoey cleared her throat. "Back to breaking kayfabe . . . Chester, you sharing whatever secrets you know would destroy the reality Lucas and these other people have created. It would ruin the character they're portraying or the illusion they've created. If they really feel threatened, they might lash out."

"I never said I was going to share anyone's secrets," Chester said. "Just that I was threatening to."

"Whether you do it or not, just be careful, bro." Zack put his hand on Chester's shoulder. "Breaking kayfabe comes with consequences. Even the threat of breaking it could come back and hurt you."

"Zack's right," Zoey said. "Some people are willing to go to the extreme to protect their secrets."

Chester waved off Zoey's and Zack's concern. "I'm not worried about it."

THREE

"I've had a few clients cancel because of the holidays, so I've got some open slots during the next couple of weeks," Bernadette Sullivan said as she turned on the coffee pot. She then set out a basket of sugar packets and a stack of Styrofoam cups on the counter of the small kitchenette. "And you've put off talking about Devon for long enough."

Zoey began seeing Bernadette for therapy sessions not long after ending her relationship with Devon Isler. That had been just over seven years ago. The year-and-a-half relationship with Devon had been toxic. He had verbally, mentally, and emotionally abused her. When she tried to leave him, the abuse turned physical. Zoey just barely escaped the relationship with her life. Had it not been for the next-door neighbors who broke into the apartment and dragged Devon off her, he most likely would have killed her.

After the physical assault, Zoey retreated into herself. She hardly left her parents' house, and she suffered from debilitating anxiety attacks. Her mother, Roxanne, forced her to go to therapy. At first, Zoey had been reluctant to talk to a stranger about her personal life. Bernadette waited her out. After weeks of discussing nothing but pro wrestling, Zoey opened up. It had taken a few years, but Bernadette helped Zoey work through her experiences and come to peace with herself.

With Zoey's approval, the prosecutor agreed to drop the attempted homicide charge if Devon pled guilty to the aggravated assault. He had been a horrible boyfriend to her, but he was kind enough to spare her from having to sit through a trial. After serving his five-year sentence, Devon was released.

A year after he was released, Devon saw Zoey wrestle at a show in Kissimmee, Florida. The next day, he followed her back to Pennsylvania. She hadn't known that he was back in her area until he showed up at the Linville Association of Wrestling's August event. Seeing him again had caused Zoey to nosedive. Her anxiety issues came rushing back full force, and she started to fall apart. In a matter of hours, all of Bernadette's hard work had nearly been undone.

But Devon's return to her life—and the wrestling ring—had been short-lived. Zoey found his dead body in the parking lot not long after his match ended. Finding his body had been traumatizing enough. But the experience had only been made worse when she immediately vaulted to the top of the suspect list. Since then, both Bernadette and her mom encouraged Zoey to schedule some therapy sessions. Deep down, Zoey knew she needed to deal with the shock of Devon's brief return and violent death. She was just too stubborn to admit it to anyone.

"I talked about Devon more than enough years ago," Zoey said. She grabbed another folding chair and added it to the growing circle that she was setting up in the middle of the tattoo shop's basement. "I spent more time trying to get over him than I did dating him. I do not want to talk about him anymore."

"Oh, Zoey . . ." Bernadette shook her head, setting into motion the miniature red ornament balls that decorated her beehive of braids. Green ribbons were twisted among the braids, and a gold star topped off the ridiculous hairstyle. "You'll never fully move on until you confront what happened."

"I have confronted it." Zoey slammed the chair's metal legs against the floor. The thin layer of commercial carpet absorbed the blow. "Devon is in my rearview mirror, and I am not looking back."

"But you're not looking forward either." Bernadette smiled, showing off the gap between her front teeth. "What happened to that cute detective who asked you out? Have you heard from him lately?"

"You mean the guy who arrested my twin brother?" Zoey snorted. "No, I haven't heard from him since he released Zack from custody. That was months ago. I guess he wasn't as interested in me as he claimed."

"Have you tried reaching out to him?"

"Nope."

"Maybe he's waiting for you to make the first move."

"Bernie . . ."

"Oh, Zoey . . ." Bernadette chuckled. "When you get over this stubborn streak and finally want to talk, I'll be here. It's past time you moved on from all this. If you don't put this thing with Devon to rest you'll never move on in your love life."

"I'm fine, Bernie." Zoey plucked a homemade chocolate chip cookie off the platter and bit into it. "Really."

Bernadette's right eyebrow crept upward, drawing attention to her lime green eyeshadow. "Do I need to remind you who you're talking to?"

Zoey stuffed the rest of the cookie in her mouth. After chewing and swallowing, she said, "I haven't had a nightmare about Devon since before Thanksgiving. Instead, I'm back to having my regular nightmares about high school. That's an improvement, right? Well, not really. But at least I'm not dreaming about Devon anymore. His return was an unfortunate setback. But I'm over it. I just hope I never find another dead body."

Turning away from the kitchenette—and putting the temptation of eating another cookie behind her—Zoey faced the rest of the basement. She had to hold back a scream when she came face-to-face with Chester.

Zoey slapped her hand against her chest and willed her heart rate to slow down. "How do you walk around in those combat boots without making any noise?"

Chester shrugged. "I learned a long time ago that being quiet attracts less attention."

Zoey thought his answer was cryptic, but she didn't ask for an explanation. Chester was an expert at avoiding talk of his personal life and deflecting questions that he didn't want to answer.

Instead, Zoey asked, "Do you need something?"

"I'm . . . uh . . . I'm done for the night." Chester traced the toe of his boot along a carpet seam. "I was wondering if I could sit in on the session. If that's okay with you."

"Of course, you're welcome to join us," Bernadette said.

Almost every Monday night for the past four years, Zoey and Bernadette had hosted meetings for a victim's support group. The first few sessions had been held at Bernadette's office. The rest were held in the basement of the tattoo shop. Many people cycled through the group sessions over the years. Some came for only one or two meetings. Others stuck around for months. One woman had only missed a half dozen sessions in the three years she'd been attending. Some of the participants were Bernadette's patients. Others found out about the group either online or by word-of-mouth.

Chester had just grabbed a cup of coffee when a group of people came downstairs. Bernadette waited a few more minutes for any stragglers before she got the session started by introducing Chester and asking him to tell the group why he was joining them for the evening.

"I, uh, I . . ." With wide eyes, Chester glanced wildly around the basement. Zoey, along with the other attendees, waited for him to speak. Chester set his coffee cup on the floor and then rubbed his hands up and down his thighs. "I, uh, I didn't have a great childhood, and, you know, I suffered from anxiety and depression . . . I was also suicidal."

Chester yanked up his left sleeve to reveal a forearm that was covered in tattoos. The tattoos partially obscured the scars that crisscrossed his flesh between his wrist and elbow. The raised skin of some old scars stood out under the basement's harsh artificial lighting. Zoey had a vague memory of Chester wearing long sleeve shirts year-round while in high school. She assumed he had used the sleeves to hide fresh cuts and scars.

Continuing, Chester said, "Mom was . . . Well, she always treated me good. But my old man, he and I never got along. He wasn't a, uh . . . a very nice guy to me. Or to my mom. I was a major disappointment to him, and he never let me forget it. He wanted a son who played sports, you know. Not a 'sissy' son who was into drawing and painting and poetry. He kicked me out right after high school graduation. Said his parental obligations to me were done. This is my first time back to the area in twelve years . . ."

When Chester trailed off, Bernadette asked, "Why did you come back?"

"Personal reasons. I don't really want to get into it." Chester glanced over at Bernadette before shifting his gaze to Zoey. "It hasn't been easy being back. It's stressing me out and bringing back a lot of memories that I'd rather have forgotten. Lately, I've been feeling really depressed. I mean, more than my usual depression. And that's caused suicidal thoughts—"

Interrupting, Bernadette asked, "Have you self-harmed recently?"

"And ruin this artwork?" Chester held out his arms so that everyone could see the highly detailed, brightly colored tattoos. "You have no idea how much money or how many hours I spent in the chair to cover up the old scars. I'm not about to slice them up."

"There are other ways of self-harming aside from cutting," Bernadette said.

"I know," Chester said as he tugged his sleeves back into place. His voice was hard and flat. "But I'm hanging in there. Today was just harder than others. I, you know, thought I'd sit in with the group . . ."

"What triggered you today?" Bernadette asked.

"An old friend stopped by to see me," Chester said. Zoey noticed that he was clenching his hands so tightly that his knuckles had turned white. "His name is Lucas, and we grew up together. We are both the only child. So we were, like, practically brothers back when we were little kids. Then, when we got to middle school, Lucas ditched me. He wanted to be part of the popular crowd, and there was no way his new friends were going to let me hang around since I was a 'freak' for dressing differently and . . . Well, you've all been in high school. You know what it's like for kids who are different. Lucas was never outright mean to me after that, but he didn't stand up for me either. It was a total betrayal. Like a knife to the back. Or heart. We weren't friends anymore after middle school. Seeing him today . . . It brought back even more memories. Some of them are good memories. But most are bad."

Chester shot Zoey a wide-eyed look that she assumed was a plea for help.

Zoey cleared her throat. "I also went to school with Chester and Lucas, and I saw Lucas today as well. He was kind of a jerk to me back then. And he was a jerk today, too. Seeing him again brought back some bad memories from high school for me . . ."

For the rest of the session, the group members discussed high school. Most of them had either been bullied or suffered in some other way. Chester didn't say anything else over the course of the next two hours, and his body language conveyed that he was uncomfortable. He couldn't seem to sit still and continuously wrung his hands as he watched the clock.

When Bernadette wrapped up the meeting just after eight o'clock, Zoey figured Chester would be the first to bolt up the basement steps. Instead, he lingered behind while the others made their way upstairs.

"I'll help clean up," Chester said as he grabbed one of the folding chairs and leaned it against the wall.

"I appreciate it." Zoey turned to Bernadette and said, "We got this. You can head home."

"All right, but I'm going to pencil in some sessions for you in the next couple of weeks."

"Yes, Bernie . . ." Once Bernadette had made her way upstairs, Zoey turned to Chester and asked, "You all right?"

"For the most part." Chester ran his hands over his face and back along the shaved sides of his head. "Being back here is hard. I mean, you and Zack are great. And being around the two of you and working here are the only things making it bearable. But my safe haven has been violated. Quincy's been giving me a hard time—"

"I noticed Quincy has been acting like a jerk towards you."

Quincy Durand was one of the other artists at 3 Count. Zoey and Zack had met Quincy in the cafeteria on their first day of middle school. As one of the only other kids wearing a pro wrestling t-shirt, the twins had naturally gravitated to him. Zack and Quincy had bonded over their shared love of pro wrestling and art. They'd been best friends ever since. But, over the last year, the friendship had become strained.

Three-and-a-half months earlier, Quincy had been involved in a motorcycle accident a few blocks down the street from the shop. Thanks to someone tampering with his motorcycle, the brakes failed as he approached a red light heading into downtown Linville. Unable to stop, he laid down the motorcycle to avoid hitting a car as it made a left-hand turn across the intersection.

Quincy had spent the past few months recuperating from his various injuries. He had returned to work just last week. On his first day back, Quincy jokingly asked Chester why he had changed his name and what he had been up to for the past twelve years. When Chester only gave him vague answers, Quincey became more insistent with his questions. His comments had also become borderline hostile. Quincy had gone so far as to accuse Chester of having committed a crime and then changing his name to elude the police. Had Zoey not gotten between them this past Friday, Quincy and Chester probably would have come to blows. Zoey and Zack had both yelled at Quincy for his cruel remarks, but that had not stopped him from pestering Chester.

"What's up between you and Quincy?" Zoey asked.

"Heck if I know." Chester shrugged. "But it goes back to high school. Quincy didn't like me back then either."

"He didn't?" Zoey asked. "I don't remember that."

"He never came out and said anything. It was just a feeling I had," Chester said. "But he doesn't seem to like me any better now. I think he sees me as a threat. Or that I'm trying to steal his spot."

"But he's the co-owner . . ." Zoey said. When they had opened the shop, Zack and Quincy had been equal owners. Recently, Quincy had signed over part of his ownership to make good on a debt that he owed Zack. "I'll talk to him."

"Thanks, but it doesn't really matter," Chester said. "With the way things are looking in my personal life, I probably won't be around too much longer."

Zoey gasped. "You're not planning to kill yourself, are you?"

"What? No." Chester tipped his head back and stared at the ceiling. "That did not come out the way I intended. I'm not planning to kill myself. I mean that I'm probably not going to be in Linville much longer."

"Why? What's going on? Why did you come back if you weren't planning to stay?"

"I may as well tell you since I told Zack back when he hired me. Honestly, I'm surprised he hasn't told you."

"Zack knows how to keep a secret. Unlike some people."

"Is that a dig?" Chester crossed his arms over his chest and leaned back against the wall. "The truth is . . . The only reason I'm here is because my mom is dying. She has stage four metastatic ovarian cancer—"

"Oh my God, I'm so sorry."

Chester nodded. "This is the second time she's had ovarian cancer. The first time was back when I was in high school—"

"You never told us that."

"There's a lot of things I didn't tell you. Or Zack. Or anyone." Chester let his arms fall away from his chest. "Between surgery and chemotherapy,

Mom's cancer went into remission. Now it's back, and it's spread to her liver and intestines. The doctor gave her six to twelve months. That was a couple months ago. When she told me, I decided to come back home to be with her. Once she passes away, I plan to go back to Los Angeles and try to forget about my interval here."

"Is it really that hard being back?"

"You have no idea." Chester smacked his palms against the wall. "All these old memories keep coming back. It's got me thinking about people who I haven't thought about in years. I'm second guessing every decision I've ever made. Wishing I'd done some things differently. There's someone I loved a long time ago. I hurt her really bad and then I ran away from her like a coward—"

"Do I know this person?"

Chester nodded. "You wouldn't believe me if I told you. I just wish I could see her one more time. Tell her how sorry I am. And that I never stopped loving her."

"Who is she?" Zoey asked. "Maybe it's not too late."

"I'd have to break kayfabe to tell you." Chester gave Zoey a weak smile. "And it's not just her. I ran into another of our former classmates the other week and I found out that I'm . . . Well, let's just say I learned something that could have totally changed my life. Something that's really pissed me off because I was lied to. And I have no idea what to do about it. I could say something, but then an innocent person would get really hurt. I don't think I could do that to the poor . . . person."

"Jeez, Chester. I had no idea you had all this stressful stuff going on in your life."

"And it seems to be getting more and more stressful every day," Chester said. "Lucas showing up today . . . That just might be my breaking point. I really don't know how much more I can take."

FOUR

Tuesday December 4th, 2018

"ARE YOU SURE YOU don't want to get a Christmas tree?"

"Bah humbug." As they drove past Baumgardner's Home and Garden Center, Zoey glared at the rows of various sized pine trees that were lined up in the store's parking lot. Even if she wanted a Christmas tree—and she did not—she didn't think her cat would tolerate it. No, Lita would climb the branches and knock off the ornaments. Heck, knowing Lita, she'd probably knock the entire tree down. Zoey turned to face her sister-in-law and asked, "Since when have you gotten all gung-ho about Christmas?"

"Since your brother and I had a kid," Arielle said. Her blonde hair, which was streaked with red and green highlights, was pulled back into a ponytail. "And I would appreciate it if you could fake some Christmas spirit for Paige's sake."

"I'll see what I can muster up for my future tag team partner. But it won't be easy." For her nearly two-year-old niece, Zoey would do just about anything. And that included acting excited about Christmas even though she was not a big fan of the overly commercialized, consumer-driven holiday. "In the nearly twenty years that we've known each other, can you recall a time when I was excited about Christmas?"

Arielle shook her head. "I remember you being excited about some of your presents. Especially that time your dad got you all *WrestleMania* tickets. And you were always thrilled about getting a week off from school. But when it came to the actual holiday . . . No, I can't really remember you ever being excited about Christmas. Halloween, on the other hand . . ."

"Is a far superior holiday."

Before they became sisters-in-law, Zoey and Arielle had been best friends. Arielle Coleman was the new kid in town when she met Zoey on the first day of eighth grade. Jim, Arielle's dad, had uprooted his family in northern New Jersey, and moved them to southcentral Pennsylvania so that he could take over as the Linville Chief of Police. Because Arielle wore punk-style clothes, had pink highlights in her blonde hair, and suffered from the unfortunate distinction of being the 'new kid,' she wasn't readily accepted by many of her new classmates. Since Zoey had already been deemed a social outcast by the popular crowd, she was much more welcoming to the new girl.

A year later, when her new best friend had hooked up with her twin brother, Zoey felt betrayed. Zack had been her partner in crime since birth. She was worried if Zack and Arielle would still have time for her, or would they be so focused on each other that Zoey no longer mattered? She had also worried about what would happen if the relationship soured and Arielle and Zack broke up. Would Zoey lose her newfound best friend? Would it alter her relationship with her twin? A year later, when Zoey began dating his best friend, Zack had similar worries. But, unlike Zoey and Quincy, Arielle and Zack had worked out. They had gotten married seven years earlier.

"You ready to work up a sweat?" Arielle asked as she pulled into the parking lot at the Linville Fitness Club. She worked part-time at the gym teaching classes.

"I'm ready to be warm," Zoey said as she slipped out of Arielle's toasty car and was bodyslammed by the chilly air. The temperature was a few degrees above freezing, and the cold sliced right through her thin zebra-print leggings. "I am not cut out for cold weather."

"You think anything below sixty degrees is cold."

Zoey dramatically shivered as she followed Arielle across the parking lot to the gym's front entrance. "I forgot to check today's schedule. What classes are you teaching?"

"First is the combo cardio and strength training," Arielle said. "And then yoga."

"Oh, yay, cardio . . . My *favorite*."

Inside the gym, the temperature was oppressive, and the air reeked of stale sweat, antiseptic, and old shoes. The Linville Fitness Club was housed in what used to be The Gutter Ball. The bowling alley had gone out of business when Zoey was a kid. After sitting empty for several years, the building was converted into a gym. The lanes were ripped out to make room for the exercise equipment, the arcade was turned into a private room where fitness classes were held, and the old concession stand was repurposed into a smoothie bar.

Zoey followed Arielle to the private room where a group of people was already waiting for class to begin. She might not enjoy cardio, but Zoey knew how important it was to her physical wellbeing. It helped her stay physically fit and kept her heart healthy. Cardio also helped keep her endurance level up—something that was crucial for her as a wrestler. Whether a match lasted for three minutes or for thirty, she had to make it to the end without becoming winded or worn out. Yoga, on the other hand was good for both her physical and mental wellbeing by keeping her flexible and helping her relax.

Following the yoga class, as Zoey and Arielle walked past the smoothie bar on their way to the exit, they heard someone shouting their names. They spotted one of their former classmates waiting in line to place her order.

"Oh, great . . . The class gossip," Zoey muttered as she waved at Natasha Bowman. They'd barely interacted in high school, but Natasha always greeted Zoey like they were long-lost best friends. "Since when has she joined the gym?"

Arielle shrugged. "This is the first time I've seen her here."

"Bad enough I have to avoid her every time I stop by the library," Zoey said as they waited for Natasha to finish placing her order. Natasha had been working at the Linville Public Library for the past few years, and she had recently been promoted to director. Zoey was an avid reader, and she made frequent trips to the library. She always tried to get in and out without running into Natasha, but she was rarely successful. "Now I have to avoid her at the gym. And I'm here almost every day."

"Oh, she's not that bad," Arielle said. Because she took Paige to the kids' story hour that was held at the library every Thursday afternoon, she ran into Natasha more regularly than Zoey did. "She just likes to talk."

"The talking I can deal with. The prying into my personal life is what gets annoying. That, and the fact that she will not move on from high school."

Natasha had been their class president in both middle school and high school. She had also headed up nearly every committee and joined several clubs. How Natasha had time to sleep or do her homework remained a mystery to Zoey.

Whenever Zoey ran into her, Natasha always wanted to reminisce about high school. According to Natasha, those had been the best four years of her life. Zoey, on the other hand, had no desire to relive the nightmare known as high school. But it was almost impossible to get Natasha to talk about anything else.

Natasha also had a bad habit of gossiping about their former classmates and asking overly personal questions about matters that were none of her business. Zoey had been purposely avoiding the library since August because she didn't want to get grilled by Natasha about her ex-boyfriend's murder. She had also ignored the numerous messages that Natasha had sent her over the past few months.

"Hey, Natasha," Zoey said as she returned the other woman's hug. She tried to smile, but she knew it probably looked more like a grimace. "We haven't seen you around here before. When did you join the gym?"

"This morning." Natasha brushed her frizzy black hair away from her face and then gestured towards her baggy gym clothes. "I put on some weight recently. Figured it was cheaper to join the gym than buy a whole new wardrobe."

"We have some personal trainers who can help you come up with a workout plan," Arielle said. "And you're welcome to come to any of my fitness classes."

"Order for Natasha!"

"Oh, that's me!" Natasha grabbed a tray containing four smoothies off the counter. She then turned back to Zoey and Arielle. "If you've got a minute, come over and say hi to the other girls. It'll be a mini reunion."

Without giving them a choice, Natasha got behind Zoey and Arielle and herded them across the smoothie bar's seating area. As they wove their way through the tables and chairs, Zoey looked around for the "girls" and noticed two more of their former classmates seated at a table by the picture windows. The windows provided a view of the gym's parking lot and the backside of the shopping center that was across the street.

"Oh, great, my two favorite frenemies . . ." Zoey whispered to Arielle. "What did we do to deserve this?"

"Be nice."

"Tell that to Brittany and Michelle."

Brittany Patterson and Michelle Harris had bullied Zoey from the first day of kindergarten all the way up through graduation. While Zoey was not the only recipient of their ridicule and pranks, she always felt that she had received the worst of it. Brittany and Michelle had picked on her for watching pro wrestling, for wearing clothes that were not "trendy," and for a long list of other made-up infractions. Zoey had hoped to never see either of them again after graduation. Unfortunately, Brittany and Michelle still lived in Linville, and Zoey ran into them on a frequent basis. Michelle worked afternoons at one of the local banks, and Brittany made her own hours at her in-home hair salon. They could be found at the gym most mornings, but Zoey rarely saw them using the equipment or participating in any of the fitness classes.

Even though it had been twelve years since they had graduated, Brittany and Michelle had changed very little. Yes, they had knocked off the childish pranks, but their veiled insults and judgmental comments had only gotten worse—and Zoey was still a recipient of the verbal abuse. She tried to kill them with kindness, but, more often than not, she wound up sinking down to their level and exchanging insults. They had always brought out the worst in her, and they continued to do so.

"Who's sitting across from Brittany?" Arielle asked as she followed Zoey past a table of beefy, college-age guys who were engaged in an arm-wrestling competition. "I feel like I know her from somewhere."

"Me, too . . ." Zoey eyed-up the slender woman who had perfect posture. She was racking her memory to determine if the woman was a regular at the gym when recognition hit her like a clothesline to the chest. "It's Jocelyn Hershey."

Arielle grunted. "The queen bee has returned to the hive."

"Brace yourself," Zoey said as she squared her shoulders. "I can't imagine that Jocelyn's gotten any less malicious since high school."

Zoey and Jocelyn had not gotten off to a good start when they first encountered each other in middle school. On either the second or third day of seventh grade, they had worn the same t-shirt. Zoey had picked up the mass-produced shirt at the mall over the summer. Yes, it had come from one of the "trendy" stores where the popular crowd shopped, but Zoey had not bought the shirt to follow a current fad or copy the popular kids. She got it because she saw the pale purple shirt in the window display and decided she liked it. Jocelyn did not like seeing Zoey dressed in the shirt—especially on the same day as her. At the end of the school day, as they headed outside to the buses, Jocelyn confronted Zoey and instructed her to never wear the shirt again. Otherwise, there would be consequences.

Zoey had not taken Jocelyn seriously. After all, what kind of "consequences" could a twelve-year-old girl dish out? She had worn the shirt again a week or two later. While walking by Zoey's table at lunch, Jocelyn dumped a tray of spaghetti down the front of Zoey's shirt. The marinara sauce permanently stained the pale purple fabric.

Zoey reported the incident to the teachers who monitored the cafeteria. She had hoped to get Jocelyn in trouble for ruining her new shirt. Instead, Jocelyn talked her way out of any punishment by claiming she had tripped over a backpack and "accidentally" spilled her lunch all over Zoey. Jocelyn had been given a replacement lunch while Zoey was forced to wear her oversized, smelly gym shirt for the rest of the day.

Along with humiliating Zoey, the lunchroom incident had cemented Jocelyn's spot at the top of the food chain. Brittany and Michelle—and the rest of the "popular" girls—fell in line. Up through graduation, they followed Jocelyn around and did her bidding. Brittany's and Michelle's juvenile antics had paled in comparison to what Jocelyn was capable of, and they had been the top two worker bees in Jocelyn's gossip campaign against Zoey. Brittany and Michelle had provided some of the ammunition and helped spread the rumors that Jocelyn made up about Zoey. Thanks to the three of them—and the rest of their friends—Zoey's middle school years were mostly miserable. High school had not been much better.

"Look who I found," Natasha said as she set down the tray and handed out the smoothies. Because Natasha had been Jocelyn's lackey, the overachieving brainiac had been tolerated by the rest of the popular crowd.

Had it not been for her friendship with Jocelyn, Natasha most likely would have been one of the outcasts along with Zoey and Arielle.

"Hi, Brittany. Hi, Michelle," Arielle said. "And Jocelyn, I don't think we've seen you since graduation."

"Why would you?" Even though Jocelyn was seated, she still managed to look down her pointed nose at Arielle and Zoey. After high school, she had moved to Saratoga Springs to attend Skidmore College. Natasha had provided Zoey with occasional updates about Jocelyn, but, because she didn't really care, Zoey hadn't paid much attention. "We weren't friends in high school. Did you really think I would have kept in touch with either of you after I escaped this hicktown?"

Zoey, Arielle, Michelle, and Brittany all grumbled while Natasha said, "You know, Jocelyn, some of us still live in this hicktown."

Jocelyn scowled at Natasha. "I was destined for better things. It's not my fault you didn't set your sights any higher than small-town librarian."

"I'm the director of the library. It's an important job." Natasha's shoulders slumped forward as she slid down in her seat. "And I had dreams. I just burned out in college."

"That's because you peaked in high school. You had nowhere to go after that but downhill." Jocelyn put her arm around Natasha and gave her a hug. "Don't feel bad. There just isn't enough room on the stage for everyone. Some people like you ladies have to sit up in the cheap seats."

Insulted, Zoey said, "You're as charming as ever, aren't you, Jocelyn?"

"What? It's the truth."

Brittany slammed her plastic smoothie cup onto the table. "Not trying to be a drama queen or anything, but you didn't exactly keep in touch with me or Michelle either, Jocelyn. Until a few days ago, I don't think we've seen or heard from you in the past ten years. And we were supposedly your best friends in high school."

"You guys were totally my besties." Jocelyn reached across the table and clasped Michelle's and Brittany's hands.

Natasha loudly cleared her throat.

"And you're still my best friend for life," Jocelyn said, earning a look of pure adoration from Natasha. "But the life of a professional dancer . . . It was so hectic. Between practices and performances and all the travel, I barely had time to breathe much less keep up with my old friends. Teaching isn't nearly as hectic, but it is time consuming. And it's not like I was able to make it back to Linville all that often over the years. And there didn't seem to be much of a point to coming back after my parents moved away."

"What are you doing back in town now?" Arielle asked.

"The *prestigious* dance academy I teach at in the Big Apple is closed for winter break," Jocelyn said. "Since my parents are off on some Caribbean cruise, I figured I'd come spend some time with Natasha. This is the first extended break I've had in years, and I plan to make the most of it."

"Jocelyn isn't our only former classmate who's back in town," Brittany said. She tucked a strand of her gingery red hair behind her ear. "Michelle was just telling us about how she ran into Lucas Jennings yesterday."

"I was stunned when you added him to our group message last night," Natasha said to Michelle. "I've tried to keep tabs on everyone from high school, but I lost track of Lucas after he retired from minor league baseball."

"Zoey and Arielle already know Lucas is back." Michelle nudged Zoey in the side and said, "I heard you had a run in with him, too."

"Yeah, Lucas stopped by Zack's tattoo shop yesterday," Zoey said. "Where did you see him at?"

"The bank. He came in to open an account. Since the manager was busy, I wound up helping him." Michelle lowered her voice to a whisper. "Don't tell anyone I said this . . . because I could lose my job for gossiping about a client . . . but Lucas is almost broke. He told me his ex-wife took him to the cleaners, and she got almost everything in the divorce."

"You shouldn't be sharing Lucas's confidences," Arielle scolded Michelle. "His financial situation is none of our business."

"Lighten up. We're just talking," Michelle said to Arielle. She then turned to Zoey and asked, "Can you believe how bad Lucas looks?"

"None of us look like we did twelve years ago. We've all changed. Some of us have gotten tattoos." Zoey held out her arms to show off the colorful tattoos that covered her arms from shoulder to wrist. She then gave Michelle and Brittany knowing looks as she said, "And others have gotten plastic surgery—"

"It was medically necessary," Brittany said as she rubbed a hand over her misshapen nose. She'd had a nose job years ago, and the plastic surgeon botched it. "I had a deviated septum. My nose may look like crap now, but at least I can breathe."

"And what I've had done to my body is nobody's business but my own," Michelle said. She crossed her arms over her silicone-filled breasts. She might have also glared at Zoey, but it was hard to tell because all the botox had left her facial muscles rigidly fixed in place. "And Lucas got fat. Like, super fat."

"Yeah, totally obese," Brittany added as she held her arms out to the side. "Michelle took a selfie with him, and she just showed it to us."

"I never would have known it was Lucas if Michelle hadn't said so," Jocelyn said. "He has three chins!"

"You know, it's not nice to make fun of people," Arielle said. "Lucas might have some kind of health issue, and it's not his fault he put on weight."

"Or he stuffed his face with junk food since retiring from baseball," Brittany said.

"You and Lucas were the cutest couple ever," Michelle said to Jocelyn. "I couldn't believe it when you broke up with him. I always figured you two would eventually get married."

Jocelyn laughed. "Lucas probably wishes that I had stuck with him. With me by his side, he would have made something of himself. He could have been a famous baseball player. Without me pushing him to succeed, he wound up as just another nobody."

"And you're somebody?" Zoey rolled her eyes. "But here's your chance to turn Lucas's life around, Jocelyn. It sounds like he's single and ready to mingle. After insulting me for still being into pro wrestling—"

"Oh my God . . ." Jocelyn laughed. "You're still into that stupid stuff? I bet you still think dinosaurs are cool and—"

"Oh, she definitely does." Michelle poked Zoey's left thigh. "She's got a tattoo of a dinosaur on her leg. It's the ugly one with the horns."

"Triceratops," Brittany murmured.

Michelle whipped around to face Brittany. "How do you know that?"

"I have a twelve-year-old son who still isn't over his dinosaur phase. He's obsessed."

"Thank God, I only have daughters."

"I have a daughter," Arielle said. "And she likes dinosaurs."

Jocelyn snickered. "I bet you two still listen to the Backstreet Boys, too. My God, you need to grow up."

"We've been telling them that for years," Michelle said. "But they won't listen."

"Just because it's your *opinion* that wrestling is stupid does not, in fact, mean it is stupid," Zoey grumbled. She didn't reply to the comment about the Backstreet Boys. Yes, she still listened to them. And, like fine wine, they had only gotten better with age.

"Everyone *knows* wrestling is stupid." Jocelyn tugged on the scrunchie that held her hair back in a messy bun. The waist-length caramel-colored hair cascaded about her shoulders. In a condescending tone, she asked, "You do know it's fake, right, Zoey?"

"Don't say that!" Brittany playfully smacked Jocelyn on the arm. "Now Zoey will lecture us on how wrestling isn't fake. It's fixed."

"Same difference," Jocelyn said.

"And she'll try to tell us what's so great about it," Michelle added.

Zoey cleared her throat. "As I was saying, before I was so rudely interrupted, Lucas asked me out on a date."

"You wish he asked you out." Jocelyn snickered. "But you must have misunderstood him. You know Lucas only dates *pretty* girls. Unless he's significantly lowered his standards since high school, he doesn't date tattoo-covered freaks like *you*."

Zoey mentally kicked herself. Why had she even said anything? After all the years she had been picked on by Jocelyn, Michelle, and Brittany, she should have known at least one of them would make a mean comment. Why would they care that Lucas had asked her out? Zoey didn't even care, so it wasn't like she was bragging.

"That's enough, Jocelyn." Arielle slammed her fist against the table. "If anyone needs to grow up, it's you."

"Me?" Jocelyn pressed her hand against her chest in mock innocence. "What did I do?"

"Insulting people and causing drama. Just like you've always done," Zoey said. "I'm not going to hang around here just to be disrespected."

"Neither am I," Arielle said. "I have to go pick up my daughter from my mom's house."

"And I have to get to work," Zoey added.

"Hold on. We aren't done talking to you." Michelle grabbed the back of Zoey's shirt and prevented her from walking away. "When I talked to Lucas yesterday, he mentioned that Chester Hartman is also back in town. And that he's working at your brother's tattoo shop."

Jocelyn grunted, and a pink flush crept over her pale skin. "Chester should have stayed under whatever rock it was he crawled under."

"Whoa . . ." Zoey said to Jocelyn. "What's gotten into you?"

Joelyn glared at Zoey as she shoved her chair back. She then stood up and stomped off without saying another word to any of them. She left her smoothie on the table and her purse and coat hanging over the back of the chair. She shot Zoey and Arielle one last glare before she walked outside wearing nothing but a tank top and leggings.

"What's up with her?" Zoey asked Natasha.

"Jocelyn doesn't owe you an explanation." Natasha scurried to gather up hers and Jocelyn's belongings. "But where has Chester been all these years? He was the only person in our graduating class who I totally lost track of. It was like he fell off the face of the Earth."

"He was out in LA. And he goes by Chester Neidigh now," Zoey said. She had yet to figure out when or why he had changed his last name. "He's been back in town and working for Zack for about three months."

"And we're only hearing about this now because . . ." Natasha said.

"Because it's none of your business," Zoey said.

Brittany grabbed a napkin out of the metal dispenser and tore the thin paper into strips. "I ran into Chester a few weeks ago—"

"What? And you didn't tell me?" Michelle turned to face Brittany. "Oh my God, do you remember how he used to creep on you during senior year? Didn't Rodney—"

"Please don't mention my ex-husband," Brittany said.

"But didn't Rodney beat up Chester for creeping on you?"

"Yes, he did," Brittany snapped. "And Chester wasn't creeping on me. He was my lab partner in physics. We were working together."

"I remember that," Zoey said. "Rodney shoved me out of the way so he could get to Chester. He yelled something about how Chester needed to leave you alone and then sucker punched him."

"And then Zack jumped in and broke it up," Arielle added. "He almost got suspended because the principal thought he was part of the fight."

Michelle laughed. "But, ugh, Chester Hartman, what a freak!"

"Knock it off, Michelle," Brittany shrieked. Her raised voice drew the attention of the other people who were seated at the tables or were standing in line at the smoothie bar. Brittany shoved her chair back and stood up. "It's not nice to call him a freak. We aren't in high school anymore."

Brittany grabbed her purse and her coat. She then hurried towards the exit.

"What the heck is her problem?" Michelle asked.

"Other than you bringing up her ex-husband?" Natasha asked as she finished gathering up Jocelyn's belongings. "You know she hates that."

After saying a quick goodbye to Zoey and Arielle, Michelle and Natasha followed Jocelyn and Brittany outside.

"That was bizarre." Arielle said. "Why would Jocelyn be all worked up over Chester? They had nothing to do with each other in high school. At least not that I remember."

Zoey shrugged. "Brittany seemed a little upset, too. Then again, Chester told me yesterday that he knows things about some of our former classmates. Things that they wouldn't want anyone to know. Maybe he knows some of Jocelyn's or Brittany's secrets."

"And maybe they know some of his."

FIVE

"I'M SURE CHESTER WILL be here any minute."

Leaving Chester's client twiddling his thumbs in the office, Zoey scurried across the hall and knocked on Zack's door.

"Sorry to interrupt," Zoey said as she pushed open the door and stepped into the small room. "Can I have a word with you?"

Zack looked up from prepping his client for a tattoo. "What's up?"

"In private." Zoey gestured for Zack to come out into the hallway. "It's about Chester."

"I'll be back in a minute," Zack said to his client. He then stripped off his latex gloves as he followed Zoey out into the hallway. "What's going on with Chester?"

"That's the problem. I don't know." Zoey stepped to the side so that Zack could see into the office. "Chester's client is here for their appointment. But Chester has yet to show up."

Zack grabbed Zoey's phone out of her hand so that he could check the time. "It's only twelve-thirty. Have you tried calling him?"

"Of course, I've called him. I've also texted him. Nothing."

"He's never been late before."

"Yeah, this is totally unlike him." Zoey snatched her phone back. "He's always here before we open."

"Maybe he had car trouble—"

"Then he would have called to tell me that," Zoey said. "I'm getting worried. What if Chester, you know, *hurt* himself?"

"He used to cut himself back in high school." Zack made a slicing motion across his left forearm. "I don't think he does it anymore, but . . . I should have paid better attention to him. I could tell he hasn't been in a great place mentally. Especially this past week or so."

"He told me that Quincy giving him a hard time definitely isn't helping."

Zack cursed Quincy. "When did Chester say that?"

"Last night. At the abuse survivor's support group—"

"Seriously? Since when has he been attending the meetings?"

"Yesterday was the first time," Zoey said. "I guess seeing Lucas really rattled him, and he wanted to talk to someone about it—"

Zack snapped his fingers. "That could be it. Maybe Chester met up with Lucas and got distracted. I don't know about you, but I got the feeling there was some unfinished business between them when Lucas stormed out of here yesterday."

"I guess that's possible."

"Or you're worried about nothing." Zack put his hand on Zoey's shoulder and gave her a gentle squeeze. "Chester could have overslept. You've done that a few times."

"Not funny." Zoey ducked her head so Zack couldn't see her blush. Because of her chronic insomnia, she had a bad habit of turning off her alarm and going back to bed if she hadn't gotten much sleep the night before. "Chester also told me about his mom. Maybe something happened to her."

"If his mom died or was in the hospital, I think Chester would have said something," Zack said. "That he hasn't answered your calls or responded to any of your texts . . ."

"I don't know why, but I have a really bad gut feeling right now. I'm going to check on Chester. I'm worried about his mental and emotional state. Last night, he assured me he was okay. And he swore to me that he wouldn't act on his suicidal feelings. But who knows what happened after he left here . . ." Zoey brushed past Zack as she headed for the staircase that led upstairs to her apartment. She stopped halfway up the stairs. "You'll have to tell me where Chester lives."

"In the shipping container community to the east of town. He's in number thirteen."

"I'm on it."

Zoey rushed upstairs to grab her coat. She then hustled out to where her purple Jeep Grand Cherokee was parked behind the building.

It was a quick five-minute drive to where Shippington Way was located on the eastern outskirts of Linville. Zoey thought the community's name was a tad pretentious considering the rental units were old shipping containers. The two dozen units were about the same size as single-wide trailers. She guessed they were twelve feet wide and about twenty-five feet long. The front yards were smaller than a wrestling ring, and the side yard provided only enough room for a metal carport and a small patch of dead grass.

Chester's home was easy to find since his beat-up yellow car was parked under the metal carport. Because there wasn't enough room for her Jeep in the driveway, she drove a little further down the road and parked in a small lot that was designated for visitors. The only other car in the lot was a red truck. Mud splatter along the bottom of the truck partially concealed the countless rust spots, and an oversized political bumper sticker across the tailgate left little doubt who the owner would be voting for in the next election. Zoey thought the truck looked familiar, but she couldn't think of where she had seen it before.

"Chester couldn't have gotten far without his car," Zoey said to herself as she walked back to his house. If Chester had car trouble and opted to walk to work, Zoey would have driven past him. There was no way she would have missed seeing that purple mohawk. "Unless he got a ride from someone else . . ."

After confirming that there was not a door or any windows along the side of the container that overlooked the carport, Zoey stepped up onto the narrow front porch. A door sat in the middle of the short side of the container.

"Chester! It's Zoey!" she shouted as she knocked on the door. "Is everything okay? You're late for work."

After a minute passed with no response, Zoey knocked again. It was possible that Chester was asleep and didn't hear her knock the first time. Or he could be in the bathroom.

"Come on, Chester." Zoey bounced on her toes and tried to stay warm. "Open up."

When Chester still didn't come to the door, Zoey looked around to see if maybe he had taken a walk around the drainage ditch that was in the center of the small community. She didn't see him anywhere, but she did notice an older man watching her. He stood between her Jeep and the red truck. Zoey waved at him and called out to ask if he knew Chester. The man stared at her for a few more seconds before he climbed into the truck and drove off.

"That was rude," Zoey muttered as she turned back to the door. She knocked one more time. "Where the heck are you, Chester?"

Pushing up on her tiptoes, Zoey tried to look through the three small windows that lined the top of the door. She was too short to see anything other than a section of the ceiling and the top of the wall cabinets that were to the left of the door. One of the cabinets was open.

Zoey had never physically been inside any of the shipping container homes, but, because Marlon had renovated the interiors, she'd seen plenty of pictures. If she remembered correctly, the wall cabinets were part of the kitchenette. Beyond that would be a small dining area. To the right of the door would be the combined bathroom and laundry room.

"May as well take a look around."

Zoey jumped off the porch and walked along the side of the container to the back where a wooden platform served as a tiny deck and provided a scenic view of an eight-foot-high wooden fence. She climbed the cinder-block steps, stepped over an ashtray that overflowed with cigarette butts, and then knocked on the sliding glass door.

After waiting a few seconds for a response, Zoey tried looking inside. Chester had drawn the vertical blinds across the door, but she found a couple gaps where she could peek inside at the combined living room and bedroom. A loveseat sat facing a low dresser. Most of the dresser drawers were pulled out. Clothes spilled out of the drawers and lay heaped on the floor.

On the far side of the dresser was the bed. She could see that the bed was empty, and Chester had not bothered to straighten up the sheets. A blanket hung off the edge of the bed, and one of the pillows was on the floor. Since the bed was empty, that meant Chester hadn't overslept. But then where was he? It's not like there were many places to hide in the shipping container. And, even if he was in the bathroom, he should have heard her knocking and yelling.

And why were there feathers scattered everywhere? Had a pillow exploded or was Chester working on some bizarre piece of artwork? Zoey didn't know if he still created any art aside from tattoos. She'd tried asking him a few times, but, per habit, Chester evaded the question.

"What a mess." Zoey wrinkled her nose in disgust. She hated clutter and disorder. Aside from his desk, Chester's private room at the tattoo shop was usually immaculate. It didn't appear that he was as neat and orderly at home.

Zoey looked over the sliding door and tried to find another gap between the blinds. Along the bottom of the door, a couple of the blinds had gotten caught on the edge of a welcome mat. It provided a larger area for her to look through. She knelt and pressed her face against the glass. It wasn't easy to see much at floor level—especially with the coffee table's legs and piles of clothes blocking part of the view. It would have been next to impossible to see anything if Chester hadn't left some of the lights on.

"What the . . ." Zoey muttered as she finally caught sight of Chester. Between the coffee table's legs, she could see the lower half of his body lying on the floor in front of the kitchenette. His upper half appeared to be in the bathroom. Her gut had been right. Something was wrong with Chester. "Oh, shit!"

Zoey grabbed ahold of the door handle and used it to pull herself upright. She was surprised when the patio door slid open.

"Chester?" Zoey asked as she tiptoed inside. "Are you all right?"

Chester did not respond.

Tiny feathers scattered as Zoey crept towards the front of the narrow shipping container. She was careful about where she placed her feet. She did not want to step on anything that could be considered evidence or disturb too much of the destruction.

Instinctively, she knew that Chester's home was now a crime scene. She should not be inside at all. And, if it wasn't for Chester, she wouldn't have ventured inside. His silence and lack of movement indicated that he was dead. But Zoey knew there was a possibility that he was just unconscious. She had to be sure.

As she made her way over to Chester, Zoey glanced around the shipping container. Stuffing spilled from the loveseat, and there were countless feathers coating the mattress and floor. The trashcan next to the kitchenette was overturned, and one of the chairs at the small table lay on its side. The kitchenette had also been ransacked. The sink was full of dirty dishes, empty beer cans, and a stack of thawing microwave ready meals. The items that had once been inside the fridge and the cabinets lay scattered on the tiny counter and stovetop. Every package had been torn open, and the contents lay scattered on the floor. Cereal and chips crunched under her boots.

"Chester!" Zoey nudged his leg with her foot, knocking chips and cardboard containers off his legs. She couldn't see the upper half of his body because it was inside the bathroom. "Please be okay. Please just be drunk."

Zoey braced her right hand against the wall and then reached around into the bathroom with her left arm. She felt around on the wall until she found the light switch.

After gathering up her courage, Zoey leaned to the side and peeked into the blood-spattered bathroom. Her eyes were drawn to the knife that protruded from Chester's chest.

"Oh, no . . ."

Zoey squeezed her eyes shut to block the image of Chester's bloody body sprawled across the tile floor. Her head spun, and lunch threatened to make a reappearance.

After a few calming breaths, Zoey opened her eyes and looked around the tiny bathroom.

A smear of dried blood on the edge of the toilet led her to believe that Chester had fallen and hit his head. There was also a large pool of blood on the floor surrounding his head and upper body, and droplets were splattered all over the floor and walls.

The fact that food and empty packaging were piled on top of him proved that someone else had searched the apartment after Chester had died or was, at least, incapacitated.

"Chester . . ." Zoey stepped into the bathroom and knelt next to his prone body. She peeled off her gloves and then pressed her fingers to his wrist. His skin was cool, and she couldn't detect a pulse. "Who did this to you?"

SIX

"IF YOU WERE FINALLY ready to take me up on the offer of buying you a drink, you could have just called," Detective Tyler Gates said as he joined Zoey in the back of the police cruiser. "You didn't have to go to the trouble of finding another body."

Zoey had been stuck in the cruiser since the responding officer had arrived at Shippington Way about an hour earlier. The officer had taken her phone and her purse but had been considerate enough to leave the engine running and the heater on. Instead of looking at the detective, she tipped her head back and stared at the assortment of stains on the cruiser's ceiling. A few reddish-brown spots looked suspiciously like dried blood.

"Trust me, I was not trying to find *another* dead body." Zoey groaned. "And I didn't exactly go looking for the first one, either."

"I know." Gates reached over and patted Zoey's clenched fist. "But, in all seriousness, we really do need to stop meeting at crime scenes."

Zoey had first met Detective Gates not long after she discovered her ex-boyfriend's dead body in the parking lot behind the local VFW Hall. That had been four months earlier. Within minutes of her calling 911, officers from the Linville Police Department swarmed the scene. As the only detective on the force, Gates was put in charge of the investigation. He had recently moved to Linville from Philadelphia, and he was under the impression that the small-town had a low crime rate. Devon's murder had been the first one in twenty years.

Despite the macabre circumstances under which they had met, Zoey had felt an immediate attraction towards Detective Gates—and it had not been a welcome thought as she stood mere feet away from her ex-boyfriend's body. She hadn't seriously dated anyone since breaking up with Devon. Sure, she'd gone on some dates over the years. Some of those dates had gone very well and showed potential of becoming more. Zoey always walked away before that could happen. Because she was still haunted by the emotional and mental trauma caused by Devon, she was scared to get involved in another serious relationship—but she also wasn't dead, and she took notice of a handsome man when she came across one. Admittedly, she also had a weakness for blonde-haired, blue-eyed heartthrobs who, once upon a time, looked like they could have been the lead singer of a boy band. Devon Isler had fit that description, and so did Detective Gates. The difference between the two was that the detective did not flaunt his good looks or have an ego of gigantic proportions—at least not that Zoey was aware of.

Zoey's attraction had wavered when Detective Gates accused her and both of her brothers of being involved in Devon's death. He had initially suspected the Wilde siblings of working in cahoots to kill Devon—that Justin had sent Devon outside to meet Zoey, and that she then distracted the victim while Zack attacked him from behind. It was a plausible theory, but it was not what had happened.

At first, Zoey hadn't been all that mad at the detective for suspecting them. Sure, she'd been a little insulted and upset. After all, it was unflattering to be considered a suspect, or, at least, Zoey didn't find it flattering. Her grandmother, Vivian, would have been thrilled to make it onto the suspect list. But Vivian—who had an alibi for the time of death—was also a tad eccentric and was obsessed with watching true crime shows. Her steadfast interest in the murder investigation had led to Zoey asking questions and sticking her nose where it did not belong. She had also put herself in danger when she accidently confronted Devon's killer.

Zoey's attraction may have cooled after Detective Gates accused her of being involved in Devon's murder, but it was put down for the three count when he wrongfully arrested Zack for the crime. That being said, she'd frequently thought about him over these past few months.

Seeing him again renewed the physical attraction—or maybe it was Zoey's subconscious way of dealing with the trauma of finding another dead body. Focusing on Detective Gates's good looks gave her something else to think about when her imagination was stuck on the image of Chester's bloody body.

As her adrenaline wore off, shock settled in. She'd spent the past hour coming to terms with Chester's violent death. Sometime between him leaving the shop around eight-thirty last night and her arriving at his shipping container house just after one in the afternoon, someone killed Chester by plunging a knife into his chest. It was so unfair. He had come back to the area to be with his mother during her final months, but he wound up losing his life.

No, Zoey thought, *he'd had his life stolen from him*.

Zoey squeezed her eyes shut and whimpered.

"Are you all right?" Gates moved closer. "Talk to me."

"Why is this happening to me?" Zoey had been holding it together pretty well up until now. Like a wrestler finding his second wind just before the ten count, her anxiety sprang to life. "Did I piss off the universe? Is finding dead bodies my punishment?"

"I don't think you're being punished." Gates put his arm around her shoulders and gave her an awkward, one-armed hug. "You were just at the wrong place at the wrong time again."

"Two dead bodies in Linville in less than six months. And I find both. I know both victims . . . What are the odds?"

Zoey opened her eyes and pulled away from Gates. It was difficult to put much distance between them in the close confines of the backseat, and she was only able to shift a few inches closer to the door. But the hug had breached the walls of her defense, and the anxiety oozed in. A single tear slid down her cheek. It was soon followed by a torrent.

"Shhh. It's going to be all right." Gates drew her closer. "Is there anything I can do?"

Zoey pressed her face to the front of his leather coat and howled, "Get me out of here."

Shoving Gates away from her, Zoey spun around to face the door. With trembling hands, she grasped the door handle and yanked. She normally did not have any issues with confined spaces. but it felt like the steel mesh separating her from the front seat was creeping closer. The heat was also getting to her. She appreciated that the officer had left the heater on, but the inside of the cruiser now felt like a sauna.

"Why won't the door open?" Zoey asked as she continued tugging on the door handle. She could hear a slight buzzing sound that steadily grew louder. "Why won't you let me out?"

"Hang on, Zoey. I'll get you out."

Having left the other door cracked, Gates was able to exit the vehicle. He then sprinted around to the other side and opened the door. Zoey scrambled out of the cruiser. She would have tripped over her own feet had Gates not grabbed her around the waist and kept her upright.

The cold breeze felt good against the exposed skin on her face as it dried the sweat and tears. After a few seconds, Zoey began to shiver. The temperature was in the low forties, but heavy clouds blocked the sun and made it feel colder.

As she clung to the detective, Zoey glanced wildly around the scene. While in the cruiser, her back had been to Chester's shipping container home. She hadn't seen the responding officer hang up crime scene tape around the perimeter of Chester's small yard. She also hadn't seen the other Linville police officers arrive. There were also State Police cruisers parked nearby along with an ambulance and the coroner's van.

A crowd was gathered in front of the shipping container. Most were identifiable by their uniforms. Zoey spotted Zack standing alongside his father-in-law, who was the Chief of the Linville Police. Jim Coleman had held the position for close to twenty years. Farther down the road—on the other side of a temporary roadblock—neighbors and a crew from one of the local news stations gathered.

"Zack . . ."

Letting go of the detective, Zoey took a step in her brother's direction. Her legs wobbled, causing her to stumble. Gates caught her as her knees gave out and she sank to the ground.

Not again . . . Zoey thought as the anxiety attack washed over her. The slight buzzing suddenly roared louder than the crowd at *WrestleMania*, and black dots swarmed in front of her eyes and clouded her vision.

Aside from a couple episodes back in August, Zoey had not had an anxiety attack of this magnitude in years. Her body was temporarily shutting down in response to the onslaught, but her brain was still working just fine.

She was aware of someone's arm wrapped around her shoulders and another person holding her hand. Above the roaring sound, she could hear voices—possibly multiple voices—but she couldn't make out what any of them were saying. She could also hear a high-pitched keening that seemed to be coming from inside her. It took Zoey a few moments to realize that she was the one making the noise.

Just keep breathing. Everything will be okay. Just breathe.

She wasn't sure how much time had passed—it could have been seconds or minutes—but the roaring abruptly faded, and her vision returned.

Zack, Jim, and Detective Gates were crowded around her. There was also an EMT squatting in front of her. The EMT held her hand as he monitored her pulse.

"She has an elevated heart rate. And her blood pressure drastically dropped," the EMT said. "I recommend taking her to the hospital for further evaluation. She could be going into nervous shock."

"I'm fine." Zoey yanked the blood pressure cuff off her wrist. "It was just an anxiety attack."

"Are you sure?" Zack asked. "Maybe you should go to the hospital. What if it's something more serious than an anxiety attack?"

"I'm fine. It's Chester that needs help."

"Chester is way past needing medical attention," Zack said. He pulled her in for a hug. "I am so sorry, Zoey. I should have taken your gut feeling more seriously and come with you."

"It's not your fault. You couldn't have known he'd be . . ." Zoey trailed off as she squirmed out of her brother's smothering grip. The hug was comforting, but, for the moment, she couldn't stand being touched. She scooted away from Zack. "What are you doing here?"

"I picked him up on my way here," Jim Coleman said. Zoey had known Linville's Chief of Police since she was a teenager. Over the years, she'd watched Jim's brown hair turn gray and the wrinkles carve their way across his face. "When I heard that you'd called in about the body, I figured I better get Zack. Just in case . . . you know . . ."

"Your brother filled me in on what you're doing here," Gates said. "He also identified the victim and gave us some information about him."

"What little I have," Zack muttered.

"Thanks for getting him," Zoey said to Jim. She then looked over at Gates. After meeting his concerned gaze, she glanced away. She was embarrassed that so many people had seen her breakdown—especially the detective. She hated showing any type of weakness. "Sorry about that. I just—"

"There is nothing to apologize for." Gates squeezed her hand. "I just want to be sure you're okay."

"I will be." Zoey took a few deep breaths. "I think I can get up now."

"Are you up for answering a few questions now?" Gates asked as he helped Zoey to her feet. "Or would you prefer to go home and rest? I can come by later to get your statement."

"I'd rather get it out of the way now." Zoey looked back at the cruiser and shuddered. "But can we do it somewhere other than the backseat?"

"We can walk over to my place." Gates pointed at the shipping container that was four spots down from Chester's. The metal was painted red, and the only Christmas decorations were a lopsided wreath and some icicle lights along the porch roof. "It's not much bigger than the cruiser, but it'll be more comfortable."

Zoey linked arms with the detective and allowed him to lead her over to the shipping container.

"How long have you lived here? Did you know Chester?"

Gates shook his head. "I saw him around a few times. That purple mohawk was hard to miss. But I don't think I ever talked to him except maybe to say hi. And I had no idea he worked at the tattoo shop. To be honest, I haven't really gotten to know any of my neighbors. Living here is only temporary until I find a house. But finding one is harder than I anticipated. I've been living in the shipping container for eight months now, and that's about five or six months longer than I'd originally planned when I first moved to Linville."

The layout of Gates's home was identical to Chester's. The kitchenette cabinets were a different color, but the flooring was the same. Gates's home was much neater than Chester's, but it also lacked any personal touches. There weren't any knickknacks sitting around or pictures hanging on the walls. Zoey spotted a "World's Greatest Uncle" mug on the counter next to the coffeemaker, but that was it for personal items.

"I only have the one chair," Gates said as he led Zoey to the far side of the shipping container. He gestured for her to have a seat in the leather recliner. He then handed her a small remote. "But it has a built-in heater and massager."

"Fancy," Zoey said as she played with the remote. It gave her something to focus on so she wouldn't gawk at Gates's home. Yes, the shipping container was more comfortable than the cruiser. But it was also more intimate. She felt like she was invading Gates's personal space, and it made her uncomfortable. "Got any tissues?"

"Of course." Gates spread a blanket over her lap. He then handed her a box of tissues, a bottle of water, and a packet of peanut butter sandwich crackers. "Take a few minutes to collect yourself."

Zoey held up the water bottle. "I could use something a little stronger than this."

"I'm not much of a drinker, so I normally don't keep anything in the house." Gates turned around and looked over at the kitchenette. "It's possible I have a bottle of whiskey tucked away somewhere."

"It's okay." Zoey held out her hand. "I'm not much of a drinker, either. But after today . . ."

"My offer to buy you a drink still stands."

Zoey ducked her head and looked at the detective out of the corner of her eye. "Are you asking me out on an actual date?"

"Yes, I'm asking you out," Detective Gates said. "And it doesn't have to be for drinks. We could go to dinner or the movies. Or . . . I'm sure there are plenty of other things to do around Linville . . ."

"What about when you asked me out the first time?" Zoey asked. "Were you really asking me out on a date then, too?"

A couple days after Devon's murder, Detective Gates had ambiguously asked her out by offering to buy her a drink in exchange for hearing some of her wrestling stories. That wasn't long after he'd accused her of being involved in Devon's death.

"I was."

"But I was still a suspect."

"Yeah, it wasn't my most professional move." Detective Gates gave her a lopsided smile. "For all I knew, you were a murderer. But I was willing to take the risk."

"Or maybe you were hoping a little alcohol would loosen my tongue, and I would confess to something."

"No, I'm not that devious."

"Well then . . ." Zoey took a sip of water. She hoped the cool drink would help ease the flush that warmed her cheeks. "I'm tempted to take you up on the offer."

"Does that mean you've forgiven me for arresting your brother?"

"Not quite."

"You know I was just doing my job," Gates said. "Zack had a good motive and no alibi. There was also circumstantial evidence."

Zoey waved her hand in a dismissive gesture. "I know. I know."

"Unfortunately, you also know the drill." Gates flipped open a notebook to a fresh page. He then pulled a recording device out of his pocket and turned it on. "Tell me about what happened today."

Zoey explained why she was at Shippington Way looking for Chester.

"Since Chester's car was here, I figured he must be inside. Or, at least, close by. I knocked a few times. When he didn't answer the door, I went around back and looked in through the sliding door. That's when I saw Chester lying on the floor by the front door. Since the door was unlocked . . ."

"It's all right."

"But I disturbed the crime scene. And I might have messed up some of the evidence."

"Like I said, it's all right. You were checking to see if he was still alive. You had no way of knowing if he was dead or unconscious until you checked," Detective Gates said as he reached over and squeezed her hand. "Did you notice anything suspicious?"

"Other than that his place is trashed?" Zoey snapped her fingers. "No . . . Wait. There was an older man lurking nearby. He was parked next to where I am. He's probably just a neighbor. Or a neighbor's guest. But, I mean, he could be the killer, right? He could have heard me knocking on the front door and slipped out the back."

"That could explain why both the front and the back doors were unlocked . . . But if that's the case, he spent hours in the victim's home. It appears that Chester has been dead since late last night or early this morning. The coroner will, hopefully, be able to narrow down the time of death," Gates said. "What can you tell me about the guy?"

"I didn't get a particularly good look at him. He had his coat zipped up to his chin and he was wearing a hat. The only reason I know he's older is because he had white stubble on his cheeks. Or it could have been light blonde, I guess." Zoey shrugged. "I might not recognize him, but I would recognize his truck. It was an older model in that burgundy color. He had an American Flag decal over the back windows and a big political bumper sticker on the back."

"Let me know if you can think of any other details. Partial license plate. Damage from an accident. Another bumper sticker. Anything that could help me better identify the truck and confirm if it belongs to one of the neighbors." Detective Gates handed her a notebook. "Go ahead and write out your statement. Include everything that you can remember. While you do that, I'm going to talk to the coroner and the forensic techs that the State Police sent over to help collect evidence."

SEVEN

ZOEY WAS READING THROUGH her statement for the second time when Detective Gates returned to his shipping container home. Zack was with him.

"Are you all right, Zoey?" Zack asked. He knelt next to the recliner and grasped her hand. "I am so sorry. I never should have let you come over here by yourself."

Zoey pulled her hand away. "I already told you it's not your fault."

"But I should have known something was wrong when Chester didn't answer your calls or texts." Zack stood up and turned to face the detective. "Can I take my sister home now?"

"I have a couple more questions, and then you can go." Detective Gates had a seat at the dinner table. "Prior to today, have either of you been inside the victim's home?"

"No," the twins said in unison.

"Shoot." Gates threw down his pen. "I was hoping one of you could look around and tell if anything obvious was missing. Or if there was something hanging on the wall above the bed. I took a closer look around and I noticed that there are two nails in the wall. The victim could have hung something on the wall, and that's what the killer took."

"Chester was an artist. Maybe he'd hung up an old painting or drawing, and the killer thought it might be valuable," Zack said. He tapped his forefinger against his chin. "But if the killer was after something that was hanging on the wall, why trash the place?"

"To make it appear he or she was searching for something else," Gates suggested. "Or it could have been a botched burglary. Chester came home and found someone going through his things. That led to an altercation . . ."

"But why take the time to go through all the frozen dinners and the medicine cabinet?" Zoey asked. "From what I saw, it looks like the killer went through everything Chester owned. I mean, I guess it's possible he had . . . I don't know . . . a flash drive that had something incriminating saved on it hidden in the medicine cabinet. Or bundles of money in his sock drawer. Or millions of dollars in uncut diamonds stashed in his freezer."

"I highly doubt he had uncut diamonds," Zack said. "But, let's face it, Chester could have had a secret life that neither of us knew anything about. It's not like he was very forthcoming in sharing personal details."

"Can you think of anyone who would want Chester dead?" Gates asked.

Zack shrugged. "Chester claims he hasn't been back in the area in twelve years. And he's been keeping a low profile since coming back. He didn't want anyone to know he was back in town since he was only planning to stay for a few months."

"Why is that?" Gates asked.

"His mom is dying of cancer. He moved back home for a few months to be near her," Zack said. "And with a new name . . . I'm not sure how many people would have realized that Chester Neidigh was Chester Hartman."

"But who knows who he was talking to or what he was doing when he wasn't at the shop," Zoey said. She pushed herself out of the comfortable recliner and faced the detective. "Chester was also threatening to break kayfabe."

Gates tilted his head to the side and looked at Zoey. "I know what kayfabe means. But how does it relate to Chester? He wasn't a wrestler, was he?"

"What she means is that Chester allegedly knew things about some of our former classmates and teachers. At least, that's what he told us yesterday," Zack said. "He threatened to expose the secrets of at least one of our former classmates."

"One of them came by the shop to see Chester yesterday," Zoey said. "They into an argument, and Lucas threatened Chester—"

"He told him to keep his mouth shut," Zack said. "We asked Chester what was going on, and that's when he told us that he knew some secrets."

"Arielle and I also ran into four other classmates at the gym this morning—"

"Let me guess," Zack said. "Brittany and Michelle. But who were the other two?"

"Jocelyn Hershey and Natasha Bowman. The prestigious—Jocelyn's word, not mine—dance academy that she teaches at is closed for the holidays. She's in town visiting. And, of course, Natasha is hanging closer to Jocelyn than her shadow."

"I thought I heard cloven hooves last night. I figured Krampus was a couple nights early. Turns out it was just Jocelyn strutting around town." Zack chuckled. "But how do the four of them know about Chester?"

"Michelle ran into Lucas sometime yesterday. He told her that Chester is also back in town. Brittany already knew, and she seemed really freaked out about it. And Jocelyn got angry and stormed out of the gym. I was going to ask Chester why Brittany and Jocelyn would be upset that he's back in town, but now I can't . . ."

Detective Gates's phone dinged. He looked down at it and groaned. "I want to hear more about these former classmates, but Chief Coleman needs me to go with him to break the news to the victim's parents. How about we get together tomorrow morning, and you can fill me in on these classmates? And anything else you can think of."

Gates escorted Zoey and Zack out of his shipping container house. He then walked them over to where Zoey's Jeep was parked. She was glad that her car had not been roped in by the crime scene tape. It had been considered part of Devon's crime scene, and the police had held on to it for a couple days while it was processed for evidence.

"One more question," Gates said. "Where were the two of you last night?"

"I was at the tattoo shop till around eight," Zack said. "Then I went home. I helped put my daughter to bed, and then my wife and I watched wrestling."

"I had the domestic abuse survivors' group," Zoey said as she handed her keys to Zack. "Chester came to that. We talked for a little after it was over. When he left, I headed over to my parents' house. I was out in the barn with

Justin, Hannah, Mort, and Eli until about one in the morning. Then I went home and worked on a few things for the upcoming LAW show."

"We didn't kill Chester," Zack said. "We had no motive."

"At the moment, I have no reason to suspect either of you," Detective Gates said as he held open the passenger side door for Zoey. "But I had to ask."

After Detective Gates dismissed them, Zoey turned on the seat warmer and hunkered down in the passenger seat. The leather quickly heated up, warming her backside, but it wasn't enough to penetrate the cold knot that had formed in her core. She glanced over at Zack who was behind the wheel. She never let anyone drive her Jeep, but, today, she was willing to make an exception. She didn't feel up to driving, and she was thankful that Jim Coleman had the foresight to pick up Zack and bring him to the crime scene.

"I can't believe Chester is dead . . . That someone murdered him."

"I can barely believe it either . . ." Zack trailed off as one of the police officers moved the roadblock out of the way so they could get past. The reporter tried to prevent them from leaving, but Zack gestured for her and the cameraman to get out of the way. "Are you sure you're all right? Because you definitely do not look all right. And that episode—"

"It was an anxiety attack."

"Whatever it was, I can tell it kicked your butt. Are you sure you don't want to go to the hospital and get checked out."

"Yes, I'm sure." Zoey blinked back another round of tears. "I'll be okay. It's just . . . It sucks. This is the first time Chester has been back to the area since we graduated . . ."

"That we know of." Zack pulled onto the road and headed towards Linville. "For all we know, he could have been lying about that."

"Why would he?"

"Heck if I know. But something was clearly up with him. I was trying to respect his privacy, but I should have asked more questions. I should have dug deeper and tried to find out what was going on."

"Why did he want to keep such a low profile? He was fine with us knowing he was back, but he sure didn't seem to want anyone else to know."

"Again, I have no idea," Zack said. "I don't even know when he changed his name. Or why. My best guess is that he wanted to leave the past behind him."

"He could have done that without changing his name."

"True." Zack shrugged. "Maybe he just didn't like his last name."

"Or maybe he was running from someone or something," Zoey said. "And changing his name seemed like his only option . . ."

The twins fell silent as Zack turned onto South Market Street and drove past the collection of strip malls on the southeastern side of Linville. Both of the town's grocery stores were located along the half-mile long commercial section, as were a handful of fast-food restaurants, pizza shops, gas stations, and various other stores and businesses.

Heading into Linville proper, they passed the Mount Rose Cemetery. Christmas-themed parade floats were lined up along the road that looped through the cemetery. The floats reminded Zoey that the Linville Christmas parade was scheduled for the next evening.

"Do you know if Chester had a criminal record?"

"He didn't," Zack said. "Before I hired Chester, I had Jim run a background check. Other than a couple parking tickets and a speeding ticket, nothing came up under either of his names."

"So, he wasn't running from the law over an old warrant like Quincy implied."

"Quincy can be such an idiot at times."

"You don't need to tell me that. Remember, I dated him for almost four years."

"He may be my best friend, but you definitely deserved better."

Changing the subject, Zoey asked, "Any idea who might have killed Chester?"

"I have no clue. I guess it could have been anyone."

"I'm thinking it was someone Chester knew. I don't think he would have opened his door to just anyone. Especially late at night."

"He might not have let the person inside," Zack said. "Like the detective said, it's possible the killer was already inside when Chester got home. Chester might have walked in and surprised a burglar as he or she was tearing apart his place."

"But what was the person looking for?"

"Again, I have no clue. It could have been anything, I guess."

"You think Chester decided to break kayfabe?" Zoey asked. "Or threatened the wrong person? He claimed to know a lot of secrets. If someone really thought Chester was going to break kayfabe, they might have killed him to keep him quiet."

"I warned him that breaking kayfabe came with consequences. And you know what else comes with consequences? Sticking your nose in police business." Zack turned into the alley that ran alongside 3 Count Tattoos. "Leave it up to the detective to figure out, Zoey."

"I plan to. Gates seems pretty smart. I'm sure he'll figure it out."

"He can't be *that* smart. After all, he arrested me for Devon's murder."

"But you have to admit he had a good reason for suspecting you."

"Yeah, yeah." Zack pulled into the small lot behind the tattoo shop and parked. He shut off the engine and then handed the keys to Zoey. "I'd tell you to take the rest of the day off, but I need you to call Chester's clients and tell them what happened. I already called the other two clients he had on the schedule for today, but he's booked solid for the rest of this week. Can you at least call the people who are on tomorrow's schedule?"

"I'll be okay," Zoey said as she tucked her keys into her purse. "I'd rather be doing something than sitting around doing nothing. This will be a distraction. I need to stay busy. Otherwise, I might have another breakdown."

Zack reached across the console and squeezed Zoey's arm. "I know my schedule is packed through the end of February, but Santino and Quincy might have time to fit some of Chester's clients in. And I know this is going to sound callous . . . But I'll also have to start looking for another tattoo artist. We can keep the lights on with just three of us. But I'd feel better having a fourth artist."

Considering she was the one who took care of paying the shop's bills, Zoey would also feel a lot better having a fourth artist working in the shop. Quincy's extended time off had caused a drop in the shop's income.

After climbing out of the Jeep, the twins walked around the side of the building and entered through the French doors that opened into the breakroom. As she walked down the hallway to the front office, Zoey paused outside Chester's private room. The desk was a mess of paperwork, but the rest of the room was tidy. Zoey grabbed the doorknob and pulled the door shut. She assumed Detective Gates would want to search the room before any of them went through Chester's sketches and cleaned out his personal items. The door wouldn't keep anyone out, but there was no way of locking it from the outside.

In the office, Zoey had a seat at her desk and brought up the weekly schedule on her laptop. Zack was right; Chester was booked solid from Wednesday starting at noon until the shop closed at eight on Saturday night. He had eleven tattoos scheduled over four days, plus a handful of consultations.

Zoey was debating what to tell the clients when Quincy Durand limped into the combined office and reception area. Including extensive road rash all along his left side, Quincy had suffered several injuries during a motorcycle accident back in August. The worst of the injuries had been two fractures to his tibia—one of which was a compound fracture. The doctors at Hershey Medical Center had inserted a titanium rod in Quincy's leg to stabilize the shattered bone. The doctors had also performed surgery on his dislocated shoulder to repair the damaged rotator cuff. Quincy's other injuries included chipping a piece of bone out of his hip, breaking his wrist, and fracturing three ribs. Quincy had spent the past few weeks recuperating and rehabbing his arm and leg. His first day back at work had been last Monday.

"Is it true?" Quincy held up his black cane that had a silver dragon's head handle. The overhead lights flashed against the dragon's ruby eyes. "Is Chester really dead?"

Zoey nodded. "Someone stabbed him either late last night or early this morning."

"Damn . . ." Quincy shuffled over to one of the leather couches and had a seat. "I'm probably the last person who saw him alive. Aside from whoever killed him."

"I last saw him at the same time you did."

Last night, following the domestic abuse group survivors' meeting, Zoey and Chester had stayed downstairs in the basement and talked for about half-an-hour. When they came upstairs, Quincy was the only person still working in the tattoo shop. He left at the same time as Chester, and Zoey left a few minutes later to head over to her parents' house.

Quincy ran his fingers through the scraggly brown beard that reached halfway down his chest. He had rapidly lost his hair while in his late-twenties, and he'd been hiding his bald head with various types of hats ever since. In response to his premature hair loss, he'd grown a bushy beard that he rarely trimmed and only perfunctorily groomed. Zoey hated it.

"No, I saw Chester after he left here. I followed him back to his place—"

Zoey joined Quincy on the couch. "Why did you do that?"

"To apologize." Quincy leaned back and looked over at Zoey. "You were right the other day when you told me I had no reason to give him a hard time. I've just . . . I've been in a bad mood for years. Between Elena leaving me and taking the kids, the gambling addiction, and then my accident . . . I've been under a lot of pressure. I guess hassling Chester over the past week was a way to relieve some of the stress."

"So, you were basically being a jerk?"

"Pretty much." Quincy moaned. "Plus, I think I came back too early. I was fine during my first tattoo last Monday. But, after that, my left shoulder really got to hurting. I never realized how much I used my left arm while tattooing until now. Plus, sitting hunched over didn't help my shoulder or my ribs. Part of me wants to throw in the towel and take some more time off. But I really need the money . . ."

"I'd say I told you so, but that would be mean," Zoey said. Both she and Zack had warned Quincy that they thought he was coming back too soon, but Quincy had insisted that he would be fine. "So, you're in pain and upset with yourself . . . I think it has more to do with than just that. Chester said something to me about how you used to give him a hard time back in high school. What did you have against him?"

"I don't know . . ." Quincy shrugged. "Back in high school, he was weird—"

"You weren't exactly 'normal' back then either."

"But there was something about Chester . . . I just didn't like him back then. And I don't—didn't like him any more now. I don't trust him. I mean, I didn't trust him. And there was something about him that gave me the creeps." Quincy let his cane slip through his fingers, and the rubber tip thudded against the refinished hardwood flooring. "And why did he just suddenly show up out of nowhere? No one has seen or heard from him for years, but he shows up just when Zack is looking to hire another artist. You think that's a coincidence? Because I don't."

"If Chester had wanted you to know why he was back, he would have told you."

"Oh, so you know something." Quincy shifted closer to Zoey. "Why did he change his name? What's he been up to the past twelve years? You know, aside from tattooing. Was he wanted by the law? Was there a hit out on him?"

Zoey scooted to the far end of the couch. "Later, Zack and I can fill you in on some stuff. For now, I want to know why you followed Chester back to his place."

"Like I was saying, I wanted to apologize for being a jerk." Quincy pulled off his knit hat and ran his hands over his bald head. "He wasn't too happy about me being there at first. But then he invited me inside. We had a couple beers. Talked. Watched a little TV—"

"TV?" Zoey asked. "Chester had a TV?"

"Yeah, it was sitting on his dresser."

Zoey shook her head. "Not anymore. I guess the killer took it."

"Most likely." Quincy shrugged. "Anyway, like I was saying . . . We got a few things settled."

"What time did you leave?"

"Around eleven-thirty, I guess."

"How did his place look? Was it neat? Was it a mess?"

"A little messy, but not out of control," Quincy said. "Why?"

"Because whoever killed Chester trashed the place. Detective Gates thinks the killer was looking for something. We have no idea what. But it had to be something small—"

"Probably drugs."

"That's crazy. Why would you . . ." Zoey smacked Quincy across the chest. "Chester was the 'friend of a friend' who got you the painkillers, wasn't he?"

While convalescing, Quincy began abusing prescription painkillers. After taking all the pills that the doctor had prescribed, he somehow got his hands on more. Luckily, his mother did some snooping and uncovered the baggie full of various painkillers hidden in his sock drawer. They were able to handle his addiction before it got out of hand. Despite being asked countless times, Quincy refused to say where the pills came from. All he would say was that a friend of a friend had gotten the pills for him.

"Why did you ask Chester to get you drugs? And when? Where did he get them?"

"Right after Zack hired him, he brought Chester by to go over some of my sketches. When Zack stepped outside to take a call, I asked him if he had any of his old connections—"

"What old connections?"

"Don't act dumb," Quincy said. "It was a well-known secret that Chester was a drug dealer back in high school."

"Yeah, but just marijuana."

Quincy shook his head. "It was *way* more than marijuana. He sold pills. Mostly uppers and downers. He also sold steroids to the athletes. I knew about the steroids because some of my teammates on the football team used them."

"Seriously? I had no idea." Zoey sat up straighter. Because she hadn't smoked marijuana or wanted anything to do with it, Zoey ignored Chester's extracurricular activities. She'd worried that Chester would get caught selling marijuana to the other students and she might get dragged into the mess because she was friends with him. It was easier to turn a blind eye and pretend it wasn't happening. Clearly there had been a lot more going on than she had realized. "Did Zack know about Chester dealing more than marijuana?"

"I don't know. I mean, it was hush-hush. No one really talked about it. At least, I never heard anyone openly talking about it. There was just this general understanding that if you needed something, Chester Hartman could probably get it for you."

"Did he sell drugs to Lucas Jennings?"

"I think so."

"Interesting . . . Where did Chester get the drugs? Who was supplying him?"

"That I don't know. All I know was that he had connections. And, considering how quickly he got me that bag of painkillers, I assume he still had those connections."

"Or made some new ones since returning to the area."

"Either way, whoever killed him might have done so because of the drugs."

"You have to tell Detective Gates about this." Zoey went over to her desk and grabbed the cordless phone out of its charging station. "He's going to ask if you have an alibi—"

"After I left Chester's place, I went back to my parents' house."

Following the motorcycle accident, Quincy moved back in with his parents since it was almost impossible for him to get up and down the steps to his second-floor apartment. He was still residing at his parents' house as a cost-saving measure. Because of a previous gambling addiction, Quincy had fallen into debt. He was trying to get it paid off.

"Were your parents still awake when you got home?"

Quincy shrugged. "They were in bed, so I don't know if they heard me come in. But I did turn on the alarm. And I stayed up playing video games—"

"They weren't gambling games, were they?"

"No, I deleted all of the card and casino games off my phone and game console."

"And you're done going to casinos?"

"I'm cured of my gambling addiction. I swear I will never step foot in a casino again."

"Or play in any private games?" Zoey asked. "Or gamble online?"

"No, I won't do any of that either." Quincy glared at Zoey. "As I was trying to say before you interrupted . . . The people I was playing with should be able to alibi me."

Not if you killed Chester and then trashed his place before heading home, Zoey thought. She hated suspecting Quincy. Her romantic feelings for him were dead and buried, but he was still her friend. She didn't want to think he could kill anyone. But if they had gotten into a fight over drugs—Quincy wanted more painkillers, and Chester refused to get them—it was possible that Quincy had snapped and killed Chester.

Zoey handed Quincy the phone. "One other question . . . Did you notice anything hanging on the wall above Chester's bed?"

"Yeah, there was a painting. It was hard to miss," Quincy said as he held his arms out to the side. "The canvas was about four-foot high by three-foot wide. It was a painting of a nude woman done in acrylics. Really good work, but it didn't seem to be Chester's style. It was elegant and hyper realistic. And I remember Chester's painting style as being raw and more abstract. I asked him about it, and he said it was an old project. Why do you ask?"

"Because whoever killed him also took the painting."

EIGHT

"WHY WON'T YOU PEOPLE leave me alone," the older woman hissed at Zoey and Zack as she peered at them through the narrow crack between the door and the doorframe. All they could see of her was a bloodshot eye and a sliver of her face. "I already told you I don't got nothing to say to you."

"We're not the press, Mrs. Hartman." Zack got the toe of his boot wedged in next to the doorframe and prevented the woman from slamming the door in their faces. "You are Imogene Hartman, right?"

The woman opened the door a fraction of an inch wider. "What's it to you?"

"We're Chester's friends," Zoey said.

Imogene yanked the door open and stared up at them. She was dressed in a faded yellow bathrobe that was at least two sizes too big for her skeletal frame. Her short, auburn hair was a tangled, greasy nest, and her crepey skin caused her to look more dead than alive.

"You must be Zack and Zoey. Chester told me about you." Imogene gave them a ghost of a smile. "You were nice to him in high school."

Imogene shuffled away from the door, dragging her feet through the detritus that covered the worn carpet. Crumbled-up pieces of newspaper were tossed about the living room, and there was a small army of porcelain dolls crammed together on the dining room table. The dolls' lifeless eyes gave Zoey the creeps. She hadn't played with dolls when she was a child. Instead, she had played with pro wrestling action figures. Any dolls she had received as gifts—usually from her maternal grandparents who disapproved of her tomboyish nature and tried to bully her into being a 'little lady' by buying her girly toys and frilly dresses—remained in their original packaging. The one Christmas that she had asked them to buy her dolls—specifically the Spice Girls' "Girl Power" collection—they thought she was joking.

"I'm sorry the place is a mess. I'm packing up my doll collection. If I don't give 'em away now, Oscar will just haul 'em to the dump once I'm dead," Imogene mumbled as she shuffled through the center section of the doublewide. After making her way through the maze of cardboard boxes, she collapsed onto the couch and drew a crocheted blanket over her lap. "I've only got a few months left . . ."

Zack gestured for Zoey to join Imogene on the couch. She glared at him in return. She hadn't been keen on visiting Chester's parents so soon after they had learned about his murder. She'd tried to talk her brother into waiting until tomorrow to visit the Hartmans, but Zack insisted they come tonight.

Zoey made her way across the crowded room and had a seat next to Imogene. The couch's plastic cover squeaked as she tried to find a comfortable spot on the hard, lumpy cushion. "Is your husband home?"

"No." Imogene grabbed a tissue and waved it through the air. "Oscar went to work. He's a second shift supervisor at the feed mill up the road."

"Your husband just found out that his son was murdered, and he went to work?"

Imogene snorted. "Oscar doesn't care. The way he sees it, Chester has been dead to him since the day he graduated from high school. That was the day his parental responsibilities ended. Oscar hated . . . well, I shouldn't say hated . . . he was indifferent to our son. Oscar played football when he was younger. He was in the Army. He calls himself a 'manly man.' He wanted a son just like him. He didn't know what to do with Chester. Our son was sensitive. He was quiet. He was terrible at sports. That's not to say he didn't try to play the ones that Oscar signed him up for. But he just wasn't any good at 'em. And Oscar punished him for it. What Chester was good at was art. And art was something that Oscar had no use for. By the time Chester was a teenager, Oscar had pretty much given up on him.

They coexisted, but they had nothing to do with each other. Of course, everything was my fault. I coddled Chester too much as a kid and that made him soft. And, since I was unable to have any more children, I was a failure as a wife . . ."

Zoey grimaced. "I guess Chester and your husband haven't spent the past few months repairing their relationship."

"Oh, no. Oscar didn't know Chester was back," Imogene said. "Of course, he found out earlier today when that detective came by to tell us about Chester. After he left, Oscar accused me of going behind his back and betraying him. I think that's the reason he went to work. He was so mad he couldn't stand to be in the same room as me."

Zoey's heart went out to Imogene. It sounded like her husband was a brute.

Changing the subject, Zack asked, "What happened to Chester after high school? We asked, but he never really told us anything."

"No, he wouldn't have. Chester was always very private. He kept everything to himself. Even as a child." Imogene perked up a bit. "But, after high school, Chester moved to Saratoga Springs to attend Skidmore University. He was studying studio art."

Zack whistled. "That's impressive. I had no idea he'd even applied there."

"Chester was so excited when he received the acceptance letter." Imogene beamed with pride for a few seconds. Then her shoulders crumpled, and she collapsed back against the couch cushions. "But he dropped out after his second year. He couldn't handle the pressure or other people telling him how to create his art. He just wanted to paint."

"Did you ever go to Saratoga Springs to visit him?" Zoey asked.

"Once." Imogene blew her nose and then tossed the used tissue onto the floor. "I took the train. But I got so confused changing trains in New York City. It was too overwhelming. After that, Chester and I would meet in Philadelphia. I could manage getting there since I didn't have to change trains along the way. Chester would meet me at the station, and he'd find somewhere for us to go. Oscar never approved of the visits . . ."

After a few moments of uncomfortable silence, Zoey asked, "Aside from going to school, what else was Chester up to in Saratoga Springs?"

Imogene shrugged. "All I know was that he seemed content. He had a girlfriend for a while. I never met her, and he never said too much. But

I gathered he was in love with her. Then something happened, and they broke up. Chester was devastated. It wasn't long after they broke up that he dropped out of school and took off for California."

"Did Chester ever say why he changed his name?" Zoey asked.

Imogene shook her head. "Neidigh was my maiden name. I guess I should have been flattered . . . But, when I found out he changed his last name, I figured he was cutting his remaining ties with his father. He changed it right after he moved to California."

Zoey glanced over to where Zack was perched on the edge of a straight-backed wooden chair. The twins' thoughts were usually along the same brainwaves, and Zoey assumed Zack was currently having the same feelings as her. They'd expected Chester's parents to tell them more about him and what he'd been up to since high school. Imogene was only able to fill in some basic information and left them with more questions than answers.

Turning back to Imogene, Zoey asked, "Did you ever visit Chester in California?"

"Once. About a year or so after he settled there. I thought taking the train was bad. Flying was even worse. I told Chester I couldn't do it for a second time. We didn't see each other again until a few months ago when he came back." Imogene grabbed another tissue and used it to wipe away the tears that dribbled down her sunken cheeks. "Oh, I told him not to come back. I didn't want him to see me like this. It was bad enough the first time I had cancer. He took it so hard. I didn't want him to have to relive it. Especially knowing I'm not going to survive it this time. But Chester came home anyway. He wanted to be with me. It was so nice having him around after not seeing him for all those years. But now he's dead, and I'm still alive."

"Do you . . ." Zack trailed off as Imogene blew her nose. "Who all knew Chester was back in the area?"

"No one other than the three of us. And that other boy from high school that works with you. The one who had the motorcycle accident."

"Quincy Durand," Zack said, supplying the name.

"Yes, Quincy. Chester told me Quincy was still in a lot of pain from the accident, and his doctor wouldn't prescribe any more pain medication." Imogene focused on tugging the loose thread from her sleeve. It was almost a foot long, and the fabric along the seam was puckering. "My doctor prescribed me pain medication, but it took four tries to find one that worked. The first one made me so dizzy I could barely get out of bed. The second did nothing at all. And the third made me sick. I know it was wrong, but I gave Chester those old pills for his friend."

Zoey and Zack exchanged wide-eyed looks. After finding the bag of prescription painkillers in her son's sock drawer, Carol Durand had demanded the twin's help in staging an intervention. Carol had also shown Zoey the bag of pills. It had contained almost a hundred pills, and there had been three different varieties.

"Did you tell Detective Gates about the painkillers?" Zoey asked.

Imogene gasped. "Oh, no. I didn't say a word. I wouldn't want the detective to know that I . . . I gave away those pills. He could arrest me—"

"I'm sure he won't do that," Zoey said. She didn't know Detective Gates all that well, but she couldn't imagine he would arrest a terminally ill woman. "And I doubt it has anything to do with Chester's murder. But Quincy mentioned that Chester got the pills for him. We were worried Chester had connections with a drug dealer, and that could be why he was murdered."

"I can see why you would think that." Imogene tugged on the loose thread and broke it free from the robe. "I'll call the detective in the morning and tell him about the pills."

"Speaking of drugs . . ." Zack cleared this throat. "Back in high school—"

"Chester sold drugs to some of your classmates." Imogene leaned forward and pressed her hands over her face. "He got them from my brother. He worked for a drug dealer, and he supplied Chester with marijuana and . . . and . . . other drugs. I didn't find out until after my brother got arrested. That was a couple years after Chester graduated."

"Where is your brother now?" Zoey asked. If Imogene's brother or any of his old connections were still around, it was possible one of them killed Chester. "Did he know Chester was back in town?"

Imogene shook her head. "My brother died in prison three years ago. And, like I said, no one else knew Chester was around. He certainly wasn't advertising his presence."

"Lucas Jennings knew Chester was back," Zack said.

"He stopped by the tattoo shop yesterday," Zoey added. "And I ran into another classmate earlier today who said that she's seen Chester around Linville a few times."

"I don't know about this other classmate," Imogene said. She slid off the couch and then gathered up the used tissues littering the floor. "But I saw Lucas's parents the other day. They live across the road. They told me that Lucas was moving back home, and I told them Chester was back, too. They must have told Lucas . . ."

"There seemed to be some animosity between them," Zoey said. "Lucas made a threatening comment as he was leaving."

"I can't imagine why." Imogene shuffled over to the kitchen and disposed of the tissues in an overflowing trash can. "It was Chester who was mad at Lucas for throwing him over when they got to middle school. They were the best of friends up until then, and Chester never forgave him for the betrayal . . . I don't know what Lucas would have been mad at Chester about."

Before Zoey or Zack could respond, the front door swung open and crashed against the coatrack. A gaunt, older man who was bundled up in a worn winter coat and hat stepped inside and slammed the door behind him.

"You're home early," Imogene said as she scurried across the room and helped the man out of his coat. "Was something wrong at the plant?"

"Compassionate leave." The man gestured towards Zoey and Zack. "Who are they? And what are they doin' here?"

"Oscar, this is Zack and Zoey Wilde. They were friends of Chester's back in high school. Chester was working at Zack's tattoo shop—"

"None of that explains what the hell they're doin' here," Oscar snapped. He yanked off his hat and tossed it at his wife's face. "Or why you let them inside. You know I don't like havin' strangers in the house."

"We came to offer our condolences and to see if there was anything we could do for you." Zack stood up and moved to stand between Oscar and Imogene. "Like your wife said, we're Chester's friends."

"My son didn't have friends. Now get out." Oscar opened the door and gestured for them to leave. "The last thing my wife needs is people like you hasslin' her. And we sure as hell don't need your pity."

As Zoey scurried out onto the lopsided front porch, Oscar slammed the door shut behind her. The door clipped the heel of her boot, causing her to stumble into her brother. Beneath the dim glow from the overhead light, she and Zack exchanged exasperated looks.

"Not exactly a nice guy," Zoey whispered as she steadied herself. She then followed Zack around the side of the house to where he had parked along the street. She came to a halt when she spotted a burgundy truck parked in front of Zack's Jeep. "That's the truck I saw at Chester's."

"Are you sure?"

"Pretty sure. I told Detective Gates that I probably wouldn't recognize the man since I only saw him from a distance. But I would recognize the truck." Zoey jogged around to the back of the truck and then pointed at the oversized political bumper sticker that was slapped across the tailgate. "I guess this means Oscar knew Chester was back in the area."

"You know, I think I've seen Oscar before," Zack said. "It was a couple weeks ago at the shop. I went outside to get something out of my car and found Chester arguing with an older man. The man took off around the corner as soon as he saw me. I asked Chester what the argument was about, and he said it was just an old guy hassling him about his hair and tattoos. I didn't think much of it since it happens to me all the time . . ."

"Happens to me, too."

Zoey turned on her heel and headed back towards the trailer. Zack grabbed the back of her coat and forced her to stop walking.

"Where are you going?"

"To ask Oscar what he was doing at Shippington Way this morning."

"No, you're not." Zack dragged Zoey over to his Jeep. "For all we know, Oscar was there because he killed Chester. I'm not going to just stand around while you confront a murderer. And, even if Oscar was there for a perfectly innocent reason, I still don't want you questioning him. That's the detective's job. Not yours."

"Yeah, you're right. But at least let me take some pictures of the truck to send to Detective Gates."

Zoey pulled her cell phone out of her purse and used it to take multiple pictures of the truck. She then texted the pictures to the detective. She also let him know that Zack had seen Oscar at the shop a few weeks earlier. As she did so, a train rattled past on the other side of the street as it traveled north along the Susquehanna River. A chain-link fence and a row of trees and dead undergrowth separated the road from the train tracks.

"If you're looking to steal a car, I recommend finding one better than that old clunker."

"What the . . ." Zoey spun around in search of the disembodied voice. "Who's there?"

On the other side of the street stood an historical home. It was hard to get a good look at the house in the dark, but Zoey could see that the original part had been built of bricks. In more modern times, a large addition had been added on the back of the house.

"We're not looking to steal anything," Zack said as he took a few steps out into the street. "We were just visiting with the Hartmans."

"The Hartmans don't welcome visitors," the voice said. "At least, the husband doesn't. The jerk won't even wave or say hello to the neighbors."

A man stepped out of the shadows alongside the old house and moved to lean against the picket fence that encircled the property. Zoey could see that he was probably close to her father's age. The stub of a cigar stuck out of the side of his mouth.

"Their son died last night," Zack said. "We came to offer our condolences."

"Chester is dead? Damn . . . We only just found out the other day that he was home." The man exhaled a cloud of smoke. "My wife said the Linville Police were here earlier. Guess that was why. The poor kid . . . And poor Imogene . . . First the cancer and now this . . ."

Zoey walked across the street so they didn't have to shout. She also wanted to get a better look at the man. Up close, she could see the resemblance.

"You're Lucas Jennings's father."

"Guilty as charged." The man grinned at her. "Did you go to high school with him?"

Zoey nodded. "I ran into him yesterday. He told me he moved back home to take over your used car dealership."

"Take over . . ." Mr. Jennings knocked the ashes off the end of his cigar and then popped it back in his mouth. "He's not taking over anything. At least not until he's proven himself. And, considering how badly he's screwed up everything else. His baseball career—

"Lucas told me he blew out his arm," Zoey said.

"Blew out his arm . . . He broke his elbow during some drunken off-season shenanigans. Fell off the top of a golf cart or something." Mr. Jennings shook his head. "He's screwed up every job he's had since then. And he screwed up his marriage. His wife finally got tired of supporting him and left. She got the house and everything else. Lucas had nowhere else to go.

So he came home, begging us for a place to stay and a job. He's my only child. I love him and want to help him . . . but I doubt he'll be wildly successful at the dealership."

"If he's not taking over, then what is he?" Zack asked. "A salesperson?"

"No. For now, he's working a desk in the service department."

"It doesn't sound like you have too much faith in your son," Zoey said.

"You wouldn't either," Mr. Jennings said. "Not if you knew him as well as I do. He had such promise, and he pissed it away."

Before Zoey could ask Mr. Jennings what he meant, Zack elbowed her in the side. He then asked, "What can you tell us about Chester?"

"Aside from the fact that he was a weird little kid?" Mr. Jennings chuckled. "Honestly, I can't tell you much. He and Lucas were best friends in elementary school. The kid was over here all the time. I think our house was a refuge for him. But it's not like I got to know him that well. Kid hardly ever said a word to anyone. But I did feel bad when Lucas stopped hanging out with him at school. Chester never had a chance . . . You went to school with him. I'm sure you know how much a weird kid like him got picked on."

"You said they stopped hanging out in school," Zack said. "Does that mean they were still friendly outside of school?"

"I don't know if 'friendly' is the right word. But Chester was still over here a lot. I paid him to tutor Lucas. My son was no genius, and he needed all the help he could get in some of his classes. What I didn't know was that Chester was providing extra help by doing most of Lucas's homework so that my son could focus on playing sports. And carry on with that stuck-up girl he was dating . . . What was her name?"

"Jocelyn Hershey."

"That's it. She was a real piece of work." Mr. Jennings sighed. "So, how did Chester die? Was it at overdose or . . ."

"He was murdered," Zoey said. "The Linville police are investigating."

"Murdered?" Mr. Jennings muttered a few curse words under his breath. "Well, shit . . . I wouldn't be surprised if his old man killed him. Not saying my relationship with my son is all that great, but it's darn near perfect compared to the relationship that Oscar and Chester had. I never knew a father could hate his son so much and for such stupid reasons . . . I wouldn't be surprised if the old bastard killed him . . ."

NINE

"LOOKS LIKE YOU'VE GOT a case of ring rust, son."

"Well, Dad, that's what tends to happen when wrestlers retire," Zack said. "And I don't think I'm *that* rusty. Right, Zoey?"

"Uhhhh . . . I plead the fifth," Zoey said. Zack frowned at her, and she gave him a sheepish smile in return. "You're still good. You're just not as good as you used to be. And I should know considering we've been wrestling each other since we were in the womb."

Zack, who was lying on his back in the middle of the ring, rocked back onto his shoulders. He drew his knees up to his chest and then kicked his legs up in the air. Using the momentum, Zack raised the rest of his body upwards. His body awkwardly arched as he brought his feet down. Zoey winced as Zack botched the kip up and tumbled over backwards. Before he'd hung up his boots, Zack had been able to execute the move flawlessly.

The ring was set up in an old barn that sat at the back of the Wildes' property on the northwestern edge of Linville. The barn was two-stories tall and covered with weathered red siding. Marlon had converted the barn into a gym years earlier. Zoey and her brothers had nicknamed it the Wilde World of Pro Wrestling. For years, Marlon hosted a pro wrestling school to train new wrestlers. He gave up the school a few years earlier to focus on his home remodel business. Despite shutting down the school, Marlon still opened the gym every Sunday morning so that local wrestlers could train in the ring. He also rented the gym to other wrestlers for practice sessions or to host wrestling schools.

"Ok, maybe I am a little rusty." Zack stood up and brushed himself off. He then tugged up his sweatshirt to reveal that his abdomen was now covered in a thin layer of fat. "I'm also out of shape."

"You should be hitting the gym," Marlon said as he climbed up onto the edge of the ring. He wore an old corduroy coat over his bathrobe and flannel pajamas. "And you should seriously think about getting back in the ring. And not just to practice with your sister."

In the two years since he'd had shoulder surgery, Zack had gotten into the ring only a handful of times to wrestle with either Zoey or Justin. He was paranoid about reinjuring his surgically repaired shoulder or suffering another injury, and it took a lot of coaxing to get him to step between the ropes.

Tonight, it had been Zack's idea to get in the ring. After wrapping up their conversation with Lucas Jennings's father, the twins headed over to Zack's house. They'd spent an hour talking to Arielle about Chester's murder before walking next door to their parents' property and sneaking into the old barn. Zoey and Zack had excessive energy and frustration that they needed to burn off, and spontaneously throwing together a match was one way to do so. It also gave them something else to think about besides Chester. Putting together a match on the fly took concentration and ring-awareness. Distractions—both internal and external—could result in an injury. It could also mess up the dynamics of the match.

"Dad . . . Not you, too. Zoey's been hinting at it. Justin said something about it earlier. And now you."

"It's just one match, son."

"And that match leads to another one. And another one. And next thing you know, I'm back doing it full time." Zack groaned. He leaned against the ropes and bowed his head. "Look, I'll admit that I miss wrestling. A lot. But, after my shoulder surgery, I had to choose between wrestling and being a tattoo artist. If I didn't have Arielle and Paige to think about—"

"You had to go with the sure thing. And that was tattooing." Marlon reached over the ropes and squeezed Zack's shoulder. "It's just . . . I watched you kids grow up in the sport. And, considering I'm the one who trained you, it's tough for me knowing how hard you worked and how much you sacrificed over the years. I had such high hopes for you, Zack. I really wanted you to make it."

From birth, Zoey's and Zack's lives had revolved around professional wrestling. As soon as they could walk, they were bouncing around the ring and tussling with each other. Their official training began when they were still kids. Roxanne frequently reminded them that she had been against Marlon teaching them to wrestle at such a young age, but Marlon had ultimately won the argument by insisting it was for the best. Zoey and Zack were already trying to emulate what they saw on TV and at live shows, and Marlon wanted to train them how to work together and execute the moves correctly. He believed that training them would, hopefully, prevent them from doing something stupid and getting injured.

By the time they were teenagers, Zoey, along with her brothers and a couple of their friends, were putting on monthly shows in the barn. Because there were so few participants, they would wrestle multiple times as different characters throughout the home-produced events. Other weekends—when a promoter would allow the teenagers to get in the ring—Zoey and Zack performed during intermission at their dad's events.

At eighteen, when they made their official debuts on the independent scene, Zoey and Zack had more in-ring experience than some of the veterans who they wrestled against.

"Excuse me . . ." Zoey planted her hands on her hips and scowled at her father. "You do know that Justin and I are still actively wrestling, right?"

"I'm aware. And we all know that while Justin is good, he doesn't have the discipline to make it beyond the indies. Not without you or Zack there to babysit him. As for you—"

Interrupting, Zack said, "Good luck getting hired at your age."

"Thirty isn't ancient," Zoey snapped.

"It's not young either."

Zoey stuck her tongue out at Zack. "What I am is . . . experienced."

"You're both right," Marlon said as he stepped between the ropes. "But most women wrestlers have already had their big break before they reach thirty."

"Heck, most of the women we know have hung it up by their mid-thirties," Zack added. "I'm sure you've realized that you're one of the elder statesmen on the circuit now."

Zoey was aware that she was one of the older female wrestlers in the mid-Atlantic region. There were some other women in their early to mid-thirties who continued to wrestle. But the majority of the women she currently competed against were in their twenties.

"Back when you were a kid, I actually hoped you wouldn't want to pursue a career in pro wrestling." Marlon put his arm around Zoey's shoulders. "Not with the way they were treating the female wrestlers at that time."

"You mean when they degraded the women by making them compete in those disgusting bra and panties matches?" Zoey asked. "Not to mention all the other crap they put those women through."

"Exactly," Marlon said. "Now, by the time you moved to Orlando, things had somewhat improved for the women . . . And I really thought you had a chance of getting picked up by the WWE."

"Yeah, well . . . Back then they were mainly hiring cheerleaders and models. I didn't exactly fit the mold."

Zoey ducked her head and stepped away from Marlon. She had been in her early twenties when she and Devon Isler moved to Florida and settled near the home base of World Wrestling Entertainment's developmental program. Believing that his career was more important—and that he had a better chance of getting hired by the WWE—Devon had relegated Zoey's career to the back burner. She had only wrestled at a handful of shows during the six months they had lived in Florida. But it was at one of those shows where Zoey had gotten noticed by a WWE talent scout. The scout offered her a once-in-a-lifetime opportunity to try out for the WWE. He had also encouraged her to part ways with the "mediocre wrestler" that she was valeting for.

The invitation to try out had been the kick in the butt Zoey needed to finally end her toxic relationship with Devon. She had a chance to make it to the big league, and she was not going to let her possessive and jealous boyfriend hold her back. Her dream was within her grasp, and all she had to do was reach out and grab it; Devon had ultimately ruined it for her.

Zoey missed her scheduled audition because she was in the hospital recovering from Devon's beating. Due to the circumstances, she had been offered another audition. But Zoey let her second chance slip away. Following the assault, she had developed PTSD. For a year, she had been unable to wrestle because getting physical with another person would trigger a panic attack. By the time she was able to get back in the ring, her opportunity for a tryout with the WWE was long gone.

Years later, the missed opportunity still haunted her, and she continued to obsess over what might have been. She knew a successful tryout did not mean she would have been offered a contract. There was a good chance that nothing would have come from the audition, but that didn't stop her from feeling like she had failed her brothers and the four generations of wrestlers who had come before them. Being a fifth-generation wrestler meant she had a lot to live up to. So far, she'd had a successful career on the independent circuit. It was something to be proud of. But she still felt like a failure because she had never made it to the very top. The weight of her family's history in professional wrestling sat heavily on her shoulders.

"I hate to say it, Zoey, but it might be time to start thinking about what's next," Marlon said. "Realistically, you've probably only got a few more years left to wrestle. Then what?"

"If running LAW works out, I can keep doing that," Zoey said. Lately, she had been thinking more and more about her future. "I'm also thinking of holding a bootcamp. Maybe take on some more students."

Once or twice a year over the course of several years, Marlon held a weeklong bootcamp for potential wrestling students. As they got older, Zoey and her brothers helped out at the bootcamp. Marlon had given it up a few years earlier when he'd decided he no longer wanted to train any new wrestlers. Zoey had taken on couple women as students since then. Justin also had trained people.

"Bringing back the bootcamp isn't a bad idea," Marlon said. "But I'm not just talking about your future in the wrestling world. I'm talking about your overall future. What's your plan? What do you want to do with the rest of your life?"

"Run Zack's tattoo shop in exchange for a place to live," Zoey joked.

"Zoey . . ." Marlon shook his head. "There's got to be more to it than that."

"It works for me," Zack said. "As long as Zoey is actually at the desk and not off somewhere."

Marlon ran his hands over his face. "You two are impossible."

"If you think we're impossible, I'd hate to know what you think Justin is." Changing the subject, Zoey nudged Marlon in the side and asked, "What are you doing up so late, old man? Isn't it past your bedtime?"

"Normally, yes." Marlon rubbed his side. "But I'm waiting up for your mom and nana to get home. When I saw the lights on out here, I figured I better check who was in my barn."

Zack climbed out of the ring and collapsed on a folding chair. André the Giant, Marlon's chocolate lab, charged over and leaped onto Zack's lap. After Marlon, Zack was André's favorite person.

While fending off kisses from André, Zack asked, "What are Mom and Nana up to that they're only getting home at midnight?"

"They went on their annual bus trip to New York."

"I forgot that was today," Zoey said as she jumped down to the floor. Every December, Roxanne and Vivian went on a bus trip to New York City. They tried to get Zoey to tag along, but she always turned them down. "I was wondering why Nana didn't show up at the shop to ask us a million questions about Chester."

"Nosy old lady," Marlon mumbled.

Vivian had an unhealthy obsession with murder. She watched countless hours of true crime shows and considered herself an expert on homicides and criminal investigations. Her passion led her to sticking her nose in Devon Isler's murder investigation—and dragging Zoey along with her. Zoey had received multiple threats warning her to stay out of it, but Vivian continued with her amateur investigation. Her persistence had almost gotten her and Zoey killed.

"If you don't want interrogated, I suggest getting out of here," Marlon said. "I talked to your mom right before I came out here, and she said they'd be home in about fifteen minutes. I told her about Chester, and I'm sure she told your nana."

Zoey grabbed her purse so that she could check her phone. In the past ten minutes, Vivian had called her three times and sent over a dozen text messages.

"Yeah, I better get out of here," Zoey said. "You, too, Zack."

Zoey and Zack were putting on their coats when one of the barn doors slid open.

"Too late," Zack said. "They're here."

After shoving aside the oversized door, Vivian paraded into the barn wearing a knee-length, pink faux-fur coat. The overhead lights reflected off the rhinestones that she had glued to her white orthopedic shoes.

"I go out of town for one day," Vivian shouted. "And I miss all the excitement."

Zoey groaned. "Nana, I would hardly call it exciting."

"It was more exciting than the day I had."

"Now, Vivian, we had a lovely time in New York," Roxanne said as she trailed her mother-in-law into the barn. She was dressed much more conventionally in a red wool peacoat. Her hair, which was dyed a dark brown to hide the gray strands, was tucked up under a knitted hat. "And stop being a ghoul and hassling the poor kids."

"Can it, Rox. You're just as curious as I am." Vivian turned to Zoey and asked, "Did you really find the body? Tell me everything."

"Not now, Nana."

Roxanne pulled Zoey in for a hug. "Your dad told us about what happened. Are you all right?"

"I don't want to talk about it."

"But you need to." Roxanne pulled away so that she could look Zoey in the eye. "Maybe Bernadette . . ."

"I'll call her tomorrow," Zoey said. She smiled at her mom, but she knew it probably looked forced. "How was New York?"

"Full of people," Vivian said. "Times Square was packed."

"Times Square is full of people regardless of the season," Roxanne said to her mother-in-law. She then turned back to Zoey and said, "We saw the Christmas Spectacular at the Radio City Music Hall."

"I don't know why we had to pay all that money to watch women kick their legs up in the air. We could have stayed home and watched me do it for free."

Vivian took a couple steps back and then kicked up a leg. Her coat prevented her from lifting her leg up above knee-height. She stumbled and would have fallen over had Marlon not reached out and steadied her.

Ignoring Vivian, Roxanne said, "We also saw the tree at Rockefeller Center. And we did some shopping."

"I got you a present, Zoey," Vivian said. She reached into her massive leather purse and pulled out a bundle of leopard print fabric. "It's a hat. I was going to save it for Christmas, but considering today's events, I better give it to you now."

Zoey turned the leopard print hat around a few times as she looked it over. Semi-circular bills covered in faux leather jutted from the front and the back. A glittery black bow on top of the hat held up the fleece-lined earflaps.

"It's a . . ." Zoey tried to think of a polite word to describe the monstrosity. She was too tired to come up with anything appropriate. "It's interesting."

"It's your sleuthing hat." Vivian reached into her purse and pulled out a matching hat. She pulled it down over her gray curls and then tugged on the bow to release the flaps. "I was lucky to find these. Otherwise, we would have been settling for some ugly Sherlock Holmes tweed hat."

"Ooohhh," Zack grabbed the hat out of Zoey's hands and then placed it on her head. "It's a deerstalker hat."

"Yeah, that's what I just said. They're our sleuthing hats." Vivian pushed Zack aside so that she could adjust Zoey's hat. "Now that we're on the case—"

"We are not on the case, Nana."

"We need to look the part," Vivian continued. "Now, tell me everything. How was Chester killed? Who are the suspects? What do we know?"

Roxanne groaned. "Vivi, I warned you in the car—"

"Not to interfere. I know, I know," Vivian said as she flapped her hand in her daughter-in-law's face. "But if we hadn't gotten involved last time, Zack could still be sitting in prison for a murder he didn't commit."

"That was different, Nana," Zoey said. "We had to get involved to clear Zack's name."

"Stay out of it, Ma," Marlon said as he linked arms with his wife and drew her towards the door. "You know what I said last time . . . If you keep sticking your nose where it doesn't belong, I'll send you to a nursing home. And not a nice one."

Vivian directed a rude gesture at Marlon's back as he and Roxanne disappeared outside. She then spun around to face Zoey and Zack. "Chester was your friend. And how do you know that handsome detective doesn't suspect either of you? He is on the case, right?"

"Yes, he is," Zoey confirmed.

Vivian moved closer to Zoey and whispered, "Did you ever find out if he's single?"

"He better be," Zack said. "He asked Zoey out on a date."

Vivian whooped in excitement. "If I was only thirty years younger . . ."

"If you were thirty years younger, you'd still be fifteen years too old for the detective."

Vivian gave Zack a dirty look. "Heck with age. Maybe I should be a cougar . . . You think I could pull it off, Zoey?"

"No."

"You're no fun." Vivian glanced back and forth between her grandchildren. "Now, would one of you please tell me what happened?"

Zoey pressed her hands over her face and groaned. She could try to claim that Detective Gates had forbidden her from discussing the specifics of Chester's death. Vivian wouldn't take that for an answer. No, she would just continue to hound her granddaughter until Zoey finally broke down and told her everything.

"He was stabbed."

"How many times?"

Zoey glared at her nana. "Seriously? It's not like I took the time to count the individual stab wounds. That's the coroner's job."

"You said 'wounds.' That means he was stabbed more than once," Vivian said. "Would you say he was stabbed more or less than ten times?"

"More."

Vivian's jaw dropped. "More than fifty?"

"I don't know. Maybe. All I can tell you is that he was stabbed a whole bunch of times in the chest and neck."

Vivian huffed. "I hope Chester put up a fight."

"I'm sure he did," Zack said as he ushered Zoey and Vivian out of the barn.

"No, he didn't," Zoey said. She tugged at the bow on top of her hat and released the ear flaps. The hat might be ugly, but it was useful. "At least, I didn't see any defensive wounds on his hands or arms."

"You didn't get that good of a look at him," Zack said as he guided Zoey down the driveway away from the barn. Vivian hustled along at their heels. "And you also said it looked like he hit his head on the toilet. Maybe he was unconscious and couldn't fight back."

"If that's the case, stabbing him fifty times seems unnecessary," Vivian said. "And, speaking of cases, who are our suspects?"

"I never said it was fifty times." Zoey whirled around to face Vivian. "And we don't have any suspects. Detective Gates has suspects. We are staying out of it, and I am going home."

"I'm coming with you. You shouldn't be alone after the day you had."

"Nana was right . . ." Ever since she was a kid, Zoey had been in the habit of talking to herself. She did so even more often now that she lived by herself. "I shouldn't be alone."

Giving up on falling asleep, Zoey rolled over in bed so that she could check the time on her phone. It was almost two-thirty in the morning. She'd been in bed for just about two hours and, despite taking the prescription medication that was supposed to combat her chronic insomnia, she had yet to doze off. She wasn't surprised that she hadn't fallen asleep. Her overactive imagination was running at full speed, and, every time she closed her eyes, she pictured Chester's mutilated body and his blood-spattered bathroom. In fact, it was probably a good thing that she couldn't fall asleep. Not when her subconscious would twist around the day's events and produce nightmares.

Zoey sat up and then fumbled around on the nightstand until she found the switch for the zebra print table lamp. The lamp's low-wattage bulb cast a soft glow around the small bedroom, giving the various brightly colored sugar skulls and other Day of the Dead décor a sinister appearance that it would not have had in the daylight.

At the foot of the bed, Zoey's short-haired orange cat lifted her head and rewarded her owner with an irritated meow.

"Enough with the attitude, Lita. I had a horrible day."

Lita chirped in response.

"Oh, please, I know you spent most of the day sleeping." Zoey nudged Lita with her foot, causing the cat to pounce on her lower legs. Not only did Zoey talk to herself, she also carried on full conversations with her cat. "And it's almost time for your middle of the night zoomies. Why don't you run around and do your thing?"

Lita blinked her green eyes a few times before she jumped off the bed and took off running. Her small feet padded on the hardwood as she raced throughout the apartment.

"And she's off . . ." Zoey groaned as she fell back against the pillows. "Who killed you, Chester? And why? What did you have that someone wanted so badly they would kill you and then ransack your place? Who was so determined to keep their secrets that they had to kill you?"

She'd meant it when she said that she didn't want to get involved in Detective Gates's investigation. She also didn't want to go behind his back and conduct her own inquiry—even though she and Zack had already done that when they'd exploited the condolence call to question Imogene Hartman, but that was more about satiating their curiosity concerning the past twelve years of Chester's life than figuring out who killed him.

Zoey knew she had no business sticking her nose where it didn't belong. She'd done that after Devon's murder, and it had almost gotten her killed. But Vivian was right. Chester was her friend. She owed it to him to do whatever she could to help find his killer.

She grabbed a pen and notebook out of the nightstand's top drawer. Now that she'd had time to get over her anxiety attack and process what had happened, she recalled more details. Whether those details were crucial to the case would be up to Detective Gates to decide.

After writing down everything she could remember about the crime scene, she turned to a clean page and wrote "Suspects" across the top. Below that, she wrote "person unknown." She'd have to ask Vivian for the exact statistics, but she knew that most murder victims were killed by someone that they knew—whether it was a family member, friend, or acquaintance. That being said, some people were murdered by strangers. She couldn't discount that Chester's killer was unacquainted with him—especially if it was someone who broke in looking for something valuable to pawn.

But that didn't explain all the stab wounds. Chester had been stabbed far more times than was necessary to kill him. Overkill took rage. The killer must have hated Chester, and they unleashed that hatred using a knife. A stranger—unless he or she was high on drugs—wouldn't have had any reason to stab Chester repeatedly.

"Oscar Hartman is at the top of the list. Imogene made it clear that he disliked his son," Zoey said as she jotted down Oscar's name. "And, I mean, what was he doing there? Especially when Imogene told us that he didn't know Chester was back in the area. Obviously, Oscar was lying. But why?"

Below Oscar's name, she made a note that she hadn't seen any blood spatter on his clothes. Yes, she had only seen him from a distance. But she wasn't that far away from him that she wouldn't have been able to see dried blood on his clothes. Considering the amount of blood that was pooled on the bathroom floor and sprayed on the walls, the killer would have gotten blood on himself. Zoey had to admit that Oscar's bulky winter coat could have concealed any dried blood spatter on his shirt, but what could Oscar have been doing in Chester's home for all that time? If Chester had died around midnight, that left Oscar with twelve hours alone in the house before Zoey got there. It couldn't have taken Oscar around twelve hours to ransack the shipping container. The place wasn't big enough, nor were there enough hiding spaces to keep someone occupied for that long.

Whether Oscar was the killer or not, it was suspicious that he happened to be lurking around the shipping container on the morning after his son was murdered. Zoey made a note to remind herself to ask Detective Gates if he'd received the text messages she'd sent to him along with pictures of Oscar's truck.

Moving on, Zoey added Quincy's name to the list. Suspecting him made her feel sick to her stomach, but she would be a fool to leave him off the list.

Over the past week, Quincy had antagonized Chester at every opportunity. When she'd questioned him about it, he claimed he'd only done it because he didn't like or trust Chester. In Zoey's opinion, that hardly seemed like a good reason to constantly harass someone.

Quincy had also admitted to being at Chester's place in the hours before Chester was killed. Yes, Quincy claimed that Chester was alive and well when he left, but he could have been lying. It was possible that the two had argued about the painkillers—Quincy wanted more, and Chester refused to supply them—and the verbal altercation turned physical. Rage could have driven Quincy to repeatedly stab Chester and then search the house for drugs. When he didn't find what he wanted, Quincy could have returned to his parents' house and spent the rest of the night playing video games like he claimed.

"And then there's Lucas, Brittany, and Michelle," Zoey said as she added their names to the list. "They all knew Chester was back in the area. And

Chester admitted to knowing some of our classmates' secrets. Considering the way Brittany was acting this morning, I bet Chester knew something about her. And he claimed to have known what really happened to Mr. Jennings's Lamborghini. Speaking of the car . . ."

Zoey tossed the notebook aside and climbed out of bed. Dodging around Lita who was still racing around the apartment, she headed over to the office nook by the front door and grabbed her laptop off the desk. She'd started keeping a journal when she was ten years old. For years, she had written in it every day—and she continued to do so on a regular basis. Not only had she written about her life, but she also kept detailed notes on the pro wrestling events that she had attended as well as the wrestling that she watched on TV. After high school, when she finally got a laptop, Zoey switched over to typing the journal. She'd then gone back and typed up all the handwritten journals.

"I must have written something about the robbery at the Jenningses' house," Zoey said as she took the laptop back to her bedroom and climbed into bed. As the laptop booted up, she watched Lita saunter back into the bedroom. Talking to the cat, Zoey said, "I remember hearing about the robbery on the news over the summer. And everyone was talking about it on the first day of school."

Zoey found the document that covered the summer of 2005. Using the search feature, she searched for Lucas's name. She clicked through the journal entries until she found the right one. At the time, social media was in its infancy. And, since she was not friends with the popular crowd, she had not been kept in the loop. She'd had to rely on the news and gossip to learn about what had happened to Lucas that summer.

Based on what she had written, the robbery took place in early August of 2005. Mr. and Mrs. Jennings had been on a European vacation. While they were gone, one of Lucas's grandmas stayed with him. Zoey figured that his parents had not trusted Lucas enough to leave him home alone. They had done that earlier in the summer, and Lucas used the opportunity to throw a party at the house. One of the neighbors called the police, and the party was raided. Almost the entire group of popular students got busted for underage drinking.

Zoey made a note to tell Detective Gates about the party. Since he lived across the street from the Jenningses', it was possible Chester was the one who had called the police. If he had, and their classmates found out about it, they could have sought revenge. The underage drinking charges would have gone on everyone's juvenile record. There could have also been other types of fallout. Their parents certainly wouldn't have been happy with them. They'd probably been fined. College scholarships could have been negatively affected. The high school might have even punished them somehow.

Turning her attention back to the journal, Zoey read over what she'd written about the robbery at the Jenningses' house. According to what she'd heard on the news, Lucas's grandma had left him home alone the one night so that she could attend the weekly bingo game at her church. While she was gone, two masked men broke into the house. They beat up Lucas and left him hogtied. The robbers then ransacked the house and stole a bunch of valuables including jewelry, Lucas's game console, a laptop, and some other small electronics. The robbers also took the Lamborghini.

The next day, the car was found in a ravine a couple miles up the road from Buckhannon. The front end of the car, which had struck a tree, was totaled. The jewelry and electronics were discovered in the trunk of the car.

"What really happened, Lucas?" Zoey asked. She recalled that Chester had said Mrs. Jennings might forgive her son for what really happened to the Lamborghini, but there was no way that Mr. Jennings would. "What Chester said implies that you're the one who crashed it. Is that what happened? Did you take the car out for a joy ride while your grandma was at bingo? You lost control and ran off the road into the ravine? Then . . . Then you called up Chester and asked him to help you stage a robbery? That sounds farfetched. But I guess it could be what really happened."

Zoey jotted down her theory.

"I don't know how helpful this will be. But it's worth a shot," Zoey said as she opened up the journal that covered the year she started high school. She scrolled down until she found the entry for the first day of school. "At best, I'll find something about Chester that breaks this case wide open. At worst, I'll stir up memories from high school and provide my subconscious with more material for nightmares."

TEN

Wednesday December 5th, 2018

"I HAVE NOTHING TO SAY to him."

"Come on, Arielle," Zack said. He stepped in front of his wife, blocking the way as she paced back and forth across the cramped confines of Zoey's combined kitchen and dining room. "In all the years I've known you, you've never held a grudge against anyone. Not even against the person who broke into your car and stole Paige's stroller."

Arielle harrumphed. "Well, in all the years I've known you, no one has falsely accused you of murder and then arrested you."

"You can't really blame Detective Gates for suspecting me. Heck, even your dad thought I might have killed Devon. And he was there when the detective arrested me. Are you holding a grudge against Jim, too?"

"Maybe my dad suspected you. But only for a hot second," Arielle said as a flush crept up her neck and across her cheeks. "And, no, I haven't exactly forgiven Dad for it yet."

Zack ran his hands through his long hair. "Hunny, we've talked about this I don't know how many times. Detective Gates was doing his job. Yes, he arrested me. It sucked. But, given the circumstances, I would have arrested me, too. I had a motive and no alibi."

"Don't forget that your fingerprints were all over the murder weapon," Zoey pointed out as she passed between Zack and Arielle. Lita indignantly meowed and nipped at Zoey's heels as she herded her owner towards the small, L-shaped kitchen. "And you were overheard threatening to bash Devon over the head with it."

"Your fingerprints were all over the murder weapon, too, Zoey," Arielle said. "But the detective didn't arrest you."

Zoey stood on her tiptoes and grabbed one of the cans of cat food that was piled on top of the refrigerator. "Honestly, I'm still kinda surprised that he didn't."

"Me, too," Zack said. "Either way, the detective got it right in the end—"

"No, your sister and grandma got it right." Arielle said. "If they hadn't stuck their noses in the investigation, who knows if the detective would have figured it out."

"There you go, Lita." Zoey finished dishing out the shredded salmon and shrimp. She then set the bowl on the floor. "I'm sure Detective Gates would've eventually gotten it right, Arielle. Besides you're the one who begged me to do something to prove Zack's innocence—"

"My husband had just been arrested for murder. You can't expect me to think rationally at a time like that." Arielle put her hands on her hips and glared at Zoey. "And I didn't ask you to confront the killer and almost get yourself killed."

"I didn't know he was the killer when I confronted him."

Zack cleared his throat, causing Zoey and Arielle to look over to where he had taken a seat at the dinner table. "Enough. Arielle, do I need to remind you *why* we're meeting with the detective this morning? It's so we can provide him with whatever information we have on Chester. You do remember Chester, right? He was murdered sometime yesterday—"

"You don't need to remind me," Zoey said. "I'm the one who found him."

"You're right, Zack. This is about Chester. I can put aside my personal feelings for the greater good." Arielle spun around and then stomped into the living room. "But that doesn't mean I will *ever* forgive the detective for arresting you."

"You do remember that he also saved mine and Nana's lives, right?" Zoey asked. After watching Arielle flop down on one end of the dark purple sectional, Zoey turned to Zack and raised an eyebrow in question. "What's gotten into her? Normally, she's the calm and rational one."

"She's been acting nutty ever since I was arrested." Zack stood up and took a couple steps closer to his sister. "You probably shouldn't tell her that the detective asked you out. Considering how she feels about him, I don't think the news will go over very well."

"How do you feel—"

Before Zoey could finish asking Zack how he felt about her going on a date with Detective Gates, she was interrupted by a knock at the door. Leaving the question for another time, she walked over to the exterior door that opened onto a deck. A half-wall next to the door created a small foyer and separated the entryway from the office nook under the window. Spread out across the desktop were Zoey's notes for the upcoming LAW show.

"Hi, Tyler." Zoey swung open the door and gestured for the detective to come inside. "How's the case going?"

"Abysmally. You and Zack weren't kidding when you said the victim was an enigma." Gates shrugged out of his coat. In the process, he stepped too close to Lita. The cat hissed and swiped at him. One of her claws snagged on the cuff of his gray pants. "Whoa. Hey there, kitty."

"Lita!" Zoey used her foot to nudge the cat back towards her food bowl. Lita gave her owner a halfhearted hiss before she resumed inhaling her food. "Sorry about that. She's just very defensive of her food bowl."

Going on four years ago, Zoey had found Lita trapped in one of the tattoo shop's garbage cans. After rescuing the half-starved kitten, Zoey cleaned her up and adopted her. Despite her current life as a spoiled housecat, Lita seemed to have never gotten over the first few months of her life when she'd been forced to fend for herself.

"I don't know what you're eating, kitty. But I can assure you that I do not want it," Detective Gates said to Lita. He then looked up at Zoey and said, "Thanks for sending me those pictures of the victim's father's truck. And for letting me know that Zack saw him around the shop. I have one of the officers looking into it. I want to gather up as much information and solid proof that I can get before I confront Mr. Hartman again. When I spoke to him yesterday afternoon, he claimed he had no idea that his son was back in the area."

"Sounds like Chester's dad is your top suspect," Zoey said as she led the detective into the living room that was overrun with wrestling memorabilia. Action figures lined the top of the entertainment center, and the walls were covered with framed photos and posters. "Do you have any other suspects?"

"Not really," Detective Gates said. "I spoke to the people who live on either side of Chester. One of them was outside smoking an illegal substance around eleven-thirty, and he saw Quincy leave. The neighbor said that Chester was still alive at the time. So, if Quincy's alibi checks out, he's off the suspect list."

Zoey sighed in relief. She hadn't wanted to suspect Quincy, but she would have been negligent not to.

"Any idea when Chester was murdered?" Zack asked.

"Most likely around midnight. The neighbor on the other side of Chester is a college student. She was up late studying for a final and, around midnight, overheard two people arguing. She figured it was the people on the other side of her. They're newlyweds, but they fight all the time. I checked, and they were not home the night of the murder. My assumption is that the argument the college student overheard was between Chester and his killer."

"Too bad the college student didn't call the police," Zack said.

"She said she would have had she realized it wasn't the quarreling newlyweds." Detective Gates had a seat on the sectional and flipped open a notebook. "I'm hoping the three of you can provide me with some more information on the victim and clue me in as to why anyone would want to kill him."

"Honestly . . . there's not that much we can tell you about Chester." Zack's shoulders slumped as he sank back against the couch cushions. "And I'm not sure if whatever we can tell you will be all that useful."

"Anything helps." Gates looked around the room. Zoey sat next to him, and Zack and Arielle were diagonal. Arielle had moved to the far end of the sectional to put as much possible distance between herself and the detective. Lita had also followed them into the living room and was eyeing up the detective from her perch on top of the cat tree. "Let's start with Chester's professional life. Did he have any problems with a client? Maybe a client who wasn't satisfied with a tattoo?"

"I'm usually the one who talks to the clients before they leave," Zoey said. It was her job to hand out aftercare instructions. She also took pictures of the tattoos to post on social media. "And the only complaint I heard was that he was too quiet."

"Some clients like having us talk to them while we work," Zack said. "It keeps them distracted. But Chester wasn't one for small talk."

"Doesn't seem like much of a reason to kill anyone," Detective Gates said. "But I would still like to speak with his clients and hear what they have to say. It's possible one of them is the killer. Could one of you put together a list of the clients and their contact info?"

Zoey held up her hand. "All of the clients' info gets entered in the system, so I can easily print off a list for you."

"If there's nothing recent you can think of . . ." Detective Gates paused for a few seconds as he looked back and forth between Zoey, Zack, and Arielle. "You mentioned yesterday that you went to school with the victim. Does that mean you've known him since kindergarten?"

"No, we went to different elementary schools," Zoey said. She named the five elementary schools in the Linville Area School District. "Zack and I went to Strohm Mill Elementary. Chester went to Buckhannon Elementary."

Gates looked over at Arielle. "What elementary school did you attend?"

"My family moved here the summer before I started eighth grade," Arielle grumbled. She refused to look at the detective and instead stared at her reflection in the TV. "But my little sister went to Linville Elementary for sixth grade. It's the one down the street from the high school."

"Zoey and I didn't encounter Chester until middle school," Zack said. He nudged Arielle with his elbow, and, when she turned to face him, gave her a pointed look. "But they kept us divided into sections. None of us were in a section with Chester in seventh or eighth grade."

Zoey clarified that there were approximately three hundred students in each graduating class. At the middle school level, the students were split into ten sections with roughly thirty kids in each group. Aside from homeroom each morning, in the hallways between classes, and at lunch, they had not really interacted with the students outside of their sections during school hours. Because Zoey and Zack had been in different sections, they hardly saw each other during the day while in middle school.

Zoey and Arielle had been in the same section in eighth grade. It was how they met and became best friends. Arielle also helped make eighth grade bearable for Zoey. Thanks to Jocelyn Hershey and her vengeful minions, the two years Zoey spent at Linville Area Middle School had been miserable.

In high school, the students were no longer separated into sections. Instead, they were able to sign up for classes of their choosing—though they were limited to what classes were offered for each grade level. The students took eight classes a year—four in the fall semester and another four in the spring.

"In ninth grade, all three of us signed up for the Foundations of Art class," Zack said. He stood up and plucked Lita off the cat tree. He then sat back down and scratched Lita under the chin. "It was the basic level art class. It was also a prerequisite for the rest of the art classes. Most of which Chester and I took."

"The only reason Arielle and I signed up for Foundations was so we could take the print photography classes offered to eleventh and twelfth graders."

"Hey," Arielle picked up a leopard print throw pillow and playfully tossed it at Zoey. "I also took the jewelry making class."

"I forgot about that." Zoey lobbed the pillow back at her sister-in-law. "I wonder if they still have print photography classes or if it's all digital now."

"They do. But it's only one class." Zack swatted the pillow away from Arielle. Lita leapt off his lap and pounced on the pillow. "Only reason I know is because our cousin, Lil' Schmitty, took it last year. I helped him with one of his projects."

Detective Gates cleared his throat. "Getting back to when you befriended Chester . . ."

"Oh, yeah. It was the first day of ninth grade," Zack said. "Arielle, Zoey, and I all had that art class together. The teacher let us sit wherever we wanted. Obviously, the three of us sat together. And, since we had an extra seat at our table, I invited Chester to sit with us. The only other empty seat was at a table with three preppy girls . . ."

"After that, we basically adopted Chester. If we had the same lunch period, he sat with us. If we were in the same class, he sat next to us. If there was a group project, one of us worked with him. The rest of our friends tolerated him, but none of them really went out of their way to make him feel welcome or include him in anything. Not like we did." Arielle looked directly at Detective Gates for the first time since he'd entered the room. "I assume I don't have to explain high school cliques to you."

Gates shook his head. "I was a jock. I played football and soccer."

"Because we dyed our hair and wore punk-style clothes, we got lumped in with the 'outcast' group. You know . . . the freaks, the goths, the emo kids . . . the ones who significantly differed from the established norm." Arielle kicked off her shoes and drew her long legs up onto the couch. After settling into a cross-legged position, she said, "Chester was the stereotypical loner kid. He was quiet and kept to himself. Most of our classmates thought he was weird and ignored him. He probably would have gone through high school unnoticed if the popular kids hadn't singled him out and relentlessly picked on him."

Zoey scooped up Lita and settled the cat on her lap. "Chester always sat at the back of the classroom. He never raised his hand. If he had to speak out loud or in front of the class, he would mumble or talk too fast. He hated being the center of attention."

"The only times when Chester actually seemed comfortable or showed any confidence was in art class," Zack said. "He was good. And I mean really good. The guy had serious talent."

Detective Gates looked up from his notebook and asked, "So what you're saying is that Chester was awkward as a teenager. And that the three of you were his only real friends."

"Not that we knew him all that well." Zack stood up and went over to the entertainment center. He picked up a random pro wrestling action figure and examined it. "Like Arielle said, Chester was quiet. He hardly talked to anyone. And he rarely shared anything personal. I knew him a little better than Arielle and Zoey, but that's because I was with him the most. We had most of our classes together."

"I'm guessing you remained in contact with Chester after graduation—"

"No, we didn't," Zack said. "Until he showed up here, none of us had heard from Chester since right after we graduated. I'll admit I tried to find him on social media. And, every once in a while, I'd search online or ask some artist friends if they'd heard of him. But I never found him."

"Honestly, I kind of forgot about him over the years," Arielle said.

"Me, too," Zoey added. "That is, until he walked into the tattoo shop . . ."

"That's what I mean when I say that we can't really help you," Zack said. "Aside from knowing he spent the past ten years working at a tattoo shop in Venice Beach, we have no idea what Chester has been up to. We know next to nothing about his personal life. We talked about it last night, and none of us have any idea what Chester could have been hiding or who would want to kill him. It could have been someone from his past or someone more recent."

"What about these former classmates you mentioned?" Gates asked. "You said a couple of them recently threatened Chester. Can you think of a reason why one of them might have wanted him dead?"

"More like the other way around," Arielle said. "They're the ones who tormented Chester in high school. I can't remember him doing anything in retaliation."

"Who are these classmates?"

"Lucas Jennings is one of them. He stopped by here on Monday, and we overheard him warn Chester to keep his mouth shut about something," Zack said as he motioned between himself and Zoey. "According to Chester, he and Lucas were best friends in elementary school. Then, when we all got to middle school, Lucas ditched Chester for the popular crowd. I don't recall Lucas every really picking on Chester in high school. But he didn't try to stop the other kids from picking on him either."

"I don't remember Lucas really acknowledging Chester's existence at all," Arielle said.

"But they were interacting outside of school," Zack said. "Chester told me and Zoey that he did Lucas's homework so that Lucas could focus on playing sports. He also mentioned something about Lucas's dad's car—"

"I read over my old journals last night, and I wrote about Mr. Jennings's car," Zoey said. "Apparently, Lucas told the police that someone broke into his parents' house and stole the car and some other valuables. Chester insinuated that Lucas was lying about that. I'm thinking that Lucas took the car out for a joy ride and crashed it."

"And . . . what?" Zack asked. "Chester helped him fake the robbery? That's kinda crazy."

"I know it's crazy," Zoey said. "But it's not totally unbelievable. Something happened to that Lamborghini. And whatever happened to it is not what wound up in the official police report. Chester knew what really happened. And Lucas might have killed Chester to keep him from telling the truth. Based on what Mr. Jennings told us last night, Lucas is at rock bottom. If Mr. Jennings finds out that Lucas is the one who crashed the Lamborghini, he's probably kick Lucas out of the house and fire him from the dealership. Then where would Lucas be? I have to think Lucas is pretty desperate to make sure his dad never finds out the truth."

"I'll look into the police report," Gates said. "And I'll also talk to Lucas."

"Chester also said that he knew some of our other classmates' secrets. Whatever else he knew might have been worth killing over," Zoey said. She, Zack, and Arielle had talked about it last night, and they had no idea how Chester had learned anyone's secrets or what those secrets might be. They also couldn't imagine any of their former classmates confessing their secrets to Chester; it was possible that Chester had overheard a private conversation or witnessed something happening. "On Tuesday morning, Arielle and I ran into four classmates at the gym. One of them claimed she knew Chester has been back in town for at least a couple weeks. And she seemed a little rattled by it. And another one seemed overly upset when she heard Chester was back in town."

Detective Gates handed Zoey his notebook and asked her to write down the names of her former classmates. "I'd like to speak with them. And any other former classmates who live in the area who might have had a run-in with Chester over the past few weeks. Are the three of you still friends with anyone from high school?"

Zoey laughed. "Heck no. Aside from Quincy, we don't associate with anyone we went to school with—"

Cutting her off, Arielle said, "What Zoey means is that we don't hang out with any of our former classmates. But we do occasionally run into some of them around town . . . like at the gym, the grocery store, the library . . . You know, places like that."

Gates took the notebook back from Zoey. "Did you attend any of your reunions."

"No!" Zoey said with more force than necessary. "We didn't even know about the five-year reunion."

"Let me guess . . ." Detective Gates said. "The invitation got lost in the mail."

"There were no invitations." Zoey explained that, sometime after graduation, Natasha Bowman started a private Facebook group for their class. Natasha then invited select people to join the group. Zoey, Zack, and Arielle had not been part of the chosen few. It was on the private group page that Natasha and the other class officers shared the information about the reunions. "The only reason we found out about the ten-year reunion was because an old friend from elementary school made a public post about it. I asked her what was going on, and she invited me to join the group. I then invited Zack and Arielle."

Zack snorted. "And I immediately left the group."

Detective Gates perked up. "How often does anyone post in this private group?"

"Since the ten year reunion . . . hardly ever," Zoey said. Occasionally, Natasha shared some news concerning a former classmate or teacher. She'd also posted pictures of the high school's new football stadium and the renovations at one of the elementary schools. "The only time anyone really posts anything is if they have some major news or if someone dies."

"Do me a favor, and keep an eye on the page," Detective Gates said to Zoey. "And let me know if anyone posts about Chester."

ELEVEN

"THANKS FOR CALLING 3 Count Tattoos. How can—"

"Yo," the caller barked, cutting Zoey off. "Is it true one of y'all got iced?"

Zoey drew in a deep breath and then exhaled. "Yes, Chester Neidigh died—"

"What's that mean for me? I'm supposed to get tattooed by him next Friday."

Zoey asked for the man's name and then confirmed that he had an appointment with Chester scheduled for the next week. She was slowly making her way through Chester's appointments and contacting his clients. She'd made it most of the way through next Wednesday, but she still had a long way to go to get to his last scheduled appointment at the end of January.

"I'm working on rescheduling Chester's clients," Zoey said. "We have three other artists here, but their schedules are already booked—"

"I want my tattoo."

Forcing herself to be polite, Zoey said, "Like I said, I'm working on—"

"Yo, your shop is totally unprofessional to be canceling on people at the last minute."

Losing what little patience she had left, Zoey said, "It's hardly the last minute. And I can assure you that Chester was not planning on getting murdered. But I do apologize that his death is such an inconvenience to you. It was also untimely to him."

"I get that, but—"

Zoey ended the call and then tossed the phone onto her cluttered desk. She usually kept it organized, but she'd had to pull out all the paperwork she had on Chester's former and upcoming clients and make copies of them for Detective Gates. The papers were spread out all over the desk, and the mess was adding to her irritation.

"If I have to deal with one more jerk . . ."

The phone rang. Zoey checked the caller ID and saw that the man she'd just hung up on was calling back.

Giving in to her frustration, Zoey sprang out of her chair and stomped over to the leather couch. She grabbed one of the throw pillows, pressed it to her face to muffle the sound, and screamed. She'd spent the last two hours calling clients and fielding calls from nosy people. Most of the clients had been polite and understanding. There were a few—like the last guy—who had been outright rude. Reporters from the local news stations and the Lancaster County newspaper had also called, and none of them wanted to take "no comment" for an answer. It was only after two o'clock, but she'd had about all she could take for the day.

When she was finished screaming, Zoey whacked the pillow against the arm of the couch a few times. Her actions did little to ease her aggravation.

"Having a bad day, *Chica*?"

Zoey flung the pillow onto the couch and then spun to face the doorway. Peeking around the door frame was Santino Cruz. His brown eyes swept over her with a mixture of concern and amusement.

Santino started working at the shop two-and-a-half-years earlier. Before that, he'd worked at a shop in Lancaster City. The atmosphere at the previous shop had been toxic, and Santino was actively searching for a new job when he met Zack at a local tattoo convention. The two hit it off, and Zack invited Santino to come work at 3 Count. Santino specialized in the traditional tattoo style, and, despite being a sarcastic and disorganized goofball, he'd become an asset to the shop.

"I wouldn't exactly call it a good day, Tino," Zoey said as she returned to her desk. "I'm sick of dealing with people and their tactless questions about Chester. It really makes me wonder what the heck is wrong with some people."

"*Chica*, some people just ain't right."

"I'd say they were raised by wolves, but wolves would have done a better job," Zoey said, stealing one of her nana's favorite insults. She leaned back in her chair and asked, "Did you talk to the detective?"

"Yep." Santino nodded, causing the tight, black curls along his forehead to bounce. Over the past few months, he had grown out his buzz cut. The tiny ringlets that popped forth from his scalp reminded Zoey of a Chia Pet. "He just left."

Zoey slumped farther down in her chair. She knew she shouldn't be upset that Detective Gates had left without saying goodbye—after all, he was in the middle of a murder investigation—but she still felt a tinge of disappointment.

"What did you tell Detective Gates?"

"That I barely knew Chester." Santino tugged up the sleeves of his gray track suit, revealing a left forearm that was covered in tattoos. His right arm was bare, but he was talking about getting a tattoo on his forearm soon. He propped his elbows on the counter and looked down at Zoey. "I didn't like him or trust him neither."

"Have you been talking to Quincy?"

Santino's handsome face screwed up in disgust. "You've gone *loca*, *Chica*. You know I ain't 'bout to agree with Quincy on nothing. *Nada*."

Throughout the time Santino worked at 3 Count, he and Quincy developed a friendly rivalry. They disagreed on just about everything and enjoyed antagonizing each other. The ribbing was meant as harmless fun. Occasionally, things got heated, and one of them would cross the line. Zoey or Zack then had to jump in to mediate and restore peace to the shop.

"Yeah, Quincy's been running his mouth 'bout Chester since last week. But you know I ain't gonna believe nothing he says," Santino stated. He picked up the Shawn Michaels action figure and played with his jointed arms and legs. "Besides, I'd already figured out there was something not right with Chester way before Quincy came back."

"Was there something in particular that made you not trust him?"

"Well . . . At first, I just got this weird vibe from him, you know. But that might have been because he was so . . . What's the word I'm looking for?"

"Aloof?"

"Exactly. He had that attitude that he didn't want to be bothered. And I was like, all right, man, I'll leave you alone." Santino leaned over the counter and whispered, "Then, a few weeks ago, I figured out he was up to some shady shit."

Zoey scooted her chair closer to the desk and asked, "Like what?"

"Blackmail."

"Chester told me and Zack that he knew some, uh, sensitive information about some of our former classmates and teachers. But he swore to us that he wasn't actually blackmailing anyone." Zoey pushed her chair backwards. "What makes you think he was?"

"Because I heard him on the phone threatening people," Santino said. "And, like three weeks ago, I saw him arguing with some lady out in the alley."

Santino's private room was sandwiched in between the front office and the breakroom. The single window overlooked the small side porch and the alley. It was the smallest of the four rooms, but Santino preferred not having to hear someone else's tattoo gun humming through the walls while he worked.

"Was she a client?" Zoey asked.

Santino shrugged. "No clue. All I know was that I had just finished up a tattoo. I was disinfecting, and I cracked the window to air out the room. I heard a car pull up in the alley. Didn't think nothing of it till I heard raised voices."

"And, because you're as nosy as my nana, you looked outside."

"Duh . . ." Santino grinned. "There was this soccer mom van parked in the alley. And Chester was arguing with the lady behind the wheel. From what I overheard; it sounded like he was blackmailing her. She was begging him not to tell anyone 'bout something. Said it could ruin her life. He said he didn't care. Also said something 'bout not owing her nothing. She told him to think of her son and what it could do to him. They got quiet after that, and I couldn't hear nothing else. A minute or two later, she drove off and Chester came back inside."

"What did the lady look like?"

"I didn't get a good look at her face. But she had red hair."

Zoey sat up straighter. "What color was the van?"

"That trendy bluish color." Santino tugged down the zipper on his jacket to reveal a black t-shirt. He pointed at the teal logo printed across the chest. "Not quite this color. But close."

Zoey knew a redheaded woman who drove a teal van.

She grabbed her laptop and opened Facebook. Because she was friends with Brittany Patterson, it only took her a few seconds to find the other woman's page. She then clicked on Brittany's profile picture—a selfie that highlighted her crooked nose.

Zoey turned the laptop around so that Santino could see the screen. "Could this be the woman you saw?"

"Maybe . . ." Santino studied the enlarged picture. "Like I said, I didn't really see her face. But the hair's the right color. Who is she?"

"Brittany Patterson," Zoey said. "She was one of the popular girls in my graduating class. She used to pick on Chester."

"And you think she's the lady I saw Chester arguing with because . . ."

"Because she has red hair, she still lives in Linville, and she drives a teal van. She also has a son."

"Doesn't mean it was her."

"Arielle and I ran into Brittany and a couple other classmates at the gym on Tuesday. We were talking about another classmate when one of them brought up Chester."

Zoey thought back to the encounter at the gym. Brittany had been an active participant in gossiping about Lucas Jennings. But, as soon as Michelle mentioned Chester, Brittany became visibly uncomfortable. She'd also gotten angry with Michelle for bringing up her ex-husband. Zoey could commiserate with Brittany on that—she still got upset whenever someone mentioned Devon Isler. But why had Brittany yelled at Michelle for calling Chester a freak? Back in high school, calling their classmates "freaks" was one of Brittany's go-to insults. Zoey recalled Brittany labeling her a freak on countless occasions. She was positive that Brittany would have used the same insult when referring to Chester.

Continuing, Zoey said, "Brittany said she knew Chester was back in the area and admitted to having seen him around a few times. For whatever reason, she seemed pretty worked up about it."

"I would be, too, if someone was blackmailing me." Santino cracked his knuckles. "Any idea what he'd be blackmailing her 'bout?"

Zoey shook her head. "You only saw her that one time?"

"Yep. But I overheard Chester threatening someone over the phone. I didn't hear the whole conversation, but it sounded to me like he was blackmailing someone. Could have been this Brittany lady. Or it could have been someone else."

"What exactly did you overhear?"

"Chester was asking how much the person was willing to pay him to keep their secrets. Or what the person was willing to do to keep their secrets. Something like that. He also said high school wasn't that long ago."

"Was that before or after the argument with the woman in the alley?"

"Before, I think." Santino thought about it a few seconds and then nodded. "I went in the breakroom to grab my dinner. Chester was sitting at the table talking on the phone. As I walked in, he made the comment 'bout high school. I told him he needed to get over whatever happened back then. He gave me the finger and then went outside."

"Was it just the one phone call you overheard?"

Santino shook his head. "Nah, it was three or four. I have no clue if he was talking to the same person or someone different. For all I know, he was blackmailing a dozen people."

"When was the last time you overheard Chester threaten someone?"

"Monday afternoon. I got no clue who he was talking to, but he was heated. Told the person that if they didn't leave him alone, he'd ruin the guy's life."

Out in the foyer, the front door swung open.

"That's my client," Santino said.

"One more question, Tino," Zoey said. She reached across the counter and grabbed his arm to prevent him from walking away. "Did you tell Detective Gates about this?"

"Yeah. I told him to check Chester's phone and see who he was talking to. The detective said he'd do that as soon as they found Chester's phone. I guess it wasn't at his place," Santino said before he walked out into the foyer and greeted his client.

"Interesting . . ." Zoey whispered to herself.

Not only had the killer taken the painting of the naked lady from Chester's shipping container home, he or she had also grabbed Chester's cell phone. That was a good indication that Chester had been in contact with his killer, and the killer wanted to cover their tracks—or there was something on Chester's phone that the killer wanted access to.

Zoey studied Brittany's profile picture. "What secret from high school could Chester have been blackmailing you about? And why would Chester sharing that secret affect your son but not your daughters?"

Zoey scrolled down Brittany's profile page. Years earlier, she'd gotten sick of the other woman's incessant postings and unfollowed her. As she scrolled, Zoey confirmed that Brittany still posted multiple times a day. Her current posting trend revolved around Christmas, and included cookie recipes, gift and craft ideas, and links to local holiday events.

It took some scrolling, but Zoey finally came across a personal post.

"Oh my God, Brittany, could you have found uglier Christmas sweaters?"

The previous weekend, Brittany had dressed her husband and four children in matching holiday sweaters and then dragged them to the local mall to get a family photo with Santa. According to the lengthy description, Brittany's four-year-old-twins had been overjoyed to see Santa, but her eighteen-month-old had been terrified. Brittany also lamented that her twelve-year-old son, Ashton, was too old to believe in Santa and had spent the day complaining about how embarrassed he was to be seen in public in the matching sweaters. Zoey commiserated with him.

In the picture, Brittany and her husband, Peter Adams, stood on either side of Santa's green velvet armchair. Peter held the unhappy looking toddler while the smiling twins perched on Santa's lap. All three girls had inherited their father's curly brown hair. Ashton, who stood next to Brittany, was a carbon copy of his mom. His hair was the same shade of gingery red, and he also had her pasty skin and abundance of freckles. Even the annoyed face he was making was an exact imitation of his mom.

"Can't blame you for being embarrassed, kid," Zoey said as she enlarged the picture to get a closer look at Brittany's son. There was something about Ashton that looked familiar, and she had a feeling that she had seen him recently. Yes, she occasionally ran into Brittany and her family around town, but the last time that happened was over the summer at the Linville Fair. She'd seen Brittany multiple times since then, but not her family. So why was she convinced that she had seen Ashton recently? "All right, Ashton. Why do you look so familiar? Where have I . . . Oh! You're the kid from Chester's picture!"

Zoey jumped to her feet, sending her desk chair crashing into the wall.

Her thick socks slid across the wood floor as she circled around her desk and then sprinted down the hallway to Chester's private room. Earlier, Detective Gates had posted a sign on the door stating that everyone needed to stay out until he had a chance to search the room for evidence. Ignoring the sign, Zoey rushed inside.

"Where is it?" Zoey muttered as she flipped through the piles of papers that covered Chester's desk. She found numerous other pictures scattered across the desktop, but she didn't find the one of the boy. She finally found it buried under a pile of sketchpads in the bottom desk drawer. "Oh, yeah, that's definitely him."

"Him who?"

"Gah!" Spinning around, Zoey came face-to-face with Zack. "What are you doing in here? Aside from giving me a heart attack?"

"I could ask you the same thing. Or does the detective's sign not apply to you?"

"Tyler said we could come in if it was an emergency. And this is an emergency." Zoey held up the picture. "Remember this from Monday? Chester was looking at it right after Lucas left."

"Yeah. And . . ."

"It's Brittany Patterson's and Rodney Dissinger's kid."

Brittany and Rodney had been high school sweethearts. They'd gotten married not long after graduation and divorced about five years later. Brittany then married her current husband.

"Okay . . ."

Zoey waved the picture in her brother's face. "Why would Chester have a picture of their kid?"

"I don't know. Maybe Rodney or Brittany was having Chester draw up a portrait tattoo."

"I don't know about Rodney . . ." Zoey snorted. "But Brittany's been giving me grief over my tattoos since I got my first one when I was seventeen. Heck, she was giving me a hard time about them just the other day. There's no way she'd suddenly change her mind and decide to get a tattoo. And, even if she did, why would she get one of just her son? She also has three daughters."

"How should I know? I don't know how Brittany's mind works."

"Neither do I. But I'm going to find out."

"No. You're not." Zack grabbed Zoey by the arm and forced her to look at him. "You need to stay out of this. What if that kid has something to do with why Chester was killed? What if he broke kayfabe and . . . Well, I don't know what secret Chester might have known about the kid. But if that kid is somehow involved—"

"I need to find out."

"No, Zoey. You need to give the picture to the detective and let him figure it out."

Zoey pulled away from her brother. "But Tyler asked for my help."

"No, he asked you to keep an eye on Facebook. He didn't ask you to stick your nose in his investigation. You know, you're almost as bad as Nana."

"Oh, please. I am not."

"Trust me, you are." Zack hustled Zoey out to the hallway, slamming the door shut behind them. "Speaking of Facebook, I saw you posted something about Chester on the shop's page. Did you also post something on the high school page?"

"No, Natasha Bowman beat me to it. Last time I checked, the only person who'd reacted to the post was Arielle." Zoey headed back to her office and had a seat at her desk. She brought up the private Facebook page and checked Natasha's post. Earlier, Natasha had posted a link to a local news article about Chester's murder. Since then, she added Chester's senior photo. "There are a dozen sad reactions. And a few comments."

"Anything suspicious?"

"Wesley Cummings says he doesn't remember Chester." Zoey looked up at Zack and asked, "Do you remember this Wesley guy from high school?"

Zack shrugged. "Name does not sound familiar."

"We did have a graduating class of three hundred. No way we knew everybody." Zoey turned back to the laptop and read over the next few comments. "Let's see . . . Michelle made a comment about Chester working here. Aww, isn't that sweet . . . She tagged me in her comment."

"She only did that because she's hoping you'll reply and share what you know." Zack came around the desk and leaned over Zoey's shoulder. "Michelle's husband responded to her comment. What did he say?"

Zoey scrolled down so that she could read the comment left by Kevin Sensenig. "Kevin says he's glad the freaks stuck together."

"I guess that means you, me, and Chester."

"Ugh, what a jerk."

"He hasn't matured any since high school." Zack looked up at the retro clock that was mounted on the wall above the desk. "I better get back to work. I have to finish up this sketch before my three o'clock appointment. And you need to get back to calling Chester's clients."

"I know, I know." Zoey closed Facebook and brought up the shop's calendar. "I want to get through the rest of next week's clients by the end of the day."

Zoey tried to focus on contacting the clients, but she kept getting distracted by the picture of Brittany's son. Why did Chester have the picture? And what was he blackmailing Brittany about? She knew she should do what Zack recommended—hand the picture over to Detective Gates and let him figure things out—but she also didn't want to waste the detective's time on something that could turn out to be nothing. She didn't think it would be a problem if she asked a few innocent questions.

Before she could allow her sensible side to talk herself out of being impulsive and nosy, Zoey picked up the phone and called Brittany's hair salon.

"This is Brittany. How can I help you."

"Hey Brittany, it's Zoey Wilde."

"What do you want?"

"I . . . uh . . ." Zoey stammered. She scrambled to come up with a reason for calling. She couldn't ask about the picture or the blackmail over the phone. Brittany would just hang up. No, she needed to ask her questions in person. "I desperately need a haircut before—"

"I have an opening tomorrow at ten. It's all yours."

Brittany hung up before Zoey could reply.

Zoey tossed the phone onto her desk and then picked up the picture of Brittany's son.

"Zack's right. I am as bad as Nana."

TWELVE

Zoey had turned her attention back to Chester's upcoming appointments when the front door swung open, and Lucas Jennings barreled into the office.

"I just saw Natasha's Facebook post." Lucas leaned against the front of Zoey's desk and wheezed. "Is it true? Is Chester really dead?"

"You only just found out?" Zoey asked. "Aren't you living with your parents? Didn't they tell you?"

Lucas shook his head. "I haven't been home. Or at the dealership. I've been . . . busy. Mom tried calling me last night and this morning, but I didn't answer. And the group chat was blowing up, but I . . . Well, it doesn't matter what I was doing. All I want to know is if Chester is dead?"

Zoey nodded. "He was murdered on Monday night. I found his body early yesterday afternoon."

"Holy shit." Lucas stumbled over to the leather couch and collapsed. "It's over. It's finally over. I'm free."

"What's over?" Zoey asked as she had a seat on the coffee table in front of Lucas. "What are you free from?"

"What?" Lucas stared at Zoey as if he had never seen her before. "Nothing. I'm just . . . It's nothing."

"Was Chester blackmailing you?"

"Blackmail?" Lucas's eyes darted around the room as he looked at everything except for Zoey. "Are you nuts? What could Chester have been blackmailing me about?"

Zoey shrugged. "You tell me."

"I can't tell you about something that wasn't happening." Lucas tried to stand up, but Zoey leaned forward and crowded him back against the couch. "Chester wasn't blackmailing me."

"Oh, really? You and Chester lived across the street from each other until we graduated high school. You were best friends up until middle school. You're telling me that he didn't know any of your secrets? That he didn't know something about you that you wouldn't want anyone else to know."

"I'll admit he knew some embarrassing things about me." Lucas dabbed at the beads of sweat dotting his forehead. "But it wasn't anything that was worth blackmailing me over. I mean, Chester knew that I had a bed-wetting problem until I was seven or eight. Sure, it's embarrassing. But it's not something I'd let him blackmail me over."

"Then what was it that Chester was supposed to keep his mouth shut about?"

"I don't know what you're talking about."

"On Monday, before you left, you said something to Chester about how if he knew what was good for him, he'd keep his mouth shut."

"I never said that." Lucas scooted down the couch so that he could get away from Zoey. "You need to get your hearing checked. Getting slammed around the ring must have damaged your eardrums."

"My hearing is just fine." Zoey moved around the coffee table and blocked Lucas as he tried to head for the door. "Chester told me that he used to do your homework—"

Lucas laughed. "Who would care about that anymore? I mean, what would the high school do? Take back my diploma? Besides, my parents paid Chester well to 'tutor' me. And I slipped him some more cash for the papers and projects. I'd have paid him to take the tests for me too if I could have. And I'm not the only person who copied Chester's homework. I bet you and Zack copied him at some point in high school."

"We might have." Zoey recalled copying some of Chester's homework when they had geometry together in tenth grade. Zoey had always done well in other math classes, but she'd never been able to grasp the finer points of geometry. "I also know that Chester sold you steroids and other drugs."

"Oh, like you never bought pot off him."

"I've never smoked weed at any point in my life."

"Seriously? What about steroids? I thought all pro wrestlers use steroids."

"Some do," Zoey said. She knew a few wrestlers who admitted to using steroids, and there were others that she suspected of using them. "But not me. And not my brothers."

"Oh. Okay." Lucas tried to edge past Zoey, but she continued to block him. "I'll admit I used steroids off-and-on back in high school. I thought they would give me an edge playing football. It was dumb, I know. But I admit I did it. So, once again, Chester couldn't have been blackmailing me over it."

"Then what was he supposed to keep his mouth shut about?"

"Nothing. It was nothing. Forget I even said it."

The bells above the front door jangled. Zoey glanced over her shoulder to see who had entered the tattoo shop. Bernadette stood just inside the door.

Taking advantage of the distraction, Lucas pushed past Zoey and headed for the door. Zoey let him go without a word.

"I guess you heard about Chester?" Zoey asked Bernadette.

"I heard about it on the news this morning." Bernadette removed her coat and hung it up on the wall-mounted rack. "This is the first break I had in my schedule. I wanted to come see how you all are doing."

"We're hanging in there."

"At least you didn't find his body."

"Actually . . ."

"Oh, girl." Bernadette crossed the room and pulled Zoey in for a hug. "You sit right down and tell me everything."

Because Bernadette was short on time, Zoey gave her a condensed summary of everything that had happened since Monday night's meeting of the abuse survivor's group broke up. She also shared her short list of suspects and their motives.

"I agree with you that someone might have killed Chester to stop him from exposing their secrets," Bernadette said once Zoey had finished her account. "If whatever Chester knew really had the potential to ruin someone's life, he or she might have felt compelled to silence him for good. And it could also explain why Chester's home was searched. If he had some kind of physical evidence—"

"Zack and I warned him about breaking kayfabe," Zoey muttered. "We told him it came with consequences."

"It seems he'd already set that ball into motion long before you and Zack cautioned him." Bernadette patted Zoey on the knee. "Now I don't want to trivialize what happened to Chester, but I've only got a few more minutes before I need to head back to my office, and I think we need to discuss Detective Gates."

Zoey pressed her hands over her face. "What about him?"

"Is there still a spark between the two of you?"

"Yes."

"And . . ."

Zoey let her hands fall away from her face. "He asked me out on a date."

"Excellent," Bernadette clapped her hands and grinned. "When? Where are you going? What are you doing?"

Zoey shrugged. "We didn't get that far yet. He is in the middle of a murder investigation after all. His love life isn't exactly the top priority at the moment."

"Good point." Bernadette frowned. "Promise me that you want self-sabotage—"

"I don't—"

"Yes. You. Do." Bernadette enunciated each word. "You refuse to see it, but, since I first met you, you've sabotaged every chance you've had at a romantic relationship. It was understandable at first. After what Devon put you through . . . But it's time to stop, Zoey. Stop pushing people away when they start getting close to you. Give the detective a chance. A real chance."

Zoey nodded. "Yeah. All right."

"Come on. Let's speed this darn thing up."

"Stop complaining, Zoey. You're worse than the kids," Roxanne said as she handed her daughter a mug of hot chocolate. "It'll get here when it gets here."

"Will that be before or after I freeze to death?"

"You can't freeze to death if the temperature is above freezing. Stop being dramatic."

"I'll show you dramatic," Zoey muttered. She turned to the Krampus animatronic that stood next to her. "Why are they having the parade tonight anyway? It's *Krampusnacht*. This is supposed to be your night."

Krampus's bulging red eyes flickered in response.

The animatronic was roughly six feet tall, and his exposed body parts were covered in matted brown hair. Two massive horns protruded from his forehead and extended upward until they brushed the porch ceiling. The creature's mouth hung open in a snarl, showing off his yellowed fangs and allowing his foot-long forked tongue to hang down his hairy chest.

Zack had constructed Krampus years earlier as part of a float for the annual Christmas parade. The organizers loathed the concept and refused to include the *Krampusnacht* float. They also banned Zack from future participation in any Linville holiday parades. In protest, Zack set Krampus up on the tattoo shop's front porch every year. The parade organizers, neighbors, and some of the townspeople hated Krampus, and every year they received complaints about the half-goat, half-demon.

Leaning over the porch railing, Zoey peered down Market Street towards the southeastern part of town. The annual Linville Christmas Parade had started ten minutes earlier. She could hear the parade—specifically the high school's band—as it made its way towards downtown, but, thanks to a bend in the road, she couldn't yet see it.

Zoey had no interest in the parade, and much rather would have gone upstairs to her apartment and crawled into bed. But Roxanne insisted it was a family tradition to watch the parade and dragged her unenthusiastic daughter outside.

Roxanne, Marlon, and Vivian were seated on the porch steps along with Quincy's parents. Zack, Arielle, and Justin had set up lawn chairs on the sidewalk in front of the shop. Quincy, his ex-wife, and their two kids sat nearby.

"Here it comes!" Quincy's seven-year-old daughter, Brooklyn, screamed. She jumped up and down and waved her arms. "Here it comes!"

"Still going to take another five minutes to get to us," Zoey said as she watched a teenager come around the bend and leisurely march up the street. A snare drum hung from a harness around the teenager's neck. "Come on, kid, walk a little faster . . ."

As the Little Drummer Boy crept closer to the tattoo shop, Zoey watched the rest of the parade emerge from around the bend. Behind the teenager was a bright red, vintage convertible. Seated in the back seat was Linville's mayor. He waved and blew kisses at the people crowding the sidewalk on both sides of the street.

Next came two of the Linville Police Department's cruisers. Chief Jim Coleman was behind the wheel of the first cruiser. He honked the horn and flashed the emergency lights as he rolled past the tattoo shop. Following the cruisers were three firetrucks and one of the town's refurbished electric trolley cars.

The rest of the parade was made up of trucks and SUVs towing decorated flatbed trailers. The floats included three Nativity scenes, a gingerbread house, a train locomotive made from painted plywood, an igloo made from Styrofoam coolers, and a toybox bursting with vintage toys. People in costumes—including nutcrackers, snowmen, reindeer, penguins, and gingerbread men and women—either rode on the floats or walked alongside. A group of people dressed in Victorian Era apparel sang Christmas carols. There were even a few people on horseback, and a handful of Shriners drove by in their miniature cars.

Santa Claus and his elves brought up the rear of the parade. This year, Santa's float was an oversized sleigh. The truck towing the float had massive plastic antlers mounted on the roof. "Here Comes Santa Claus" blasted out of a speaker mounted in the truck bed.

"With that, I wish you all a good night," Zoey said as Santa passed by the tattoo shop. "I'm going to bed."

After saying goodbye to everyone, Zoey slipped inside and headed up the stairs to her apartment. When Marlon renovated the old house, he'd walled off both sides of the staircase. The walls split the upstairs into two sides—the living room, kitchen, and dining room were on one side and the bedroom, bathroom, and laundry room were on the other. After shedding her layers of winter gear, she headed for the bathroom and jumped in the shower.

When Zoey emerged from the steamy bathroom a short while later, she sensed that something was not quite right in her apartment. The lights were on in her combined kitchen and dining room. She distinctly remembered turning those lights off after she'd hung up her coat in the closet.

After tucking the towel more tightly around her, Zoey went in search of the person who had invaded her apartment. She found Vivian stretched out on the sectional with Lita curled up on her lap. For what had to be the millionth time, Zoey cursed herself for giving Vivian a key to her apartment. Vivian took it as an open invitation to stop by anytime. Zoey considered asking for the key back, but she knew it would hurt Vivian's feelings and make her believe that her only granddaughter didn't want her around. Vivian also claimed that hanging out at Zoey's apartment gave her a break from Marlon and Roxanne. She'd been living with them since her husband died, and she claimed that her son and daughter-in-law 'cramped her style.'

"What are you doing?"

"Petting your cat."

"I mean what are you doing here?"

"You're the one who asked me to spend the night. Don't you remember? We planned for this on Sunday," Vivian said. She nudged Lita off her lap and stood up. "You said we need to figure out what we're doing at this Saturday's show. And I want to see what you have planned for LAW next weekend."

Zoey pressed her hands over her face and groaned. She'd forgotten that she'd asked Vivian to spend the night. The past few days had been chaotic, and she hadn't gotten enough sleep. Truthfully, she hadn't had a good night's sleep in years. But that was because she had chronic insomnia.

"You're right," Zoey said. "We do need to figure things out for this Saturday. Not that you ever follow the script."

"I like to improvise."

"No, you just like doing whatever the heck you want to do."

On Saturday night, Zoey was scheduled to wrestle in Newark, New Jersey. It would be her first time wrestling for the Newark Organization of Pro Wrestling, and she wanted to make a solid debut. She was being brought in to wrestle NOPW's top female babyface, and their rivalry would stretch out over the next few shows. Zoey was excited to play the heel. Lately, she had only gotten to play the "good guy" role, and she was getting tired of it. She had always preferred being the villain.

When NOPW's booker had contacted her, he begged her to bring Vivian along. He'd seen footage of Vivian's antics at LAW events, and he wanted Zoey to use the loudmouthed elderly woman as her manager. Zoey was leery of having Vivian at ringside—after all she caused more than enough commotion just sitting in the audience—but she couldn't deny her nana the chance to officially be a part of the show. Knowing what her nana was capable of, Zoey made it clear to the NOPW booker that she would not be held responsible for anything that Vivian said or did while at ringside.

"You can stay," Zoey said as she tightened the towel to keep it from slipping. "But on one condition . . . No talking about Chester."

"But you need—"

"I don't need to do anything."

"But I want to know—"

"No. It's an active police investigation. Detective Gates doesn't want me talking about what I saw or what I know with anyone. That includes you."

Vivian pouted. "You talked to Zack about it."

"That's different."

"I don't see how—"

"Trust me, it is."

"I just want to know what happened. How else am I going to help you investigate."

"You're not," Zoey said. "Because I'm not investigating."

"Then why do you have this out?" Vivian grabbed Zoey's yearbook off the coffee table and held it up. Lying next to the yearbook was Zoey's laptop and a notebook. Zoey had brought everything upstairs after closing the tattoo shop prior to the start of the parade. "I overheard—"

"You mean eavesdropped."

"Zack telling Arielle about how you were putting together a list of suspects."

"It's not . . ." Zoey paused as her muddled brain struggled to find the right words. "I was Facebook stalking some of my former classmates to see who still lives in the area."

"Do you think one of them killed Chester?"

"I don't know. Maybe." Zoey grabbed the yearbook out of Vivian's hands. She then tossed it on the coffee table. "We are done discussing it."

"All right, I promise I won't talk about it tonight," Vivian said. "But you'll have to tell me about it eventually."

"No. I don't."

Zoey spun on her heel and stomped out of the room. Lita trailed Zoey to the bedroom and watched as she changed into a pair of flannel pajamas. The cat then herded her owner to the kitchen and waited impatiently as Zoey dished out a can of wet food.

In the living room, Zoey collapsed on one end of the sectional. Vivian picked up the laptop and held it out to Zoey. "The Hillbillies posted their promo."

"Did they call out Zack?"

"They did."

"Splendid." Zoey laughed. "I love it when a plan comes together."

"Has Zack agreed to do it?"

"Not yet. But he will." Zoey brought up LAW's Facebook page and clicked the link that Bubba had shared. Twangs from an out-of-tune-banjo emanated from the laptop's speaker, and the image of an outhouse filled the screen. "Well, that's different. Normally, they film their promos in front of the moonshine still."

Zoey and her brothers had known Mama, Bubba, and Tiny for over ten years, but she knew very little about them. She only recently confirmed that they really did hail from the backwoods of West Virginia. She also finally learned their real names. The different surnames failed to prove or disprove if they were siblings or cousins—over the years, they had claimed to be both. It was possible that none of them were related, and they could just be claiming kinship as part of their gimmick. That being said, Zoey wasn't even sure whether the hillbilly personae was an actual gimmick or not. Either they were always in character or the characters they portrayed were based on their real-life personalities.

After the obligatory banjo music, Mama and Tiny entered the frame from opposite sides. Mama was dressed in a ratty coat made from various animal pelts, and she had her hair pulled back in messy, lopsided pigtails. Tiny—whose nickname was a misnomer since he was seven-feet tall and skinny as a ring post— approached the outhouse. He tentatively knocked on the door and asked Bubba what was taking so long and if last night's deep-fried possum upset his stomach. Bubba yelled something back and then kicked open the outhouse door. He took two steps across the snow-covered ground before his camouflage pants slipped down to his ankles and hindered his forward progress. Beneath the camouflage pants, Bubba wore a faded red union suit.

"Oh for the love of Shawn Michaels . . . Please, please, please don't have a butt flap."

Vivian snorted. "Of course, it has a butt flap. And you know Bubba didn't bother to button it. I just saw way more of that boy than I ever wanted to."

Zoey swore and then turned her attention back to the video in time to watch Bubba announce that the local granny woman—Appalachia's term for the local healer and midwife—had cleared him for action. Bubba then proceeded to challenge Zack to come out of retirement for a night to have one more six-person tag team match between the Wildes and the Hillbillies. Once he finished throwing down the gauntlet, Bubba returned to the outhouse and the video faded to black as the banjo once again began to play.

"That'll put Zack on the spot." Zoey grinned. "He can't say no now."

Zoey had just started rewatching the video when her phone alerted her to a new text message. It was from Zack.

"*Nice try. I'm still not doing it.*"

Zoey rolled her eyes. "But you will, Zack. I know you, and I know you'll do it."

THIRTEEN

Thursday December 6th, 2018

"ARE YOU EVER GOING to tell me about what happened to Chester?"

"Nope."

"You're so mean." Vivian crossed her arms over her chest and pouted. "You're now my least favorite granddaughter."

"I'm your only granddaughter."

Vivian grumbled something under her breath. "I followed your rules last night. I didn't bring up Chester after you told me not to. And I didn't say anything about him this morning."

"You want a trophy or something?"

"No. I just want to know what happened."

After making sure that her seat warmer was turned on, Zoey pulled out onto Market Street and headed towards the southeastern end of town. Sunrise was a few minutes away, but, thanks to the heavy cloud cover, there was little sign of it aside from a faint brightening of the sky towards the east. Headlights and streetlamps illuminated the busy street.

"You ever think that maybe I'm traumatized after finding Chester's body?" Zoey asked as she eased to a stop at the redlight near Mount Rose Cemetery. The Christmas parade floats were no longer parked among the tombstones. "Maybe that's the reason I don't want to talk about it."

"But I want to know the details."

"Why?"

"Because . . . because . . ."

"Because you're a nosy old lady."

Vivian harrumphed. "All right, yes. I'll admit I'm nosy. There's no need to point out that I'm also old. I'm reminded of that every time I look in the mirror."

"Well, there you have it. That's why I won't tell you the details."

"Because I'm old?"

"No, because you're nosy." When the light turned green, Zoey hit the gas and drove through the intersection. "And, from past experiences, I know you won't be satisfied with just knowing the details of Chester's murder. It'll be like when Devon was killed—"

"No, it won't."

"You're telling me you won't stick your nose in this investigation?"

"I did what I had to do back in August. You and your brothers were suspects. And, if it wasn't for me, that handsome detective might never have figured out who killed Devon."

"I'm sure Detective Gates would have figured things out eventually."

"But, until he did, Zack could have been stuck sitting in jail."

"Good thing Zack and I aren't suspects this time."

"Exactly. I have no reason to stick my nose in the investigation. I just want to know what happened."

Zoey glanced at Vivian out of the corner of her eye. Her nana was bundled up in the pink fur coat, and the leopard print deerstalker hat mashed down her gray curls. Bright red lipstick emphasized Vivian's pout.

Turning her attention back to the road, Zoey made her way through the congested commercial section of town. She noticed long lines at the fast-food drive-throughs as people grabbed coffee and breakfast on their way to work.

"You're telling me that you won't put together a list of suspects and their motives?"

"I have no idea who would want to kill Chester. I barely knew him. I only talked to him a handful of times."

"True . . ." Zoey pulled off Market Street and then turned onto the side street that ran behind a shopping center. "But what's to stop you from picking my brain to see who I suspect."

"Ah-ha! You admit you've made up your own suspect list."

"I might have a short list of people I suspect could be the killer."

"Are you going to question them?"

"I . . . umm . . ." Zoey thought about her appointment with Brittany later in the morning. She'd made that appointment to specifically ask Brittany why Chester had a picture of her son and what he'd been blackmailing her about. "I plead the fifth."

Vivian laughed. "You're as nosy as I am."

"Hardly."

Zoey pulled into the nearly empty parking lot at the Linville Fitness Club and parked next to Arielle's car. The gym had only opened a few minutes earlier, and Arielle's first class of the day was scheduled to start at seven-thirty.

Inside, Zoey and Vivian split up. Zoey headed for the fitness room to find Arielle, and Vivian made her way towards the row of treadmills. While Zoey participated in the yoga class, Vivian would spend the morning taking a leisurely walk and ogling the young men who were working out. The regulars were used to Vivian, and, as far as Zoey knew, they didn't mind that the older woman hung around while they worked out.

"You look like you're about to fall asleep on your feet," Arielle said when Zoey walked into the fitness room. So far, they were the only two people in the small room. "Did you sleep at all last night?"

"Nana and I were up until almost two," Zoey said as she unrolled her purple yoga mat. "And then it took me another hour to fall asleep."

"Did you and Vivi spend the night putting together a suspect board?"

"No." Zoey stretched out on the mat and closed her eyes. "I banned her from talking about Chester."

"And she actually listened?"

"I distracted her with wrestling stuff."

Arielle chuckled. "Zack told me that Chester had a picture of Brittany's son. What's up with that?"

"No idea." Zoey opened her eyes and looked up at Arielle. "But I'm going to find out."

"How?" Arielle had a seat on the floor next to Zoey. Because two other women had entered the room, she whispered, "Don't tell me you're planning to ask Brittany about it."

"I have an appointment with her later this morning."

Arielle gasped. "You're going to let her cut your hair?"

"No!" Zoey sat up and placed her hands over her head. "No. I'm just going to show her the picture and ask her why Chester had it."

"And you think Brittany will tell you?"

Zoey shrugged. "If she doesn't, I'll give the picture to Detective Gates and let him question her."

"That's what you should be doing in the first place. It's not your job to figure out why Chester had the picture. I mean, that picture could be the reason why he's dead." Arielle drew in a deep breath and then exhaled. "If Brittany is the one who killed him, she's not going to appreciate you snooping around. She might even attack you."

"Pretty sure I can take her."

"Brittany allows all sorts of people to come into her home during the day. I'm sure she takes some sort of precaution to protect herself. She has a plethora of sharp objects at hand. She might even have pepper spray or a gun. Do you really want to tangle with something like that?"

"Not really."

"Promise me that you'll cancel the appointment and let Detective Gates question Brittany," Arielle said as she stood up. "That goes for Chester's father—"

"And Jocelyn, Michelle, and Natasha."

"Them, too. And anyone else you might suspect." Arielle nudged Zoey with her foot. "Promise me."

"All right, all right." Zoey pushed Arielle's foot away from her. "I promise."

"I don't believe you." Arielle stood up. "Oh, and by the way, Zack is close to giving in and agreeing to the match."

"Yes!" Zoey pumped her fists in the air. "I knew I could wear him down."

Arielle made her way to the front of the room and got the class started. Zoey tried to clear her mind as she worked through the different yoga poses, but her thoughts kept circling back to Chester's murder. Arielle was right, she really should not be questioning Brittany or anyone else. It was not her job to find the killer, but no matter how much she tried to convince herself to drop it, she just couldn't bring herself to do it.

After class, Zoey said goodbye to Arielle and then went in search of Vivian. She had just spotted her nana over by the free weights when

Michelle and Jocelyn stepped out from between two pieces of exercise equipment and cut her off. Zoey almost bumped into them.

Jocelyn scowled at Zoey. "Watch where you're going, freak."

"Really?" Zoey asked. "We're thirty years old, but you're still that immature that you need to call me a freak?"

"If the shoe fits. Right, Michelle?"

"Definitely."

Zoey rolled her eyes. Forgetting about her promise to Arielle, she asked, "Did you hear about Chester getting killed?"

"Yeah," Jocelyn said. "Who cares?"

"Seriously? Our former classmate is murdered, and that's the attitude you have?"

"It's not like I was friends with him."

Michelle frowned. "Have a heart, Jocelyn. The poor guy was murdered."

"What did you have against him anyway, Jocelyn?" Zoey asked.

"That's none of your business."

"It is if it's the reason Chester was killed."

"From what I understand, Chester was already dead by Tuesday morning." Jocelyn flung her long hair over her shoulder. Her spandex shorts and sports bra showed off her muscular legs and toned core. Years of dancing had kept her physically fit. "How could I have killed him when I didn't even know he was in town until *after* he was already dead?"

"I never accused you of killing him," Zoey said.

"But I told everyone he was back on Monday night in the group chat," Michelle said. "Didn't you—"

"No, I didn't," Jocelyn snapped. "I turned off the notifications for that stupid group chat. I never wanted to be added to it in the first place, but Natasha insisted."

"Who all is in this group chat?" Zoey asked.

"Oh, you know, just some of us who are still local," Michelle said. "Obviously, Kevin and I are in it. Brittany. Olivia and Jeremy Smith. Anthony Groff. Blair Albright. Sidney Hager. Garrett Zimmerman and his wife, Vanessa. She graduated the year after us. One of her friends is in the group, too. And, of course, Natasha is in it. She's the one who started it."

Zoey turned to Jocelyn and asked, "When did Natasha add you to it?"

"Sometime over the weekend."

"And I added Lucas on Monday afternoon," Michelle added.

"What exactly did you say about Chester?"

"Just that he was back in town and working at your brother's tattoo shop."

"Did anyone ask about him?"

"Not really. Someone asked how I knew, and I said Lucas saw him," Michelle said. "You know, Zoey, you're assuming that we cared more about Chester than what we really did. I mean, we wouldn't be discussing him now if he hadn't gotten killed."

"Michelle's right," Jocelyn said. "We didn't care about Chester in high school. And we certainly do not care about him now."

"I kind of care," Michelle said. "I mean, it's awful that he was murdered. And I hope they catch the person who did it."

Jocelyn huffed.

Zoey glared at Jocelyn. "Why not tell me what you had against Chester?"

"Fine," Jocelyn said, dragging out the word. "Senior year, Lucas arranged for Chester to write a paper for my World Lit class. Between dance practice and competitions, I just didn't have time to read *Anna Karenina* and then write a paper about it. Chester totally screwed me over. The paper he wrote was horrible, and Mr. Stokowski failed me. You remember what a hardass he was? I couldn't admit that Chester had written it. Who knows what Mr. Stokowski would have done to me. That paper was the only thing I ever failed in school. And, thanks to that F, I got a B minus in World Lit. I had straight As in all my other classes throughout high school."

"And you're still mad about this twelve years later?" Zoey asked.

Jocelyn stamped her foot. "Chester ruined my grade point average."

"Were you at the top of our class?" Zoey asked. "Would you have been valedictorian otherwise?"

"No. Between all the extra credit and brown-nosing, Natasha had already secured that honor."

"And, by then you'd already been accepted at Skidmore . . ." Zoey said. "So, who cares about one lousy B?"

"That's the attitude of someone who settles for second best. Unlike you, I'm not happy with mediocrity."

"What's that supposed to mean?"

"I don't follow professional wrestling, but, occasionally, I see commercials for that WWE company." Jocelyn leaned closer to Zoey and said, "I haven't seen you on any of those."

Michelle giggled. "She makes a good point, Zoey."

Zoey glared at Michelle before turning back to Jocelyn. "And I haven't seen *you* starring for any famous ballet companies. In fact, I couldn't find any evidence of your dance career."

Jocelyn's upper lip curled in disgust. "Are you stalking me?"

"Hardly. I just did a quick search to see what you've been up to since graduation. I couldn't find anything," Zoey said.

"You wouldn't have. I use a stage name."

"I did find your Facebook page. It doesn't look like it's been updated in ten years."

"Unlike some people, I don't feel the need to share everything on social media." Jocelyn pointed at her left ankle that was laced up in a stabilizing brace. "And, if you must know . . . I broke my ankle in a car accident. I had to take a couple years off from my dance career to fully heal. That's why I've been teaching."

"What's the name of this *prestigious* dance academy that you teach at?"

"It's called none of your business."

When Jocelyn tried to push past her, Zoey stepped to the side and blocked her.

"Can I ask you something about Lucas?"

Jocelyn held up her hand with her thumb and forefinger about an inch apart. "Does that answer your question?"

"No. Because that's not what I'm asking about," Zoey said. She was glad she was still a little flushed from yoga class, and that her reddened face hid her blush. "I was wondering if you know what really happened to Lucas's dad's Lamborghini the summer before we graduated?"

"Someone broke into the Jenningses' house, beat up Lucas, and stole the car. They also stole all of Lucas's mom's jewelry and some other valuable stuff. But that's ancient history. Why are you asking about it?"

"Because Chester implied that something else happened to the car."

"I was taking lessons at a dance academy in California for most of that summer. All I know is what Lucas told me when I got back." Jocelyn shrugged. "Maybe the person who broke into the Jenningses' house was Chester. He was super shady."

"No, he wasn't."

"Trust me, he was. If you'd only seen his true colors . . ."

"What about when you were going to Skidmore?" Zoey asked. "Did you ever see Chester around campus."

"A few times. But it's not like I hung out with him."

Jocelyn shoved past Zoey and then headed for the women's locker room. Michelle grabbed Zoey's arm and prevented her from going after Jocelyn.

"Don't bother," Michelle said. "If she won't open up to me or Brittany, she sure isn't going to tell you anything."

"Jocelyn hasn't told you anything about her personal life or her dance career?"

"No. She gets real defensive if anyone brings it up." Michelle stepped away from Zoey. "You know, I forgot how much of a major bitch Jocelyn could be. I'm not even sure why Brittany and I have been hanging out with her the past few days. It makes me feel like I'm back in high school. And, unlike, Natasha, I have no desire to relive those days."

"Neither do I."

"Zack and Arielle are right. This is a dumb idea," Zoey muttered as she pulled up in front of Brittany Patterson's house. Since leaving the gym, she'd debated over cancelling the appointment. It was none of her business if Chester had been blackmailing Brittany, nor was it up to her to figure out why he had a picture of Brittany's son. "But I guess it's too late to back out now that I'm here."

Zoey climbed out of her purple Jeep and then surveyed the two-story house. A ten-foot-tall inflatable snowman dominated the front yard, and Christmas lights were strung around the windows and front door. Parked in the driveway was a teal minivan. She took a picture of the van and sent it to Santino along with a message asking if the van looked familiar.

Following the signs for the salon, Zoey wandered down the driveway and around to the back of the house where a sliding door led into the walk-out basement. She slid the door open and entered the in-home salon. At the far end of the compact room was a desk and a display cabinet packed with hair products and Christmas decorations. Beside the desk,

French doors opened into the rest of the finished basement. Zoey spotted Brittany's youngest daughter taking a nap in a pack and play. Nearby, the twins hosted a tea party for their dolls.

"You weren't kidding about desperately needing a haircut," Brittany said as she walked through the French doors. "I can see your split ends from here."

"Seriously?" Zoey grabbed a hunk of hair and held it up in front of her face. She couldn't see any split ends. Then again, she wasn't sure what a split end looked like. "Is it that bad?"

"Well, it's not good. When was the last time you got your hair cut?"

"Uhh . . ." Zoey flung the lock of hair over her shoulder. Her hair was currently the longest it had been since she was a kid. The ends fell to about mid-waist. "Sometime over the summer."

"Good Lord, Zoey . . . You need to take better care of your hair. No wonder it always looks like a hot mess." Brittany picked up an emery board and waved it around. "What kind of shampoo and conditioner do you use? How often do you wash your hair? Do you blow dry it?"

"I'm . . . uh . . . I'm not actually here about my hair," Zoey said as she pulled her hair back into a sloppy ponytail. "And, considering what happened in first grade, I don't exactly trust you holding a pair of scissors anywhere near my head."

Brittany gave her a blank look. "What happened in first grade?"

"You tried to scalp me with a pair of kid's safety scissors." Zoey patted the top of her head. "I had to wear a side ponytail for the rest of the school year to hide what you did."

"I do not remember that. Are you sure it was me?"

"Yes, I'm sure it was you."

Brittany snickered. "Michelle probably put me up to it."

"Was Michelle behind all the other mean things you did and said to me back when we were kids?" Zoey asked between clenched teeth. "Was she the mastermind behind all those stupid pranks you pulled?"

"Zoey, I have no idea what you're talking about. I remember picking on you for being into pro wrestling. And maybe some other things. I'll admit that I wasn't always very nice to you. But you weren't exactly nice to me either."

Zoey opened her mouth to protest, but immediately snapped it shut. Brittany was right. The animosity between them went both ways. In Zoey's mind, Brittany and Michelle were the villains and she was an innocent victim. Yes, they had relentlessly picked on her and played mean pranks, but Zoey had done the same in retaliation.

"Now, if you're not here to get your hair cut, why are you here?" Brittany asked. "I've got a business to run. I can't be wasting time on . . . on whatever it is you're here for."

"I know. I know." Zoey held up her hands in a placating gesture. "It's just . . . I'm sure you heard about Chester's murder—"

Brittany slammed the emery board down on her appointment book. "Yeah, I heard. What does it have to do with me?"

"At the gym you mentioned seeing him—"

"Yeah, I ran into him at the grocery store a few times." Brittany picked up the emery board and attacked her nails. "It was nothing."

"It if was nothing, why did you get all freaked out when Michelle brought him up?" Zoey asked. "And why did you visit him at the tattoo shop?"

"I . . ." Brittany glanced up at Zoey. "I never came to the tattoo shop."

"You were seen—"

"Whoever claims to have seen me is either lying or has got me confused with someone else." Brittany pointed towards the sliding door. "I don't know what game you're trying to play, but I'm over it. You need to leave."

"I'll leave if you want me to. But I need to show you something first." Zoey reached into her purse and pulled out the picture of Ashton Dissinger. She held up the picture and said, "Chester had a picture of your son—"

"Give me that!"

Brittany lunged across the desk and tried to snatch the picture out of Zoey's hand. Zoey jumped backwards and held the picture out of Brittany's reach.

"I caught Chester looking at this on Monday. It was right after Lucas left . . ." Zoey trailed off. Could Lucas have given the picture to Chester? But why would Lucas have a picture of Brittany's son? Unless . . . "Is Lucas your son's real father?"

"What?" Brittany shook her head. "No, Lucas is not Ashton's father. Why would you think that?"

"Like I said, I caught Chester looking at the picture right after Lucas left—"

"So, you just assume that means Lucas is Ashton's father?" Brittany huffed. "You always did have an active imagination."

"Then why *did* Chester have a picture of your son?"

"Because . . ." Brittany snapped the emery board in half. "Because Chester is Ashton's father."

FOURTEEN

"Oh my God . . ." Zoey stumbled backwards a few steps and collapsed in the styling chair. "You're serious? How did that happen? I mean, I know *how* it happened. But, how . . ."

"Congrats, Zoey. Now you know my dirty little secret." Brittany grabbed a tissue and wiped away the tears that streamed down her face. "You're going to tell everyone, aren't you?"

"No, I'm not." Zoey's stomach churned with guilt until she reminded herself that Chester was dead, and the picture of Ashton might have something to do with why he'd been murdered. "I swear—"

"Yes, you will. You'll have it all over Facebook by the end of the day," Brittany screeched. "It's obvious you've spent years dwelling on all the mean things I allegedly did to you. This'll be the perfect revenge. Tell everyone that Chester Hartman is my son's birth father and ruin my life. But let me tell you something, Zoey. It won't just be my life that you're ruining. You'll be ruining my son's life, too. And he—"

"Mommy?" One of the twins stepped through the French doors and tugged on Brittany's arm. The other little girl huddled behind her. "Mommy, what's wrong?"

"Mommy's okay, sweetheart." Brittany knelt to hug her daughters. "Go back to playing."

"But you're crying," the other twin said.

"Sometimes mommies cry. Now be good girls and go back to your tea party." Brittany gave her daughters a gentle push towards the basement. She waited until the twins returned to their dolls before she spun around to face Zoey. "Are you going to blackmail me first? Or are you going to skip that step and just tell everyone?"

"It would be the perfect revenge." Zoey walked over to the desk and handed Brittany the picture. "But I'm not going to tell anyone. Unless you killed Chester. Then I have to tell the police."

"No, I didn't kill him." Brittany blew her nose. "I had no reason to after I convinced him to keep his mouth shut—"

"Just because he agreed to keep his mouth shut now doesn't mean he wouldn't have changed his mind in the future."

"You're right." Brittany balled up the used tissue and tossed it into the trash. "But I didn't kill him. Come on, you've known me forever. Do you think I'm capable of killing someone?"

"To protect one of your kids, yes," Zoey said. "Do you have an alibi for Monday night?"

Brittany shrugged. "I was up until midnight wrapping everyone's Christmas presents."

"Can anyone back that up?"

"No, I was down here by myself," Brittany said. "The girls were in bed. And Peter and Ashton were upstairs watching football till sometime after eleven. I normally don't let Ashton stay up that late on a school night, but the Eagles were playing. They're his favorite team. Ashton and Peter were both in bed by the time I finished up with the presents and went upstairs."

"So, you have no way of actually proving that you never left the house that night?"

"Other than my word, no. But I swear I didn't kill Chester."

Zoey wasn't about to take Brittany's word. She knew from personal experience that Brittany was a pathological liar. She was also manipulative.

"What about Rodney?" Zoey asked. "Could he have killed Chester?"

Brittany shook her head. "Rodney was at the football game in Philly. He facetimed Ashton from the parking lot afterwards. And, as far as I know, he was stuck in the stadium traffic until after midnight."

"Then I guess Rodney couldn't have killed Chester."

"No, he couldn't have. Besides, if Rodney had found out that he isn't Ashton's birth father . . . I'm the one who would be dead." Brittany sat down and pressed her hands over her face. "Rodney loves Ashton, but he still accuses me of getting pregnant on purpose. And blames me for ruining his life."

"I never could figure out what you saw in him."

"He was cute and popular. In high school, not much else mattered."

"But he was such a jerk. Except maybe to you."

"No, Rodney was a jerk to me, too," Brittany said. "But I was naive and didn't know any better. I put up with his crap because I thought I was in love with him."

"You're preaching to the choir when it comes to toxic ex-boyfriends." Zoey walked over to the sliding door. "I'm sorry about all this, Brittany. I promise I won't tell anyone—"

"Wait! I've never been able to talk to anyone about this. Not my parents or my husband. Not even Michelle, but that's only because she couldn't keep a secret if her life depended on it. But since you now know . . ." Brittany came around the desk and grabbed a nylon cape. She then gestured for Zoey to have a seat in the styling chair. "Besides, you really do need a haircut."

"That's not necessary."

"Trust me, it is."

"I . . . uh . . ."

"I promise I won't scalp you. After all, I have a reputation to uphold."

Zoey sat down and allowed Brittany to drape the nylon cape around her shoulders. "Just cut off a couple inches."

"Let me try something different," Brittany said as she dipped the chair backwards. "Maybe some layers . . ."

"Don't you dare give me bangs."

Zoey remained silent while Brittany shampooed and conditioned her hair. She wanted to hear Brittany's story, but she couldn't force the other woman to talk. She had to be patient. Brittany would share when she was ready.

After toweling away the excess water, Brittany ran a comb through Zoey's hair. It got caught in a knot, and Brittany yanked it free.

"Ouch." Zoey leaned away from Brittany. "Remember, you promised *not* to scalp me."

"It's not my fault. The ends are all tangled." Brittany giggled. "This is unbelievable."

"Oh, come on, my hair is not that bad."

"I mean this whole situation," Brittany said as she worked on another knot. "I can't say you're the last person I thought I would tell my secrets to, but you're pretty far down the list."

"You'd be nowhere near the top of my list either." Zoey turned to look at Brittany. "So, what happened. How did you wind up hooking up with Chester?"

"It was right after Rodney dumped me during the spring of senior year. He told me he didn't see our relationship lasting past high school and that we may as well break up so that he could focus on baseball. A week later he hooked up with that trashy freshman Elouise . . . You know, he's married to her now. He went running back to her the second I kicked him out."

Steering the subject away from what she suspected was still a sore spot for Brittany, Zoey asked, "How did Chester get caught up in all this?"

"We had physics together during the spring semester. The teacher drew names out of a hat to assign lab partners. I got paired up with Chester. I never would have talked to him otherwise." Brittany separated Zoey's wet hair into sections. She then picked up a pair of shears and began snipping away the split ends. "At the time, getting stuck with the class freak was so embarrassing. But it wound up being a good thing. I couldn't wrap my head around physics, and I probably would have failed if it wasn't for Chester. Of course, if it wasn't for Chester, I also wouldn't have gotten pregnant . . ."

Brittany fell silent as she snipped Zoey's hair. With her back to the mirror, Zoey could not see what Brittany was doing to her. She grew increasingly alarmed as the clippings piled up on her lap and on the floor.

Forcing her thoughts away from her hair—after all, it would grow back—Zoey said, "So . . . You and Chester were lab partners . . ."

"Chin up." Brittany tapped the comb against Zoey's chin. "I was a mess after Rodney broke up with me. I couldn't stop crying or complaining about him. Chester was trying to make me feel better. You know, telling me I deserved better and all that. He might have looked like a total freak. But he was really a sweetheart."

"You know that old saying about how you can't judge a book by its cover?" Zoey asked. "Well, you also can't judge a person by their clothes, hair, or tattoos."

"I know that now. But I was so shallow back then."

"Sometimes you still are."

Brittany grumbled something under her breath. "Like I was saying, Chester was way nicer to me than I deserved considering how I'd been such a bitch to him over the years. Heck, he was nicer to me than Rodney ever was, and Rodney was my boyfriend."

"Is that why you hooked up with him?"

"Yeah, I guess. I mean, it was just one of those things that happen. Chester was over at my house helping me study for a physics test. I made the first move. And . . . it happened. It was awful and awkward and . . . and you do not need to know the details."

"Was it just the one time?"

"Yeah. But once is enough." Brittany ran her fingers through Zoey's wet hair. She then continued snipping away. "After that, I threw myself into helping plan the prom, the spring carnival, our senior trip—"

"None of which I went to," Zoey said. Despite having no regrets about skipping the prom, she frequently dreamt about it. "On prom night, Zack and I wrestled at an event in Delaware."

"Always pro wrestling with you . . ." Brittany shook her head. "Prom night was supposed to be magical. Instead, it turned into a nightmare when I realized I was pregnant."

"Yeah . . . I heard there was a lot of drama at the dance."

"Drama is putting it mildly." Brittany snorted. "I made Michelle promise she wouldn't tell anyone—"

"I'm guessing she broke that promise."

"Yeah, as soon as we got to prom, Michelle ran off to find Rodney. On her way to find him, she told everyone that I was pregnant. Hence why I don't tell her any of my secrets anymore." Brittany tossed the shears onto the counter and then grabbed a tissue. "It was awful. In front of everyone, Rodney accused me of poking holes in his condoms so I would get pregnant. He said it was all part of my evil plan to trap him in a permanent relationship. Then he called his parents. And they called my parents . . . Let's just say that things got ugly real fast—"

"Did Chester ever ask you if he might be the father?"

"He did. I told him it wasn't possible, and that Rodney was the father." Brittany moved around the chair to stand in front of Zoey. "Looking back, yeah, I should have said I wasn't sure who the father was. It would have saved me from those five years of hell spent married to Rodney. But put yourself in my shoes. I was eighteen. My parents were furious, and they kept screaming at me for being irresponsible. Rodney and his parents were accusing me of getting pregnant on purpose. Plus, I knew everyone at school was laughing at me for getting knocked up . . . If I admitted to hooking up with the class freak . . . No, I couldn't do that."

"You still didn't have to rush down the aisle two weeks after graduation."

"It was five weeks. And our parents didn't give us much choice."

Brittany brought an end to the conversation when she picked up a hairdryer and turned it on. Zoey's hair was thick, and, even with a hairdryer, it took a long time for it to dry. Zoey had a lot to think about while she waited. She also had a lot of questions.

As soon as Brittany turned off the hairdryer, Zoey asked, "When did you figure out that Chester was Ashton's father?"

"A few months after Ashton was born." Brittany grabbed a curling iron and wrapped a strand of Zoey's hair around it. "I took Ashton to the doctor for a checkup. The nurse was going over his paperwork with me, and she asked if I'd made a mistake when I filled out mine and Rodney's information. I insisted that I hadn't. The nurse left the room, and then the doctor came in. He asked me about our blood types. Ashton's is B. Rodney and I both have type A. If Rodney was Ashton's birth father, then Ashton's blood type would either be A or O. Chester was the only other possibility, so . . ."

"You still didn't say anything after that?"

"I didn't know what to do. So, I kept my mouth shut. I mean, I was married to a man who pretty much despised me. We were living in his parents' basement. Rodney's dad was cool, but his mom was a total psycho. Sure, I would have loved to get out of that situation. But my parents were still furious with me, and I had my baby to think about."

"I guess I understand. Plus, it's not like anyone knew what happened to Chester."

"Jocelyn knew where he was."

"That's right . . . They both went to Skidmore." Zoey shifted in the chair so that she could look back at Brittany. "How did you know Chester was also going to Skidmore? Did Jocelyn tell you?"

"The summer after we graduated, everyone was back in town. Me, Jocelyn, Michelle, Natasha, and some of the other girls got together to catch up." Brittany nudged Zoey's shoulder and forced her to turn back around. "Someone pulled out our yearbook, and we started gossiping. Jocelyn mentioned Chester. She told us that he was going to the same college as her. I tracked him down, but I couldn't bring myself to contact him."

"You just let it go."

"Like I said, I didn't know what to do," Brittany said. "By the time Rodney and I split up, Chester had moved on from New York and I had no idea how to find him. It's not like he was on social media. So I figured it was a sign. Plus, I really didn't think I would ever see him again—"

"Until you ran into him at the store and just blurted out that he's Ashton's birth father?"

"God, no." Brittany turned off the curling iron and then set it aside. "And the first time I ran into Chester was at Schmitt's. We went there for dinner one Sunday. Chester was there with an older woman—"

"Probably his mom."

Brittany shrugged. "Chester recognized me and came over to say hi. He took one look at my son and knew he was Ashton's father."

"But Ashton looks exactly like you."

"No, he has my coloring. He has Chester's blue eyes and facial structure. If you look at pictures of them side-by-side, you'll see the resemblance."

"How did Chester react when he realized he has a son?"

"How do you think he reacted?" Brittany brushed the hair off the nylon cape and then removed it from around Zoey's shoulders. "At first, he was devastated. Then he was pissed. And he threatened to tell Rodney."

"But you convinced him to keep his mouth shut."

"Yep. That's what I was doing that day at your brother's tattoo shop. Begging Chester not to ruin my son's life. It took some convincing, but he finally agreed. And that's the last time I saw him."

"I have to ask . . . How have you managed to live with yourself knowing that Rodney isn't really Ashton's birth father?"

"It's hasn't been easy." Brittany sniffled. "I live in constant fear that Rodeny will somehow find out. Or Ashton will someday want to learn about his family history and take one of those DNA tests. Then what am I going to do? Act like I had no idea? Or confess that I knew all along?"

"That's a tough one," Zoey said. She did not envy Brittany's situation. "But you made your decision back when Ashton was a baby. Someday you might have to face the consequences."

"Don't remind me . . . But thank you for listening. It feels good to finally be able to tell someone. It's just—"

"I won't tell anyone," Zoey said. "Not because I feel any loyalty to you. But your son doesn't deserve it. He's innocent in all this."

"Thank you." Brittany spun the chair around so that Zoey faced the mirror. "Ta-da!"

"Whoa." Zoey turned her head from side-to-side and admired her new haircut. Brittany had layered her hair, leaving it longer in the back and cutting it shorter around her face. She had also curled Zoey's hair. "Your hair cutting skills have improved immensely since elementary school."

FIFTEEN

"Zoey?" Imogene Hartman peered around the doorframe into the front office of 3 Count Tattoos. "Can I come in?"

"Of course." Zoey stood up and waved Imogene into the room. She appeared even more haggard than she had two days earlier. Deep purple bags stood out beneath her bloodshot eyes, and it looked like she hadn't combed her hair in days. "Did you want to see me or Zack? Because he's in the middle of a consult right now."

"Lucas Jennings's mother drove me here, and I don't want to keep her waiting. She already spent most of the morning at the hospital with me and the afternoon helping me plan Chester's funeral." Imogene grabbed a tissue and dabbed at the tears streaming down her cheeks. "I just wanted to let you know that Chester's service will be at the Cozma Funeral Home at ten next Wednesday morning. Mr. Cozma said we shouldn't advertise the service. That way reporters and other nosy people won't show up."

"That's a good idea." Zoey jotted down the date and time. "Zack and I will be there."

"I'm glad it won't just be me. I don't know if Oscar will even go," Imogene said. "I also wanted to say sorry for the way my husband treated you the other night."

"You don't have to apologize for your husband's actions."

"I know." Imogene pulled a glove out of her coat pocket and then twisted it between her hands. "Oscar ain't always like that. He just doesn't like strangers."

"Is he taking good care of you?"

"Oh, yes. He's been real good to me since the cancer came back. It's the best he's treated me in years." Imogene used her glove to wipe away a tear. "It's just . . . Now he's mad at me for going behind his back to see our son. Not that he would have been happy if I'd told him Chester was back—"

"But Oscar knew Chester was back for at least the past couple weeks."

Imogene's head snapped up. "Oscar only found out that Chester was back when the police . . . when the police told us that Chester had been murdered."

Zoey shook her head. "Zack saw him here a few weeks ago. Chester and Oscar were out in the alley arguing. And I saw him at Shippington Way right before I found—"

"No." Imogene slapped her glove against the countertop. "You and Zack are wrong."

Zoey reached over the counter and grabbed Imogene's hand. "I know—"

"You don't know nothing." Imogene pulled her hand away from Zoey. "And now you're making up lies about my husband."

"I'm not making up anything. Zack and I both know what we saw," Zoey said. She took a deep breath. "Do you know where Oscar was late Monday night? Was he at work?"

"No, he went to the bar with some of his coworkers after their shift ended," Imogene said. "He didn't get home till almost three in the morning."

"Is it possible Oscar lied to you about being at the bar? Could he really have been at Chester's place?"

Imogene gasped, and what little color she had faded from her sunken cheeks. "You think my husband killed our son?"

"You told us that Oscar hated Chester—"

"But he never would have killed him."

"Are you sure about that?"

"Yes, I'm sure." Imogene shot Zoey a look filled with disdain before she shuffled out into the foyer. "My husband's right. I don't need you hassling me. Or your pity."

Imogene opened the heavy wooden door and then slammed it shut behind her.

A few minutes later, Zack and his client emerged from the front room. After showing his client out, Zack walked into the office.

"Was that Imogene Hartman I saw storming out of here?"

Zoey nodded. "She wanted to thank us for being Chester's friends and apologize for the way Oscar acted on Tuesday night."

"What did you say to upset her?"

"I told her that Oscar is lying to her," Zoey said. "He's claiming that he didn't know Chester was back in the area until the police came to tell them that Chester was dead. I told her that you saw Oscar here a few weeks ago, and that I saw him at Shippington Way on Tuesday."

"I think Imogene only believes what Oscar tells her to believe."

"He does seem rather bossy," Zoey said. Oscar's domineering attitude reminded her of her ex-boyfriend. According to Devon, he was always right. And he wanted everything his way. Zoey's opinions, wants, and needs hadn't mattered all that much to him. She suspected the same was true for the Hartmans. "I also asked Imogene where Oscar was on Monday night."

"Does he have an alibi?"

"Oscar told her that he was at a bar with some coworkers," Zoey said. "Imogene claims he didn't get home until almost three in the morning."

"His wife is dying, but he's staying out late at the bar?"

"Maybe drinking is how he's coping with her cancer."

Zack huffed. "He can get drunk after she's dead. Right now, he should be with her."

"I agree with you," Zoey said. "But what if Oscar is lying about the bar?"

"You really think he killed Chester?"

Zoey shrugged. "Don't you? I mean, he clearly hated his son. And it's weird that he was lurking around Chester's place on Tuesday afternoon."

"Yeah, that is weird. But, honestly, I don't know what I think. I'm glad it's not my job to figure it out." Zack leaned his elbows on the counter and sighed. "How's it going with contacting Chester's clients?"

"I'm down to the last week of January."

"Are you still getting bombarded with calls from the press?"

"Yeah. But not as many as yesterday." Reporters from two of the local news stations had called, as well as a journalist for Lancaster County's lone newspaper. "Nana called a few times pretending to be from the local news stations."

"You know, sooner or later, you're going to have to tell her about what happened. She's not going to stop bugging you until you do."

"I know, I know." Zoey walked over to the leather couch and sat down. "I'm going to be stuck with her most of the day on Saturday. Once she has me trapped in the car, I won't be able to avoid her."

"Who are you wrestling? And where is the show at?"

"Persephone," Zoey said, naming her opponent. She'd known Persephone for a few years, and they had wrestled each other a handful of times. The last time they had competed against each other had been in a Tables, Ladders, and Chairs Match at the September LAW show. "And the show is at a youth center in Newark."

"Is Justin booked at the same show?"

"No, he's wrestling somewhere in Northern Virginia."

Zack sat down next to Zoey. "Who's going to Newark with you and Nana?"

"Mort."

Zoey never traveled to shows alone. If she and Justin were not booked on the same show, she asked one or more of Justin's students to accompany her. If none of Justin's students were available, Marlon would tag along. Zoey was confident in her ability to protect herself, but she liked having someone along to watch her back and her belongings. Not all promoters were trustworthy, and sometimes the other wrestlers or the fans might try to start something in the parking lot after the show. Zoey carried pepper spray and a knife for protection.

Zack's phone dinged, and he pulled it out of his sweatshirt pocket.

"It's Thor Gunderson. He's texting to let me know he's available to talk."

"Thor Gunderson? Sounds like a Viking. Is he a client?"

"No. He's a tattoo artist. Chester worked for him out in California. We've been texting about Chester since Tuesday evening, but our schedules didn't line up for an actual conversation until now. Do you want to talk to him?"

"Duh."

"I'll FaceTime him."

Zack played around on his phone, and, a few seconds later, an image of Thor filled the small screen. Upon hearing Chester's former boss's name, Zoey pictured him as a burly man with a bushy beard. She was slightly disappointed to see that, instead of looking like a stereotypical Viking, Thor was an aging flower child with scraggly gray hair and a scrawny build beneath his tie-dyed shirt and beaded necklaces.

After Zack made the introductions, Thor said, "Man, what a bummer about Chester. It totally blew my mind when the fuzz called and told me he'd gotten himself killed. Have they found the guy who did it?"

Zoey pressed her hand over her mouth to stifle her giggles. She was used to the current slang words—some of which she had to look up the meaning of online. Hearing slang from the 1960's era was both amusing and refreshing.

"The police are still investigating," Zack said. "But my sister thinks she's Nancy Drew and has been conducting her own amateur investigation."

"Far out."

"Chester was working for you for the past ten years, right?" Zoey asked Thor. "You must have gotten to know him pretty well during that time. What can you tell us about him?"

"Not much. Chester hid his secrets better than I hide my stash." Thor chuckled. "In all seriousness, I might have known Chester for years, but I really didn't know him that well. He never really shared anything personal with me."

"We went to school with Chester," Zack said. "And we didn't know him that well either."

"How did you and Chester meet, Thor?" Zoey asked.

"My shop, Psychedelic Tattoos, is on Ocean Front Walk in Venice. Been here since my old lady and I split Haight-Ashbury and headed farther down the coast in the late sixties." Thor picked up his phone and turned it so that Zoey and Zack could see Venice Beach through the shop's front window. They also got a glimpse of the tie-dye painted walls of the shop. "Around ten years ago, after one of my artists flaked on me, I hung a 'help wanted' sign in the window. Next day, Chester showed up. I wasn't looking to take on an apprentice, but I could tell he had potential. So, I hired him on the spot. He's been with me ever since."

"Do you know where Chester lived?" Zack asked. "Or what he did in his free time?"

Thor pointed upwards. "He lived above the shop. Farrah and I are on the second floor. Chester was on the third. He was the best tenant I've ever had. As for free time . . . All the boy did was paint or sketch. He converted part of his apartment into a studio. He always had multiple projects going at once. I told him he needed to relax and hit the beach. He never did."

"Did Chester sell any of his paintings?" Zack asked.

"Oh, yeah. Some of the smaller ones he sold in the shop." Thor stood up and moved over to the far side of the room. Hanging on the wall were multiple canvases that featured paintings of the ocean and other iconic landmarks of Venice and the surrounding area. There were also some paintings of old school style tattoos. Zoey thought that the paintings were well done, but there wasn't anything special about them. "Chester also sold paintings out of a fancy gallery in downtown LA. And he did some commissioned pieces. You'd have to get in touch with his art dealer if you want to know more about that. All I know is that he made some serious bread selling those paintings. I always told Chester that he was wasting his time as a tattoo artist. Not that tattooing ain't a form of art . . . But the boy had real talent."

"You ever see a painting Chester did of a nude woman?" Zoey asked. She thought back to what Quincy had told her of the painting he'd seen hanging on Chester's wall. "It was done in acrylics and was super realistic. I think it was something he did for art school."

"Yeah, I've seen it. He's got a whole wall of paintings featuring that woman. He called her his muse, but I nicknamed her the Foxy Lady because, you know, she was foxy."

"Did Chester ever tell you the woman's name?" Zoey asked. She grabbed the phone out of Zack's hands and held it closer to her face. "Or anything about her?"

"Nah. Just that he dated her for a while when he was in college. But then she broke his heart, and he split."

"Unfortunately, neither Zack nor I saw the painting. All we know is that whoever killed Chester stole it from his place. There must be a reason why the killer took it."

"Maybe the killer thought it was valuable," Zack said.

"That's a possibility," Thor said. "You know, Chester has a portrait of the Foxy Lady tattooed on his chest. I inked it right after Chester started working for me."

Chester's body from the neck down had been almost entirely covered in tattoos. A handful of tattoos had been reproductions of famous paintings.

On Chester's back was Vincent van Gogh's 'Starry Night.' He also had Edvard Munch's 'The Scream' on his right arm, one of Edgar Degas's ballerinas on his calf, and numerous characters from Hieronymus Bosch's 'The Garden of Earthly Delights' scattered about his body.

"Chester showed us a lot of his tattoos, but I don't remember seeing his chest piece. Zack, did you ever see it?" Zoey asked. When Zack confirmed that he had not seen the tattoo, Zoey turned back to the phone. "Thor, do you have a picture of the tattoo?"

"Probably somewhere around here. I'll look for it." Thor glanced off to the side before turning his attention back to his phone. "I've got customers I need to take care of. We can talk more next week when Farrah and I fly in for Chester's funeral. Maybe we'll think of something that'll help you solve the case or identify the Foxy Lady. Peace out."

Zoey ended the call and then handed Zack his phone.

"Not sure if we really learned anything from Thor that would be related to Chester's murder," Zoey said. "But now I really want to figure out the identity of Chester's muse."

"And just how do you plan to do that? He dated the woman while living in Saratoga Springs. Are you going to wander the Skidmore campus and ask the faculty if they remember Chester Hartman from over ten years ago? Even if you find someone who remembers him, do you think they'll remember who he was dating and give you her forwarding address?"

"Well . . . When you put it that way . . ." Zoey slumped back against the couch cushions. "I ran into Jocelyn and Michelle this morning at the gym. Jocelyn admitted to running into Chester around campus when they were both at Skidmore. Next time I see her, I'll have to ask if she knew his girlfriend."

"I can't see Jocelyn really caring if Chester had a girlfriend. I'm surprised she even remembers seeing him around campus."

"Or that she would have even acknowledged him." Zoey tipped her head back and looked up at the ceiling. "This is so frustrating. I don't know what to do."

"It's not your job to figure out who killed him." Zack patted Zoey on the knee. "How many times do I have to tell you to leave it up to your boyfriend—"

"Don't call Detective Gates my boyfriend," Zoey said. The word 'boyfriend' made her nervous. It had been years since she'd last been in a serious relationship, and she still wasn't sure if she was ready to try at another one. She wanted to take it one step at a time with Gates. "We haven't even gone out on a date yet."

"All right, all right. All I'm saying is that it's his job to investigate what happened to Chester. Tell him what you've learned and let him decide what to do with the information."

"I have been keeping him informed. For the most part." Zoey got up and went over to her desk. She grabbed her yearbook and a notebook that she had brought downstairs with her earlier that day. "Speaking of passing along information . . . Have you thought of anything from high school? Like maybe someone who Chester had a problem with back then?"

"It was over twelve years ago. I barely remember who I had problems with. How am I supposed to remember who Chester might have had a beef with?"

"Look through this and see if anything jogs your memory," Zoey said as she handed her brother the yearbook. "I also tracked down most of our former classmates—"

"Seriously? What did you do? Facebook stalk them?"

"Well . . ."

"For the love of Macho Man Randy Savage, you did."

Heat spread from Zoey's chest up her neck to her face. The flush left her pale skin a bright pink. "I just wanted to see who still lives in the area and might have run into Chester sometime over the past three months."

Of the 298 students in their graduating class, 203 of them were members of the private Facebook group. Tracking down the remaining students was a headache. Some were easy to find. Others were impossible. There was a handful who she had been unable to locate on Facebook or anywhere else.

"How many still live around here?" Zack asked.

"Way more than I thought. I guess if we had kept in touch with more people, we would have known that."

"There really wasn't anyone I wanted to keep in touch with."

"Me either."

"If Chester didn't keep in contact with us, I highly doubt he remained in contact with anyone else."

"Unless he really was blackmailing someone. He did admit to us that he knew some of our classmates' secrets."

"He also denied that he was blackmailing them."

"True . . . But even if he wasn't actually blackmailing them, they might have felt threatened because he knew their secrets. Chester definitely knew something about Lucas. Brittany, too."

"Did she tell you what that secret is?"

Zoey nodded. "I promised to keep it kayfabe."

"Pinch me," Zack said as he held his arm out to Zoey. "I must be dreaming. There is no way you would ever keep a secret for Brittany Patterson."

Zoey swatted her brother's arm away. "All I'm going to say is that Brittany has a darn good motive and no alibi. And she knew Chester was back in the area."

"You think she killed him?"

Zoey shrugged. "I don't know. She swears that she didn't. But, from experience, I know not to trust anything she says."

"She always was a pathological liar," Zack said. "But how would she have figured out where Chester lived?"

"Easy. She knew he worked here. All she would have had to do was follow him home. Lucas could have done the same thing." Zoey snapped her fingers. "And Michelle—"

"I hope she's on your suspect list. She's malicious enough to kill someone just for fun."

"I wouldn't put it past her," Zoey said. Even though she had included Michelle on her suspect list, she hadn't really given her much thought. It was possible that Chester had known something about Michelle, and that Michelle had killed him for it. But she'd been too flippant about him on Tuesday morning. Why bring up that she knew he was back in the area if she had killed him the night before? Not mentioning Chester at all would have been the smart thing to do. "Michelle told me and Arielle that she saw Lucas when he came into the bank that she works at on Monday afternoon. He told her about Chester, and she mentioned in some group chat—"

"Who all is in this group chat?"

"If you could stop interrupting me, I would tell you," Zoey said before listing off everyone who was in the group chat. "Did Chester have problems with any of them?"

Zack nodded. “Oh, yeah. Kevin, Rodney, and Garrett used to pick on Chester a lot.”

“And Quincy said that Chester sold steroids to a lot of the jocks. Especially the ones who played football. Those guys might have been Chester’s customers.”

Zack flipped through the yearbook. “You know, if the killer is someone from high school it’s not necessarily someone from our graduating class. It could be someone from the classes before or after us. Chester would have interacted with some of those students. Especially if they had an art class with us. Or if Chester sold them drugs. It could also be a teacher or someone else on the faculty.”

“Instead of eliminating suspects, we keep adding to the list.” Zoey groaned. “One other thing, Zack . . . About the match.”

Zack glared at her. “You’re not going to stop, are you?”

“Nope.”

All right. I’ll do it. But that’s it. One match. And it counts as a Christmas present.”

Zoey pumped her fists in the air. “I knew you’d come around eventually.”

SIXTEEN

Friday December 7th, 2018

"YOU'RE STILL HESITATING BETWEEN spots, Mort." Zoey placed her hand over her mouth to stifle a yawn. Last night, she'd spent a few hours working on stuff for the upcoming LAW event. It was after two when she went to bed. She'd only gotten a few hours of restless sleep before having to get up and rush over to her parents' house for the practice session. "With each pause, you're making it obvious to everyone watching that you're getting yourself in position and setting up for the next move. It doesn't look good."

"I know." Mortimer Cozma grabbed a towel and rubbed it over his face. It was chilly inside the barn, but Mortimer had worked up a sweat over the past hour. "I can't help it. It's like the more I try *not* to hesitate, the longer I pause. And the longer I pause, the worse I look."

"It's because you're overthinking things," Dwight Walters said. Dwight, who went by the ring name of the Masked and Mighty Gladiator, had been wrestling on the independent circuit for the past thirty years. Zoey had known him since she was a little kid. "It's a mistake that every rookie makes. Back in the day, I would hesitate between spots. Occasionally, I still do."

"Same here," Zoey said. Of course, because her dad had started training her at a young age, she'd been well past the hesitation phase long before she made her official debut. "It's also a matter of ring awareness. You need to know where you are in relation to your opponent, the ref, and the ropes. You want everything to appear seamless. You know, like a choreographed dance."

"That's why we're putting together our high spots and running through the match ahead of time. Then, when we get in front of the audience, you will be prepared," Dwight added. As he neared retirement, Dwight had expressed a desire to work with the younger wrestlers and help them gain experience. Zoey had him booked to wrestle Mortimer at next Saturday's LAW event. "You also need to have more confidence in yourself. You know the moves. You just have to trust yourself to pull them off. And you need to have faith in your opponent—whether it's me or someone else—to work with you to make everything come together."

"Practice makes perfect," Zoey said as she climbed out of the ring. "Mort, you're way better than you were a year ago. You just need to get out of the habit of hesitating. And remember to sell. A move or submission might not hurt too much, but you need to make the fans believe that you're in excruciating pain."

When the scrawny eighteen-year-old began hanging out at Marlon's open gym two years earlier, few of the other wrestlers took him seriously. Mortimer had only recently gotten into professional wrestling, and he knew very little about it. Because he kept showing up week after week, Justin took Mortimer under his wing and started training him. It seemed like a wasted effort at first, but gradually, Mortimer caught on.

Thanks to Leland Freeman, Mortimer was forced to make his in-ring debut long before he was anywhere near ready. At last April's Linville Association of Wrestling show, one of the wrestlers had car trouble and called at the last minute to let Leland know that he wasn't going to make it. In desperate need of a replacement—and against the advice of Zoey and Justin—Leland decided to throw Mortimer into the match simply because he was the only other wrestler in attendance who wasn't already on the card.

During the pre-show, Mortimer ran the few blocks down the street to his parents' house to change into his wrestling gear. He returned just before the show got underway wearing a cheap vampire costume of black pants, frilly white shirt, and a red cape. He'd even glued plastic fangs to his incisors. Because Mortimer was such a slow learner, no one had bothered to discuss character development with him. That hadn't stopped Mortimer from creating an in-ring personae based on his obsession with vampires and death.

Because he'd been utterly unprepared, Mortimer's debut match had been a borderline disaster. Not only had he botched multiple spots, he also accidently swallowed one of his fangs and his cheap costume pants tore down the side from hip to ankle. All four hundred plus people in the audience got a glimpse of his superhero underwear. The only thing that saved the match was the experience of his opponent.

Since his debut match, Mortimer's in-ring skills had improved. He'd also gotten new ring gear and had veneers professionally adhered to his incisors.

"Let's run through the match one more time," Dwight said. "Zoey, how about you film the match on Mort's phone. That way he can watch it later. Then you and I can run through the match while Mort films it. That'll give him something to compare his match to."

"Sounds like a plan." Zoey grabbed a ten-foot-tall stepladder and set it up next to the ring. She then climbed up the steps and set Mortimer's phone on the top cap. After making sure that the phone's camera would record the entirety of the ring, she called out, "Ding! Ding! Ding! Start the match."

In the ring, Dwight and Mortimer lunged at each other. Their match was scheduled to last roughly three minutes, and Dwight spent most of that time on the offensive. That allowed him to control most of the match. Mortimer only had the upper hand at the beginning and the end of the match. From the ladder, Zoey played the role of referee by calling out the count whenever Dwight or Mortimer went for a pin.

"How did I do that time?" Mortimer asked after the short match. "Was I still hesitating?"

"Yes," Zoey said as she stopped the recording and made sure that the video saved to the phone. "But you're getting better. It wasn't quite as noticeable as it was before. But you hesitated too long before hitting The Impaler."

Mortimer used a diving elbow drop as his finishing move. While his opponent would lay prostrate in the ring, Mortimer climbed up onto the top turnbuckle. He would then take a diving leap towards his opponent. As he landed, Mortimer would drive his elbow into his opponent's chest as if he were impaling them.

"A brief hesitation is understandable before any aerial maneuver," Dwight said to Mortimer. "You need to get yourself balanced on the turnbuckle. And you have to determine where your opponent is before you jump."

"Always look before you leap," Zoey added. "I mean, I would never go for my finisher, or any other high-flying move, without looking to see where my opponent is. I want to land on top of my opponent. I don't want to overshoot or undershoot the distance. Otherwise, it looks bad. And I could wind up hurting myself or my opponent if I land wrong. And, obviously, I don't want to do that."

"Just because we make it look like we're beating each other up doesn't mean we actually want to injure anyone." Dwight glanced at the clock on the wall and then said, "Let's take a quick break. I need to call one of my clients. He just updated his accounting software and needs me to talk him through the new payroll process. It shouldn't take long. Then we can run through the match, Zoey."

While Dwight went upstairs to the viewing platform that was above the locker rooms, Zoey and Mortimer sat in the ring and watched the match. Zoey pointed out what Mortimer had done right and what still needed improvement.

After watching the video for a second time, Mortimer turned to Zoey and asked, "That guy who got killed earlier this week . . . You knew him, right?"

"Yeah, Chester and I went to high school together," Zoey said. "And he was working for Zack for the last three months."

"His memorial service is going to be at my parents' funeral home next Wednesday."

"I know. Imogene Hartman stopped by the shop yesterday and gave us the details."

Mortimer untied his wrestling boots and loosened the laces. "I feel really bad for Mrs. Hartman you know. She was in a month or two ago to plan her own funeral. Her husband came in with her, but my mom said he wasn't any help. He kept asking for the cheapest options and wouldn't let Mrs. Hartman get what she wanted. He talked her out of a burial and into a cremation since that is way cheaper. But then he didn't want to spend fifty bucks on an urn. Mr. Hartman kept saying that he had an old coffee canister that could do the job just as well."

"What a jerk." Zoey muttered a swear word as she balled up her fist and punched the ring. "Please tell me your parents aren't going to put Imogene's ashes in a coffee can."

"No! No, they would never do that," Mortimer said. "Mom was just gonna give Mrs. Hartman the urn that she wanted. Like I said, it didn't cost all that much. But then the son came in and paid cash for his mom's funeral. Now Mrs. Hartman is getting the burial that her husband claimed was too expensive."

"What about Chester? Is he going to be cremated or buried?"

"Cremated. Mrs. Hartman wanted to bury him next to her, but she said she can't afford the second plot or the casket. Mom is going to hold on to the son's remains, and, when Mrs. Hartman passes away, she's going to place the cremains in her casket."

"Your mom will probably have to sneak the ashes into the casket," Zoey said. "I have a feeling that Oscar will protest if he sees them."

"It won't be the first time we've snuck cremains or some type of memento into someone's casket that a spouse, child, or other family member doesn't want in there." Mortimer leaned closer to Zoey and whispered, "We keep a list of all the weird stuff we've been asked to sneak into caskets. I could show it to you sometime."

"You should show it to my nana. It sounds like something she would be interested in."

Zoey wondered if her family was on Mortimer's list. They had ultimately cremated her grandfather, but, for the memorial service, they had Kazimir "The Wilde Man" Wilde laid out in the flashiest casket that the Cozma Funeral Home had available for rent. They'd had him dressed up in an old animal print jacket that he used to wear out to the ring. They also placed one of Kazimir's championship belts around his waist.

"Did the county coroner send over Chester's body yet?"

"They dropped the remains off last night." Mortimer kicked off his boots. "Whoever killed him went overboard. They stabbed him at least forty-two times in the chest. And there were five stab wounds to his neck. One severed his carotid artery."

Zoey whistled. "That's overkill."

"Some of the stab wounds punctured his heart. But the majority were right here." Mortimer placed his hand over the right side of his chest. "The knife pierced his lung and obliterated the portrait tattoo on his right pectoral. I don't know if it was intentional, but it kinda looks like the killer was trying to destroy the tattoo."

"Too bad the killer ruined it," Zoey said. "Apparently, it was a portrait of Chester's ex-girlfriend. He got it a while after they broke up."

"He must've really had a thing for her." Mortimer turned to Zoey and gave her a wide-eyed look. "Maybe the ex-girlfriend killed him. That could explain why the killer destroyed the tattoo. She didn't want anyone to know the tattoo was of her."

Zoey was about to respond when Dwight walked over and said, "It's always death with you, isn't it, Mort? Don't you have any interests aside from death, vampires, and pro wrestling?"

"Not really," Mortimer said as he stood up. "But you try growing up in a funeral home and not developing an unhealthy obsession with death."

Dwight patted Mortimer on the back. He then turned to Zoey and asked, "You ready to run through this match?"

"Let's do it."

Because Zoey had watched Dwight and Mortimer rehearse the match at least a dozen times, she knew all the high spots. Dwight helped her keep everything in order by calling out the moves—most of which were basic ones that she could have performed in her sleep. Zoey barely broke a sweat during the brief match.

"I'll watch these videos later," Mortimer said as he climbed down from the ladder. "Right now, I need to get to work. Those bodies aren't going to embalm themselves."

"He's a good kid. Overly morbid. But a good kid," Dwight said as he watched Mortimer hustle out of the barn. He then turned to Zoey and asked, "You got a minute? Or do you need to get to work?"

Zoey checked the time. It was almost ten. The tattoo shop didn't open until noon.

"I've got time."

"I hope you don't mind some unsolicited advice from an old workhorse." Dwight had a seat on a folding chair. He then gestured for Zoey to sit beside him. "And some constructive criticism."

"Fire away."

"You've been in the business so long that I doubt there's anything I can tell you that you don't already know," Dwight said. "But I wanted to tell you that I think you're doing a great job running LAW on your own. I know you were the backbone of the organization even before Leland took off. And I know you handled a lot of the stuff he didn't want to be bothered with."

"Yep. He might have booked the wrestlers and scheduled the matches. But I did all the promotion. Uncle Leland was too lazy to pound the pavement and hang up flyers. And his technology skills were lacking. If not for me, LAW probably wouldn't have had any social media presence."

"Leland wasn't just lazy when it came to promoting," Dwight said. "He was lazy, period. And a narcissistic know-it-all. He wanted everything how he wanted it. It's good to see you working with the wrestlers and letting them have some say. You can't stand back and let the inmates run the asylum. But you also can't hold total control like Leland did."

"I'm trying to be flexible."

"That's good. Just don't make Leland's mistake and let your ego get in the way."

"What ego?"

Dwight snorted. "Keep in mind that you're straddling the fence between talent and corporate. Some of the other women you hire might get angry if you keep holding on to that title. They'll think you're using your position as booker to keep the title on you."

"You're not the first person to say something." Zoey ran her fingers through her ponytail. "And I'm planning to drop the title at the February show."

Dwight stood up. "Just remember that, at the end of the day, you have to keep the fans happy. You need the wrestlers to put on a show. But you need an audience for them to perform in front of. Keep the fans happy, and they'll keep showing up."

The Linville Public Library was located on Market Street half a block from the town square. The two-story, red brick building was sandwiched in between a consignment shop with a garish chartreuse exterior and a realtor's office that occupied an historic building crafted out of locally quarried stone.

Zoey hadn't planned on visiting the library on her way home from her parents' house. She really didn't have time since she wanted to take a shower before opening the tattoo shop, but, as she drove past the library, she felt compelled to make a quick stop to see if Natasha Bowman was working. In high school, Natasha had made a point of knowing everyone's business. It was possible she knew something about Chester's personal life that Zoey, Zack, and Arielle hadn't known. She might also remember who Chester had problems with while in high school or even have an idea on who he could have been blackmailing.

Skipping the on-street parking that would require her to parallel park, Zoey cut down one of the side streets and then took a right onto Peach Alley. For several blocks, the alley ran behind the stores and businesses on the western side of Market Street. Down by the tattoo shop, Peach Alley was a narrow one-way street. Closer to downtown, the alley widened and provided access to the backside of the buildings, public parking lots, and the old warehouses and factories that had been renovated into apartment complexes and office buildings.

Zoey parked in the lot behind the library and then headed for the rear entrance. She had always preferred the backside of the building because, when she was a kid, the rounded tower and turret at the one corner reminded her of a modern-looking castle. Even as an adult, she still sometimes referred to the library as "the book fortress."

Inside, to the left of the door, was the circulation desk. Behind that was the staff's breakroom and Natasha's office. The children's picture books were in the tower. The age level of the books increased section-by-section up to the young adult books that were at the front part of the building. Also, downstairs were the public computers, periodicals, and reference books. There was also a small room that could be used as a classroom or for book club meetings. The room was currently decorated with garland and other Christmas decorations. In the corner, next to an armchair, was a sign announcing that Mrs. Claus would be reading children's Christmas stories that night during Linville's annual Christmas Festival.

"Can I help you with something, miss?" a volunteer asked Zoey as she stood up from behind the circulation desk. The elderly woman wore a red velvet dress that had white lace at the collar and cuffs. A nametag introduced her as "Mrs. Claus." She held out a candy cane. "Do you have a book on the reserve shelf? Or are you looking for the adult fiction section? That's upstairs along with the non-fiction books."

"Actually, I'm looking for Natasha Bowman," Zoey said as she slipped the candy cane into her purse. "Is she working today?"

"She . . . Well, she's . . ." Mrs. Claus looked Zoey up and down, taking in her messy ponytail, baggy sweatpants, and puffy winter coat. Zoey had a feeling the woman wouldn't think too highly of her if she could see the tattoos that were hidden beneath her clothing. "Do you have an appointment with Ms. Bowman?"

"No. We're old friends from high school. One of our classmates was murdered earlier this week. I just wanted to stop by and . . . and . . ." Zoey trailed off as she scrambled to come up with a plausible purpose for her visit. "To let Natasha know when the funeral will be."

"Oh! You mean the young man who was murdered down in Shippington Way?" Mrs. Claus's face paled, leaving two circular spots of bright pink blush staining her cheeks. She pressed her hand to her ample chest as she whispered, "My grandson lives in one of those shipping containers. Not locally. He's out in California. But we've been talking about the murder all week. Natasha never mentioned that the victim was her classmate."

Zoey thought that was odd. Considering how much Natasha loved to gossip, Zoey figured she would be telling anyone who would listen that she used to go to high school with the victim. She'd probably also embellish the truth and tell everyone that she had been best friends with Chester when, in reality, she hadn't interacted with him more than a handful of times.

"So . . . Is Natasha here?"

Mrs. Claus nodded. "She's downstairs setting up for tonight's used book sale. She told us not to interrupt her unless it's an emergency. And we're not supposed to let anyone in the basement unless it's during one of the times when it's open to the public. But, seeing as how you're Natasha's friend—"

"I appreciate it."

Before Mrs. Claus could change her mind, Zoey hustled to the center of the library where a staircase descended to the basement. She squeezed past the sign that advertised the book sale and then headed downstairs.

The Linville Public Library held a used book sale on the first Friday of every month. It coincided with the town's First Friday events that had been held every month for the past eleven years. Market Street from the town square to the VFW Hall was blocked off to traffic, and vendors set up in the street. The local businesses and restaurants extended their hours and remained open throughout the event. Most of them also offered discounts or other specials to lure in the public. The library held the used book sale. There was usually a band or some other type of entertainment on a stage set up in the town square. Food trucks congregated in the VFW's parking lot while an arts and crafts show was held in the building's banquet hall.

"Natasha?" Zoey called out when she reached the bottom of the steps. She glanced around the basement but didn't see anyone. Tables covered in books were lined up across the large room. Signs hanging from the ceiling advertised what genres were on each table. "Are you down here?"

"I'm right here." Natasha popped up from between two tables. She cradled a stack of paperback books in her arms. "Oh, hi, Zoey. What are you doing here?"

"I, uh, I just wanted to stop by and let you know that Chester's funeral will be at the Cozma Funeral Home at ten next Wednesday morning," Zoey said. "I saw the post you made about Chester getting murdered on the class Facebook page. Maybe you want to—"

"Announce his funeral. Of course. I don't know if anyone will show up. Chester wasn't exactly Mr. Popularity. But I'll be sure to come." Natasha tossed the books aside and then came around the table to hug Zoey. "Are you and Zack okay?"

"I, uh . . . It was a shock."

"I can't even begin to imagine." Natasha released Zoey and stepped back. "It's just crazy. I found out on Tuesday morning that he was back. And to think he was murdered just a few hours before that."

"I thought you found out he was back on Monday evening," Zoey said. "Michelle told me that she announced it in your group chat."

"Oh, yeah." Natasha walked over to a nearby table and began to tidy up the rows of science fiction books. "Yes, Michelle mentioned Chester was back on Monday night. But then she added Lucas to the group chat, and we were all so busy catching up with him. I didn't even think about Chester again until Michelle mentioned him at the gym on Tuesday morning. What was Chester doing back in town anyway?"

"His mom has cancer. She's dying."

"Oh, that's terrible," Natasha said. "Do the police have any idea who killed him?"

Zoey shrugged. "I figure he knew the person who killed him. He was . . . Well, there was a lot of rage involved in the murder. A stranger wouldn't have bothered with . . . with the overkill. Plus, whoever killed Chester ransacked his place and stole one of his paintings."

"How do you know all this?"

"Because I found his body."

"Oh my God . . ." Natasha pressed her hand over her mouth. "Who all knew he was back? I mean, before Michelle mentioned him in our group chat. Aside from his parents, and you and your brother, did anyone else know?"

"Zack and I didn't kill him."

"I wasn't accusing you. I'm sorry it came out that way."

Zoey accepted the apology. "Brittany mentioned running into Chester a few weeks ago."

"You can't honestly think Brittany killed him. She's the sweetest person. She wouldn't hurt a fly."

"Are we talking about the same Brittany? Because Brittany Patterson was a holy terror in high school. It was Britt Trousdale who was the sweetheart," Zoey said. "And Lucas knew—"

"Oh, I hardly think Lucas would have killed him."

"Why not? He came by the shop on Monday. And he made a threatening comment to Chester as he was leaving."

"I highly doubt that. You must have misunderstood Lucas."

"I know what I heard." Zoey propped her hip against a table and crossed her arms over her chest. "Plus, Chester told me that he knew some of Lucas's secrets. And some of our other classmates' secrets as well. Did he know any of yours?"

Natasha laughed, and the shrill sound echoed in the room. "I don't have any secrets. But, even if I did, how would Chester have known any of them? We weren't friends. I didn't hang out with him. I don't even remember having any classes with him."

"Well, he was blackmailing someone—"

"The only friends Chester had in high school were you, Zack, Arielle, and your other weird friends. It has to be one of the people in your friend group that he was blackmailing. That's *if* he was even blackmailing anyone." Natasha grabbed a box of books and dumped them onto the table. "No one else wanted anything to do with Chester. How could he have learned anyone's secrets when no one would willingly interact with him?"

"By listening. I'm sure he overheard plenty. Most people treated him like he didn't exist. I'm sure some of our classmates forgot he was there and said stuff in front of him," Zoey said. "And he clearly knew something about Jocelyn—"

"Jocelyn didn't kill him!"

Zoey held up her hands in a placating gesture. "I never said she did."

"But you implied—"

"What did Chester do to Jocelyn?"

Natasha slammed a hardback book against the table. "What happened between them is none of your business."

"Jocelyn told me that she 'hired' Chester to write a paper on *Anna Karenina* for her during senior year. He purposely didn't do a good job, so she got a bad grade," Zoey said. "I find it hard to believe she's still holding a grudge over that. Did something else happen between them in high school? Or was it when they were both attending college in Saratoga Springs? Jocelyn mentioned hanging out with him a few times."

"Because she felt bad for him." Natasha took a step in Zoey's direction. "What else do you know about them going to the same college?"

"Not much. Chester never even brought it up—"

"He didn't talk about Jocelyn at all?"

"Not that I remember," Zoey said. Chester had barely talked about high school, and, aside from a couple comments, she hadn't bothered trying to discuss it with him. "Should Chester have mentioned Jocelyn? What's going on? What happened?"

"Like I said, it's none of your business." Natasha turned back to the books. "Anyway, none of us in the group chat could have killed Chester. We didn't know where he lived."

"But you knew where he worked—"

"And, what? You think one of us went to the tattoo shop, followed Chester home, and then killed him? That's crazy. None of us cared enough about him to kill him." Natasha herded Zoey towards the stairs. "Now, I'm going to have to ask you to leave. I have a lot of work to do before tonight's book sale. And you're not even supposed to be down here."

SEVENTEEN

As she turned into the alley that ran alongside 3 Count, Zoey almost crashed into the back of Oscar Hartman's truck. The house next door had hidden it from her view as she drove down Market Street. It wasn't until she was already committed to the turn that she realized the truck was parked in the alley.

"Oh, crap!"

Instinctively, Zoey slammed on the brakes. The seatbelt tightened across her chest and yanked her back against the seat as her car came to an abrupt stop a few inches short of Oscar's rusted, dented bumper.

After making sure that the back end of her Jeep was not sticking out into the street, Zoey relaxed her white-knuckle grip on the wheel and then pressed her hands over her chest. Beneath her palms, her heart raced.

Zack and Oscar, who stood nose-to-nose in the narrow space between the truck and the porch, stopped arguing and looked over at her.

"You!" Spittle flew out of Oscar's mouth as he yelled. He stomped over to Zoey's Jeep and yanked open the driver's side door. "I just spent the night in the slammer thanks to you."

"Oh yeah?" Zoey climbed out of the car. "Please explain how that is my fault."

"Because you ran your mouth and told that damn detective I killed my son."

"I never told Detective Gates that you killed Chester." Zoey crossed her arms over her chest and returned Oscar's glare. "All I told him was that I saw you lurking around Chester's place on Tuesday afternoon. And don't even try denying it was you. I recognized both you and the truck."

"I ain't denyin' I was there," Oscar said. "But if you hadn't gone blabbin'—"

"What was I supposed to do?"

"You shouldn't have said nothin' at all. Bad enough you talked to that detective. But did you have to tell my wife I was there? When she got home yesterday, she was up my ass wantin' to know what I was doin' at Chester's place and askin' how I found out he was back in town. She ain't shown that much spirit in years."

"Probably because you destroyed whatever spirit she had," Zack muttered.

Oscar glared at Zack before turning his attention back to Zoey. "It was almost a relief when those officers showed up and hauled me to the police station."

"You still haven't answered my question," Zoey said. "What were you doing at Chester's place on Tuesday?"

"You sound like that detective. 'What were you doing at your son's house? Did you kill him? How long have you known your son was back? Where were you Monday night?' When I didn't give the detective the answers he wanted to hear, he threw me in the slammer. I spent the night sharin' a cell with a drunk who kept quotin' the Bible and tryin' to save my soul." Oscar paced alongside his truck. "And then that detective grilled me again this mornin'. He finally released me an hour ago."

"And you headed straight here—"

"No. My lawyer took me home. I figured Imogene would start naggin' me the second I walked in the door. But she wasn't there. I had a few minutes of peace before Ruth Jennings waddled over and told me that Imogene went to the hospital in an ambulance last night—"

"Is she okay?"

Oscar shrugged. "Ruth said Imogene had chest pains or somethin'. I dunno. I'm on my way to the hospital, but I figured I'd stop here first and give you both a piece of my mind. And let you know it's your fault my wife is in the hospital. If you'd just kept your dang mouths shut."

"You still haven't told us what you were doing at Chester's place," Zoey said.

"What I was doin' ain't none of your damn business."

"Did you kill him?"

"No!" Oscar lunged towards Zoey. His hands slammed into her shoulders. "I've got an alibi for Monday night."

Zoey stumbled backwards into the porch. Her ponytail cushioned the back of her head as it hit one of the wooden posts.

"Don't touch my sister!"

Wrapping his arms around the older man's waist, Zack drove Oscar into the side of the truck. Oscar yelped in pain when the driver's side door handle dug into his back.

"Zack, stop!" Zoey shouted as she pushed away from the porch. She grabbed her brother by the back of the coat and tried to get between him and Oscar. "Everyone just calm down."

"I'm good. I'm good," Zack said as he allowed Zoey to drag him away from the cowering older man. "But you should call the cops. This scumbag needs another night in jail to cool off and learn some manners."

"I ain't spendin' another night behind bars." Oscar's face was flushed a deep red, and saliva foamed at the corners of his mouth. "And I don't gotta answer to you."

"No, you don't. But I think I deserve some answers." Zoey leaned against the driver's side door and prevented Oscar from opening it. "So, you really were at a bar with your coworkers on Monday night?"

"What I was doin' Monday night ain't none of your business. All you need to know is that I wasn't killin' my son."

"Then what were you doing at Chester's place?"

"Oh, hell, I may as well tell you. I already told that detective." Oscar reached into his coat pocket and pulled out a crumpled packet of cigarettes. "I ain't gonna lie . . . I hated my son. But not enough to kill—"

"Chester was your only child," Zack said. "As a father, I just don't understand how you could hate your own kid."

"Because Chester was a disappointment." Oscar lit a cigarette and took a long drag. "I had all these expectations, and he didn't meet a single one of 'em. I wanted a son who played sports. I got one who liked to fingerpaint."

"Chester was an extremely talented artist," Zack said. "You should have been proud of him. And encouraged him."

Oscar grunted. "What use do I have for art? It's as useless as he was."

Zoey stamped her foot. "Enough insulting Chester. I want to know when you found out he was back. And what you were doing at his place."

Oscar exhaled a cloud of smoke in Zoey's face. "I found out he was back when the funeral home called the house and left a message that Chester had paid for Imogene's funeral. Imogene didn't know I heard the message, and I didn't say nothin' even though I was pissed at her for goin' behind my back. I knew she was up to somethin', but I didn't think it was that."

"Your wife had every right to see her son," Zoey said.

"Yeah, yeah," Oscar snarled at her. "I followed Imogene to her next meetin' with Chester. Then I followed him here—"

"Is that the day I caught you two arguing in the alley?" Zack asked. "It was about a month ago."

Oscar nodded. "That was a couple days after I found out Chester was back. I told him I'd let him see his mama. Figured I couldn't deny her that. But I made it clear I didn't want him in my house. I didn't want nothin' to do with him, and I told him that he better head back to La-La Land once Imogene died."

"How thoughtful of you," Zoey said. She was being sarcastic, but she wasn't sure that Oscar picked up on that. "How many times have you seen Chester since then?"

"That was it." Oscar dropped the cigarette and ground it out with his heel. "Next time I saw him, he was dead."

"What were you doing at his place on Tuesday?"

Oscar sighed. "I went to talk to Chester before he left for work. I wanted to make peace with him. Like a truce, you know. I could see how all the sneakin' around was wearin' Imogene out. I figured if I put up with Chester for eighteen years, I could make nice another few months for my wife's sake. I went to his place to tell him that, but I was too late. He was already dead."

"Chester should have been here by noon," Zack said. "If you wanted to talk to him before he left, you had to get there around . . ."

"It was quarter after eleven when I got there."

"And I didn't get there until about a quarter to one," Zoey said. She jabbed Oscar in the chest. "What were you doing lurking around for an hour and a half? Were you inside?"

"Yeah, I was inside when you showed up." Oscar lit a second cigarette. "When Chester didn't answer the door, I looked in through the little windows in the front door. I saw him on the ground. Since the door was unlocked, I let myself in—"

"Why didn't you call the police?" Zoey asked.

"I was goin' to. But I figured I may as well look around first."

"Look around for what? The place was trashed . . . Or are you the one who trashed it?"

Oscar used the remains of his cigarette to light a third one. "Chester paid for his mama's funeral with cash. I figured there was more where that came from. So, I decided to look in the hidin' spots I'd taught him 'bout when he was a kid. I don't trust banks, and I keep cash hidden . . . Well, it ain't your business where I keep my money. When I didn't find nothin' in the usual hidin' spots, I tore the place apart."

"You robbed your own son?" Zack asked. "That is about as low as you can get."

"I ain't proud of what I did. But I needed the money. Not that I found much," Oscar said. "I don't make much workin' at the feed mill, and my insurance is crap. It was only a few years ago that I finally finished payin' off Imogene's medical bills from the first time she had cancer. We've been practically livin' paycheck to paycheck. When the cancer came back . . . Well, any money I'd managed to save went towards doctor bills. I needed money. I went through Chester's stuff, and I took what I could find. It ain't like he was gonna need it."

"What about the painting hanging above the bed?" Zoey asked. "Did you take that, too."

Oscar shook his head. "There wasn't no paintin'. And, even if there was, I ain't got no use for art."

"What about his phone?" Zack asked. "And his TV?"

Oscar nodded. "Yeah, I took those. Got a few bucks for them from the pawn shop."

"Let me make sure I have this right," Zoey said. She pushed away from the truck and had a seat on the porch steps. "You went to make peace with Chester, but you found his body. Instead of trying to get him help—"

"He was dead. Wasn't nothin' I could do for him," Oscar said. "And I was gonna call the police when I was done lookin' around."

Zoey cleared her throat. "As I was saying . . . Instead of immediately calling the police, you tampered with the crime scene and raided his place for cash and anything you could pawn. You then snuck out the back door when I showed up."

"I couldn't let you catch me in there with his body." Oscar swung open the driver's side door and then climbed in his truck. "Now, stay away from me and my wife. You pesterin' and interferin' is gonna kill her before the cancer gets a chance."

After watching Oscar drive away, Zoey muttered, "If Oscar didn't kill Chester, who did?"

"It's not our job to figure it out," Zack said. "And you need to stop asking questions. I found a . . . Well, it's a threat. But it's an unusual one."

Zoey turned to look at her brother. "What is it?"

"Go see for yourself." Zack pointed towards the street. "It's on the front porch."

Zoey hustled around to the front of the building and ran up the porch steps. She glanced around the narrow porch and spotted an addition to the Krampus animatronic. Seated at Krampus's furry feet was a four-foot-tall plastic doll. Like Zoey, the doll had brown hair and brown eyes. Red paint had been spattered on the doll's leopard print pants and purple t-shirt, and a pocketknife protruded from the cloth body. The knife held a piece of paper pinned to the doll's chest. Printed across the paper in bold black letters was a warning.

"STOP ASKING QUESTIONS OR YOU'LL END UP LIKE CHESTER."

"You're right. It is unusual." Zoey knelt next to the doll to get a closer look. "It was on the porch when you got here?"

Zack nodded. "I got here about twenty minutes ago. I'd just found the thing when Oscar pulled up, so I don't think it's one of Imogene's dolls."

"No, her dolls are porcelain. And antiques." Zoey pulled her phone out of her purse and took a picture of the doll. She sent the picture to Detective Gates. "This is a cheap, plastic doll. Something that Brittany's or Michelle's daughters would play with."

"Makes sense . . . This reminds me of something they would do. And I wouldn't put it past either of them to stab you for real." Zack gave Zoey a pointed look. "I told you to stay out of it and let Detective Gates do his job. But, no, you just had to go sticking your nose where it doesn't belong."

"Let's look on the bright side . . . At least it's not a voodoo doll."

"HO, HO, HO! MERRY CHRISTMAS!"

Zoey trailed behind her family as they exited the queue line and joined Santa Claus in front of his North Pole workshop. The workshop—a small brown shed that had been decorated with gigantic plastic candy canes, peppermints, and gumdrops so that it resembled a gingerbread house—was set up on the southern corner of the town square in front of the Aloysius Scholz Pretzel Factory Museum.

"Were you all good little boys and girls this year?" Santa asked as the Wildes gathered around him. "Or will I find your names on my naughty list?"

"I can assure you that this one has been a good little girl." Zack picked Paige up out of her stroller and then plopped her down on Santa's lap. "Haven't you, Paige?"

Paige nodded, causing her brown curls to bounce.

Santa looked down at the toddler and asked, "What would you like for Christmas?"

"Belt!" Paige squealed. "I wanna belt."

Santa looked up at Zack. "Did she say she wants a belt?"

"A title belt. You know . . . The kind that the pro wrestlers have."

"That's a new one." Santa leaned closer to Paige and asked, "Are you sure you don't want a nice dolly?"

"Belt!"

"Gather around everyone. We've got a long line of people who still need to see Santa," the photographer said as he pushed Paige's stroller off to the side. The photographer then directed the Wildes on where to sit or stand as they crowded around Santa. "Say 'sugarplum' . . ."

The camera's flash momentarily blinded Zoey, and she still had dark spots hindering her vision as she followed her family into the town square where Market Street and High Street intersected. The square was packed full of people who had come out for the combined Christmas Festival and

First Friday event. On the other side of the town square, the Linville Area High School's chorus sang "Frosty the Snowman."

Clapping her gloved hands over her ears, Zoey said, "Christmas music should be outlawed. It's cruel and unusual punishment."

"Some of us enjoy Christmas music," Roxanne said.

"You're the only person in the family who enjoys it."

"Your father listens to Christmas music."

"No, Dad listens to Neil Diamond sing Christmas songs. There's a difference."

Marlon cleared his throat. "I also listen to Chicago's Christmas albums. And Elvis."

Zoey rolled her eyes. "What I'm saying is that you're selective when it comes to Christmas music. You don't listen to just anything. You only listen to certain singers."

"And I can recall a time when you listened to Hanson's Christmas album year-round," Roxanne said to Zoey. "You used to get so excited about Christmas. You'd help me decorate the house and bake cookies—"

"I still help with the cookies."

"You'd beg us to take you to see Santa," Roxanne continued. "We'd drive you kids around and look for Christmas lights."

"Back then, Christmas meant a week off from school and a pile of presents," Zoey said. "It lost it's magic as I got older and realized that Santa doesn't—"

"Don't say it!" Arielle yelled. "Not in front of Paige."

"She's not even two." Zoey looked down at the stroller to see that her niece was staring at her. "She's not going to understand or remember anything I say."

"But there are other kids who will," Roxanne said as she gestured at the people gathered around them. Zoey noticed that there were a lot of children running around the town square. "Don't ruin it for them."

Zoey grimaced. "All I'm saying is that as I got older, I became indifferent to Christmas."

"You promised me you'd fake some Christmas spirit for Paige," Arielle said.

"I made that promise before I found Chester's body," Zoey said. "That destroyed any Christmas spirit that I might have been able to fake."

"You still haven't told me anything about what happened to him," Vivian said.

"And I don't plan to."

"I'll make you tell me tomorrow," Vivian said. "You'll be trapped in the car with me and won't be able to escape. Or ignore me."

"Knock it off, Ma," Marlon said.

"What's everyone's plans for the rest of the night?" Roxanne asked. She then turned to Zoey and scowled. "I already know your plan, Miss Scrooge. Now that we've taken the annual family photo with Santa, you'll probably head home."

"No, I'm headed to the food trucks to grab dinner," Zoey said. "Then I'm going home. I've got some sleep to catch up on."

"Zack and I are coming with you to the food trucks, Zoey," Arielle said. "Paige needs to eat soon, or she'll get cranky. And then she'll be miserable for the rest of the night."

"Paige is just like her aunt." Zack tugged on the end of Zoey's ponytail. "She gets hangry and turns into a raging monster. Then we're all in trouble."

"Ha-ha." Zoey smacked Zack on the arm. "Very funny."

"Zoey's been hangry for the past hour," Roxanne said. "What about the rest of you? Are we sticking together?"

"No can do. Hannah and I are meeting some friends at the Black Bear Tavern." Justin unzipped his coat and revealed a hideous—and borderline inappropriate—holiday sweater. "They're having an ugly sweater contest."

"And then they're having a Christmas karaoke competition." Hannah Stoltzfus flung her long, strawberry-blonde hair over her shoulders. Her hair clashed with her hot pink leather jacket. "I already signed up to sing 'Santa Baby.'"

Hannah, who was twenty-one, was Zoey's protégé and her biggest fan. They'd met following Zoey's debut match at the Linville VFW Hall. Zoey had been eighteen at the time, and Hannah was only eight. During the show's intermission, little Hannah approached Zoey and asked the teenager to train her when she was old enough. Zoey agreed that she would, and, ten years later, she followed through on that promise.

Justin and Hannah started dating back in August. At first, Zoey was leery of the relationship. Justin rarely took relationships seriously and had a bad habit of jumping from woman to woman. Zoey did not want to see Hannah get her heart broken. She also did not want to get dragged into the middle of the resulting drama. Much to her surprise, Justin was taking the relationship seriously. Hannah had been an unexpectedly good influence on Zoey's immature and selfish little brother. Unfortunately, Justin's legion of simpering female fans drove Hannah crazy. More than once, Zoey had to hold Hannah back and prevent her from going after a woman who flirted with Justin or even tried to feel him up while at an event.

"What about you, Vivi?" Roxanne asked. "Do you want to check out the arts and crafts show with me?"

"I've got to get over to the historical society," Vivian said. "I'm stuck answering questions about the items in the antique toy display—"

Interrupting, Justin asked, "Is that because you played with some of the toys when you were a kid, Nana?"

Vivian smacked Justin on the back of the head. "For that, I'm returning all of your Christmas presents, young man."

Roxanne shook her head. "Looks like it's just you and me tonight, Marlon."

"Can't I go home with Zoey? You know I hate these things. It's the same vendors every time and—"

"Oh, it is not." Roxanne grabbed Marlon's hand and dragged him away. "Besides, I'll need you to carry my bags."

"Let's go." Zack used Paige's stroller to force his way through the crowd. "Paige and Zoey aren't the only ones who will be hangry if they don't eat soon. I haven't eaten anything since before we opened the shop at noon."

It was slow going as they walked the three blocks down Market Street to where the food trucks were set up in the VFW Hall's parking lot. The street had been blocked off to vehicular traffic, but it was teeming with people as they made their way between the shops and restaurants. Many of the businesses along Market Street had put up Christmas or winter-themed displays in their front windows. Groups of people moved from building to building to admire the decorations. Tents had also been set up in the street for vendors, and there was a live nativity scene in front of the Saint Hedwig Catholic Church.

"There's no funnel cake truck!" Zoey had spent all week looking forward to getting a funnel cake at the festival. She tried to eat healthy most of the time, but she allowed herself to indulge occasionally. Funnel cakes were one of her weaknesses. "But they've got a snow cone vendor. Who wants a snow cone in December?"

"Considering how many people I've seen eating snow cones, I'd say the vendor is doing some steady business." Zack pointed to the far end of the parking lot. "They might not have funnel cakes, but there is a cookie truck down there."

"I do love cookies," Zoey said as she rubbed her hands together. "Hopefully, they have something with extra chocolate."

Arielle knelt next to the stroller and asked, "What do you want to eat, Paige?"

"Chickee nugs!" Paige screamed as she kicked her legs around. "Chickee nugs!"

Arielle sighed. "This kid and her chicken nuggets. Breakfast, lunch, and dinner . . . That's all she wants to eat."

"It looks like they have chicken tenders at the one truck. Is that good enough?"

"It'll do." Arielle steered the stroller over to the front of the VFW Hall where a family of four had just vacated a wooden bench. "And I'll eat whatever Paige doesn't."

"What about you, Zoey?" Zack asked. "Do you want anything? Or are you just going to stuff your face with cookies?"

"Get me a cheeseburger."

Zoey pushed her way through the crowd to get to the back of the parking lot. Luckily, the line at the cookie truck was short, and she didn't have long to wait. As she made her way back to the street—with a half-dozen freshly baked chocolate chip cookies in hand—she heard someone shouting her name. She looked around the crowd and spotted Detective Gates.

"Hey, Tyler," Zoey said. "You taking a break from investigating Chester's murder?"

"Actually, I'm looking for you and Zack. I stopped by the tattoo shop, but Santino told me that you all were at the festival. I figured I'd walk up and try to find you. I didn't realize how big of an event this is until I got here." Gates held up a soft pretzel log that had been stuffed with ham and cheese. "I was going to call it a day, but I got distracted by the food trucks."

"Oh man, the soft pretzel truck is here. How did we miss that?" Zack asked as he joined them. He handed Zoey a cheeseburger wrapped in foil. "Hey, Gates, did you hear about the mutilated doll that someone left on my shop's front porch?"

"Zoey sent me a picture. And Chief Coleman showed me the doll when he got back from collecting it. We sent it off to the state's crime lab for processing," Gates said. "But that's one of the things I wanted to talk to you about, Zoey. Considering the warning, I assume you've been . . . uhh . . . interfering in my investigation?"

"No, she's conducting her own," Zack said, prompting Zoey to elbow him in the ribs. "Ask her to show you her notes."

Detective Gates groaned. "Zoey . . ."

"What? You basically gave me permission to snoop around."

"No, I didn't. And you know that." Gates gave Zoey a stern look. "The only thing I asked you to do was keep an eye on that Facebook page. I never told you it was okay to question any of your former classmates about Chester's murder."

"I can't help that Lucas came into the shop," Zoey said. "And I ran into Michelle and Jocelyn at the gym."

"But you sought out Brittany and Natasha," Zack added.

"I expect you to fill me in on everything you've learned," Gates said. "And allow me to handle any further questioning."

"I have every intention of doing so," Zoey said. "But you're the one who hasn't returned any of my calls or texts since Wednesday evening."

"I was busy dealing with Oscar for most of yesterday and this morning," Gates said. "I also wanted to talk to you two about his visit to the shop. Since he put his hands on Zoey, I can charge him with assault."

"That's not necessary," Zoey said. She gestured for Zack and Gates to follow her as she made her way to the front of the VFW Hall. "It's not like he actually hit me."

"No, Zoey, you should do it," Zack said. "If it wasn't for your ponytail, you would have cracked the back of your head on that post."

"But if I press charges against him, he could then press charges against you."

"Who's pressing charges against Zack?" Arielle asked. She scooted down the bench and made room for Zoey. "What did I miss?"

"Oscar Hartman came by the shop earlier," Zack said. He handed Arielle a Styrofoam box that contained the chicken tenders. "He pushed Zoey. So, I shoved him against his truck."

"You got into a fight?" Arielle asked. She ripped apart a chicken tender and then held out a piece to Paige. "Why are you only telling me about this now?"

"It barely qualified as a scuffle." Zack grabbed a handful of fries out of the Styrofoam box. "Zoey pulled me off Oscar before I had a chance to actually hit him."

Zoey looked up at Gates. "Oscar said he has a solid alibi for Monday night. Was he really at a bar with some of his coworkers?"

"It was just one coworker in particular," Gates said. "Her name is Wanda, and they've been having an affair for over a year."

"What a rat bastard!" Zack said.

"Basta!" Paige screamed as she snatched another piece of chicken. "Rat basta!"

"Nice job, Zack," Arielle said. "You know she repeats everything we say."

Gates chuckled. "I confirmed that Oscar and Wanda were at the bar until about twelve-thirty. They then went back to her place. Wanda's son told me they got home around one, and that Oscar left just after two-thirty. There's no way he could have killed Chester."

"Then what was he doing at Chester's place when Zoey got there?" Arielle asked.

"Oh, you're going to love this, hunny," Zack said. "He was ransacking the place for stuff that he could pawn."

"He claims he was going to anonymously call the police after he was done helping himself to Chester's belongings," Zoey added.

"Son of a—" Arielle glanced over at Paige. "You know what I mean."

Zoey nudged Gates. "Did you get back the stuff that Oscar pawned?"

Gates nodded. "It took us a while since he went to three different pawn shops around Harrisburg. He pawned the TV, a game console, cellphone, tablet, a watch, and a couple other small things. Oscar managed to wipe the memory on the phone and tablet. The State Police's forensics team have them, but they don't think they can recover any of the data."

"What a horrible person . . ." Zoey said. "I can't comprehend how he could steal from his dead son. I mean, Chester's body was lying right there the whole time."

"Try not to think about it," Gates said.

"Have you made any other headway on the case?" Zack asked.

"Some. Chief Coleman confirmed that the redheaded woman who Santino saw arguing with Chester outside the shop is Brittany . . ." Gates snapped his fingers. "You know, the former classmate that you told me about."

"Brittany Patterson," Zoey said. "Her married name is Adams."

"Yeah, her," Gates said. "She was also seen at Shippington Way by Chester's neighbors. But that was a couple weeks ago."

"What?" Zoey smacked her hand down on the bench's metal arm. "I talked to Brittany yesterday and she never mentioned that she knew where Chester lived."

Gates grumbled something under his breath. "The chief also talked to Lucas Jennings."

"What did he have to say for himself?" Zack asked.

"Lucas admitted that he stopped by the tattoo shop on Monday," Gates said. "I shouldn't be telling you this, but . . . He denies threatening Chester. He claims you misunderstood him."

"No, we didn't." Zoey balled up the cheeseburger wrapper and tossed it in a nearby trash can. She then grabbed a chocolate chip cookie. "Lucas definitely threatened Chester."

"Chief Coleman also asked about the Lamborghini," Gates said. "Lucas stuck to his original story. But he also insinuated that Chester might have been one of the two burglars."

"Oh, please . . ." Zoey said. "Going off what Chester said, Lucas is lying about what really happened that night. Maybe I could try asking Lucas—"

"Absolutely not," Detective Gates said at the same time Arielle asked, "Are you nuts?"

"Here's your chance, Zoey . . ." Zack pointed down the street. "Lucas is headed this way. We're about to have an impromptu high school reunion."

"Tell me you're joking."

Zoey peered around Paige's stroller and locked eyes with Jocelyn Hershey as she led a group of their former classmates down the sidewalk. Jocelyn glared at Zoey, and her upper lip curled in disgust. Vying for Jocelyn's attention were Natasha and Lucas. Zoey also spotted Brittany and Michelle along with their husbands. Garrett Zimmerman and his wife were also part of the group. Zoey's former best friend, Olivia Kreider, and her husband brought up the rear. Olivia was pregnant, and she was struggling to keep up with the others.

"Hey, look." Kevin Sensenig let go of Michelle's hand so that he could point towards where Zoey and the others sat. "It's the class freaks."

"Oh, for heaven's sake, Kevin," Olivia's husband, Jeremy Smith, said. "We're not in high school anymore. Stop calling people freaks."

"They were freaks back then," Kevin said. "And they still look like freaks now."

Zoey shrank back against the bench as her anxiety swelled. She could deal with running into Michelle and Brittany on a semi-regular basis. She had been putting up with them for twenty-five years and was used to their harassment. But now she was faced with a whole group of people who had made her middle school and high school years a living hell. And Kevin, at least, seemed to want to pick up where he had left off with the nasty comments and the bullying.

"Knock it off, Kevin!" Michelle shouted at her husband before she hugged Zoey. "Natasha just told us that you found Chester's body. That must have been so traumatizing."

"Almost as traumatizing as you hugging me," Zoey said as she broke free from Michelle. "But, yes, I did find him."

"That's just crazy," Michelle said.

"Yeah, why didn't you tell us?" Brittany said as she gave Zoey a pointed look.

"I . . . uh . . ." Zoey stammered. "The police asked me not to say anything."

"Can you tell us anything now?" Michelle asked, prompting the others to bombard Zoey with questions. None of them had shown this much interest in Chester when he was alive. Now that he had been brutally murdered, they suddenly cared.

Zoey glanced at Detective Gates out of the corner of her eye. He slightly shook his head.

"No, not really," Zoey said. "As far as I know, they're still investigating."

Saving Zoey from further interrogation, Arielle pushed her way into the crowd and asked, "What are you all up to this evening?"

"Natasha planned a bar crawl for us," Michelle said.

"I should really be at the library to oversee the book sale." Natasha wrung her hands and looked down the street towards the library. "But

Jocelyn wanted me to organize a get-together tonight. So here we are."

Michelle linked arms with Zoey and Arielle. "The three of you should join us. Your friend is welcome to come, too."

"Yeah, Wilde, you should come," Garrett Zimmerman said to Zack. He was wearing his old high school wrestling jacket. The leather sleeves were cracked around the shoulders and elbows. "We could finally have that rematch you owe me."

"Oh my God, Garrett," Vanessa whined. "It's been how many years? Just let it go."

"He owes me, Nessa." Garrett glared at his wife before turning to Zack with a fake smile. "Come on, Wilde, what do you say?"

"Not gonna happen," Zack said as he moved away from Garrett. "Besides, it would end the same way as last time . . . with you humiliated."

"You got lucky that time, and you know it."

"I beat you fair and square," Zack said. "Like your wife said, you need to get over it."

Gates stepped closer to Zoey and asked, "What's that guy's problem?"

Zoey rolled her eyes. "That's Garrett Zimmerman. He was the star of the high school's wrestling team, and he absolutely hated everything about professional wrestling. He hassled us almost every day from the first day of seventh grade until about a third of the way through twelfth grade. That's when Zack humiliated him during the wrestling team tryouts. Garrett wouldn't acknowledge us after that."

The twins had met Garrett in homeroom on the first day of seventh grade. As soon as he found out that they were pro wrestling fans—and that their dad was a wrestler—he showered them with disdain. He also regularly harassed them about how pro wrestling was "fake." The harassment got old fast, and it wasn't just Zoey and Zack who grew sick of it, but Garrett had a massive ego and could not be stopped.

After years of ignoring Garrett's insults, things finally came to a head in the late fall of twelfth grade. During the morning announcements, the student newscasters were listing when the winter sports tryouts would be held. Garrett got in Zack's face and dared him to come to the wrestling tryouts so he could see what "real" wrestling was. Zack finally had enough of Garrett and decided to take him up on the challenge.

"Zack showed up dressed like Macho Man Randy Savage and cut a promo on Garrett . . ." Zoey struggled to keep from laughing as she recalled the moment. "Zack called out Garrett and challenged him to an amateur wrestling match. Garrett couldn't really say no. Not in front of his teammates and coaches."

"Zack beat him?"

"To quote Macho Man . . . OH YEAH! Garrett was humiliated. He kept insisting he wasn't ready, and that Zack cheated. So, Zack challenged him to a best out of three. Garrett couldn't say no to that either, and Zack beat him two more times. Garrett's teammates never let him live it down. And the coaches tried to recruit Zack, but he wasn't interested."

Gates threw his head back and laughed.

"Well, are you coming along on the bar crawl or not?" Michelle asked as she looked back and forth between Zoey and Arielle. "We're meeting some more of our classmates at the first stop, and we don't want to keep them waiting."

"Not interested." Arielle grabbed Paige's stroller and pulled it in front of her. "And, even if I was, I'm not taking my kid on a bar crawl."

"Why not?" Jeremy patted Olivia's belly. "Liv and I are bringing our kid."

Olivia smacked Jeremy's hand and then furiously whispered something in his ear.

"Are either of your parents here?" Brittany asked. "Can't you just ditch your kid with them? That's what Michelle and I did with our kids."

"We are not ditching our kid," Zack said as he used the stroller to push his way out of the group. Paige leaned around the side of the stroller and waved at everyone. "Come on, Zoey."

"Actually . . ." Detective Gates said as he wrapped his arm around Zoey and pulled her against his side. "Zoey and I will tag along."

EIGHTEEN

"We will?"

"Sure, we will. It sounds like fun." Detective Gates pressed his lips against Zoey's temple and whispered, "Play along. I want to hear what they have to say about Chester."

"You're going to owe me big time for this," Zoey hissed. She then faked a smile and said, "I guess Tyler and I will join you."

"Great!" Michelle clapped her hands. "Let's go. Our first stop is the Vineyard at the 'Ville. They have a tent set up in my bank's parking lot."

As she and Gates followed the others down the street, Zoey glanced back at Arielle and Zack who were gawking at her as if she'd just made an unexpected heel turn on her tag partner and aligned herself with the enemy. She could understand their confusion. Aside from Olivia, Zoey couldn't really stand anyone in their graduating class's popular crowd, and she never would have willingly hung out with any of them. She didn't want to hang out with them now, but Gates hadn't given her much choice. Not that he really had to twist her arm considering she also wanted to hear the gossip about Chester.

"What do you want me to do?" Zoey asked. "Am I supposed to just bluntly ask if any of them killed Chester and hope one of them confesses?"

"That's probably not the best approach." Gates drew Zoey back so that they were walking a few feet behind Olivia and Jeremy. "If they don't bring him up—"

"Oh, trust me, they will. The only reason they invited us along is because they're hoping I'll share more details with them. You better tell me what's okay to divulge and what isn't."

"Don't tell them anything that I shared with you about the police investigation. I wasn't supposed to tell you about any of that." Gates pulled Zoey to the edge of the sidewalk to avoid a group of teenagers who weren't paying attention to where they were walking. "But you can say that Chester told you that he knew some of your former classmates' secrets and that he was blackmailing at least one of them. Pay attention to how they react and what they say. One of them might let something slip—"

"You know, it was only about fifteen minutes ago that you gave me attitude for interfering in your investigation. Now you're encouraging me to question possible suspects."

"When I told you to butt out of my investigation, I didn't know this prime opportunity was about to fall into my lap. And I don't want you to interrogate them. Just get them talking about Chester and maybe ask some leading questions. That's if you want to—"

"Of course, I want to," Zoey said as she veered off the sidewalk and into the bank's parking lot. An enormous white tent with cathedral window sidewalls had been set up in the lot. Signs on either side of the entrance welcomed them to the Vineyard at the 'Ville's popup location. "But you do remember that mutilated doll and threatening note that someone left on the shop's front porch earlier today? I'm betting the person who left it is one of them."

"Oh, shoot. I did forget about that." Gates held back the tent flap. "You're right, this is a bad idea. Maybe we shouldn't—"

"Oh no. We're committed now." Zoey walked into the tent. "I'm just not looking forward to the fallout. Even if none of them killed Chester, they're going to be furious when they find out who you really are. I guess it's a good thing I'm not actually friends with any of them."

Inside the tent, the air was significantly warmer thanks to a few strategically placed space heaters. A makeshift bar had been set up at the back of the tent, and there were tables and chairs scattered throughout the rest of the open space.

Two more of her former classmates were waiting for them at a table in the corner. Zoey had bumped into Anthony Groff a few times over the years, but she hadn't seen Rodney Dissinger since a year or two after they graduated.

Feeling like an outsider—a status she had gotten used to during her schooldays—Zoey hung back as the others greeted each other. No one stepped forward to hug her, and she received more curious glances than heartfelt welcomes as she awkwardly hovered on the fringes. She was almost thankful when Michelle drew her and Gates into the group.

After shushing everyone, Michelle said, "On our way here, we ran into Zoey and her . . . uhh . . . friend?"

"Boyfriend." Gates draped his arm around Zoey's shoulders. "I'm Zoey's boyfriend."

Stammering a bit, Zoey said, "Yeah . . . This is my boyfriend, Tyler."

"Careful," Kevin said to Gates. "One of her ex-boyfriends got murdered last summer. And another one was in a motorcycle accident. Dating Zoey may be hazardous to your health."

"That's enough, Kevin," Michelle said. She then turned to the rest of the group and said, "But speaking of murder, I'm sure you all heard about Chester Hartman, right? Well, Zoey is the one who found his body."

Zoey was once again bombarded with questions. She was spared from having to answer when a server came over to take their drink orders. The Vineyard at the 'Ville had a selection of red, white, and rosé wines available. They also had a collection of fruit-flavored sparkling wines and ciders. Zoey had been to the vineyard for several events over the years—including Zack's and Arielle's wedding—and she knew which of their wines she liked and which ones she didn't.

After placing his order for a glass of peach cider, Gates leaned closer to Zoey and said, "One of the Linville police officers is over by the bar. I'm going to say hi to him before he comes over here and outs me."

After waving Gates off, Zoey turned to Brittany and asked, "What are Rodney and his wife doing here? I thought they lived in Philly."

"It's their weekend to have Ashton. I told them about the bar crawl, and they decided to stick around for it before they take him home." Dropping her voice to a whisper, Brittany asked, "You're not going to say anything about Ashton, right?"

"I already told you I wouldn't," Zoey said. "But why didn't you tell me that you knew where Chester lived?"

"I didn't—"

"Cut the crap. You were seen at Chester's place by a few of his neighbors."

Brittany squeezed her eyes shut. "Okay . . . I was there. But that was weeks ago. I told you I ran into him at Schmitt's while I was out to dinner with my husband and kids. I could tell by the way Chester reacted that he knew Ashton was his son. I couldn't let him say anything in front of my family, so I gave him one of my cards and told him to call me. The next day, he invited me over to his place to talk about it. That's when he threatened to tell Rodney. We yelled at each other on his front porch before I drove off. That must be when his neighbors saw me."

"Why didn't you just tell me that?"

"I don't know . . . Maybe because you were accusing me of killing him."

"You didn't happen to go to his place on Monday night and—"

"No! I didn't go to his place. I didn't kill him."

"Hey," Michelle said as she pushed her way in between Zoey and Brittany. "What are you two whispering about?"

"Nothing," Zoey and Brittany said simultaneously.

"Uh huh." Michelle gave Brittany a questioning look before she turned to Zoey and asked, "So where did you find the stud muffin? And why have you been keeping him a secret?"

"I, uh, I met him at one of my wrestling events over the summer," Zoey said as she accepted the plastic tumbler of black raspberry cider from the server. She also grabbed Gates's drink. "I don't normally date my fans, but . . . He, uh, he's a nice guy."

Michelle giggled. "He's definitely nice to look at."

"So, you really are seeing someone." Lucas sidled up to Zoey and leered at her. "On Monday, I figured you were lying about that."

"Why would I lie?"

"Because you're still pissed at me for turning you down in seventh grade."

"I got over that a long time ago."

"That's not the impression I got the other day. You still seem pretty upset about it."

"Trust me, I'm not." Zoey sipped her cider. "You know, Chester told me about what really happened to your dad's Lamborghini."

Lucas, who had just taken a sip of his wine, spewed the dark red liquid all over Jocelyn's face and white, wool pea coat.

"What the hell, Lucas?" Jocelyn shrieked, drawing everyone's attention to her.

"Oh my God!" Natasha, who was hovering next to Jocelyn, set her tumbler on the table and grabbed a handful of paper napkins. She used the napkins to sop up the wine that dribbled down Jocelyn's face. "What's wrong with you, Lucas?"

"I . . . I . . ." Lucas sputtered. Trying to speak made him cough. "Chester . . ."

Ignoring Lucas's gasping protests, Zoey said, "Chester shared some of Lucas's secrets with me. And he told me some of yours, too, Jocelyn."

"What?" Jocelyn swatted Natasha away from her and then leaned across the corner of the table to glare at Zoey. "What did he tell you?"

"Do you really want me to talk about this in front of everyone?"

"No!"

Olivia tossed a balled-up napkin at Zoey. "What's going on down there."

"Nothing." Jocelyn squeezed the tumbler between her hands, causing the plastic to crack. White wine ran through her fingers and pooled on the table. "It's nothing."

"Oh, I wouldn't call it nothing," Zoey said. She raised her voice so that everyone crowded around the table could hear her. "Chester was blackmailing at least one of our classmates over something that happened back in high school. He wouldn't tell me who. I was just asking Lucas and Jocelyn if it was either of them."

"Like I told you earlier, Zoey, Chester was probably just pulling your leg about the blackmail," Natasha said. She pried the cracked tumbler out of Jocelyn's hand. "I can't imagine Chester knowing anything about us that's worthy of blackmail."

Zoey glanced around the table and noticed nervous glances being exchanged between a couple of her former classmates. The rest looked at her with interest.

"This is getting juicy." Michelle nudged Zoey and asked, "What did Chester share with you?"

Disregarding the furious glares being directed at her from certain people, Zoey said, "Chester told me that almost all of you used to copy his homework. And that he sold a bunch of you guys drugs like weed and steroids."

Recovered from the coughing fit, Lucas said, "Natasha is right. Just about everyone at this table . . . By which I mean the ones who graduated with us . . . We all copied Chester's homework at least once in high school. But that's hardly worth blackmailing someone over."

Lucas's accusation caused a slew of finger pointing around the table. Some of them readily admitted to copying Chester's homework. Others were more reluctant.

Interrupting the others, Natasha shouted, "You all should be ashamed of yourselves! None of you should have copied Chester's work. It was cheating. And it was wrong."

"Oh, come on, Natasha," Anthony said. "It was just homework."

"Homework that you should have done yourselves." Natasha looked around the table and scowled at everyone. "I never copied Chester. Or anyone else. And I certainly never asked Chester to write a paper or do one of my projects like I know Lucas used to do."

"You always were a Miss Goody Two Shoes," Lucas muttered.

"And a hypocrite," Jocelyn added. "How many times did I copy your homework? And how many of my papers and projects did you do for me?"

"I . . . well . . ." Natasha stammered. "That was different."

"Not really." Jocelyn frowned at Natasha. "And if you had written that stupid paper on *Anna Karenina* for me, I wouldn't have had to get Chester to do it. Thanks to him royally screwing me over, I got a B minus in World Lit. I still blame you for that."

Natasha cowered. "I didn't have time. I was so busy planning the fairy tale-themed prom so that it was just how you wanted it—"

Jocelyn huffed. "You came up short of my vision."

"Your vision would have been impossible to pull off. I didn't have the budget or the manpower," Natasha said. She clasped her hands beneath her chin in a pleading gesture. "Plus, I had to plan the spring carnival and the senior trip. And I had my own homework to do—"

"It's always excuses with you, Natasha. I've been listening to them since we were in kindergarten, and I'm getting sick of it." Jocelyn then turned to Zoey and said, "And give me a break. Do you really think I would defile my body with drugs? Not only is my body a temple, it's also my livelihood."

Michelle leaned closer to Zoey and whispered, "She says that, but she smokes at least two packs a day. She claims it kills her appetite and helps keep her skinny."

"Terrible for her lungs, though," Zoey whispered back. "And you'd think she'd want to keep those healthy so she can breathe while dancing."

"But we're up in the cheap seats," Brittany said. "So, what do we know?"

Detective Gates returned to the table and plucked the tumbler of peach cider out of Zoey's hand. "Nice job. Now keep them talking. And try to remember what everyone says."

"That's going to be the hard part," Zoey whispered. "They're all talking over each other."

Anthony pounded his empty tumbler against the tabletop. "I don't know about the rest of you, but I never bought any drugs from Chester."

"I'll admit I bought weed from him on occasion," Jeremy said. Olivia, who was sitting on a plastic lawn chair, smacked her husband's thigh as she shot him an irritated glance. "But I never got any steroids. I played golf and tennis, for heaven's sake. I had no use for steroids."

"I played golf, too. And I got steroids from Chester," Kevin said. "Though that was mainly in the spring during baseball season."

"I bought weed off Chester a bunch of times," Garrett said. "And I used steroids a few times, too. But then I got really bad acne on my back from it, so I quit."

"I wish Rodney had quit using the steroids," Elouise said as she flung her dark blonde hair over her shoulder. "They left him practically infertile. His sperm count is so low it's almost negative. If I'd known Chester was back, I would have driven up here from Philly just to slug that freak in the face."

"Now, Elouise," Rodney said. "The doctor said it *might* have been the steroids. Or it could have been something else."

"If you're shooting blanks, how did you get Brittany pregnant?" Garrett asked Rodney. "Or is there something we don't know?"

Beneath the table, Brittany reached around Michelle and grasped Zoey's hand. "Obviously, Rodney wasn't infertile back then."

"Are we sure about that?" Elouise asked. "Maybe we should have Ashton's DNA tested."

"You witch!" Brittany let go of Zoey's hand so that she could throw her empty plastic tumbler at Elouise. Elouise ducked, and the tumbler hit Vanessa on the shoulder. "You're just jealous of me. You always have been."

"Maybe for a while." Elouise wrapped her arms around Rodney's waist and smirked. "But I won in the end."

"If you call Rodney a prize." Brittany grabbed Peter's arm. "I'm the one who upgraded."

"That's enough," Rodney said. "Besides, if I'm not Ashton's dad, who is?"

"Maybe it was Chester," Kevin said. "Wasn't he creeping on Brittany senior year?"

"No, he wasn't." Brittany said. Her voice was high pitched and verging on hysterical. "He was my lab partner in physics."

"Chester had a crush on you, Britt," Rodney said. "That's why I had to beat him up."

"Oh, please," Jocelyn said. "If Chester had a crush on anyone, it was me."

"Regardless of who he had a crush on, I know Brittany never would have hooked up with that freak. Not even if he was the last guy on Earth," Rodney said. "I know Ashton's my son."

"Yeah, yeah, we all know Brittany poked holes in your condoms," Jeremy said. "We've heard it a million times."

"And none of us want to hear it again." Natasha glanced at her watch. "Hurry up and finish your drinks. We need to get over to Lynch's soon or we'll fall behind schedule."

Zoey chugged the rest of her black raspberry cider and then moved around to the far side of the table to help Olivia out of the lawn chair. The chair's seat sloped back, causing her feet to dangle above the macadam. With her belly in the way, she had trouble scooting forward. Jeremy, who stood in front of her, grasped Olivia's forearms and tried to pull her out of the chair.

"Same ol' jerks," Zoey muttered as she watched the others head for the exit. While most of them had noticed Olivia's struggle, none bothered to help. "You all right, Liv?"

"Do I look all right?"

"No. You look—"

"Don't you dare say radiant. Or glowing. Or any of those other asinine things that people say to pregnant women to make them feel better. I know I look like a beached whale."

With Detective Gates on one side and Jeremy on the other, they tipped the chair forward enough for Olivia to slide free.

"I was going to say you looked uncomfortable," Zoey said as she helped Olivia adjust her coat. "But, yeah, you do kind of resemble a beached whale."

Olivia's blue eyes widened as she drew in a deep breath. She then burst out laughing.

"Zoey says that, and you laugh," Jeremy said. "But if I said it, you'd take my head off."

"You're my husband. You're supposed to lie and tell me I look beautiful even though I'm all swollen and full of raging hormones," Olivia said. "Zoey's my friend—"

"You two haven't been friends since seventh grade."

"But we've known each other since we were babies." Olivia waved Jeremy off. "Now go away and let us catch up."

"Come on, man," Gates said as he guided Jeremy towards the tent flaps. "You already dug yourself into a hole when you revealed that you bought weed from the dead guy. Don't make it any worse."

As they exited the tent, Olivia linked arms with Zoey. "Watch my feet for me. I haven't seen them in weeks, and I'm sick of stubbing my toes and tripping over things."

"Mom told me you're having a girl," Zoey said as she steered Olivia around the horde of people gathered in front of the live nativity at the Saint Hedwig Catholic Church. Even though they were no longer friends, their moms still talked on a regular basis. Roxanne had kept Zoey up to date on Olivia's life. "But I can't remember if she told me when you're due."

"Christmas Eve. But the doctor said Genevieve is good to make an appearance any time now. I'd prefer it be sooner rather than later. I'm tired of the constant kicking. Not to mention feeling exhausted all the time, the nonstop heartburn, and having to pee every half hour."

Zoey had to wait until they had walked past the chainsaw carving demonstration that was taking place in the middle of the street before she could ask, "If you feel so terrible, why are you tagging along on a bar crawl? Wouldn't you rather be at home?"

"To be honest . . . Yes, I would much rather be at home. I told Jeremy to go without me, but he begged me to come along. He reminded me that this might be the last time we get to go out before Genevieve's born, so I gave in."

Zoey gestured at their former classmates who were walking ahead of them and asked, "Do you still hang out with them?"

"Jeremy plays golf with Kevin, Anthony, and Garrett. And we all get together a few times a year." Olivia made a face. "But, personally, I can't really stand any of them."

"They were your best friends in high school."

"No, they were the people that I hung out with after my best friend ditched me." Olivia stopped walking. Because she had a firm grip on Zoey's upper arm, Zoey was forced to stop as well. "Do you have any idea how lost I was without you?"

"You hardly seemed lost. Not after you got swept up by the popular crowd." Zoey tugged on Olivia's hand, pulling her forward. "I'm the one who was lost. Between Jocelyn dumping the spaghetti all over me at lunch and then Lucas publicly humiliating me—"

"I never would have said anything to him had I known he was going to do that."

"You shouldn't have said anything to him at all."

"I was trying to do you a favor—"

"Some favor."

A whistle pierced the air, cutting through the combined racket caused by countless people talking and shouting, the ongoing chainsaw demonstration, and a contemporary Christmas song blasting out of a nearby speaker.

"Hurry up, you slowpokes," Garrett yelled as he held open the door to the brewery. "Everyone's waiting."

"This conversation is to be continued," Olivia said to Zoey. She then raised her voice and shouted at Garrett, "Don't you whistle at me like I'm a dog. I'm lugging around a tiny human being. I'll waddle along as slowly as I want."

Zoey was about to follow Olivia into the brewery when Lucas appeared in the doorway and forced her back onto the sidewalk.

"What did Chester tell you about the Lamborghini?"

NINETEEN

"Just that you're the one who crashed it," Zoey said as she moved away from the door so that another group could get inside. "And that he helped you fake the burglary to cover it up."

"Shit. When I talked to Chester on Monday afternoon, he swore he hadn't told anyone." Lucas staggered over to a bench and collapsed. "When did he tell you?"

"He mentioned it right after you left."

"I should have just left it alone . . ." Lucas ran his hands over his face. "This is going to sound terrible, but I was relieved when I found out Chester was dead. With him gone, I thought I was in the clear. That I could live the rest of my life without looking over my shoulder. That car was my dad's pride and joy. It was a 1964 Lamborghini 350 GT, and he spent a small fortune rebuilding it. He'd never forgive me if he found out that I totaled it."

Zoey had a seat next to Lucas and asked, "Was Chester blackmailing you?"

"Not exactly. I mean, he held it over my head during senior year. You have no idea how petrified I was that he was going to tell my parents the truth. I think the only reason he didn't was because he was afraid he'd also get in trouble for helping me fake the burglary."

"What about after high school? Did you guys stay in touch?"

"Our moms sometimes talked, so I knew where he was living and what he was up to. I even went to see him at that hippie's tattoo shop in Venice

Beach. That was five or six years ago. Other than that . . . I'd get a message from him every year or so. Every time something positive happened in my life, he'd ruin it by reminding me about the Lamborghini. And whenever my life was in the crapper, he'd pop up and say that he could make my life even worse."

"But he never asked you for money?"

Lucas shook his head. "He just liked to taunt me. I think it was his way of getting back at me for ditching him in middle school. I know it was awful. Chester was like a brother to me. But I wanted to be friends with the popular kids. And there was no way they were going to accept a weirdo like him. So, I kicked him to the curb."

"When did you find out that Chester was back in town?"

"Mom mentioned he was back on Friday. I called your brother's shop on Saturday and talked to Chester. He told me to meet him there on Monday afternoon." Lucas leaned closer to Zoey and said, "Don't tell the others this, but I'm just about at rock bottom. My wife got the house in the divorce. And just about everything else. I've been out of work for the past few months, and my bank account is almost tapped out—"

"Michelle's already told a few of us that you're broke."

"She never could keep her mouth shut. I just hope you can."

"I have zero interest in you or your life. And it's not like I'd benefit from sharing your secrets." Zoey pulled her coat tighter around her shoulders. "Chester didn't give me the details about that night. What exactly happened?"

"My parents went to Italy for two weeks to celebrate their twentieth wedding anniversary. They originally planned to leave me home alone, but, right after school let out, I threw a big party at their house. Chester called the police, and they showed up to bust the party. We all got charged with underage drinking."

"Do any of them know that it was Chester who tipped off the police?" Zoey gestured over her shoulder to the brewery. On the other side of the picture window, some of their former classmates were playing cornhole. "Could one of them have killed him over it?"

"I didn't know that it was Chester who called the police until years later. And I never bothered to tell anyone. But that doesn't mean that one of them didn't figure it out. As for killing him over it . . . It hardly seems worth it now. Sure, we all got into trouble. But I don't think anyone got into *that* much trouble. Do you really think one of them might have killed him?"

Zoey shrugged. "So, your parents didn't trust you enough to leave you home alone?"

"They had my one grandma come to stay with me. She was insanely strict and hardly let me out of her sight except to go to football practice. I'm fairly sure she booby trapped my bedroom door and the windows so I couldn't sneak out at night. I've never been to prison, but I imagine that's what it's like."

"If she was up your butt the whole time, how did you manage to take the Lamborghini out for a joyride?"

"Grandma's church used to have monthly bingo tournaments. The one for that month happened to be on the last night she was staying with me. Grandma tried to drag me along, but I begged her to let me stay home. I'd been to a few of those bingo tournaments, and those old ladies were brutal. I wanted nothing to do with it. After she left, I took the Lamborghini out."

"Had you ever driven it before?"

"Once. Right before they went to Italy, Dad let me coast it around the block. But he about had a heart attack when I tried to give it some speed. He didn't think I could handle it because it had a manual transmission and a V12 engine."

"Was he right?"

"He sure was." Lucas leaned forward and pressed his hands over his face. "I planned to go just a mile or two up River Road and then come back. But I was going too fast, and I sucked at shifting. I lost control going around a curve. The car slid off the road, went down an embankment, and slammed into a tree."

"How did Chester get involved?"

"I called and asked him to come get me. I then begged him to help me fake the burglary." Lucas slumped against the arm of the bench. "He left me hogtied in the kitchen and then went back to the car to put my mom's jewelry and the other stuff in the trunk. An hour or so later, Grandma came home and found me. I was so paranoid that the cops would figure out that I'd crashed the car. Or that I would get my lies mixed up and give myself away. But, somehow, I got away with it."

"Don't you feel bad about what you did?"

"Of course, I do!" Lucas pounded his fists against the bench. "The stress ruined my life. And you know how I've coped with it? By nonstop eating. And drinking. But I gave that up a couple years ago after going to rehab."

Zoey couldn't believe the depths of Lucas's selfishness.

"What about your dad?"

"What about him?"

"I'm assuming he was upset that his car was totaled."

"Oh, yeah. He was devastated. You think the dad in *A Christmas Story* was bad when the kid broke that stupid leg lamp? Well, my dad was a million times worse. He still talks about that damn car."

Zoey shifted on the cold, metal bench so that she faced Lucas. "Did you kill him?"

"What?" Lucas sat up straighter. "What did you say?"

"Chester. Did you kill him?"

"No. Do you really think I could kill someone?"

"You just admitted that you have motive."

"But that doesn't mean I killed him."

"Do you have an alibi for late Monday night?"

"Seriously?"

Behind them, someone rapped on the window. Zoey and Lucas spun around to see Natasha waving at them.

Lucas groaned. "I never could stand her."

"Aside from Jocelyn, did anyone in your group genuinely like Natasha? Or did they just tolerate her because she was Jocelyn's best friend?"

"She was Jocelyn's lap dog," Lucas said. "Don't tell Natasha, but Jocelyn didn't really like her. Had she not been so easily manipulated and willing to do whatever Jocelyn wanted, I bet Jocelyn would have kicked her to the curb the same way I did to Chester. But, as long as Natasha was useful, Jocelyn kept her around."

"Natasha's smart. You'd think she'd have figured out that she was being used."

"I think she knew. I also think Natasha had a thing for Jocelyn."

"Like a crush?"

"I don't know if I'd call it a crush. I never quite got that vibe. But she was obsessed with Jocelyn. And she always seemed to resent me because I was dating her. She used to tell me that Jocelyn would be better off without me and even tried to talk me into breaking up with her. She was also jealous of Jocelyn's female friends. Anyone who came between her and Jocelyn was a threat." Lucas stood up. "But now Natasha is acting like she wants to be my best friend. She's been blowing up my phone since Monday, asking me all sorts of personal questions like—"

"Did she ask you about Chester?"

"Actually, she did. She asked if I knew how long he'd been back in town and where he's been the past few years."

The brewery's front door swung open, and Natasha stepped out onto the sidewalk.

"If you two want to grab a beer, you better hurry up. We're moving on soon."

"We're coming." Lucas ambled over to the door. Turning back to Zoey, he said, "I know you already told the police about the car. Why else would the chief have asked me about it earlier today? But if you tell him or anyone else about what I just said, I'll tell them you're crazy and a liar and that you're trying to get back at me for turning you down in seventh grade."

Zoey rolled her eyes as she tried to follow Lucas into the brewery. Natasha stood in the doorway and wouldn't let her inside.

"What were you two talking about?"

"Oh, you know . . ." Zoey said. She decided to put Natasha on the spot to see how she reacted. "Lucas was just telling me about how you were texting him on Monday night and asking all sorts of questions about Chester."

"I . . . I might have asked him a question or two about Chester. I don't remember." Natasha pushed past Zoey and scurried down the sidewalk. Calling back over her shoulder, she said, "I need to check on the book sale. I'll meet you guys outside the library."

Inside, Zoey joined the group of spectators watching the cornhole tournament. Brittany and Peter were taking on Garrett and Vanessa at one set of boards while Michelle and Kevin faced off against Anthony and his wife.

"There you are." Detective Gates, who was talking with Rodney and Elouise, wrapped his arm around Zoey's shoulders and pulled her against his side. Lowering his voice, Gates asked, "What were you and Lucas talking about?"

"He told me about how he wrecked his dad's car, and that Chester helped him fake the burglary," Zoey said. She took a sip of Gates's grapefruit shandy and grimaced. She had never been a fan of beer. "Have you learned anything interesting?"

"Not too much." Gates drained the rest of his beer and set the glass on a nearby table. "I had a good talk with Jeremy, and I've been able to eliminate him and Olivia from the suspect list. Not that I suspected Olivia—"

"I would hope not."

"She thought she was going into labor on Monday night, and they spent a few hours at the hospital before the doctors determined it was Braxton Hicks contractions."

"Did you get alibis for anyone else?"

"Just for Anthony," Gates said. "And even that's questionable."

Anthony taught American history at the Linville Area High School and coached the boys' basketball team. His wife, who he had met while they both played basketball at Syracuse University, also taught at the high school and coached the girls' basketball team.

"I heard the boys' varsity basketball team won an away game on Monday night."

"Anthony didn't say what time the team bus got back to town, but it sounds like it was late. So, he might be in the clear. As for the others . . ." Gates shrugged. "I can't really come out and ask them what they were doing Monday night without giving myself away."

After Garrett and Vanessa finished trouncing Brittany and Peter at cornhole, the group left Lynch's Brewing Company and headed down Market Street to the Black Bear Tavern. As they walked past the library, Natasha rushed outside to join them.

The Black Bear Tavern was in an old, two-story brick building that had been constructed on the bank of the Temeyok Creek in the mid-eighteen hundreds. The deck that overlooked the creek was deserted, and there weren't many people in either the bar or the downstairs dining room. The handful of people in the dining room were crowded around the central fireplace. A sign at the bottom of the steps directed patrons upstairs to the annual Ugly Sweater Contest and Christmas Karaoke Competition. Zoey breathed a sigh of relief when Natasha led them past the stairs and into the bar—especially when she overheard someone attempting to sing "Santa Baby" in a high-pitched, childish voice. She hoped it wasn't Hannah.

While they waited for a couple busboys to push some tables together, Zoey looked over the holiday-themed drink menu. The Tavern was serving traditional drinks such as hot buttered rum, wassail, and eggnog. They also had a long list of cocktails with cutesy holiday names like Peppermintini, Jingle Juice, and Candy Cane Cooler.

Zoey was trying to decide on a cocktail when Jocelyn approached her.

"I need to talk to you in private."

"Okay . . ." Zoey handed the menu to Detective Gates. "Order me something that doesn't have any tequila. Or rum. Or whiskey. Or—"

"Why don't you just tell me which alcohols you're okay with."

"Vodka. But nothing that tastes like coconut or vanilla. Or banana."

Gates gave her a cheeky salute.

Zoey followed Jocelyn across the barroom and into the women's bathroom. After making sure that there wasn't anyone in the stalls, Jocelyn locked the door.

"What did Chester tell you about me?"

"Absolutely nothing."

"What?" Jocelyn's drawn on eyebrows shot up in surprise. "Are you serious?"

"He never mentioned you at all."

"Not even once? I can't believe it."

"Was Chester supposed to talk about you?"

"Of course not. I was just—"

"What's going on?"

"Nothing."

Jocelyn moved towards the door, but Zoey cut her off. Leaning her back against the heavy wooden door, she prevented Jocelyn from leaving.

"I know you saw Chester when you were both going to Skidmore College."

"Yeah, okay . . ." Jocelyn stomped over to the sinks and checked her makeup in the mirror. "I might have seen him around campus a few times."

"How many is a few?"

"I don't know." Jocelyn pulled a tube of lipstick out of her purse and applied a fresh layer. "It's a small campus, and there are only so many residence halls and places to eat. So we ran into each. But it's not like we hung out on a regular basis."

Zoey joined Jocelyn in front of the mirror. "But you did hang out with him?"

"A few times during our first year," Jocelyn said as she swiped on more mascara. After returning the makeup to her purse, she turned to face Zoey. "I know this will sound crazy, but it was nice to have someone from home going to the same college. Even if it was Chester. College was difficult for me at first. I was homesick, the classes were hard, and I was exhausted all the time. Plus, I went from being a big fish in a tiny pond to—"

"You always did have a high opinion of yourself." Zoey crossed her arms over her chest. "And I really don't care about how you were doing. I just want to know about Chester."

"He was struggling with some of his classes, and I was struggling with mine. We acted as each other's cheerleaders. And he came to some of my dance rehearsals."

"I'm surprised you let him come around where your new friends could see him. Weren't you embarrassed to be seen with a 'freak' like him?"

"He was also sketching me—"

"In the nude?"

"Eww! No." Jocelyn's upper lip twitched. "He sketched me while I was dancing. It was for one of his classes. He had to draw people while they were in motion. Now, if you're done questioning me—"

"I'm not." Zoey returned to blocking the exit. "And you're the one who wanted to have this private chat."

"Well, I'm done talking." Jocelyn tried to push past Zoey. "Get out of my way."

"Not until I've asked you a couple more questions."

Jocelyn took a step backwards. "About what?"

"Chester's girlfriend. Did you ever meet her?"

"Girlfriend?" Jocelyn snorted. "Who said he had a girlfriend?"

"His mother," Zoey said. "And the tattoo artist that he worked for out in Venice Beach inked a portrait of the girlfriend on Chester's chest. That was a while after they broke up—"

"That's only slightly pathetic."

"To each their own," Zoey said. "Chester thought of her as his muse.

Back in Cali, he's got an entire wall in his apartment covered in paintings and sketches of her—"

"Even more pathetic."

"He brought one of the paintings with him and had it hanging on the wall above his bed. Whoever killed him, stole it."

"Maybe the killer thought it was valuable." Jocelyn shrugged. "And, if he had a girlfriend, he never told me about her. But, my God, can you imagine how desperate she must have been to date Chester."

"Is there—"

A pounding on the wooden door interrupted them. Zoey flipped the lock and let Olivia into the bathroom.

"Told you I have to pee every half hour," Olivia said as she ducked into one of the stalls.

"Now we're done talking," Jocelyn said as she pushed past Zoey and exited the bathroom.

"One more question." Zoey followed Jocelyn back out to the barroom. She waited until Jocelyn spun around before she asked, "What did Chester do to piss you off? I know it had nothing to do with *Anna Karenina*—"

"He humiliated me in front of some of my college classmates. It was unforgivable."

While Jocelyn joined Natasha and Lucas at the bar, Zoey walked over to where Detective Gates was talking to Anthony Groff and his wife. Gates handed her a martini glass that had a coating of red sugar around the rim. A maraschino cherry floated in the lime green liquid.

"What is it?"

"It's called the Grinch."

"Fitting." Zoey took a tentative sip of the citrusy liquid. "What's in it?"

"Lime vodka, melon liqueur, pineapple juice, and ginger ale."

"It's good." Zoey sipped her drink while she and Gates chatted with Anthony and his wife. When the conversation wound down—and she finished her drink—she said, "Let's get out of here."

Zoey waited for Gates to finish his Saint Nickarita and then headed for the exit. Out on the sidewalk, she started speed walking towards the town square. The Christmas Festival was winding down, but the town square remained packed with people.

"That was awful."

"Oh, it wasn't that bad."

"Absolute torture," Zoey said. "You owe me big time."

"How about I take you out to dinner sometime soon? We could go back to the Tavern. Or how about that place?" Gates pointed across the street to the Steakhouse on the Square. "Are they any good?"

"It's the classiest restaurant in Linville."

"You got any plans tomorrow night?"

"I'm wrestling in Newark."

"Sunday night?"

"Nothing."

"Then it's a date." Gates draped his arm around Zoey's shoulders. "Now, tell me, Nancy Drew, did you solve the case for me?"

"No. But I learned some very interesting things tonight."

During the half-mile walk back to the tattoo shop, Zoey filled Detective Gates in on everything she had learned over the past few days. The only thing she didn't tell him about was that Chester was the birth father of Brittany's son. She was debating whether she should break her promise to Brittany when they reached the shop and headed down the alley towards the back of the building.

She had just made up her mind to tell him when a car engine fired. There was a blinding flash of high beams and the squeal of tires as the car accelerated down the alley towards them.

Her senses dulled by the alcohol, Zoey froze. Gates, on the other hand, sprang into action. He slammed into Zoey, knocking her sideways and sending her sprawling on the wooden steps leading up to the side porch. Her hip crashed into one step, and her upper arm hit another. Gates landed on top of her, knocking the wind out of her.

The car swerved towards them, and the passenger side mirror smashed against one of the support posts. The front right corner of the car also clipped the edge of the porch. Before Zoey or Gates could react, the car pulled out onto Market Street and raced up the road towards the cemetery.

Zoey and Gates remained sprawled on the wooden steps for another minute as they both tried to catch their breath and calm their racing hearts.

"That was close." Gates was the first to stand up. "Are you all right?"

"I think so," Zoey said as Gates pulled her to her feet. She tested her limbs. The left side of her body from shoulder to knee throbbed, but nothing felt broken. "I'd be in a lot worse shape if that car had hit me."

"Did you get a look at the car?"

"I couldn't see anything after the headlights blinded me."

"The headlights were high up. It had to be an SUV or a truck—"

"Or a van." Specifically, a teal van driven by a redheaded woman. "There's no way it was a sedan."

"Do you think the driver was drunk? Or just didn't see us?"

"No. I think they were waiting and tried to run us down on purpose," Zoey said. "And I'm betting the person behind the wheel is one of my former classmates."

TWENTY

Saturday December 8th, 2018

"WHICH ONE OF THEM do you think was behind the wheel?"

"I don't know, Nana," Zoey groaned. She lay curled up on her parents' couch with ice packs on her bruised knee, hip, and arm. "I guess it could have been any of them."

"No, it couldn't have." Vivian leaned over and tapped Zoey on her injured arm. "Let's go over the suspect list and narrow it down."

Lita, who lay sprawled across Zoey's chest, raised her head and hissed at Vivian. Vivian's tuxedo cat, Classy Freddie Blassie, hissed in response. Freddie just barely tolerated sharing the house with a dog. Having another cat in the house was an outrage.

"I don't want to talk about this anymore, Nana," Zoey said as she stroked Lita's back. "I just want to sleep. In case you forgot, I've got a match tonight."

"Right now, I think it's more important to figure out who tried to kill you."

The near miss had rattled Zoey more than she was willing to admit. Once the adrenaline faded, her anxiety took over. The pain radiating through her body—along with Detective Gates's quick thinking—prevented the anxiety from overwhelming her. Realizing that the car was long gone, Gates escorted Zoey into the tattoo shop's breakroom and got her calmed down. He'd then called the police and had them send over an officer.

As soon as Zoey was done providing her statement to the responding officer, she packed up the essentials—her cat, a toothbrush, and some clothing—and went to stay at her parents' house. If someone really was trying to kill her, there was a chance they might come back later to make another attempt. She was not about to stick around her apartment to find out.

Zoey arrived at her parents' house just after midnight and found Roxanne and Marlon waiting up for her. She'd called them ahead of time to let them know she was coming to spend the night. Naturally, they wanted to know why. They also wanted to know why she was limping.

After giving her parents a condensed version of the evening's events, Zoey spent a restless night on the living room couch. The couch wasn't the comfiest to begin with, and her various bumps and bruises made it even harder to find a comfortable position. Her racing thoughts—along with Lita's fascination with the Wildes' Christmas tree and abundance of decorations—also kept her up. Zoey was afraid that if she fell asleep, her cat would go into destruction mode and start batting the ornaments off the tree or knock the decorations off the fireplace mantle. As Zoey kept an eye on Lita, she went over and over the known facts concerning Chester's murder. If the killer was threatening her with a mutilated doll and trying to run her over, she must be getting close to discovering his or her identity.

Exhaustion finally overtook Zoey around dawn, and she was able to get about an hour's worth of sleep before Vivian came downstairs and woke her up. Vivian—who had been in bed when Zoey arrived the night before—wanted to know what she was doing there. Because her nana would settle for nothing less than the whole story, Zoey wound up having to recount the full version of events starting from when Lucas showed up at the tattoo shop on Monday afternoon through the near accident in the alley.

"Knock it off, Ma," Marlon said as he walked into the living room. "You're driving the poor girl nuts."

"No, I'm trying to solve a murder," Vivian said. "And save Zoey before she becomes the next victim."

"And we keep telling you that it's the detective's job to solve it." Marlon turned on the gas fireplace and then plopped down on a recliner. "Where are you wrestling at tonight, kiddo? And what time do you have to leave?"

"Newark," Zoey said. "And Mort's coming to pick us up around noon."

"That's not for another three hours. We have plenty of time to catch up on *Smackdown!* from last night." Marlon grabbed the remote and turned on the TV. Raising his voice, he said, "I would have watched it live last night, but someone forced me to go to a stupid craft show."

From the kitchen, Roxanne yelled, "You bought more at that craft show than I did."

Marlon grunted.

Giving up on taking a nap, Zoey sat up. She could always sleep during the drive to Newark.

The first segment was wrapping up when Zoey's cell phone rang.

"Can you pause it, Dad? Detective Gates is calling." Zoey waited until Marlon paused the show before answering. "Hey, Tyler. What's up?"

"I just wanted to see how you're doing this morning."

"I'm a little beat up. But it's not too bad. I've been in worse shape after some of my matches," Zoey said. "What are you up to?"

"I just wanted to let you know that I have Lucas Jennings in the interrogation room."

"Did he freak out when he saw you?"

"I thought he was going to have a heart attack." Gates chuckled. "Once he got over the initial shock, he started yelling about how you set him up and then demanded a lawyer. Now I'm waiting for the lawyer to get here so that I can question him."

"Any idea what kind of car Lucas drives?"

"An SUV," Gates said. "And the right front of that SUV just happens to be damaged."

"Oh, really?"

"The headlight is broken. And the passenger side mirror is dangling."

"I guess he didn't tell you how that happened."

"No. But he did tell the officer who I had pick him up. According to Lucas, he left his car in the VFW Hall's side lot during the bar crawl. When he went back to get the car at the end of the night, it was damaged. He claims someone sideswiped it in the lot."

"It could be the truth. Or he's the person who tried to run us down."

"I'm getting a warrant to collect evidence from Lucas's car. Once I have it, I will send the remains of Lucas's headlight to the state's crime lab along with the broken glass that was collected in the alley last night," Gates said. "And I'll keep you posted if there are any major developments. But, until I have someone in custody, I suggest you watch your back. If Lucas is not the killer and it turns out to be one of your other classmates, I expect that person will make another attempt once they find out that I'm with the police."

"Here comes the fallout." Zoey said goodbye to Gates and then ended the call. "Back to the show."

"Wait!" Vivian waved her arms in the air. "What did the handsome detective tell you?"

"That Lucas drives an SUV. And the right front is damaged."

"I'll add that fact to my notes."

"Give it a rest, Ma," Marlon grumbled. "Zoey and I are trying to watch wrestling."

They managed to watch another two segments before Paige burst into the room. The toddler was headed for Marlon when she caught sight of Zoey. Screaming in delight, Paige dodged around her grandpa's outstretched arms and launched herself at her aunt. Her knee slammed into Zoey's bruised hip.

"Hello to you, too, Paige," Zoey said through teeth that were clenched in pain. "How's my future tag team partner?"

Paige babbled something and then scrambled over to Marlon.

"How was the bar crawl?" Zack asked as he had a seat at the other end of the couch. "And how much alcohol did you have to drink to make those people tolerable?"

"It was awful," Zoey said. "I almost died."

"Oh, I'm sure it wasn't that bad," Arielle said.

"No, I'm serious. I almost died," Zoey stood up so that she could show off the massive purple bruise that covered her hip. "Someone tried to run me and Tyler over in the alley next to the shop."

"Zoey would be dead if the handsome detective hadn't pushed her out of the way," Vivian added. "He's a hero."

"What?" Zack asked. "Are you serious?"

"No, Zack, I'm making it up," Zoey said sarcastically.

"I knew you shouldn't have gone off with him." Arielle paced in front of the TV, causing Marlon to mutter something about how he just wanted to watch his show in peace. "I knew nothing good would come out of you tagging along on that bar crawl. I just didn't think the detective would almost get you killed! What did he do?"

"He didn't do anything." Zoey readjusted her sweatpants and sat down. "I was the one asking questions—"

"Because he forced you to do his dirty work."

Zoey rolled her eyes. "Tyler didn't force me to do anything. And we all know, whether Tyler had been there or not, I probably would have wound up tagging along on the bar crawl last night. I would have asked the exact same questions. And the outcome—"

"That's enough! I'm so sick and tired of talking about this murder," Marlon shouted. "Can we please just watch wrestling?"

"No. Now that Zack and Arielle are here, we need to go over the suspect list." Vivian held up a corkboard that she'd had leaning against the side of the couch. Tacked to the board were index cards on which she had written the names of Zoey's former classmates who had been on the bar crawl. "If the four of us put our heads together, I bet we can narrow it down. We might even figure it out."

"That's it! I'm watching wrestling in the basement."

Marlon turned off the TV and then trudged out of the room. They could hear his feet pounding on the steps as he retreated downstairs.

Satisfied that she was getting her way, Vivian pushed aside Paige's coloring books and crayons so that she could lay the corkboard on top of the coffee table. "I think we all agree that the person who killed Chester is the same person who left the doll and tried to run over Zoey—"

"Not necessarily," Zoey said. "It's possible that a different person was behind each act."

"Hmmm . . . You might be right," Vivian said. She drummed her fingers against the edge of the coffee table. "But what are the odds of that?"

"What are the odds we'll figure out who the killer is?" Zack asked. "I mean, your suspect board is impressive, Nana. But we don't know everyone's motive. Or if they have alibis."

"We don't even know if they all knew that Chester was back in the area until after he was dead," Arielle said. "And, if they did, how would they have found out where he lived?"

"The killer had to figure it out somehow," Zoey said. "In their group text, Michelle told everyone that Chester worked at 3 Count. They could have followed him home from there."

"And what?" Zack asked. "Waited around for two hours until Quincy left and Chester was all alone?"

"If the person was determined to kill Chester—"

"But we don't know if the person specifically went there to kill him." Arielle had a seat on the recliner that Marlon had vacated. "My dad told me that the murder weapon was a kitchen knife. It matched the other knives in the drawer. Dad thinks the murder was spur of the moment. That the person got angry, grabbed a knife, and killed Chester."

"Okay, there are still a lot of questions that need answered. But, for now, we can eliminate some of our suspects based on what we know." Zoey grabbed a box of Paige's crayons out of the coffee table drawer. She then used an orange crayon to draw Xs on four of the index cards. "Olivia and Jeremy have a solid alibi. They were at the hospital on Monday night. Rodney and his wife were at the Philadelphia Eagles game. And Anthony couldn't have done it either. The boys' basketball team had an away game. He was probably back in town before midnight. But how would he have figured out where Chester lived?"

"Is he married?" Vivian asked. "He could have asked his wife to follow Chester."

"Anthony's wife coaches the girls' basketball team. They had a home game. She would have been at the high school all evening." Zoey used a purple crayon to draw a star on Lucas's card. "In my opinion, Lucas is the top suspect. We know he had motive . . . He didn't want his dad to know he totaled the Lamborghini."

"Do we know that for a fact?" Arielle asked.

"Lucas told me all about it last night."

"Then there is a good possibility he tried to run you down," Zack said. "If he'd already eliminated the one person who knew his secret, he'd be compelled to take you out to make sure you didn't tell anyone else."

"But why confess everything to me?" Zoey asked. "He could have just denied it and claimed Chester was making up lies to get back at him."

Zack shrugged. "That is a good point."

"Anyway . . . Back to Lucas being the top suspect. He had motive. He also argued with Chester mere hours before the murder. And he might have known where Chester lived. It's possible that Imogene told Ruth Jennings and that she told her son." Zoey drew another purple star. "Brittany also had motive—"

"Which you won't share with us," Arielle said.

"I promised her that I wouldn't."

"I think it's pretty obvious what her motive is." Vivian jumped to her feet. "Chester is Brittany's son's father."

"No way." Zack doubled over in laughter. "No freaking way."

"Where did you come up with that crazy idea?" Arielle asked Vivian.

"Deductive reasoning. Why else would Chester have a picture of Brittany's son?" Vivian bounced around in front of the Christmas tree. "I'm right. Aren't I, Zoey?"

"No," Zoey said. She hoped she sounded convincing. She'd never been a good liar. "You're not right."

"Then why did he have a picture of her son?" Vivian asked.

"Yeah, Zoey, why did he?" Zack asked. "And why is it such a big secret?"

"Can we please just move on?" Zoey asked. She was afraid that if they kept talking about it, she would reveal what she knew. "I promised to keep kayfabe."

"Fine . . ." Vivian returned to her seat. "Does Brittany have an alibi?"

"No." Zoey said. "She claims she was wrapping Christmas presents by herself."

"What about her husband?" Arielle asked. "Do you think Peter could have killed Chester to protect Brittany. She could have told him that Chester was threatening her . . ."

"I'll add him as an option. I mean, he might have known Chester was threatening Brittany about something from the past. He could have confronted Chester and things escalated," Zoey said. She added a question mark to Brittany's card and wrote Peter's name next to it. "What about Michelle and Kevin—"

"They're malicious," Arielle said. "But I don't know if they're capable of murder."

"Michelle was the one who invited us along last night. And she was the one who initiated the conversation about Chester when we were in the winery tent," Zoey pointed out. "I don't think she would have done that if she's the killer."

"Not unless she wanted to pick your brain and find out what you know," Vivian said.

"She is that devious. And so is Kevin." Zoey drew two more green question marks. "Then there's Garrett and Vanessa . . ."

"We know Garrett is capable of holding a grudge for years," Zack said. "You heard him challenge me to a rematch last night. If something happened between him and Chester back in high school, I wouldn't be surprised if he was still upset over it."

"I'll put Garrett in the maybe column," Zoey said.

Arielle tapped the corkboard. "I can't see Natasha killing anyone. I don't think she's ever done anything bad in her life."

"Unless . . ." Zoey drug out the word. "Last night everyone was talking about how they'd copied Chester's homework in high school. Or even paid him to write a few papers or put together some projects. Natasha flipped out about how wrong that was and how they should be ashamed of themselves. It made me think of that line from *Hamlet*. The one about the lady protesting too much."

"You think Natasha got some help from Chester? I guess it's not out of the realm of possibilities," Zack said. "But do you really think she'd kill him to keep that a secret?"

"Natasha still brags about being our class valedictorian. I'm pretty sure it's her crowning achievement in life," Zoey said. "If Chester was threatening to ruin her reputation . . ."

"She would want to protect it," Zack said.

"That just leaves Jocelyn," Arielle said. "And we know she's still mad at Chester over something that happened in high school."

"Actually, it was during college. They both went to Skidmore," Zoey said. "Last night, Jocelyn told me that the reason she was mad at Chester was because he humiliated her in front of her new friends."

"Did she say what he did?" Zack asked.

Zoey shook her head. "But you know how she is. She'd take something minor and turn it into a catastrophe."

"But was it a catastrophe worth killing over?" Arielle asked.

"There's something wrong with the TV in the basement," Marlon said as he returned to the living room. He grabbed the remote and turned the TV back on. "I'm watching wrestling in here. Either you can watch with me, or you can go play Sherlock Holmes somewhere else."

"Zoey Wilde . . . I don't know how you do it, but you don't look like you've aged a day since we graduated from high school."

"The trick is to take weekly baths in the blood of your enemies."

Zoey scrambled to come up with a name as she stared at the vaguely familiar looking woman who stood in front of her merchandise table. At least the woman had provided a clue to her identity by mentioning high school.

"Samantha Paulsen," Zoey said after a few seconds had passed. If she had not recently looked through her senior yearbook or Facebook stalked her former classmates, she doubted she would have been able to put a name to the face. "It's been a minute."

"You didn't recognize me right away, did you?" Samantha laughed as she patted herself on the stomach. "That's all right. Sometimes I look in the mirror and don't recognize myself. I'm no longer the twig that I was back in high school. Having three kids in just under five years will take its toll."

"I didn't know you lived in Newark," Zoey said. "When did you move here?"

"I went to college near here, and that's where I met my husband. He's a security guard at the Newark Liberty International Airport." Samantha looked over her shoulder and then motioned for a man and three children to come over. She introduced them as her family. "See, kids, I told you that I used to be friends with one of the wrestlers."

Zoey wouldn't exactly have said that she and Samantha were friends. In high school, Samantha had hovered on the periphery of the popular crowd along with the other wannabees. Zoey recalled that they'd had a few classes together—and had gotten along well enough when they'd interacted—but she and Samantha had never actually hung out.

"Wow . . ." The older of Samantha's two sons looked back and forth between his mom and Zoey. He then took a step closer to Zoey and asked, "Can I have your autograph, ma'am?"

"Of course."

Zoey grabbed three eight-by-ten photos off her merchandise table. She usually sold them for five dollars each, but she was willing to give them to Samantha's kids for free. For this being her first time wrestling for the Newark Organization of Pro Wrestling, she'd done surprisingly well with t-shirt and photo sales.

After signing autographs for the kids, Zoey posed for a picture with them. She and Samantha also got a picture together.

"Why don't you take the kids and go find our seats?" Samantha said to her husband. "Zoey and I need a few more minutes to catch up."

Once her family had walked away, Samantha said, "I heard about Chester Hartman. Have the police arrested anyone yet?"

"Not that I know of. Hopefully, they figure it out soon."

"I don't know what shocked me more when I heard about it. That Chester had been murdered. Or that he was still living in the Linville area," Samantha said. "He always seemed like the kind of guy who would leave and never look back."

"He did move away right after graduation. He was in Saratoga Springs, New York, for a couple years, and then moved to Los Angeles. He was only supposed to be in Linville for a few months. His mom has terminal cancer, and he came back to be with her."

"Oh, wow. That makes it even more tragic."

Zoey stepped away from Samantha to sign autographs for a group of teenagers.

Returning to Samantha, Zoey asked, "How often do you come back to visit?"

"Not too often anymore," Samantha said. "After my oldest was born, Mom sold her house and moved up here to be closer to us. The last time I was back in Linville was for the ten-year reunion."

"Zack, Arielle, and I skipped it. It wasn't really our thing, and we didn't want to fork over fifty bucks for a ticket."

"Yeah, it definitely wasn't worth the money," Samantha said.

As the class president, Natasha Bowman had overseen planning the reunion. She hadn't bothered to listen to anyone's suggestions and had decided to just do what she wanted. From reading over the comments on the class's Facebook page, Zoey knew that most of her classmates had wanted to rent a private room at a local restaurant for a casual happy hour. Instead, Natasha tried to recreate their prom by renting the banquet hall in the historic barn at the Willow Ridge Estate. The reunion wound up being a formal affair with expensive catered food and a cash bar.

"And it's not like you missed anything," Samantha continued. "Natasha gave out some lame awards. A few people got drunk and made fools of themselves. At least they were mildly entertaining. And the popular crowd still acted like they were better than everyone. I know I used to want to be part of that crowd, but I got over it long ago. Instead of wanting to be one of them, I just wanted to get away from them."

"I wound up going on a bar crawl with some of them last night," Zoey said. "I was at the Linville Christmas Festival and ran into a group of them. They invited me along so they could ask me about Chester. It was pure torture."

"Then why did you go along?"

Zoey leaned closer to Samantha and said, "Chester was blackmailing at least one of our former classmates. He wouldn't tell me who. I went along on the bar crawl to see if I could figure out if it was one of them."

Samantha giggled. "Ooohhh. That's exciting."

"Can you think of anything about the popular kids that might have been worth blackmailing over? You paid a lot more attention to them than I would have."

"Not that I can think of. I mean, yeah, I could probably tell you some things about them. But if I knew about it, then other people did, too. If Chester really did know something that was worthy of blackmail, I'm guessing only he knew about it."

"You're probably right," Zoey said. "If other people knew, then word would have gotten around in high school."

"So, who all went on this bar crawl?"

Zoey rattled off the names. "Lucas Jennings just moved back to Linville. And Jocelyn Hershey is back in town because the dance academy she teaches at is closed for the holidays."

"It's not closed for the holidays. It's closed for good."

"How do you know?"

"Jocelyn was my daughter's dance instructor."

Zoey's brown eyes widened in surprise. "You take your daughter into New York City for dance lessons?"

"What? No. What makes you think the dance studio is in the city?"

"Jocelyn said something about the prestigious dance academy that she teaches at in the Big Apple—"

Samantha hooted. "That's one way to manipulate the truth. But Jocelyn always was good at that. Her studio was called The Prestigious Dance Academy. And it was in the Big Apple Shopping Plaza over near the airport. The studio was stuck in between a pizza shop and a company that sells replacement windows."

"You're talking about it in the past tense . . ."

"Like I said, it's closed for good," Samantha said. "There was a big recital right before Thanksgiving. A week later, I stopped by the strip mall to grab a pizza. I noticed that the studio was empty and that there was a 'for rent' sign in the window. I tried to contact Jocelyn through her studio's Facebook page, but she never got back to me."

Before Zoey could say anything, the speaker mounted on the wall above her head screeched with feedback. The ring announcer then gave them the five-minute warning. Fans were encouraged to find their seats, and the wrestlers were told to head backstage.

"Do you have to go?" Samantha asked.

"I should," Zoey said. "But my match isn't until after intermission. And we've already got everything worked out."

"You mean it's not real?" Samantha joked. "Don't tell my kids that."

Zoey sent Vivian backstage and instructed Mortimer to keep an eye on her merchandise table. She then turned back to Samantha.

"Tell me everything about Jocelyn."

"I really shouldn't. There are things she told me in confidence—"

"Come on, Sam . . ." Zoey said. Part of her felt dirty for pushing Samantha to gossip. Zoey hated it when she found out that people were talking about her behind her back—and it happened fairly often in the pro wrestling community. There were even some bloggers who'd spread rumors of her private life all over the internet. She shouldn't be asking Samantha to spill Jocelyn's secrets—but she really wanted to know. It was possible that what Samantha knew could help solve Chester's murder. "I'm not going to go around telling anyone. I just—"

"You're curious. And would probably like to have something to hold over Jocelyn's head after the way she treated you back in high school."

"Well . . . I'm not a saint. And she was awful to me," Zoey said. "But I want to know because it might help figure out who killed Chester."

"Did Jocelyn know he was back in Linville?"

"Not until after he was already dead," Zoey said. "But Natasha knew he was back. It's possible she killed Chester to keep him from exposing Jocelyn's secrets."

"Natasha always was overly protective of Jocelyn. I don't know how close they are anymore, but—"

"So why not tell me what you know? Especially if it's something that happened while they were both at Skidmore—"

"Oh, something definitely happened between them while at Skidmore."

Zoey grasped Samantha's arm. "Tell me."

"All right. If you insist. I might not have had anything to do with Chester, but I feel bad that he was murdered." Samantha drew in a deep breath. "I'm sure you can imagine my surprise when I took my daughter to her first ballet lesson and realized Jocelyn was the instructor. And, man, did she freak out when I recognized her. She tried to deny who she was at first—"

"Seriously?"

"Then she begged me not to tell anyone. Said she didn't want anyone to know she was running some small dance studio for kids. I asked her how she wound up in Newark and she told me she'd broken her ankle and that's why she wasn't professionally dancing anymore."

"I looked online and couldn't find any evidence of her dance career," Zoey said. "But Jocelyn told me she used a stage name, so that's probably why I couldn't find her."

"Yeah, her stage name is JoJo Mackenzie—"

"JoJo? Back in high school, she would have killed us if we'd called her anything other than Jocelyn. And where did Mackenzie come from? Was she married?"

"I think it's her middle name," Samantha said. "But even if you knew her stage name, you wouldn't have found all that much about her online. She didn't exactly have a stellar career."

"Did you look online, or did she tell you?"

"At first, she told me she'd been a member of a couple traveling dance troupes. Tried to make it sound like she was the star of the show. Later, she confessed that she was just a background dancer. She was also a showgirl in Atlantic City for a few years."

"For going to Skidmore, you'd think she'd have done better for herself. From what I understand, Skidmore has a really good dance program."

"She only went to Skidmore for two years. She got kicked out towards the end of her sophomore year when one of the teachers caught her snorting cocaine in the bathroom during rehearsals."

"Cocaine?" Zoey shoved aside a pile of t-shirts and then had a seat on the corner of her merchandise table. It was possible Chester had known about Jocelyn's cocaine problem. Imogene had mentioned that Chester dropped out of Skidmore after his second year. He would have still been on campus when Jocelyn got kicked out. "Joelyn told you that?"

"Back in September, not long after my daughter started taking ballet lessons, I went out for drinks with some of my girlfriends. Jocelyn happened to be at the same bar, and she was wasted. I noticed that she was by herself, and that some creep was trying to convince her to go home with him. I couldn't just sit there and watch this guy take advantage of her. I ditched my friends and went to sit with her. While I waited for her to sober up, she started spilling secrets. One of those secrets was her cocaine addiction."

Zoey knew that cocaine use had a long and sordid history in the world of professional dance—the same way that steroid use and painkiller addiction plagued professional wrestlers. Dancers believed that the cocaine would provide them with an energy boost and help with weight loss.

"Did she go to rehab?"

"She did. Her parents got her into some private rehab center in Vermont," Samantha said. "She was drunk and ranting the night I talked to her, so not everything she said made sense. But it sounds like her parents cut her off after she got kicked out of Skidmore."

"Did she get her life turned around?"

"For a while. But her parents cutting her off and then Skidmore refusing to take her back definitely didn't help when it came to keeping herself on the straight and narrow," Samantha said. "She got a job with a traveling dance troupe, but they fired her after a few months because the other dancers couldn't stand working with her. I guess she was being a prima donna—"

"You mean she was being her usual self?"

Samantha laughed. "She got picked up by another dance troupe and was with them for a couple years. As some point she started using cocaine again, and the second troupe fired her. After another stint in rehab, she moved to Atlantic City and got a job as a showgirl."

"How long did that last?"

"Almost five years. Then she got into a car accident and broke her ankle. That pretty much killed her career as a professional dancer, so she opened the dance studio here in Newark."

"Jeez, that's awful. Addiction is no joke," Zoey said. She was friends with people who had battled drug and alcohol addictions. She knew how much they had struggled, and that some of them were never able to put their addictions behind them. "While Jocelyn was rambling, did she mention Chester Hartman?"

"That's the thing . . ." Samantha said. "He's the one who got her hooked on cocaine."

"That must be what Jocelyn was referring to . . . Last night, she told me that Chester humiliated her in front of some of her classmates. If he's the one who gave her the cocaine, and then she got caught snorting it . . ." Zoey could see how Jocelyn would find that humiliating and unforgivable. "But it's not Chester's fault. Yes, he supplied her with the cocaine. But she willingly took the drugs."

"That's what I told her. But she kept putting the blame squarely on Chester."

"If Natasha knows about all this—"

"Which I'm sure she does."

"Then maybe Natasha decided to get revenge for Jocelyn. She knew Chester was back in town sometime Monday evening . . ."

A young man dressed in a NOPW staff shirt approached Zoey and said, "They're asking for you backstage, Miss Wilde."

"Tell them I'll be right back," Zoey said. She then gave Samantha another hug. "It was good seeing you again."

"Good to see you, too," Samantha said. "I'll send you a friend request on Facebook. And I'll send you that picture of us."

"Send me the info for Jocelyn's dance studio, too," Zoey said. "I might need to make a pit stop at the Big Apple shopping center before I head home after the show."

TWENTY-ONE

Sunday December 9th, 2018

Zoey was fairly certain that she had only been asleep for an hour when her alarm went off and interrupted a dream about the prom. Since graduation, she'd been plagued with frequent dreams about high school. For some reason, her subconscious seemed fixated on that four-year period of her life. Her subconscious also seemed to regret not attending the prom since at least half of the dreams involving high school took place there.

It was rare that Zoey could recall anything beyond a few basic details of her dreams, and this time was no different. Aside from knowing that it took place at the prom, all Zoey could remember was that Chester had been there along with some of their former classmates that she'd hung out with on Friday night.

In a semi-conscious stupor, Zoey rolled over and reached for her phone. Forgetting that she had spent the past two nights at her parents' house, she wound up plunging over the side of the couch and falling to the floor. She landed on her bruised left hip. Her left knee—which she further injured during her match last night—also struck the floor.

"Ouch . . ."

Lita, who had been sprawled out along the back of the couch, leaped to the floor and stuck her nose in Zoey's face. After confirming that her owner was still alive—and, therefore, capable of feeding her—Lita ran towards the short hallway that connected the living room and the kitchen.

Since the alarm was still blaring, Zoey untangled herself from the blanket and located her phone so that she could shut it off. Then, with a lot of grunting and groaning, she pushed herself up from the floor and headed for the kitchen. She found her parents seated at the dinner table along with Justin and Hannah.

"What's up with you?" Justin asked. "You take a bad bump last night?"

"I took a bad bump on Friday night and battered my whole left side," Zoey said as she limped over to the fridge. "Last night, I made things worse by twisting my knee."

"What happened on Friday?" Justin asked. "I thought you were heading home after hitting the food trucks."

"That was the plan." Zoey poured a glass of orange juice. "But then I ran into Detective Gates. We wound up going on a bar crawl with some of my former classmates. Afterwards, one of them tried to run us over. Gates shoved me out of the way, and I landed on my left side."

"What?" Hannah asked. A piece of bacon fell from her fingers, bounced off the edge of the table, and landed on the floor. André shot out from under the table and scarfed it up. "Are you serious? Why would they do that?"

"Because I was asking about Chester." Zoey had a seat at the table. "I'm pretty sure one of them killed him, and they didn't like that I was snooping around."

"I didn't hear you and Vivi come home last night." Roxanne set a toasted chocolate chip bagel in front of Zoey. "What time did you get in?"

"Around four."

"That's better than us," Justin said. "We only got home an hour ago."

"Eli is still passed out in the car," Hannah added.

"I don't know why he's so tired. It's not like he really did anything other than stand around at ringside. And do most of the driving." Justin poured himself a second helping of cereal. "So, Zoey, how did your match go?"

"I won." Zoey grabbed a knife and the container of butter. "But I had to cheat to do it."

"Me, too," Hannah said. "Eli distracted the ref while I took Priscilla out with a chair."

"I'm not sure how I feel about you using such underhanded tactics against my former protégé," Zoey said as she and Hannah exchanged high-fives across the table. "But nice job."

"Well, I lost," Justin said.

"You can't win them all, son." Marlon patted Justin on the shoulder. He then turned to Zoey and asked, "Did Ma behave herself?"

"Does she ever?" Zoey snatched a couple pieces of bacon off the platter. "But she followed the script. That's all that matters."

After breakfast, Zoey hobbled across the backyard to the barn for the weekly open gym. With the sun not yet up, the yard was only dimly lit by the exterior lights that were mounted above the house's back patio and the barn's double doors. The grass was covered in frost, but, as of yet, there hadn't been any snowfall aside from a couple quick flurries. Unlike the rest of her family, Zoey harbored a deep hatred of snow. She was not hoping for a white Christmas.

In the barn, Zoey grabbed a lounge chair and dragged it closer to one of the heaters. She probably would have been more comfortable on the couch or one of the armchairs that were upstairs in the loft, but there was no way she was tackling a staircase this morning. And she wasn't getting in the ring either.

With ice packs tucked in next to her knee and hip, Zoey pulled her notes for the LAW show out of her bag and settled in for some last-minute planning. She was confident that she was ready to go on Saturday night, but there were still a few minor things that she had to take care of.

Zoey spent most of the morning finalizing plans for Saturday's show. Several of the wrestlers she had booked were at the open gym, and she spoke with all of them. With tentative plans in place, Zoey later joined Justin and some of the other veterans around the ring. In the ring were the rookies—including Hannah, Mortimer, and Eli. The veterans took turns calling out attacks, holds, and maneuvers as they put the rookies through drills that were designed to keep them on their toes and help them be able to react quickly in the ring.

Around noon—just when Zoey was about to throw in the towel and head back to the house for lunch—the double doors swung open, and Olivia Kreider waddled into the barn.

"It's been a long time since I've been in here," Olivia said. "I remember when that loft used to be piled high with old junk."

"It took me, Zack, and Justin an entire summer to clear it out." Limping towards the doors, Zoey asked, "What are you doing here?"

"Jeremy got called into work. I didn't want to be alone in case I go into labor, so I had Mom pick me up and bring me to her house." Olivia groaned as she followed Zoey towards the grouping of chairs set up near the heater. "I saw your car and decided to walk over. There are a couple things I need to talk to you about."

Zoey helped Olivia get settled on a plastic lawn chair. "What's up?"

"First, I want to finish our conversation from Friday night and tell you that I really am sorry I told Lucas that you liked him—"

"Why did you? I trusted you with my secret, and you betrayed me."

"The first school dance was coming up. I thought if I told Lucas that you liked him, he would ask you to dance with him."

"Did you really think that one of the most popular guys in our grade was going to ask a freak to dance?"

"You weren't a freak!" Olivia smacked her hands against the armrests. "I know Lucas and the rest of them saw you that way. But I never did. You were my best friend. You were like a sister to me. And I loved you just how you were. I thought Lucas would see how awesome you were, too. Instead—"

"Instead, he humiliated me in front of a whole bunch of our classmates."

"I never thought he would do something like that," Olivia said. "You know I went to church with him. I've known him for almost as long as I've known you. He'd never acted like that before, and if I'd had any idea that he was going to say those horrible things to you—"

"It's all right. It's in the past," Zoey said. She could see how worked up Olivia was getting and didn't want her to overdo it. Not when she was on the verge of going into labor. "Let's just move on. What is the other thing you want to talk about?"

Olivia slumped lower in the chair. "That guy you brought along on Friday night . . . Is he really your boyfriend?"

"Not exactly. Or, I guess I should say, not yet. We are going out on a date tonight." Zoey winced. She had an idea of where this conversation was going. Since yesterday afternoon, she had received multiple angry messages from some of her former classmates. "Let me guess . . . You want to tell me that everyone now knows that Tyler is a detective and they're mad at me for bringing him along on the bar crawl."

"It's more like livid," Olivia said. "And they're not mad that you brought him along. They're upset that you didn't tell us he worked for the police—"

"It's not like anyone asked—"

"Yes, we did. When we were at the brewery and you were outside talking to Lucas, Jeremy and I talked to your . . . detective. We asked him some questions about himself and his relationship with you. He gave us some vague answers about moving here for his job and meeting you at one of your wrestling shows."

"Technically, that's all true."

"But why didn't you just tell us who he was?" Olivia asked. "Or did you purposely not tell us so that you could set us up and ask us questions about Chester?"

"It wasn't exactly a set up in the sense that we planned it out ahead of time," Zoey said. She leaned forward and propped her elbows on her thighs. "We were just standing there talking outside the VFW Hall, and, suddenly, there you all were. When Michelle invited us along, it seemed like a perfect opportunity. We both know Michelle only invited me, Zack, and Arielle because she wanted to grill us about Chester—"

"Maybe she was being friendly."

"Oh, come on, this is Michelle Harris that we're talking about. When has she *ever* been friendly to me? When has anyone in that group—aside from you—been friendly to me?"

"I guess you're right. But if you thought that they weren't nice to you before . . ."

"Are you mad at me?"

Olivia sighed. "Yes and no. I mean, I can understand why you did it. If Chester really was blackmailing someone . . . Or was that a load of crap?"

Zoey shook her head. "He was overheard threatening to share someone's secrets. And he made a reference to high school during the conversation."

"But you don't know for sure that he was blackmailing anyone?"

"No. But he knew very private things about some of our classmates. Things they wouldn't want anyone else to know," Zoey said. "I think one of them killed Chester to keep him from breaking kayfabe—"

"That's a term I haven't heard in a while."

"Yeah, because you broke kayfabe."

Olivia grunted. "I thought you were done hassling me about telling Lucas that you had a crush on him."

"I am. I am." Zoey took a few seconds to regroup. "Like I was saying, I think one of our former classmates killed Chester to keep him from sharing whatever secrets he knew. And now that person is trying to kill me because they think Chester told me. Or because I'm asking questions about Chester."

"What are you talking about? Did something happen to you?"

"On Friday afternoon, Zack found a mutilated doll on the front porch of the tattoo shop. The doll had been dressed up to look like me. And there was a knife stuck in her chest." Zoey brought up a picture of the doll on her phone and showed it to Olivia. "And then, after the bar crawl, someone tried to run me and Tyler over in the alley beside the shop."

"Are you for real?" Olivia pressed a hand against her chest. "Could it have been a neighbor? Maybe they didn't see you."

"Whoever it was waited until we were halfway down the alley before they fired the engine and gunned it. If it wasn't for Tyler's cat-like reactions, we would have gotten hit." Zoey shifted forward until she was sitting on the edge of the chair. "Did anyone leave the Tavern right after me and Tyler?"

"Yes. Me, Jeremy, Garrett, and Vanessa. The four of us had met there earlier. Garrett and Vanessa left their car in the Tavern's parking lot, and Jeremy drove us down to the VFW Hall. We parked in their side lot. At the end of the night, Garrett gave us a ride back to our car."

"What kind of car does Garrett drive?" Zoey asked. "And do you think he might have tried to run us over?"

"I'm not exactly sure what it is. But it's some kind of sports car."

"Then it couldn't have been him. Whoever tried to run us down was driving an SUV or a truck." Zoey tapped her finger against her chin. "I guess you don't know when anyone else left or where they were parked."

"Brittany, Michelle, and their husbands did the same thing as us. One of them parked at the Tavern and the other drove everyone down to the VFW Hall," Olivia said. "But, when we left the Tavern, they were heading upstairs to watch the end of the Christmas karaoke competition."

"What about the others?"

Olivia shrugged. "I have no idea where anyone else parked."

"Could they have talked about where they were parking in your group chat?"

"I guess. I don't exactly pay attention to every message. But I could go back and look."

"I'd appreciate it," Zoey said. "And do you mind rereading all the messages for the past few days? See if anyone said anything suspicious about Chester. Or about me."

"You've been the main topic of discussion since yesterday afternoon. But no one mentioned trying to run you down on Friday night. Maybe I could ask—"

"No!" Zoey jumped to her feet. "Don't say anything that might provoke them to come after you. Just read over what they said, and then pass along anything that sounds suspicious to me so that I can tell the detective."

"Hey, Tyler." Zoey greeted Detective Gates at her parents' front door. Beneath his coat, he wore gray dress pants and a dark blue sweater. "Did Lucas confess to anything?"

Gates offered Zoey his arm and escorted her down the sidewalk. "Even with his lawyer there, Lucas refused to answer my questions. But he did deny telling you about the Lamborghini. He claims you made all that up to get back at him for something that happened in middle school. He also swears that he didn't try to run us down in the alley."

"Does he have an alibi?"

"He told me that he left the Tavern with Jocelyn and Natasha. They walked around the festival until it closed," Gates said. "They back him up."

"Hmmm . . . Interesting . . ." Zoey climbed into the SUV. She then waited until Gates came around the front and got in behind the wheel before she asked, "Did you arrest Lucas?"

Gates shook his head. "I don't have enough evidence to charge him with a crime yet."

"Darn . . ." Zoey smacked her thigh. "Who else did you talk to? And did they admit to anything?"

"Between yesterday and today, I talked to Lucas, Brittany, Jocelyn, Michelle, Kevin, Natasha, and Anthony. None of them admitted to killing Chester. Brittany admitted to leaving the doll at the tattoo shop—"

"Ha! I assumed it was her."

"But none of them admitted to trying to run us down," Gates said. "Have you received any other threats? Or had any near misses since Friday?"

"Nope." Zoey grabbed her seatbelt and clicked it into place. "But I learned some interesting things about Jocelyn last night."

"Can we talk about it later?" Gates asked as he fired the engine and then backed out of the driveway. "We're finally going on a date, and I'd prefer to focus on that. I don't want to ruin it by talking about the investigation."

"But this could be pertinent to your investigation."

"All right . . . You have until we get to the restaurant to fill me in. Then I don't want to discuss any of this until the end of the date."

It typically took five minutes to get from Zoey's parents' house to the town square. The heavy traffic and the stop lights worked in Zoey's favor and extended the trip to almost ten minutes. As Gates drove, Zoey summed up everything she had learned from Samantha Paulsen.

"I already knew about Jocelyn's car accident. I came across the record when I did a background check," Gates said as he pulled into a public parking lot located near the town square. "At the hospital, they tested her blood-alcohol level. It was almost twice the legal limit."

"She was drunk? Samantha didn't tell me that part."

"Maybe Jocelyn didn't tell her." Gates pulled into an empty parking spot and shut off the engine. "I'll admit this is all very interesting, Zoey. But Jocelyn swears that she didn't know Chester was back in town until Tuesday morning when Michelle brought it up at the gym. Plus, she has an alibi."

Zoey climbed out of the SUV and slammed the door shut. "What was she doing at midnight on Monday night?"

"She was with Natasha. They were up late watching movies and putting together activity booklets that were handed out to the kids who came to the library during the festival."

"That does not sound like something Jocelyn would do."

"Maybe not the Jocelyn you knew back in high school." Gates took Zoey by the hand and led her down the sidewalk towards the restaurant. She tried to conceal her limping. "And now that we're here, let's talk about something else."

Because Detective Gates had called ahead to make a reservation, they were able to skip past the line of people who were waiting for a table to open. After grabbing a couple menus, a hostess led Zoey and Gates past the bar and into the dining room.

The whitewashed Georgian-style building housing the Steakhouse on the Square had been constructed back in the late 1700s. The building had originally served as a general store. Then, in the 1800s, it was converted into a silk factory. When the silk factory went out of business, the building was transformed into a pharmacy. Zoey had vague memories of shopping there when she was a kid. After the pharmacy shut down, the building sat empty for several years before the current owners purchased the property and turned it into the steakhouse.

Aside from refurbishing the storage rooms into a commercial kitchen, the owners of the restaurant had done little renovating to the interior of the building. They had kept the original wood floors and exposed brick walls, and they'd turned the old pharmacy counter into the bar. The owners had also located some of the original machinery from the silk factory and used it to decorate the dining room.

"This is nice," Gates said as they followed the hostess across the dining room. "I just hope the food is good."

"It was the last time I ate here." Zoey slid into the empty booth and accepted the leatherbound menu that the hostess held out to her. "As long as you're a fan of steak, you really can't go wrong."

A few minutes later, one of the servers came over to take their orders. Having eaten there before, Zoey knew exactly what she wanted—a filet mignon along with mashed potatoes and seasoned green beans. Gates's order was almost identical.

"I've been meaning to show you these for a couple weeks now." Gates pulled an envelope out of his coat pocket. Inside the envelope was a short stack of photographs. "But I wasn't sure how welcome I would be at the tattoo shop—"

"You could have stopped by."

"I thought about it a few times. But since I never heard from you, I didn't know if you were still mad at me for arresting Zack. Or if Zack was still upset about it."

"Zack's over it. Arielle isn't—"

"Yeah, I picked up on that the other day," Gates said. "But what about you?"

"I understand why you arrested Zack. I got over being mad about it a while ago. I just . . . I don't know. I guess I was waiting for you to say something. Like I needed a sign that you really meant it when you asked me out and weren't just trying to get closer to me as part of your investigation—"

"That's not why—"

"I know. It doesn't help that I overthink everything. And with what Devon put me through years ago and him getting murdered . . . I was not in a good place for a while. But I'm better now."

"Good. I'm glad." Gates reached across the table and handed the pictures to Zoey. "Over Thanksgiving, I went down to Myrtle Beach to visit my parents. They moved to South Carolina after my dad retired from the Philly police. While I was there, I looked through the old photo albums and found some wrestling pictures."

Zoey glanced at the top picture and burst out laughing. In the picture, a young boy stood alongside Marlon and Leland. Zoey guessed that Gates had been about eight years old at the time. And, judging by Marlon's and Leland's mullets and their neon ring gear, she assumed the picture had been taken in either the late-eighties or early-nineties. She only had vague memories of the mullets, and she knew Marlon had gotten rid of his by the time Justin was born. Leland had held onto the mullet for another year or two before he finally moved on to a different style.

"We still pick on my dad for that unfortunate hairdo."

"Your dad's mullet wasn't quite as bad as Leland's," Gates said. "And Leland's sleazy mustache made it even worse. He looked like the stereotypical eighties' porn star."

"Please don't ever say 'Leland' and 'porn star' in the same sentence." Zoey pretended to gag. "But I don't know what Uncle Leland was thinking when he bleached his hair and got a perm. The mullet was bad enough. Why get a perm on top of it? Then again, I've known Uncle Leland my whole life, and I have yet to figure out why he does what he does."

Zoey flipped through the rest of the photos. There were a couple more pictures of Gates with Marlon and Leland, and there were also a few shots of the tag team in the ring.

"Thanks for showing me these." She tucked the pictures back into the envelope and handed it to Gates. As she did so, she looked across the dining room and saw that Lucas was headed their way. "Oh, crap."

"What's wrong?" Gates turned to look across the room. "Where did he come from?"

"Probably the bar."

"He does look pretty drunk."

Lucas stumbled towards them. All eyes were on him as he bumped into several patrons and nearly knocked an elderly woman out of her chair.

"You!" Lucas shouted as he got closer. He pointed a shaking finger in Zoey's direction. "You set me up!"

"No, I didn't."

"Yes, you did!" Lucas pounded his fist on the table. If it wasn't for Gates's quick reaction, Lucas would have knocked over Zoey's glass of wine. "You snaked your way into going on the bar crawl—"

"Michelle invited us."

"Either way, you brought this guy along." Lucas pointed at Gates. "And you didn't bother to tell us he worked for the police. You questioned us about Chester. And then you told him what we said. Now he thinks one of us is the killer."

"Did you kill Chester?" Zoey and Gates asked at the same time.

"No!"

"What about Friday night?" Zoey asked. "Did you try to run me and Tyler over."

"No. I told your boyfriend that I was with Jocelyn and Natasha after the bar crawl."

The restaurant's manager and two busboys appeared behind Lucas.

"Sir, we are going to have to ask you to leave."

"I ain't going nowhere."

"Sir, you can either leave willing or we can call the police and have them escort you out," the manager said. "But, if we have to call the police, we will press charges against you."

"Don't bother calling the police. They're already here." Lucas made a rude gesture in Gates's face. He then leaned closer to Zoey and hissed, "I'll get you for this. We all will. You messed with the wrong people—"

"What are you going to do?"

"How the hell should I know?" Lucas spun around and stumbled back across the dining room. The two busboys followed on his heels. "But if my dad finds out about his car . . ."

"My apologies," the manager said. "He was, unfortunately, overserved at the bar."

As the manager slipped away, the server swooped in with their starter salads. Lucas's outburst cast a pall over the dinner, and Zoey and Gates picked at their salads in silence. It wasn't until they were cutting into their steaks that either of them spoke.

"Did you really hate high school as much as you've said?"

"I hated every minute of it. From the first day of kindergarten up through graduation. I couldn't wait for it to be over." Zoey set down her knife and fork. "I shouldn't say that. Honestly, there were some things about school that I enjoyed. Believe it or not, but I was one of those kids who actually enjoyed learning. Except for math class. I always hated math. Especially geometry. I still can't wrap my head around it."

"Math was not my strong suit either," Gates said. "But you must have some good memories about school. Didn't you go to any dances or football games?"

"Not really."

Because her evenings and weekends had revolved around training in the ring or attending pro wrestling events, Zoey had not gone to many after-school functions or sporting events. To support Quincy, she, Zack, and Arielle sat through a handful of home football games. They also made an appearance at their ninth-grade homecoming dance, but they'd thought it was boring and swore they'd never attend another one.

"What about field trips? You must have gone on some field trips. Weren't they any fun?"

"Well . . ." Zoey popped a piece of filet mignon in her mouth and chewed. "We had some good ones and some bad ones. I remember going to the Philadelphia Zoo in first grade. And we toured the Gettysburg Battlefield in fifth grade. And then there was that year they took us to some county park and made us play all these stupid group games likes charades and Simon Says. For some reason, we also had to wade in the creek. Everyone's shoes got ruined. It was awful."

"I went on some crappy field trips, too. But I don't remember ruining any shoes," Gates said. "But what else? You must have some other good memories."

"I remember playing a lot of that *Oregon Trail* computer game," Zoey said. "And there was also that week when Zack, Arielle, and I were the most popular kids in middle school."

"How did that happen?"

"Out of the six hundred or so kids who were in the seventh and eighth grades, we were some of the only ones whose parents let them go to the Pop Disaster tour at Hershey Stadium. There were maybe two or three others at the middle school who were also going. Everyone was jealous of us. Even some of the younger teachers were jealous."

"The Pop Disaster Tour was Blink 182 and Green Day, right? Back in 2002?" Gates asked. "I saw them in Camden. Of course, I was eighteen and fresh out of high school. I didn't need my parents' permission to go."

"Lucky you. Nana took us."

Gates laughed. "Did she know what she was getting herself into?"

"Of course, she did. She was a huge fan."

Zoey and Gates spent the rest of dinner discussing concerts they'd attended.

After declining dessert—some of which sounded delicious, but the insane number of calories convinced Zoey that none of them were worth it—she and Gates left the Steakhouse on the Square and returned to his car.

"Aside from Lucas's antics, that wasn't bad for a first date, was it?" Gates asked as he held open the passenger side door for Zoey.

"No, it wasn't." Zoey slid into the passenger seat and looked up at Gates. "I don't want to get into the details, but I have been on some epically bad first dates."

"Did any of those guys get a second date?"

"Nope."

"Will I?"

"Yeah . . . You will."

Gates grinned and then shut the car door. While he made his way around to the driver's side, Zoey pushed down the spark of panic. It was just second date. It wasn't a lifetime commitment. Zoey drew in a deep breath and let it out. She knew Bernadette was right. She needed to get past Devon and her fear of intimacy so that she could move on. She was used to being single, but she didn't necessarily want to be single for the rest of her life. She wasn't against relationships—she just didn't want anything like what she'd had before. But she'd never have any relationship if she didn't allow things to move forward. So far, she liked Gates. She wanted to see where it might lead. She just had to get out of her own way and let it happen.

Gates climbed in behind the wheel and started the engine. He then turned the heaters on to full blast. "So, what is this Holiday Trail of Lights that I keep hearing, about? Is that worth driving through?"

Zoey shrugged. "I haven't been through in years. But, if you're into Christmas lights, I guess it's okay."

For almost twenty years, the Willow Ridge Estate had been hosting the Holiday Trail of Lights every December. The estate was made up of nearly three hundred acres, and it was located on the northwestern outskirts of Linville. The estate's main attraction was an historic gothic revival-style barn. The main barn—as well as other smaller barns and outbuildings—could be rented for weddings and other indoor events. Certain spots around the extensive gardens and the vineyard could also be rented for outdoor events. Over the years, Zoey had been to the estate on several occasions—just not for her prom or ten-year reunion.

"Christmas isn't exactly my favorite holiday," Gates said. "But I guess we can drive through if you don't mind. Since I keep hearing about it, I'd like to see it."

"It's fine with me," Zoey said. "They've made some changes to it and expanded the route since I last went through. It used to be only a mile. Now it's two miles. And a few years ago, they transported an old, covered bridge to the property. It sounds like you get to drive through it."

Gates took the main road out of town and then joined the line of cars who were waiting to get into the Holiday Trail of Lights. A staff member greeted them at the turnoff into the drive. He handed them a brochure and then instructed them to follow the other cars to the booths where they could pay the admission. They crept along the road and occasionally spotted brightly colored lights through the trees and bushes.

After half-an-hour of waiting, Gates pulled up to the admissions booth and handed over twenty dollars. He then pulled around a grove of trees and, suddenly, the full display of lights was spread out in front of them.

"It's pretty nice even if you don't like Christmas."

"You're supposed to tune into that radio station," Zoey said as she pointed to a sign that marked the official start of the Holiday Trail of Lights. "They play non-stop Christmas music."

"I've got something better that we can listen to."

Gates played around on his phone. A few seconds later, a familiar song blasted out of the car's speakers.

"Blink 182? I'm not sure their music really fits."

"They just mentioned Christmas Eve." Gates smiled at Zoey before he pulled forward and followed the line of cars through the first section of lights. "In my book, that makes it a Christmas song."

Zoey threw back her head and laughed. If Gates kept doing quirky things like that, Zoey believed the relationship had potential.

TWENTY-TWO

Monday December 10th, 2018

"YOU'RE ALMOST AN HOUR late."

"Blame your mother," Zoey said as she stepped through the French doors into the tattoo shop's breakroom. She held up a half-dozen shopping bags. "She's the one who dragged me to countless stores and then the mall."

"Last time I checked, she's your mother, too."

"You know I lay no claim to Mom when she's in her crazy Christmas mood. And now that she has a granddaughter to spoil, she's gotten even crazier."

"From what I've heard, she's already bought Paige a bunch of toys and clothes for Christmas." Zack said. "Do I even want to know what else she got for my daughter?"

"This is for Paige's birthday." Zoey set the shopping bags down. She then brought up a picture on her phone to show her brother. "Mom got Paige this plastic playhouse that's shaped like a castle."

"Mom really is spoiling my kid," Zack said as he swiped through the pictures that Zoey had taken of the pink monstrosity. At Roxanne's insistence, she had even crawled inside to check out the castle's interior. "And what happened to Dad fixing up our old playhouse for Paige?"

Marlon had built the custom two-story playhouse for the twins when they were three years old. He kept it well maintained until Justin outgrew it. Since then, thanks to weather and time, the playhouse had become run-down. Several boards were missing, and the slide and swings were long gone.

"That was the plan until he realized that one of the support posts is cracked. And the crossbeam for the swing set is rotten." Zoey pulled off her hat and gloves. "Now he's planning to start from scratch with a new playhouse."

"Just as long as he gets her a plastic slide," Zack said. "You remember that metal one we had? How many times did we burn ourselves on it in the summer?"

"I hated that slide." Zoey rubbed her hands along the back of her thighs as she recalled some unpleasant childhood memories. "Remember when Justin was ten or eleven, and was going through his daredevil phase?"

"I'm not sure he's gotten past that phase yet."

"Me either." Zoey tapped her finger against her chin. There was a long list of risky things that Justin had done over the years. "But I'm talking about the time he went down the slide on his rollerblades and tried to jump over the Kreiders's plastic kiddie pool."

"How could I forget? He wound up faceplanting in the pool in front of all the kids in the neighborhood. And didn't he break his nose? Or was that the time he knocked out his front tooth?"

"I don't know. All I remember is that Justin was so embarrassed he wouldn't talk to any of his friends for the rest of the summer." Zoey laughed. "He barely talked to us."

Zack shook his head. "I hope Paige doesn't do any of the stupid stuff that we used to do."

"It was Justin who did the really dumb stuff."

"True. We were pretty tame compared to him."

"Take my advice, and don't let Paige spend too much time with her Uncle Justin."

"As if her Aunt Zoey isn't capable of getting her in trouble . . ."

Zoey raised her arms above her head and used her hands to form a halo.

"I reminded Mom that Dad is going to build Paige a new playhouse and tried to talk her out of buying the castle. But she thought it was 'just so cute,' and decided that her little princess must have it." Zoey rolled her eyes. "I think Mom's hoping Paige turns out to be a girly-girl. She missed out on that with me since I was such a tomboy."

"Your idea of a doll was those stuffed Wrestling Buddies and action figures."

"Remember how we used to fight over them?"

"I remember you stealing all my Shawn Michaels stuff."

"Duh . . . He was my favorite. Plus, the female wrestlers had hardly any merchandise when we were little kids."

"At least I won't have to worry about Paige fighting over toys with any siblings. Arielle and I have officially decided that one kid is enough for us."

"Then Paige is most likely going to be the only grandchild," Zoey said. "We both know that I will never have kids—"

"You've got a boyfriend now," Zack said. "What if Gates wants kids?"

"We had one date. He's not my boyfriend. Yet."

"But what if he wants kids? If that's a dealbreaker for you, then you better—"

"He doesn't. I asked." Zoey hadn't meant to ask such a personal question on their first date, but she'd accidentally blurted it out while they were driving through the Christmas lights. She'd felt immensely relieved when Gates had said he didn't really want to have kids. It wasn't that Zoey didn't like kids; she'd just never felt any desire to have one of her own. "I also can't imagine Justin and Hannah having any kids. I know Justin doesn't want to. And Hannah has never seemed interested."

"Arielle's sister and her girlfriend probably won't have any kids either. That would hamper their nomadic lifestyle. Paige will be Jim and Nancy's only grandchild, too. I guess I just need to accept the fact that my daughter is going to be spoiled." Zack grabbed a shopping bag and tried to peek inside. "I thought you were done Christmas shopping. What's all this?"

"It's none of your business." Zoey swatted her brother away from the shopping bags before he spotted the limited-edition Macho Man Randy Savage action figure she'd bought for him at the sports memorabilia store. "And, yes, I did all my Christmas shopping online on Black Friday. Which Mom knew. But that didn't stop her from kicking me off her couch and forcing me to go shopping with her. I only got about three hours of sleep last night—"

"La la la la la." Zack clapped his hands over his ears. "I do not need to know what you and the detective got up to after your date."

"We didn't get up to anything. And, even if we did, I don't kiss and tell." Zoey ducked her head so Zack couldn't see her blush. She had kissed Gates when he'd dropped her off at her parents' house. She'd also told Vivian about it—but that was mainly because Vivian had been spying on them from the front window and demanded to know what they'd been doing sitting in Gates's car for ten minutes before Zoey finally came inside. "All I'm saying is that you shouldn't be surprised if I fall asleep at my desk."

"Wouldn't be the first time."

"You can also blame your wife for me being late. Arielle insisted that Paige get her picture taken with the mall Santa."

"Again?" Zack smacked his hands against his sides. "We already got Paige's picture taken with the mall Santa right after Thanksgiving."

"Well, Arielle wanted another picture with him," Zoey said. "When Mom, Arielle, and Paige got in line, they were told the wait to see Santa would be about twenty minutes. It wound up being a forty-minute wait because some kid peed on Santa. He had to change his pants."

"Santa had to change his pants? Or the kid?"

"Both."

"As long as it wasn't my kid who peed on Santa."

"No, Paige behaved herself. Unlike most of the other little kids who were screaming and crying. While we were waiting for Santa to come back from changing his pants, Nana wandered off. It took us another half-hour to find her."

"She wasn't at the soft pretzel stand? That's where she usually goes when she wanders off at the mall."

Zoey shook her head. "We were at the soft pretzel stand when I lost her. When we realized how long the wait for Santa was really going to be, Nana and I went to get snacks for everyone. I took pretzels over to Mom, Arielle, and Paige. Then I went back to sit at a table with Nana. But she was gone."

"Let me guess, you found her in one of the candy stores gobbling up the fudge samples."

"It was a kiosk. And they were selling gourmet popcorn."

Zack snorted. "It sounds like you had a traumatic morning."

"I just barely survived."

Zoey had never been a huge fan of shopping. And she tried to avoid the mall unless she had to try on clothes or shoes to determine the size and fit. She preferred to do most of her shopping online—especially at Christmastime when the stores were overcrowded, overheated, and over-decorated. Worst of all was the Christmas music. If she heard that stupid song about the hippopotamus one more time today, she would lose it.

Behind Zoey, the French doors swung open, and Detective Gates stepped into the breakroom.

"Hey, Tyler. What are you doing here?" Zoey walked across the room and gave him a hug. She suddenly felt shy around him and quickly put some distance between them. "And why do you look so grim?"

"I solved Chester's case," Gates said. "But Lucas Jennings is dead."

"What?" Zoey's knees wobbled. She took a couple steps backwards and then collapsed onto a chair. She just missed sitting on one of her shopping bags. "When? How? Who killed Chester? Was it Lucas? Or did the same person kill him?"

"This is between the three of us. Don't say anything to anyone until after the official announcement," Gates said. He leaned against the kitchenette cabinets and crossed his arms over his chest. "Lucas killed Chester. And then, sometime between us seeing him last night and seven o'clock this morning, Lucas hung himself."

"Oh my God!"

"That's awful." Zack put his hand on Zoey's shoulder. "But where did you see Lucas at last night?"

"At dinner. He was in the barroom at the Steakhouse. He came into the dining room to confront us. He was drunk, and the manager kicked him out." Zoey turned to Gates and asked, "Did you talk to the manager? Did he tell you what Lucas did after they kicked him out?"

"One of the busboys took Lucas's keys to prevent him from driving while drunk. The busboy then waited outside with Lucas while he ordered a car through one of the rideshare services. Once the car came to pick him up, the busboy went back inside."

"Where did the driver drop him off?" Zack asked.

"At his dad's dealership."

"Is that where he . . ."

Gates nodded. "One of the mechanics found Lucas hanging from a car lift in the service area. It looks like he tied a noose around his neck, and then tied the other end around the platform . . . or whatever you call it that the tires sit on. Lucas then hit the button to raise the lift, and that was it."

"But why did Lucas kill himself at the dealership?" Zack gathered up Zoey's shopping bags and set them on the floor. He then had a seat. "Why not do it where he was living?"

"Because he was staying with his parents," Gates said.

"Hold on." Zoey used her hands to form the universal signal for 'time out.' "How do you know that Lucas killed Chester? Did he leave a signed confession?"

Gates nodded. "There was a note in the printer. Lucas admitted to killing Chester. He then said he couldn't live with what he had done and had to kill himself."

"Did he say exactly why he killed Chester?"

"Nope." Gates ran his hands over his face. "To be honest, the note was vague. Word for word, he wrote, '*Sorry to everyone I've hurt. I killed Chester Hartman, and I can't live with it any longer. This is the only way*.' He didn't go into any details. And he didn't even sign it."

"You'd think he'd have mentioned the Lamborghini. And apologized to his dad for wrecking it. If Lucas killed Chester to prevent him from telling anyone about what really happened . . . But if that's the case, why did he tell me about it?" Zoey asked. "This makes no sense?"

"No, it doesn't." Gates pulled out a chair and joined Zoey and Zack at the table. "I just spoke with Mr. and Mrs. Jennings, and I told them about the car. I'm not sure what Mr. Jennings is more upset about . . . His son's suicide, the fact that his son killed Chester, or that it was Lucas who wrecked his precious car. When I left, Mrs. Jennings was screaming at her husband to stop talking about the damn car."

Zoey leaned forward and grabbed Gates's hand. "Did you go through Lucas's stuff? Did you find the painting?"

Gates shook his head. "I left a couple officers at the Jenningses' house to sort through Lucas's belongings. So far, they haven't found the painting or anything else."

"Probably long gone by now," Zack said. "I bet Lucas tossed the painting in the dumpster at the dealership, and it's now lost in a landfill."

"Most likely."

"I still don't understand why Lucas would take the painting of the naked woman," Zoey said. "And what about cameras? Aren't there any security cameras around the dealership that caught footage of Lucas?"

"There are cameras. In the showroom and the garage, as well as out in the lot," Gates said. "The weird thing is that Lucas turned them off not long after he got there. And not just the ones in the garage. He turned off all the cameras. All we know is what time he got there and that he was swigging from a bottle of whiskey when he turned off the cameras."

"I'm guessing he turned the cameras off because he didn't want his dad or anyone else to see the footage of him dying." Zoey stood up. "But it's over? Case solved. I don't have to worry about someone trying to run me down or take me out some other way?"

"I'd keep looking over my shoulder if I were you." Gates pulled Zoey in for another hug. "It appears that Lucas's car really was sideswiped in the VFW's side parking lot. The pieces of headlight cover that I collected from the alley do not match with what's left of the cover on Lucas's car. I also found some paint scrapings along the porch. Lucas's car is blue. The paint chips are burgundy."

"Oscar Jennings drives a burgundy truck."

"I know. I saw it parked along the street when I left the Jenningses' house." Gates looked down at Zoey with a grim expression. "The right side of the truck has a brand-new headlight cover, and the area around it is damaged. And the passenger side mirror is now held on by duct tape. I'm working on getting a warrant to collect evidence from Oscar's truck. But that could take a while. So, if you see him at the funeral on Wednesday, don't confront him about it. And don't do or say anything that could further aggravate him. That man is a loose cannon."

ZOEY SPENT THE REST OF THE afternoon in a daze. She managed to answer the phone and greet clients. But, otherwise, she could not get herself to really focus on anything. Instead of making updates on the LAW Facebook page like she'd planned to do, she paced the floor of the front office and impatiently waited for Bernadette to arrive for the abuse survivors' support group meeting. She'd tried calling Bernadette a few times since she'd stopped by on Wednesday afternoon; but their schedules had never matched up, and they'd wound up playing an aggravating game of phone tag.

With Lucas dead—and Chester's case solved—Zoey was desperate to talk to Bernadette. No matter how many times she told herself that Lucas's suicide was not her fault, she still felt partially responsible.

Bernadette finally arrived at the tattoo shop mere minutes before the six o'clock meeting was scheduled to begin. This week, she'd woven her braids together and then wrapped them around the back of her head to form a wreath. She then decorated the hair wreath with ribbons and sprigs of holly. It wasn't as ostentatious as the Christmas tree beehive from the week before, but the hairstyle was still over the top.

"Sorry I'm late. My last session ran over," Bernadette said as she joined Zoey by the kitchenette. "But I got your message. How are you?"

"Not good."

"We'll talk later. I promise." Bernadette squeezed Zoey's arm. Then, with a cup of coffee in hand, Bernadette joined the support group attendees and got the meeting underway. "I'm sure most of you have heard about the murder that took place in Linville last Monday night. I want to confirm that the victim was the young man who joined us for last week's meeting."

The people who had attended the previous meeting turned to look at Zoey as she continued to linger by the kitchenette.

"No, Zoey will not be answering any questions or talking about it this evening. If she wants to talk to us about it someday, she can do so when she's ready." Bernadette clapped her hands together. "Now, who wants to go first."

For the next two hours, Zoey watched the minutes pass by on the clock. She didn't really pay attention to what the others had to say, and she failed to contribute anything to the discussion. She felt bad about her lack of participation. Over the years, she had gotten a lot out of these meetings and talking to some of the other abuse survivors had really helped her. She wanted to be equally helpful to the others, but, tonight, her heart wasn't in it.

Just before eight o'clock, Bernadette wrapped up the meeting. The attendees folded up their chairs and set them against the wall before they headed upstairs to leave. As soon as the last person vacated the basement, Zoey turned to Bernadette.

"Finally . . ." Zoey switched off the coffee machine and dumped the old coffee down the drain. "We can talk."

"Like I said, I got your message." Bernadette opened the box of donuts to see that there was only one left. "But you didn't quite make sense. All I picked up on is that another one of your classmates passed away."

Before Zoey could respond, there was the sound of footsteps on the stairs.

"Hey, Zoey," Zack said as he walked downstairs. "There are four angry women waiting for you in the office."

"Who?"

"Who do you think?" Zack waited for a few seconds and then said, "It's Jocelyn and her minions."

Zoey groaned. "I'd ask what they want, but I think I already know."

"Just so you know, they're furious." Zack stepped aside so that Zoey could go upstairs. "I tried to calm them down, but I only managed to get them more worked up."

At the top of the stairs, Zoey turned around and looked back at her brother. "Do they know about Lucas?"

Zack nodded. "There was an announcement on the six o'clock news. The reporters didn't go into any details. They just said that Lucas killed himself. But I think these four were already planning to come by to confront you before they saw the news. Now they just have more that they want to scream at you about."

"I guess it's for the best that they came here," Zoey said. "I'd be mortified if they confronted me in public."

Zoey squared her shoulders and then walked down the hallway to the office. She found Jocelyn, Natasha, Brittany, and Michelle crowded hip to hip on the black leather couch. When Zoey walked in the room, they all leapt to their feet and began firing off a string of accusations. Zoey couldn't possibly defend herself when all four of them were screaming at her. Not when she couldn't comprehend exactly what each one was accusing her of or blaming her for.

"Everyone calm down!" Zack stuck two fingers in his mouth and whistled. The earsplitting sound caused all of them to flinch. It also had the desired effect in making everyone quiet down. "That's enough. Screaming at Zoey isn't going to get us anywhere. Especially when you're all talking at the same time."

"But—"

"No buts, Brittany," Zack said. "Now, we're going to do this one at a time—"

"You are absolutely unbelievable Zoey," Michelle said as she jumped forward. "I invited you to join us on the bar crawl out of the goodness of my heart—"

Interrupting, Zoey said, "Cut the crap, Michelle. We all know that the *only* reason you invited me along was because you wanted to find out what I knew about Chester's murder."

"You make it sound so morbid."

"But am I wrong?"

"Well . . . I won't deny that I was curious. We all were." Michelle looked to the others for confirmation. Brittany and Natasha nodded in agreement. Jocelyn studied her acrylic nails. "But you're the one who took advantage of the situation."

"You're right, I did," Zoey said. There was no point in disagreeing with Michelle's accusation. "I suspected that one of you might be the killer. So, yes, I tagged along to see what everyone had to say about Chester."

"And you brought along your boyfriend who just happens to be the detective in charge of investigating Chester's murder." Brittany crossed her arms over her chest and scowled at Zoey. "Is that guy even your boyfriend or—"

"We're dating," Zoey said. "Not that it's any of your business."

"It certainly is our business when you bring him along and then ask us questions about Chester right in front of him. None of us would have said anything had we known who your boyfriend was. Not when he thought one of us killed Chester." Natasha put her hands on her hips. "That's . . . that's . . . Well, I guess it's not illegal. But it's certainly unethical."

"Exactly," Brittany said. "I wouldn't have talked to you at all if I'd known you were dating a cop. I trusted you—"

"I didn't share your secrets with the detective."

"I know." Brittany took a step backwards. "I'm just saying . . . Your boyfriend had me brought into the police station on Saturday so that he could question me. He knew . . . Well, he knew some things that only you could have told him. Just not, you know, *that*."

"What are you two talking about?" Michelle leaned around Natasha so that she could look at Brittany. "What did you tell Zoey? What is this big secret? Do I know what it is?"

"No," Brittany said. "It's nothing."

"It definitely sounds like something. But we can talk about it later." Michelle turned back to Zoey. "It's your fault that all of us got dragged into the police department over the weekend."

"And it's your fault that Lucas hung himself." Natasha pointed at Zoey. "If you had just stayed out of—"

"I am not responsible for what Lucas did," Zoey said. "Lucas is the one who crashed his father's Lamborghini and then got Chester to help him fake the burglary to cover it up. He's the one who killed Chester—"

"Lucas killed Chester?" Brittany asked. "They didn't say that on the news."

"They wouldn't have since it's part of an active police investigation," Zoey said. She mentally scolded herself for sharing things that Gates had told her in confidence. "But Lucas killed Chester to continue keeping the secret that he crashed his dad's car. And he's the one who decided to take his own life. I am not responsible for any of that."

"But if you hadn't gotten involved—"

"Hold on," Zack said as he pushed his way into the group of women. "Natasha, how do you know Lucas hung himself? They didn't say anything about that on the news."

"I . . . uh . . . I'm friends with one of the first responders. An EMT. He told me that Lucas hung himself from a car lift."

"Seriously?" Michelle asked. "That's awful. Can you imagine hanging there while you slowly strangle to death? If it was me, I'd want it over quick."

Zoey looked over at Jocelyn. "What do you have to say?"

"Just that you're an absolute bitch."

"Takes one to know one." Zoey smirked. "Right, JoJo?"

Jocelyn's eyes widened. "What did you just call me?"

"You heard me." Zoey felt a surge of guilt, but that didn't stop her from pressing her finger to the side of her nose to close off one nostril. She then deeply inhaled through the other nostril. "JoJo."

Jocelyn made a noise that was a combination of a gasp and a hiss. She grabbed Zoey by the arm and then dragged her out of the room and across the hall to Zack's private room. Jocelyn kicked the door shut behind them.

"What do you know?" Jocelyn asked. "What did Chester tell you?"

"I already told you that Chester never mentioned you."

"Then how do you . . ." Jocelyn tapped the side of her nose.

"I had a match in Newark on Saturday night. Samantha Paulsen was there with her family. She told me that you were her daughter's ballet instructor—"

"Did she also tell you that her daughter isn't coordinated enough to do a simple *plié*?"

"Give the kid a break. She's only in kindergarten—"

Jocelyn waved her arm through the air, silencing Zoey. "I can't believe Samantha gossiped about me. That two-faced—"

"You're the one who drunkenly confessed everything to her." Zoey leaned back against the lime green tattooing chair. "What happened to the Prestigious Dance Academy? Why did you suddenly have to close up shop?"

"The landlord raised the rent, and I couldn't afford it. Not while also paying rent for a crappy one-bedroom apartment. Plus, I was getting sick of teaching snot-nosed, no-talented brats. I was supposed to be a professional dancer. I should have been the star of a ballet company. Or been on Broadway. I was not supposed to end up like this." Jocelyn leaned back against the wall and lowered her voice. "What all did Samantha tell you about me?"

Zoey recounted what Samantha had told her—starting with Jocelyn getting kicked out of Skidmore University for cocaine use up through closing the dance studio in Newark.

"You have no idea how shocked I was to hear all that about you. She didn't talk about you too often, but Natasha always made it sound like you had this great career."

"She would . . . Natasha is the only person who knew what all has happened to me since we graduated from high school. Well, aside from my parents and some other family members. Natasha never could get past high school, and she probably wanted to make it seem like I was still . . . Like my life had turned out the way I'd planned." Jocelyn walked over to the desk and plopped into the chair. "I guess I could try to deny everything.

But what's the point? You could search 'JoJo Mackenzie' online and find references to my time with the traveling dance troupes and as a showgirl in Atlantic City. And, if you know where to look, you can find the public record of my accident."

"Was it Chester who got you hooked on cocaine?"

Jocelyn shook her head. "It was another dancer who gave it to me originally. She told me that it would help me focus and up my energy level. Chester just kept supplying me with it. I don't know where he got it, but he always had it ready when I needed it. That son of a bitch ruined my life."

"You ruined your own life."

"But he supplied me—"

"Did he force you to use the cocaine."

Jocelyn huffed. "No. But if he hadn't—"

"Stop blaming Chester for your mistakes."

"This conversation stays between us." Jocelyn jumped to her feet and stomped over to the door. "And I suggest you stay out of my way. If I find out you're spreading rumors about me—"

"What are you going to do?" Zoey pushed away from the tattooing chair. "Are you going to dump more food on me? Or spread some more rumors?"

"I could end you."

"Go ahead and try. And I'll take you down with me."

Jocelyn glared at Zoey for a few seconds. She then spun around, yanked open the door, and stalked out into the hallway. She barked at the others to follow her before heading out through the front door. Natasha and Michelle raced after her.

"Zoey . . ." Brittany lingered near the door. "I just wanted to apologize. I left the doll on the front porch."

"I know," Zoey said. "Detective Gates told me."

"I'm sorry." Brittany glanced over to where Zack and Bernadette were standing at the far end of the hallway. "I was trying to scare you into keeping your mouth shut about . . . You know. I was so afraid you'd tell someone."

"I promised I wouldn't."

"I know." Brittany wrung her hands. "I told your boyfriend about what I did. He suggested I talk to you about it and that it would be up to you if you wanted to press charges."

Zoey waved her hand in the air. "Just don't do something like that ever again."

"I won't." Brittany yanked open the front door and stepped out onto the porch. "I really am sorry."

Zoey locked up behind Brittany. She then turned to face Bernadette.

"Can we talk now?"

Bernadette nodded. "Tomorrow, I'm checking my schedule and booking some sessions for you. It sounds like you need it."

"I'm long overdue," Zoey said. "And I've got a lot to talk about."

TWENTY-THREE

Wednesday December 12th, 2018

"YOU OKAY, ZOEY?" ZACK asked. Using the rearview mirror, he made eye contact with her in the backseat. "You've been unusually quiet."

"It's been a long week," Zoey muttered as she broke the eye contact and turned to gaze out the window. She was still staying at her parents' house, and she hadn't gotten a good night's sleep in over a week. Tonight, she planned to return to her apartment. "And you know I'm not a fan of funerals."

"At least there isn't going to be a body, right?" Arielle shifted around in the passenger seat so that she could reach over the console and pat Zoey on the knee. "Didn't Mort say that Chester was already cremated?"

Zoey nodded. Mortimer had explained that Imogene didn't want to put her son on display and opted to have him cremated prior to the memorial service. Any ghouls who came to the service hoping to see Chester's body would be disappointed when they found his urn instead.

"It's not the body that bothers me," Zoey said. "Though, I'm not sure I would want to see Chester again after finding him . . . I still can't get the image of all that blood out of my head—"

"I know I wouldn't be able to." Arielle shuddered. "I don't know how you kept it together for so long after finding him. I probably would have passed out."

"Well, I do have some previous experience at finding dead bodies," Zoey said sarcastically. "At least I didn't find Lucas's body—"

"Do we have to go to his funeral?" Zack asked.

"I feel like we should," Zoey said. "For closure."

"You're not blaming yourself for Lucas killing himself, are you?" Arielle asked. "Because what he did is not your fault."

"I know it's not." Zoey stared blankly at the homes and businesses they passed as they drove down Market Street. "But maybe if I hadn't confronted him on Friday night, and then passed along what he told me about the Lamborghini to Tyler . . . Now we'll never know what really happened the night he killed Chester. And Lucas won't be punished—"

"Death seems like the ultimate punishment to me," Zack said. "And, look at it this way, we won't have to testify at the trial—"

Arielle smacked Zack on the arm.

A few seconds later, Zack turned off Market Street and pulled into the Cozma Funeral Home's parking lot. The funeral home was in an old Federal-style house that had been built in the early 1800s. A porch ran along the front of the building, and there was a second-story balcony above it. The front of the funeral home had been tastefully decorated for the holidays with wreaths hanging over the front door and all the windows.

Having heard the history from Mortimer, Zoey knew that the building had served as a residence for almost a hundred-and-fifty years. After sitting abandoned for another fifty years, Mortimer's grandfather, Serghei, purchased the house in the 1980s, and refurbished it into the second Cozma Funeral Home. The original Cozma Funeral Home was in Quarryville, and a third one was later opened in Columbia. Mortimer's parents ran the Linville funeral home, and he worked there while also attending mortuary school.

"There's Oscar's truck," Zoey said as she climbed out of the backseat of Zack's Jeep. She walked over to where the truck was parked. "And there's the damage from when he tried to run over me and Tyler."

Around the headlight, the burgundy paint was scratched, and the fender was dented. Zoey noticed that the sideview mirror had been duct taped into place on the passenger side. The mirror was also shattered. A brand-new headlight stuck out amidst the damage.

Arielle walked over to join her. "Has Gates proven that it was Oscar who tried to run you down?"

"Not yet." Zoey had talked to Gates about an hour earlier. He'd gotten a warrant to inspect the truck and was planning to serve it after the memorial service. "He's working on it."

"What are you freaks doin' here?"

Zoey spun around and watched Oscar charge out of the funeral home's side door. He headed across the parking lot towards them. Oscar was casually dressed in worn jeans and had on a plaid shirt under his winter coat. An unlit cigarette dangled from his lips.

"Remember what your boyfriend said," Zack said as he stepped in front of Zoey. "Don't confront Oscar about Friday night."

"Screw that." Zoey stomped towards Oscar. "What happened to your truck?"

Oscar glanced over at his truck as he lit the cigarette. "Hazard of parkin' on the street."

"Oh really?" Zoey crossed her arms over her chest and glared at Oscar. "You sure you didn't run into anything? Like the side porch of the tattoo shop?"

Oscar inhaled sharply and began to cough. A middle-aged blonde whose skirt was too short to be appropriate for a funeral teetered across the parking lot on her high-heeled, knee-high boots. She whacked Oscar on the back until he stopped coughing.

"You've got a lot of nerve showin' up here," Oscar said after recovering from his coughing fit. "Especially after I told you to stay away from me and Imogene."

"We're here to pay our respects to your son," Zack said. "We clearly cared about him more than you did."

"What an awful thing to say to a grieving father," the woman said.

Zack snorted. "If you think Oscar is grieving, I've got some oceanfront property out in Kansas to sell you."

The woman bared her teeth and hissed.

Arielle cleared her throat, drawing everyone's attention to her. "Where is your wife?"

Oscar gestured over his shoulder towards the funeral home. "She's in there."

"And you're not with her?" Zoey asked. "You might not have cared for Chester, but I know Imogene is devastated. Shouldn't you be in there supporting her?"

"She don't need me. She's got her friends from the cancer support group to comfort her." Oscar dropped the cigarette butt and then ground it out beneath his heel. "And even if she didn't have them, she wouldn't want me in there. She ain't talkin' to me no more."

"At least someone is offering you a shoulder to cry on." Zoey eyed up the mystery woman. "Are you Wanda?"

The woman shook her head. "I'm Margaret."

"Another girlfriend?" Zoey asked.

"She's my sister."

"What's this about a girlfriend?" Margaret spun to face Oscar. "Have you been cheatin' on Imogene?"

"Ain't like she's been fulfillin' her wifely duties the past few years." Oscar shrugged. "And she ain't gonna be around much longer. Don't hurt to line up a replacement."

"You are disgusting." Margaret slapped Oscar across the face and sent him stumbling backwards. "If you invited this woman—"

"Relax, would ya." Oscar rubbed his hand against his cheek. "I ain't dumb enough to invite her to my son's funeral."

"She better not show her face at Imogene's funeral either." Margaret gave Oscar another shove and then headed across the parking lot. Over her shoulder, she yelled, "Imogene should have left you a long time ago. She's a good woman. And you never deserved her."

"Your sister is right," Zoey said as she pushed past Oscar and followed Margaret. "You are absolutely repulsive."

Zoey entered the funeral home through the side door and stepped into the foyer. When he renovated the old house, Serghei tore down the dilapidated, detached kitchen and then added an addition to accommodate the preparation room, storage room, and a garage for the hearse. The foyer connected the addition to the original building.

"Hey, Zoey," Mortimer said as he stepped out from behind a coat rack.

"Hi, Mort." Zoey shrugged out of her coat. She'd forsaken her usual animal print clothing and dressed subduedly in a dark purple sweater and a long black skirt. "Are you on coat check duty?"

"Kinda." Mortimer took Zoey's coat and hung it on the rack. "Mainly, I'm hanging out here to make sure there aren't any funeral crashers. We get them sometimes. Especially when the decedent died from . . . unnatural causes. Mrs. Hartman told me to only let in people who can prove they knew her son."

"Have you had to turn anyone away?" Zack asked as he hung up his coat.

"A reporter from the local news station tried to sneak in. But that's it so far. We didn't exactly advertise the funeral."

"The parking lot looks pretty full," Arielle said. "Are there a lot of people here?"

"It's mainly people from Mrs. Hartman's cancer group," Mortimer said. "Santino and Quincy beat you guys here. The detective and Chief Coleman were also here, but the detective got a phone call and they went running outside. They took off just before you got here."

"I wonder what's going on?" Zoey asked.

Mortimer shrugged. "I heard the detective say something about an autopsy."

"Must be Lucas's autopsy," Zoey said. "Tyler told me that was scheduled for this morning."

"But that's it?" Zack asked. "Those are the only people who showed up?"

"There are two older ladies who claimed they used to teach art at the high school. Quincy vouched for them," Mortimer said. "And I think Willie Nelson's brother is here."

Zoey's right eyebrow crept up. "What?"

"The guy has long gray hair that he's wearing in two braids." Mortimer pointed to the sides of his head. "You know, like Willie Nelson. Except I don't think he's as old as Willie. But he might be as high. He sure smelled like weed when he walked by."

"You didn't ask who he was?" Arielle asked.

"Mrs. Hartman said he was okay."

"It's gotta be Thor," Zack said. "He and Farrah flew in late last night."

Behind them, the door swung open, and Oscar tramped inside. He tossed his coat to Mortimer, shot all of them a dirty look, and then headed up the short set of steps into the original part of the building. The thick carpet muffled the sound of his plodding footsteps.

"You guys should probably head in," Mortimer said. "The memorial service is scheduled to begin in about fifteen minutes."

"Are they in the small chapel?" Zoey asked as she followed Zack and Arielle up the steps. "Or the big one?"

"Small one," Mortimer called after them.

Zoey had been to several services at the Cozma Funeral Home, and she knew her way around the interior. The original house had contained four rooms downstairs—two parlors, a library, and a dining room. Serghei tore out the wall between the two parlors to create a large chapel. The library became a smaller chapel, and the dining room was broken down into bathrooms and a private room for family members to retreat to if they needed some seclusion. The upstairs bedrooms now served as offices and display rooms for the caskets and urns. Zoey had only been upstairs once when she'd come along with Vivian and Marlon to pick out Kazimir's urn and make the final decisions for his funeral.

After signing the guest book, they entered the chapel. Rows of chairs faced a table that had been set up at the front of the room. An urn sat at the center of the table, and it was surrounded by framed photos of Chester. Zoey noticed that there were numerous pictures of Chester from his childhood, but only a couple of him as an adult.

Imogene Hartman sat by herself in the center of the front row. Oscar hovered nearby, but she blatantly ignored him.

Zoey sat down next to Imogene. "How are you holding up?"

"Not too well." Imogene grasped one of Zoey's hands. "It's my fault Chester is dead."

"No, it's not," Zack said.

"But if I hadn't told Ruth Jennings that Chester was back in town, Lucas never would have known. The only reason I told her was because she kept bragging about how her son was coming home." Imogene blew her nose. "I still can't believe Lucas did it. He and Chester were best friends. They were like brothers."

"That was a long time ago," Zoey said.

"And all because of that stupid car . . ."

Zoey, Zack, and Arielle talked to Imogene for a few more minutes. Arielle then went to talk to Santino, while Zoey and Zack joined Thor and Farrah Gunderson. They were both dressed in black, but Zoey noticed that Thor's socks were tie-dyed, and Farrah wore an oversized peace sign necklace.

Even though it didn't really matter anymore, Zoey asked, "Hey, Thor, did you ever find a picture of the Foxy Lady tattoo?"

"I did. I also found a picture of the Foxy Lady herself. The fuzz finally came and looked through Chester's apartment yesterday morning. Don't know what they were looking for or why, but they told me and Farrah we couldn't go into the apartment until they searched it. Once they were done, I went in and looked around. I found a picture of the Foxy Lady next to his bed." Thor reached into his jacket pocket and pulled out a picture. "Don't know if it'll be much help."

"Oh my God . . ." Zoey snatched the picture out of Thor's hand and stared at the familiar face. "It's Jocelyn Hershey."

"You know her?" Farrah asked.

"We went to high school with her," Zack said. "They both went to Skidmore."

"You're sure this is the woman from the tattoo?" Zoey asked. "And all the paintings?"

"Yep. She's Chester's muse." Thor handed Zoey his phone. "Check it out."

Zoey looked at the picture that Thor had brought up on his phone. It was a grayscale tattoo of Jocelyn's face. Thor then scrolled through picture after picture that he'd taken of Chester's artwork. Each picture featured either a painting or a sketch of Jocelyn.

"Can you text these to me?" Zoey asked Thor.

"Sure thing."

"I know what you're planning to do," Zack hissed in Zoey's ear. "You need to stay out of it. It's none of your business."

"But she needs to know."

"Zack's right. This really is none of my business."

With that thought in mind, Zoey marched up the sidewalk to Natasha Bowman's front door and rang the bell.

Natasha's single-story rancher was just a five-minute walk from the tattoo shop. The only reason Zoey knew where Natasha lived was because she and Arielle had been invited to her housewarming party several years earlier. Zoey wanted to skip it, but Arielle insisted they make an appearance.

Zoey was about to ring the bell a second time when the door swung open.

"What do you want?"

Jocelyn pushed open the screen door and stepped out onto the porch. Zoey noticed that her pupils were dilated and that there was a dusting of white powder under her nose and on the front of her black sweatshirt.

"Are you high?"

"What I am is none of your business." Jocelyn slipped on a pair of sunglasses before trying to light a cigarette. Her hands trembled, and she had trouble getting the lighter to spark.

"I'm serious, Jocelyn. Are you alright?"

"No, I am not all right!" Giving up on lighting the cigarette, Jocelyn hurled the lighter at Zoey. It bounced off her coat and fell to the ground. "And I'm so sick of pretending that I am!"

"Do you need to talk to someone about it?"

Jocelyn snorted. "Give me a break. You are the last person I would ever talk to. Well, maybe not the last, but—"

"I didn't mean me. My friend Bernadette is a therapist—"

"I don't need some shrink trying to get in my head. I had enough of that crap while I was in rehab."

"Yeah, but that was years ago."

"Oh my God! Would you just drop it? You're starting to sound like Natasha. Nagging me all the damn time." Jocelyn bent down and picked up the lighter. "Now would you just tell me whatever it is you came here to say?"

Zoey drew in a deep breath. "You were his muse."

"What?"

"Chester. You were his muse. He loved you. And I think you were in love with him."

"Ha! You have no idea what you're talking about."

Jocelyn yanked open the screen door and stepped inside. She tried to slam the front door shut, but Zoey muscled it open and forced her way into the house. Zoey immediately noticed that there was drug paraphernalia and empty bottles of vodka on the coffee table.

Ignoring the mess, Zoey held up her phone so that Jocelyn could see the pictures that Thor had sent to her. She scrolled through them as she spoke. "Chester had paintings and drawings of you covering every wall of his apartment. He even had a portrait of you tattooed on his chest. Look at it!"

"I don't need to look." Jocelyn swatted the phone away. "I know what it looks like."

"When did you see it? He got it done when he was living in California. Unless you stayed in touch after you both left Skidmore—"

"You mean after he abandoned me?" Jocelyn threw herself down on the couch. "He got me addicted to cocaine, ruined my life, and then abandoned me while I was trapped in rehab. I spent eight months isolated in that stupid rehab center. Other than a half hour phone call with my parents every Sunday afternoon, I had no contact with the outside world. They wouldn't even let us watch TV or listen to the radio. It was awful. I couldn't wait to escape. And, when I finally did, I rushed back to Skidmore and tried to pick up the pieces of my life. But the dance department refused to take me back, and Chester was long gone."

"What really happened between you two?" Zoey walked over to the couch and handed Jocelyn the picture of her and Chester that Thor had given to her. "Because you look pretty chummy in this picture."

Jocelyn stared at the picture for a few seconds as tears streamed down her face. She then tore the picture in half and let it flutter to the floor.

"You're right. We were in love. He was the only person I could really be myself around. He didn't put me on a pedestal and hold me to some impossible standard like my parents did. Or Natasha. Or Lucas. I could just be me. It was liberating. But the cocaine ruined everything. I went to rehab, and he disappeared. I looked for him. You have no idea how hard I tried. But I couldn't find him." Jocelyn used her sweatshirt sleeve to swipe away the tears running down her face. "Last Monday was the first time I'd seen him in almost ten years."

"You saw Chester on Monday?" Zoey sat down on the edge of the coffee table. "Then you *did* see Michelle's text—"

"Yes, I saw the damn text! I saw the text that Chester was back in Linville, and I rushed over to your brother's shop to see him."

"Is that when he showed you the tattoo?"

"No, I didn't talk to him at the shop. I couldn't risk you or Zack seeing me. I followed Chester back to that little shipping container house. But one of the other tattoo artists followed him home, too. I had to wait for almost two hours until that guy left before I could see Chester."

"So you talked to Chester?" Zoey asked. She could feel her anxiety mounting. Zack was right. She should not have come here. Ignoring her gut feeling that she should get away from Jocelyn, she asked. "What else happened?"

"What do you think happened?" Jocelyn jumped up from the couch. She paced back and forth across the living room, taking jerky, agitated steps. "I spent the past ten years having imaginary conversations with Chester. Going over and over in my mind what I would say if I ever saw him again. At first, not a day went by where I didn't think about him. Some days I hated him. Some days I loved him. Sometimes I blamed him for what happened, and other times I blamed myself. I drove myself crazy wondering what if . . . What if I hadn't started snorting cocaine? What if Chester hadn't disappeared? What would have happened? Where would I be? Where would he be? Would we still be together? As the years passed, I didn't think about him as much. First, I would go a couple days without thinking about him. Then it would be a couple weeks. A couple months. But his ghost was always lurking in the background. Ready to pop back up and haunt me. I'd have a dream about him. Or hear a song that reminded me of him. It was like . . . like . . ."

"Like ripping off a bandage expecting to find a healed wound, but, instead, finding that the wound is still festering."

"Exactly!" Jocelyn clapped her hands. "You know what it's like, right? Natasha told me about your ex-boyfriend who beat you up. You must have gone through something similar over the years. And then when he popped back up—"

"But I didn't kill my ex."

"I didn't mean to kill Chester!" Jocelyn screamed. Her face was bright red, and her eyes rolled wildly. "I didn't mean to do it."

Zoey stood up. "You don't stab someone forty-two times and not mean it."

"I . . . I . . . When he opened the door . . . All I could ask him was why? Why did he leave me? He told me it was for the best. That I was better off without him. He made it sound like he did me a favor. Or leaving me was some kind of noble sacrifice on his part." Jocelyn reached behind the couch and pulled out a painting. The canvas was four-foot high by three-foot wide, and the painting of the nude woman was just how Quincy had described it. It was realistic, and it looked exactly like a younger Jocelyn.

It would have been a beautiful piece of artwork, but smears of dried blood were streaked across the canvas. "Then I saw this hanging on the wall. He was painting this right before my parents shipped me off to rehab. I never saw the completed painting. Seeing it that night . . . And the tattoo . . ."

"He loved you."

"He *destroyed* me." Jocelyn tossed the painting onto the floor. "I couldn't stomach listening to anything else he had to say. I tried to leave, but he reached out to stop me. I pushed him and he fell. He hit his head on the toilet, and it . . . I guess it knocked him out. After that . . . I don't . . . It's like I was outside of myself . . . I remember grabbing the knife off the counter. And I know I stabbed him. Over and over. I couldn't stop. But I wasn't stabbing him to kill him. I just wanted to obliterate the tattoo. I didn't mean to kill him. You have to believe me, Zoey."

Zoey held up her hands. "I do believe you. But I don't understand how you acted so normally at the gym on Tuesday—"

"Because it still didn't seem real. I thought it was a nightmare. It's not like I hadn't dreamed of killing him before. That's what is felt like. A dream." Jocelyn resumed pacing. "When I saw the news that he was dead . . . That's when it finally hit me that I *killed* him."

Changing the subject, Zoey asked, "What about Lucas?"

"Lucas made the perfect scapegoat."

Zoey spun around to see Natasha standing in the doorway.

"You shouldn't have stuck your nose where it didn't belong, Zoey. And you definitely shouldn't have come here. Now we're going to have to get rid of you, too." Natasha stepped inside and slammed the door shut. She locked the door and flipped the deadbolt into place. With the door secure, she reached into her purse and pulled out a gun. "Damn it, Jocelyn. How many more of your messes am I going to have to clean up?"

The bubble of anxiety that had slowly been building inside her burst. Trying to remain calm, Zoey asked, "Do you have a permit for that?"

"Yes. You know, us single women have to protect ourselves." Natasha waved the gun around. "I really don't want to shoot you, Zoey. Especially not in here. My God, the mess it will make . . . But, like I said, we need to get rid of you since . . . Well, you know too much . . ."

Determined to keep Natasha talking, Zoey asked, "When did you realize that Jocelyn killed Chester? Was it that night?"

"It was after his murder was announced on the news." Natasha set down her purse and took off her coat. She continued to point the gun at Zoey. "Somehow, I slept through Jocelyn coming home on Monday night. She was acting normal in the morning, and she'd hidden the painting. It wasn't until they revealed Chester's identity on the news that—"

"That I told her what I'd done," Jocelyn said. "Or what I thought I'd done. It still didn't seem real."

Zoey looked back and forth between Jocelyn and Natasha. "And you . . . What? Decided to help her cover it up?"

"It's what best friends do," Natasha said. "If it was Arielle—"

"Arielle would never kill anyone," Zoey said. "Well, maybe in self-defense—"

"Look, Zoey, I did what I had to do. And, at first, I didn't have to really do anything other than destroy her bloody clothes. It wasn't until you started asking questions and then brought your boyfriend around that I had to act. By the time we were brought into the police department, we knew that your boyfriend was the detective in charge of investigating the murder. We had plenty of time to make up the story that Jocelyn and I were up late putting together activity packets for the library."

"Which is a totally lame alibi," Jocelyn said. She had a bottle of vodka in hand and was drinking from it. "Anyone who knows me—"

"Oh, would you shut up!" Natasha screamed at Jocelyn. Jocelyn flicked Natasha off and then turned her attention to the bottle. "I knew it was a lame alibi. I was also worried that Jocelyn wouldn't be able to keep her mouth shut. Between the drugs and the drinking—"

"She needs serious help," Zoey said.

"I am aware that she needs help. And I'm doing my best to help her."

"Hello . . ." Jocelyn waved around the bottle. "I'm right here. Could you two stop talking about me as if I weren't standing right next to you?"

Zoey shot Jocelyn a sideways look before turning back to Natasha. "Your way of helping Jocelyn was by covering up Chester's murder and then helping her kill Lucas? When did you decide to frame him?"

"Spur of the moment," Natasha said. "Lucas was—"

"Blowing up my phone since Monday night. He was begging me to give him another chance. As if." Jocelyn snickered. "On Sunday, he called me from his dad's dealership. He asked me to meet him there for old time's sake. Back in high school, that's where we used to hook up. I wasn't going to—"

"But that's when I decided we should get rid of Lucas. We could make it look like he killed himself and leave a confession that he killed Chester."

"When we were at Skidmore, Chester told me all about the Lamborghini," Jocelyn said. "We knew Lucas had motive."

"We also knew he came by your brother's shop on Monday," Natasha said as she moved closer to Zoey. "I told Jocelyn to tell Lucas she would meet him at the dealership. I also had her tell him to turn off all the cameras."

"The dummy was absolutely shitfaced by the time we got there." Jocelyn set down the empty vodka bottle. She then laid down on the couch and flung her arm over her eyes. "He barely put up a fight when we strangled him with an extension cord."

Zoey pointed at Natasha. "And then you put a noose around his neck and strung him up on the car lift."

"It was the perfect plan," Natasha said. "And we would have gotten away—"

"No, you wouldn't have." Zoey remembered what Mortimer had told her about Detective Gates and Chief Coleman racing out of the funeral home after receiving a call about Lucas's autopsy. Whatever that call had been about must have been important, and Zoey suspected the coroner told them that he'd found proof that Lucas's death was a homicide disguised as a suicide. "Just so you know, the coroner determined that Lucas was strangled before he was hung. Detective Gates knows someone murdered Lucas and staged it to look like a suicide."

"What?" Natasha lowered the gun so that it was pointed at Zoey's midsection instead of her head. "No way. You're lying. You're just trying to save yourself."

Zoey shook her head. "You messed up, Natasha."

Jocelyn giggled. "See, Natasha . . . You're not as smart as you think you are."

"This is all your fault!" Natasha whipped to the side and pointed the gun at Jocelyn. "I've been cleaning up your messes and doing your bidding since kindergarten. And what kind of thanks do I get? Nothing! You all but forgot about me once you left for college. The only time I hear from you is when you need something. And when you show up at my door, begging me for a place to stay because you have nowhere to go . . . What do I do? I open my home to you. And you turn around and kill Chester and then drag me into helping you kill Lucas to cover it up."

"Uh, pretty sure killing Lucas was your idea."

Natasha screamed in rage and then lunged at Jocelyn. With Natasha's attention focused elsewhere—and the gun pointed away from her—Zoey was quick to act. She grabbed one of the empty vodka bottles and swung it at Natasha. The bottle shattered as it connected with the back of Natasha's head.

With a grunt, Natasha collapsed onto the couch, pinning Jocelyn beneath her.

Zoey didn't waste any time. She raced towards the door, fumbled with the locks, and then darted outside just as a black SUV pulled up to the curb in front of the house. Detective Gates was behind the wheel. Three police cars pulled up behind him.

"Zoey!" Gates yelled as he jumped out of the car. "Are you all right?"

"I'm fine." Zoey yelled as she darted around the front of the SUV and dove into Gates's arms. "But they've got a gun."

Gates shouted at the police officers to be careful approaching the house.

"Jocelyn killed Chester. And Natasha helped her kill Lucas."

"I know. The coroner found markings around Lucas's neck that did not match the rope that was used to hang him. It was obvious Lucas was strangled first and then hung. None of us noticed it at the crime scene since Lucas was wearing a hooded sweatshirt that hid his neck." Gates looked down at Zoey and said, "As for you . . . Next time, would you please listen to your brother and stop confronting my suspects?"

"I'm just hoping there is no next time."

TWENTY-FOUR

Saturday December 15th, 2018

Zoey peered through a crack in the faded red, faux velvet curtains that hung across the stage at one end of the Linville VFW Hall's banquet room. Set up in the middle of the room was the wrestling ring in which the second to last match of the night was taking place.

She wouldn't admit it out loud—mainly because she didn't want anyone to think that running her own show was too much for her—but Zoey couldn't wait for the night to be over. She'd known it would be stressful to take over the Linville Association of Wrestling, but she hadn't anticipated how taxing it would be on her both mentally and physically. It didn't help that she was still frazzled over everything that had happened since she'd found Chester's body over a week-and-a-half earlier. She'd spent most of Thursday at the police department. She'd had to provide her statement and talk to the district attorney. Then, on Friday, she'd had a therapy session with Bernadette. Talking things through helped, but Zoey knew it would be a while before she was able to put everything behind her.

Focusing on putting on the best show possible was one way to keep her mind off the unpleasant thoughts.

There had been a few small hiccups during the night, but nothing major had gone wrong, at least not yet. All the talent showed up. The matches went as planned. Well, at least, mostly as planned. Zoey had never been part of a show where absolutely everything went perfectly. Thankfully there hadn't been any injuries aside from the usual bumps and bruises. The fans also seemed to be having a good time—and that was the most important thing. If the fans didn't enjoy the show, they might not come back next month.

"I still can't believe I let you talk me into this."

"The match?" Zoey asked as she turned to face Zack. "Or the matching pants?"

"Both." Zack said as he looked down at the pair of purple and black zebra print leggings he wore. He also wore a "Wilde Ones . . . One More Time" t-shirts that Zoey'd had made as soon as he agreed to the match. She'd also had shirts made for their family and friends. "But mainly the match. After my shoulder surgery . . . When I said I was done with wrestling, I meant it. I never planned to get back in the ring again. Not for real."

"It's one match," Zoey said. "Your retirement match."

"I'm not exactly pleased about the pants either," Justin said as he flung his arms around his older sibling's shoulders. With their long brown hair, scruffy beards, and matching outfits, Zack and Justin could have been mistaken for twins. "But you need this, Zack. We need this."

"And we're honored to be part of it," Mama said as she, Bubba, and Tiny joined them. Mama wore her coat made from mismatched animal pelts over a ratty white tank top and holey jeans. Bubba and Tiny were dressed in camouflage pants and flannel shirts. "After all those matches we've had over the years . . . It's only right that your career ends with us."

"Just take it easy on me," Zack said. "I'm a little rusty. And I can't afford any injuries."

Out in the VFW Hall, the roughly four hundred fans erupted in cheers and then the bell rang three times to signify the end of the match. The ring announcer proclaimed that there was a new LAW Heavyweight Champion. A few seconds later, the former champion came through the curtains. He was soon followed by the referee and then an elated Sasquatch.

"Main event is all yours," Sasquatch said to the six of them as he squeezed past. The title belt was flung over his hairy shoulder. Zoey'd originally had the Heavyweight title match set for the main event. Sasquatch and his opponent had graciously insisted that Zack's retirement match be the final match of the night. The Wildes were the hometown heroes. They deserved to go on last. "Get out there and kill it."

Out in the VFW Hall, banjo music blasted out of the speakers. Mama and her boys took that as their cue and pushed their way through the curtains and out onto the stage.

"The following six-person intergender tag team match is scheduled for one fall," the ring announcer stated. "Making their way to the ring . . . They hail from the backwoods of West Virginia . . . Mama, Bubba, and Tiny . . . The Hillbillies!"

A few seconds later—once the Hillbillies had reached the ring—the banjo was replaced by the "Wilde Ones" punk rock style song that an old friend from high school had recorded for Zoey and Zack. That particular friend was one of the very few former classmates that Zoey, Zack, and Arielle stayed in touch with. The song always made Zoey feel a little nostalgic. When she and Zack started out as a tag team nearly thirteen years ago, this was the song they'd used as their entrance music. Over the past few months, she and Justin had used the song at the start of their many tag matches.

"Let's do this," Zack said. "One last time."

The siblings exchanged fist bumps before they flung aside the curtains and stepped out onto the stage. They were met with a deafening cheer as the fans hurled rolls of purple and black streamers at them. Zoey may have been looking forward to the end of the night, but she wanted this moment to never end. Wrestling was her passion, and she'd always been happiest when teaming with her twin brother. Now that she and Justin were getting along better than they ever had in the past, it was even more special to be sharing the ring with them. Zoey was elated to have this opportunity with her brothers . . . but also depressed that, after tonight, this would never happen again.

"Making their way to the ring . . . They hail from Parts Unknown . . . Which just happens to be right here in Linville . . . Zoey, Zack, and Justin Wilde!"

The Wildes made their way to the ring, high-fiving the fans who were seated along the metal barricade that separated the fans from the action. They briefly paused next to their family who were seated in the front row. Marlon, Roxanne, and Vivian were there, as were Arielle and Paige. Paige screamed in excitement when she saw her dad. Arielle's parents, Jim and Nancy Coleman, were also there to support their son-in-law. Hannah, who'd wrestled earlier in the show, had changed out of her Amish-themed ring gear so that she could watch the match from the audience. Even Tyler Gates was there, squeezed in between Vivian and Hannah.

Once the ring was cleared of streamers, the match got underway. The Wildes and the Hillbillies had come up with a rough plan for the match earlier in the day—one that only had Zack minimally involved in the action and didn't require him to take any big bumps or perform any high spots. That plan was almost immediately cast aside when Zack decided to go all in. He performed moves that he hadn't done in years, and, despite being a bit rusty and botching a few times, still performed almost seamlessly with his siblings. It might not have been one of their best matches, but it was one of the most meaningful. They also gave up on maintaining kayfabe. What was supposed to be a serious bout between two sets of long-time rivals devolved into a fun match between friends.

When Zack finally pinned Tiny for the win, there were tears in his eyes. Zoey and Justin both had to blink back tears of their own. Even the Hillbillies looked emotional as they bowed down to the Wildes and left the siblings to continue celebrating in the ring.

"You were both right," Zack said as he pulled Zoey and Justin in for a hug. "I needed that match . . . We need it . . . But, damn, did it make me realize how much I've missed this."

"Merry Christmas!"

"Bah humbug." Zoey rolled over to face Vivian who standing in the doorway. Turning back the other way, Zoey pulled the blanket over her head to block out the light from the hallway. "It's too early, Nana."

"It's almost seven o'clock." Vivian flipped the switch to turn on the overhead light. "Your mom's about to start breakfast. And we could get the call that Paige is awake at any moment. So get your lazy butt up or you'll miss out."

Zoey groaned as she crawled off the air mattress that she'd set up on the floor of her old bedroom. The walls were still the same shade of light purple that they'd been since she was five. All other traces of her had long since been removed from the upstairs bedroom that overlooked the front of the house. When Vivian had moved in with Marlon and Roxanne, she'd turned Zoey's old bedroom into her living room. The room that Zack and Justin had shared was now Vivian's bedroom.

After changing into her mandatory ugly Christmas sweater—a pro wrestling themed one, of course—Zoey washed her face and combed her hair. She then headed downstairs.

"I smell bacon," Zoey said as she descended the stairs into the combined kitchen and dining room. Back when they were kids, Zoey, Zack, and Justin had raced each other down the stairs every Christmas morning. One year, in an attempt at a shortcut, Justin climbed over the banister and dropped down to the floor. The opening of presents had to be delayed so that Roxanne could wrap Justin's sprained ankle. "But I don't smell turkey."

"That's because I haven't put the turkey in the oven yet," Roxanne said as she set a plate piled high with bacon on the kitchen island. Marlon, Vivian, and Justin were already seated around the island. André circled them in hopes that someone would sneak him some bacon or other tasty tidbit. "We've decided to do things a little differently this year. Instead of eating around noon, we're going to wait and eat around six instead."

"Whatever . . . I don't really care what time we eat as long as there's mashed potatoes and Nana's homemade garlic bread." Zoey helped herself to a portion of the French toast casserole that Roxanne had made every Christmas morning for as far back as Zoey could remember. The layers of bread were topped with strawberries, raspberries, and blueberries. Zoey added a copious amount of powdered sugar and drowned her plate in maple syrup. She then turned to Justin and said, "I'm supposed to be the Scrooge in this family. Why do you look so glum?"

Justin glared at her over his glass of orange juice. "You know why."

Zoey did know. It was Justin's and Hannah's first Christmas as a couple, and they were spending the day apart. Hannah, who was an only child, had gone to Baltimore with her parents to celebrate Christmas with her maternal grandparents. Justin had been invited to join them, but he'd ultimately decided to spend the day with the Wildes—mainly because he didn't want to miss out on watching his niece open all of her presents. Zoey knew that Hannah was disappointed that Justin chose his family over her—especially since Hannah spent Thanksgiving with the Wildes. Zoey hoped Justin's decisions wouldn't cause any problems between him and Hannah. If it did, Zoey was prepared to mediate.

"I just got some good news," Roxanne said as she had a seat across from Zoey. She held up her phone so everyone could see the picture of a red-faced, newborn baby. "Kathy Kreider just texted me. Olivia had her baby right after midnight. She said that both Olivia and Genevieve are doing fine."

Olivia and Jeremy wouldn't be the only people spending Christmas in the hospital. A few days earlier, Ruth Jennings had let Zoey know that Imogene had entered hospice care. After Chester's memorial service, she took a turn for the worse. Zoey and Zack had both gone to visit Imogene the previous afternoon. Before they'd left, Imogene made them promise that they'd make sure Chester's ashes were placed in her casket before she was buried. She didn't trust Oscar to fulfill her final wish.

Thinking about Imogene left Zoey feeling depressed. She ate her breakfast in silence.

After helping Roxanne clean up the kitchen, Zoey ran upstairs to brush her teeth. She then joined her family in the living room. Marlon had turned on the gas fireplace, and the flames crackled behind the grate. Hanging from the mantle were a row of personalized Christmas stockings. In front of the floor-to-ceiling windows was the Christmas tree. The colorful lights were on, illuminating the ornaments. Piled around the base of the tree were piles and piles of gift bags and various sized packages wrapped in Christmas-themed paper. The majority of the presents were for Paige—from Santa, both sets of grandparents, her only living great-grandparent, her uncle, and her aunts. Zoey would be the only aunt present, but Arielle's sister and her girlfriend had sent gifts.

Zoey was pleased with the present she and Vivian had picked out for Paige—a hot pink, battery operated, kid-sized Jeep. Zoey had plastered a Wilde Woman sticker across the hood, and Vivian sewed up a set of leopard print covers for the plastic seats. Sitting next to the Jeep was a pink tricycle from Jim and Nancy Coleman, and a gigantic stuffed unicorn from Justin and Hannah.

Zoey was about to join Justin on the couch when the doorbell rang. She detoured into the foyer and opened the front door for Jim and Nancy.

"If you're here, I guess that means Paige is up," Zoey said.

"Arielle said she's literally bouncing off the walls," Nancy said as she hung her coat on the rack by the door. "She's trying to get Paige fed and dressed, but Paige won't stop running around the house."

"You doing okay, Zoey?" Jim asked. "I know the past few weeks have been pretty rough for you."

"I'm getting through it one day at a time." Zoey leaned closer to Jim and asked, "Any updates on Jocelyn and Natasha?"

Jim shook his head. "Jocelyn's lawyer is still planning to make a case for temporary insanity. He's trying to prove she was out of her mind when she stabbed Chester."

"More like under the influence of drugs."

"Jocelyn's lawyer is also trying to put all the blame for Lucas's murder on Natasha," Jim continued. "He's claiming it was all Natasha's idea and that she forced Jocelyn to help her."

"I just hope Natasha doesn't decide to take the blame for it," Zoey said. "It would be just like her to try to protect Jocelyn."

André's excited bark brought an end to the whispered conversation as he alerted everyone that Paige, Zack, and Arielle had entered the house through the back door. With a plastic title belt clutched to her chest, Paige came charging into the living room. She slid to a halt when she saw all the presents. Her eyes grew wider and wider as she glanced around the room. Her eyes finally settled on the Jeep and she shrieked in delight. The title belt slipped out of her little hands as she ran over to her new ride. Zoey and Vivian exchanged congratulatory high-fives over their spectacular choice in presents. Paige wasn't quite old enough yet to drive the Jeep around herself, but it came with a remote control that allowed for an adult to operate it.

It took a few minutes to coax Paige away from the Jeep. After examining the tricycle and unicorn, Paige began to tear into her other presents. She was equally enthused over every gift she received whether it was clothes or toys. Zoey couldn't help but laugh as Zack grew more and more dismayed over the amount of presents that Paige received. She overhead him mumble something to Arielle about how maybe they should reconsider having another kid so that Paige didn't wind up a spoiled only child. Arielle sounded adamantly against the idea.

When Paige was finally done opening all of her presents, the adults got to have their turns. Zoey received a number of gift cards, some wrestling items, and a mint condition Spice Girls doll that Roxanne found at a local thrift store. Despite it being twenty years too late, Zoey was thrilled to finally get the doll. That being said, she had no idea what she would do with it.

Zoey's favorite and most meaningful present came from Zack when he announced that he was coming out of retirement. He made it clear that he only wanted to wrestle in tag matches with Justin and/or Zoey, and only at LAW shows. Unless they received a major opportunity, Zack had no desire to go back on the road as a full-time independent wrestler. His first commitments were to his family and 3 Count Tattoos, but he was finally ready to admit that he wasn't quite done wrestling. Zack's announcement gave Zoey a renewed optimism for the future. She was already coming up with ideas for future LAW shows.

After cleaning up the mess of shredded paper, empty bags, and discarded boxes in the living room, everyone trooped outside so that Paige could try out her Jeep and the tricycle. Paige was so enthralled with her Jeep that she refused to get out of it until the rechargeable battery gave out. After a meltdown that foreshadowed what she might be like during her terrible twos, Paige finally settled down to take a nap.

The rest of the day was spent hanging out and helping Paige try out all her new toys. In one day, Zoey spent more time playing with dolls and other "girly" toys than she had throughout her entire childhood. Halloween would always be Zoey's favorite holiday, but Paige's enthusiasm and joy reminded her of why she'd loved Christmas so much as a child. She'd started out the morning faking her Christmas enthusiasm for her niece's sake, but it didn't take long for the excitement to become genuine.

"I'm so hungry that this fake food is starting to look good," Zoey said as she held up a slice of realistic-looking pizza. One of Paige's presents from Roxanne and Marlon was a plastic tea set. Roxanne had also purchased enough play food for a five-course meal. That food and dinnerware were currently spread out across the coffee table. Glancing at the clock, Zoey saw that it was just after five o'clock. "I still don't understand why we decided to eat dinner so late."

"Because we did," Vivian said as she stared at Zoey over top of a plastic tea cup filled with water. "And it shouldn't be too much longer."

"Maybe if you'd eaten something a little more substantial at lunch you wouldn't be so hungry . . ." Arielle said. "All I've seen you eat today was cookies."

"I had French toast and bacon for breakfast." Zoey tossed the slice of pizza onto the coffee table. "And a sandwich at lunch."

"And at least two dozen cookies throughout the day," Arielle said. "Good thing I'm leading a cardio class first thing tomorrow morning. You'll need to burn off all that sugar and extra calories."

Zoey stuck out her tongue.

"Cookies!" Paige banged a tea cup against the side of the coffee table. "Wanna cookie!"

"Not until after dinner," Arielle told her daughter.

"Want. Cookie. Now." Paige screamed and then swiped half of the tea set and plastic food onto the floor. Water from the cups and tea pot immediately began to soak into the area rug. André pounced on a hot dog but quickly lost interest when he realized it wasn't real. "Now. Now. Now."

"That's enough, Paige," Arielle said. "Now clean up the mess you made."

Paige screamed louder and pounded her feet against the floor. Her face also turned an alarming shade of red as she continued to howl. André fled the living room with his tail between his legs.

"I . . . uhh . . ." Zoey jumped up and put some distance between herself and her agitated niece. "I'll just go check on dinner."

Zoey followed her nose to kitchen where Roxanne and Nancy were putting the finishing touches on the Christmas meal. The turkey was done, and the two women had mashed potatoes, green bean casserole, and other side dishes keeping warm until they were ready to eat.

Feigning that she was weak with hunger, Zoey collapsed against the island and asked, "How much longer till we eat?"

Roxanne pushed Zoey away from the island. "Should be ready any minute."

The doorbell rang, though it was hard to hear over Paige's shrieking and André's barking. The dog almost knocked Zoey over as he charged out of the kitchen and headed for the door.

"Who could that be?" Zoey asked. "Other than the people across the street coming over to complain about the noise?"

"Why don't you go answer the door and find out?" Roxanne hustled Zoey out of the kitchen. "And fix your hair. It looks like you just wrestled a match."

Zoey tidied her ponytail as she made her way to the front door. She wasn't sure who she expected, but she was both shocked and thrilled to see Hannah and her parents standing on the front porch. All of a sudden, it made sense why the Wildes were eating Christmas dinner much later in the day than the normally did. They were waiting for the Stoltzfuses to makes it back from Baltimore.

Justin—who had been in the basement with the other men as they battled to see who get the highest score on the refurbished Wrestlefest arcade machine that they'd all chipped in to buy for Marlon—came rushing upstairs when he heard his girlfriend's voice. Justin picked Hannah up and twirled her around the foyer.

Seeing Justin and Hannah together not only brought about an end to Paige's temper tantrum but it made Zoey acknowledge how lonely she was. The realization hit her like a body slam. She'd texted Gates off-and-on throughout the day, but, since he had volunteered to cover the first shift on patrol so that other officers could be at home with their families, he'd been busy. Too late, Zoey realized that she should have invited him over to her parents' house after he got done at work. It was too late to do so now, and Zoey cursed herself for the oversight. She and Gates had been on two more official dates—both of which had gone better than the first one. He'd also stopped by the tattoo shop several times after he got off work so that he could see Zoey. Meanwhile, Zoey was receptive but still hesitant to the budding relationship—and that wasn't fair to Gates. Zoey needed to make more of an effort.

Zoey was debating what to do when the doorbell rang a second time. She yanked open the door and came face-to-face with Gates.

"You're here."

"Yep. I'm here."

"But how . . ."

"I invited him. Since it didn't seem to occur to you to do it," Vivian said as she elbowed Zoey in the ribs and pushed her back from the door. That allowed Gates to step inside. "You'll have to forgive her, Tyler. Zoey's been single for a long time. She not only forgets what it's like to have a boyfriend, but that she's actually supposed to include him in things."

"That's all right, Vivi," Tyler said as he took off his coat. "The relationship isn't exactly official yet."

Vivian dug her elbow into Zoey's side a second time. "It should be."

Zoey blushed. "Hannah and her parents aren't the only reason Mom pushed back dinner, is it? You all planned this, didn't you?"

"Everyone was in on it except you and Justin." Vivian winked at her granddaughter before turning to leave the foyer. "By the way, you're standing right under the mistletoe."

Zoey glanced up to see the sprig of mistletoe hanging from the light fixture.

"I'm sorry I didn't invite you," Zoey said. "But I'm really glad you're here."

"So am I," Gates said before he kissed her. "Merry Christmas, Zoey."

Photo by Paris Bretherick

RANDEE GREEN IS THE AUTHOR OF THE Carrie Shatner Mystery series and the Zoey Wilde Mystery series. Her passion for reading began in grade school with *Little House in the Big Woods* by Laura Ingalls Wilder. She has a bachelor's degree in English Literature, as well as an MA and an MFA in Creative Writing. When not writing, she's usually reading, indulging in her passion for Texas country music, traveling, or hanging out with her dog, Daisy.

www.ingramcontent.com/pod-product-compliance
Lightning Source LLC
Chambersburg PA
CBHW011932050726
47590CB00011B/3256

* 9 7 8 1 6 8 4 9 2 3 5 6 4 *